One Night DENIED

Also by Jodi Ellen Malpas

This Man
Beneath This Man
This Man Confessed

One Night: Promised
One Night: Denied
One Night: Unveiled

One Night
DENIED

JODI ELLEN
MALPAS

FOREVER

NEW YORK BOSTON

This book is a work of fiction. Names, characters, places, and incidents are the product of the author's imagination or are used fictitiously. Any resemblance to actual events, locales, or persons, living or dead, is coincidental.

Forever
Hachette Book Group
1290 Avenue of the Americas, New York, NY 10104

www.HachetteBookGroup.com

Printed in the United States of America

RRD-C

First Edition: November 2014
10 9 8 7 6 5 4 3

Forever is an imprint of Grand Central Publishing.
The Forever name and logo are trademarks of Hachette Book Group, Inc.

The Hachette Speakers Bureau provides a wide range of authors for speaking events. To find out more, go to www.hachettespeakersbureau.com or call (866) 376-6591.

The publisher is not responsible for websites (or their content) that are not owned by the publisher.

Library of Congress Cataloging-in-Publication Data

Malpas, Jodi Ellen.
One night: denied / Jodi Ellen Malpas. — First edition.
pages; cm. — (One night trilogy)
ISBN 978-1-4555-5934-3 (softcover) — ISBN 978-1-4789-8467-2 (audio book) — ISBN 978-1-4789-2980-2 (audio download)
I. Title. II. Title: Denied.
PR6113.A47O54 2014
823'.92—dc23

2014032980

For Nan, Great-Aunty Doll, and Great-Aunty Phyllis. There's a cheeky bit of each of you in Olivia's Nan. We miss you all. xxx

Acknowledgments

A million thank-yous to the usual suspects. You all know who you are! I'm a lucky girl to have you all behind me. A special thank you to Leah, my editor, who makes editing almost pleasurable. I said almost! What is a pleasure, though, is working with you. Thank you for everything and getting my Jodi-isms. To the art department at both my U.K. and U.S. publishing houses. I'm totally crap at expressing how I want the covers to be, yet you nail it every time. Thank you!

And my ladies. I just want to take you all out and drink mojitos until we fall over!

I hope you enjoy *Denied.*

Jodi xxx

One Night Denied

Prologue

William Anderson replaced the phone slowly and thoughtfully, then reclined in his big office chair. His large hands formed a steeple in front of his mouth as he ran over the ten-minute conversation repeatedly until he was on the brink of craziness. He didn't know what to think, but he knew he needed a drink. A large one. He strode over to his drinks cabinet and lifted the old-fashioned globe-style lid. He didn't stop to consider which malt he fancied; any alcohol would suffice right now. Pouring a tumbler to the brim with bourbon, he downed half and immediately topped it back up. He felt hot and sweaty. The usually composed man had been knocked for six by today's revelations, and now all he could see were beautiful sapphire eyes. Everywhere he turned they were there, torturing him, reminding him of his failure. He yanked at his tie and unfastened the top button of his dress shirt, hoping the extra room at his neck would help him breathe. No such luck. His throat was closing up on him. The past had returned to haunt him. He'd tried so hard not to get attached, not to care. And now it was happening again.

In his world, decisions needed to be made with a clear head and objective mind—something he was usually an expert at. Usually. Things in William's world happened for a reason, and that reason was typically because he said so—because people listened to him, respected him. Now he felt all sense of control slipping away, and he didn't like it. Especially where *she* was concerned.

"I'm too old for this shit," he grumbled, collapsing onto his chair. After taking another long, healthy glug of his bourbon, he rested his head back and stared up at the ceiling. She'd sent him into a tailspin before, and he was about to let her do it all over again.

He was a fool. But having Miller Hart added to the complicated equation left him little choice. And neither did his morals... or his love for that woman.

Chapter One

My destiny has been steered by someone else. All of my effort, my cautious approach, and the protective shields I worked hard to put in place were obliterated the day I met Miller Hart. It fast became obvious that I'd reached a point in my life where it was paramount I maintained my sensible life strategies, kept my calm façade, and stayed vigilant. Because that man was unquestionably going to test me. And he did. He still is. Trusting a man, confiding in a man, and giving myself to a man was the ultimate. I did it all, and now I wholeheartedly wish I hadn't. Being frightened that he would leave me because of my history was wasted concern. That should have been the least of my fears.

Miller Hart is a high-class male prostitute. He said "escort," but you can't pretty it up by selecting a less taboo word.

Miller Hart sells his body.

Miller Hart lives a life of debasement.

Miller Hart is the male equivalent of my mother. I'm in love with a man I can't have. He made me feel alive when I'd spent too long just existing, but he took away that invigorating feeling, replacing it with desolation. My spirit is more lifeless now than it ever was before my encounters with that man.

The humiliation of being proved wrong is being drowned out

by the hurt. I can feel nothing but crippling hurt. It's been the longest two weeks imaginable, and I have the rest of my life to soldier through. The thought is enough to make me want to close my eyes and never open them again.

That night at the hotel plays over and over in my mind—the feel of the straps Miller put on my wrists, the cold impassiveness of his face as he expertly made me come, the look of raw anguish when he realized the pain he'd caused. Of course I had to flee.

I just didn't realize I'd be running right into an even bigger problem. William. I know it's only a matter of time before he finds me again. I saw the surprise on his face when he registered me, and I saw the recognition when he spotted Miller. William Anderson and Miller Hart know each other, and William will want to know how I know Miller and, God forbid, what I was doing at that hotel. Not only have I spent two weeks in hell, but I've also spent two weeks looking over my shoulder, waiting for him to appear.

* * *

After dragging myself to the shower and pulling on anything I can lay my hands on, I plod down the stairs, finding Nan on her knees loading the washing machine. I slip silently onto a chair at the table, but Nan seems to have a radar on me these days and every movement, breath, and tear is detected, no matter if she's in the room with me or not. She's caring but confused, sympathetic but encouraging. Trying to make me see the positive side of my encounters with Miller Hart has become her life goal, but I can see nothing but imminent misery and feel nothing but lingering pain. There can never be anyone else. No man will ever spark those feelings, make me feel protected, loved, and safe.

It's ironic, really. All my life I've despised that my mother abandoned me for a life of men, pleasure, and gifts. And then Miller

Hart turns out to be a male escort. He sells his body, takes money to bring women pleasure. For him, every time he took me in his *thing*, held me so tenderly in his arms, it was to erase the taint of an encounter with another woman. Of all the men in the world who could've captured me so completely, why him?

"Would you like to come to Monday club with me?" Nan asks casually while I try to choke down some cornflakes.

"No, I'll stay home." I plunge my spoon into my bowl and take another mouthful. "Did you win at bingo last night?"

Huffing a few times, she slams the door of the washing machine, then proceeds to load the tray with laundry detergent. "Did I heck! Waste of bloody time."

"Why do you bother, then?" I ask, stirring my breakfast slowly.

"Because I rock that bingo hall." She winks, smiling a little, and I mentally plead for her not to hit me with another pep talk. My plea goes ignored. "I spent years mourning your grandfather's death, Olivia." Her words stun me a little, the mention of my grandfather the last thing I expected. My stirring slows. "I lost my lifetime partner and I cried oceans." She's trying to put things into perspective, and it's in this moment I wonder if she thinks I'm pathetic for being so blue over a man I've known so briefly. "I didn't think I would ever feel human again."

"I remember," I say quietly. And I remember how I came close to multiplying Nan's grief. She wasn't even over my mother's disappearance before she was cruelly faced with the premature death of her beloved Jim.

"But it did happen." She nods reassuringly. "It doesn't feel like it right now, but you'll see that life can go on." She's up the hallway now, while I'm considering her words, feeling a little guilty for mourning something I barely had and even guiltier that she's comparing it to the loss of her husband in an attempt to make me feel better.

I slip deep into thought, running over encounter after encounter, kiss after kiss, word after word. My washed-out mind seems hell-bent on torturing me, but it's my own stupid fault. I asked for it. Hopelessness has taken on a new meaning.

The chime of my mobile makes me jump back in my chair, bringing me out of my daydream, where all of the misery is real again. I don't particularly want contact with anyone, least of all the man responsible for my heartache, so when I see his name appear, I quickly drop my spoon into my bowl and stare blankly at the screen. My heart is sprinting. I've clammed up with panic, and I'm far back in my chair, putting as much distance between me and the phone as possible. I can't move farther away because every useless muscle in my body is on shutdown. Nothing is working, except my damn memory, and it's torturing me some more, making me speed through every moment that I've spent with Miller Hart. My eyes begin to pool with tears of despair. It's not wise to open this message. Of course it's not wise to open this message. I'm not being very wise at the moment, though. Haven't been since I met Miller Hart.

I swipe up my phone and open the text.

How are you? Miller Hart x

I frown at the screen and reread the message, wondering if he thinks that I may have forgotten him already. Miller Hart? How am I? How does he think I am? Dancing on the ceiling because I got myself a few rounds of Miller Hart, London's most notorious male escort, for free? No, not for free. Far from free. My time and experiences with that man are going to cost me dearly. I've not even begun to come to terms with what's happened. My mind is a knot of questions, all jumbled up, but I need to unravel it all and get it in order before I try to make any sense of this. Just the fact that the only man I've ever shared my whole self with is suddenly gone is hard enough to deal with. Trying to fathom why and how is a chore my emotions refuse to bear on top of my loss.

How am I? "A fucking mess!" I yell at my phone, stabbing at the Delete button repeatedly until my thumb gets sore. In an act of pure anger, I throw my phone across the kitchen, not even wincing at the crash as it smashes to smithereens against the tiled wall. I'm heaving violently in my chair, barely hearing the rushed clumping of footsteps down the stairs over my angry gasps.

"What on earth?" Nan's shocked tone creeps over my shoulders, but I don't turn to see the stunned look that'll most certainly be plaguing her old face. "Olivia?"

I stand abruptly, sending my chair flying back, the screeching of wood on wood echoing around our old kitchen. "I'm going out." I don't look at my grandmother as I escape, making my way quickly down the hall and viciously snatching my jacket and satchel from the coat stand.

"Olivia!"

Her footsteps are pounding after me as I swing the front door open and nearly take George off his feet. "Morn—Oh!" He watches me barrel past, and I just catch a glimpse of his jolly face drifting into shock before I break into a sprint down the pathway.

* * *

I know I look out of place as I stand near the gym entrance, clearly hesitant and a little overwhelmed. All the machines look like spaceships, hundreds of buttons or levers on each one, and I haven't the first idea how to operate them. My one-hour induction last week did a great job of distracting me, but the information and instructions fell straight from my memory the second I left the exclusive fitness center. I scan the area, fiddling with my ring, seeing masses of men and women pounding the treadmills, going hell for leather on the bikes, and pumping weights on huge lifting devices. They all look like they know exactly what they're doing.

In an attempt to blend in, I make my way over to the water machine and gulp down a cup of ice water. I'm wasting time being hesitant when I could be releasing some stress and anger. I spot a punching bag hanging in the far corner with no one within thirty feet of it, so I decide to give it a try. There are no buttons or levers on that.

Wandering over, I help myself to the boxing gloves hanging on the wall nearby. I shove my hands in, trying to look like a pro, like I come here every morning and start my day with an hour of sweating. After securing the Velcro, I give the bag a little poke. I'm surprised at how heavy it is. My feeble hit has barely moved it. I draw back my arm and poke harder, frowning when all I get is a little sway of the giant bag. Deciding it must be full of rocks, I inject some power into my weak arm and throw some effort into my next hit. I grunt, too, and the bag shifts significantly this time, moving away from me and seeming to pause in midair before it's on its way back toward me. Fast. I panic and quickly pull back my fist, then extend my arm to prevent being knocked to the ground. Shock waves fly up my arm when my glove connects with the bag, but it's moving away from me again. I smile and spread my legs a little, bracing myself for its return, then smack it hard again, sending it sailing away from me.

My arm is aching already and I suddenly realize I have two gloved hands, so I pummel it with my left this time, smiling wider, the impact of the bag on my fists feeling good. I break out in a sweat, my feet start to shift, and my arms begin to pick up a rhythm. My shouts of satisfaction spur me on, and the bag morphs into more than a bag. I'm beating the shit out of it and loving every moment.

I don't know how long I'm there, but when I finally let up and take a moment to think, I'm drenched, my knuckles are sore, and my breathing is erratic. I catch the bag and let it settle, then take a cautious glance around the gym, wondering if my lash-out has been noticed. No one is staring. I've gone totally unnoticed, everyone focused on their own grueling workout. I smile to myself and collect a cup of water and a towel from the nearby shelf, wiping my pouring brow as I make my way from the huge room, a certain skip to my step. For the first time in weeks, I feel prepared to take on the day.

I head toward the changing rooms, sipping my water, feeling like a lifetime of stress and woes has just been knocked out of me. How ironic. The sense of release is new and the urge to go back in and pound for another hour is hard to resist, but I'm already at risk of being late for work, so I push on, thinking this could get addictive. I'll be back tomorrow morning, maybe even after work today, and I'll thrash that bag until there are no more traces of Miller Hart and the pain he's caused me.

I pass door after door, all with glass panes, and peek into each. Through one I see dozens of tight backsides of people pedaling like their lives depend on it, through another are women bent into all sorts of freakish positions, and in another there are men running back and forth, randomly dropping to the mats to do varied sets of push-ups and sit-ups. These must be the classes the instructor told me about. I might try one or two. Or I could give them all a go.

As I'm passing the final door before the women's changing rooms, I pull up when something catches my eye and backtrack until I'm looking through the glass pane at a punching bag similar to the one that I've just attacked. It's swinging from the ceiling hook, but with no one in sight to have made it move. I frown and step closer to the door, my eyes traveling with the bag from left to right. Then I gasp and jump back as someone comes into view, bare chested and barefoot. My already racing heart virtually explodes under the added strain of shock it's just been subjected to. The cup of water and my towel tumble to the ground. I feel dizzy.

He has those shorts on, the ones he wore when he was trying to make me comfortable. I'm shaking, but my shocked state doesn't stop me from peering back through the glass, just to check I wasn't hallucinating. I wasn't. He's here, his ripped physique mesmerizing. He looks violent as he attacks the hanging bag like it's a threat to his life, punishing it with powerful punches and even more powerful kicks. His athletic legs are extending in between extensions of his muscled arms, his body moving stealthily as he weaves and dodges the bag when it comes back at him. He looks like a pro. He looks like a fighter.

I'm frozen on the spot as I watch Miller move around the hanging bag with ease, his fists wrapped in bandages, his limbs delivering controlled, punishing blows time and time again. The sounds of gruff bawls and his hits send an unfamiliar chill down my spine. Who does he see before him?

My mind spins, questions mounting, as I quietly observe the refined, well-mannered, part-time gentleman become a man possessed, that temper he has warned me about clear and present. But then I retreat a pace when he suddenly grabs the bag with both hands and rests his forehead on the leather, his body falling into the now subtle sway of the punching bag. His back is dripping and heaving, and I see his solid shoulders rise suddenly. Then he begins to turn toward the door. It happens in slow motion. I'm rooted in place as his chest, slicked with a sheen of sweat, comes into view and my eyes slowly crawl up his torso until I see his side profile. He knows he's being watched. My held breath gushes from my lungs and I move fast, sprinting down the corridor and flying through the door of the changing room, my exhausted heart begging me to give it a break.

"You okay?"

I look across to the shower and see a woman wrapped in a towel with a turban on her wet head, watching me with slightly wide eyes. "Sure," I breathe, realizing I'm splattered against the back of the door. I can't blush because my face is already bright red and steaming hot.

She smiles through a frown and carries on her way, leaving me to find my locker and retrieve my shower bag. The water is far too hot. I need ice. But after five minutes of fiddling with the controls, I fail to cool it down. So I make do and set about washing my tangled, sweaty mane and soaping down my clammy body. My earlier relaxed frame of mind and body has been obliterated by the sight of him, and now the visions are replaying in my mind, too. There are hundreds of fitness centers in London. Why did I choose this one?

I haven't time to waste thinking too much or time to begin appreciating the pleasant effect of the hot water, which is now massaging my post-workout muscles, not burning my already heated flesh. I need to get to work. It takes me ten minutes to dry my body and hair and get dressed. Then I'm skulking out of the gym with my head down and my shoulders high, bracing myself for that voice to call me or that touch to ignite the internal flame. But I escape safely and hurry to the tube. While my eyes are thankful for the reminder of Miller Hart's perfection, my mind is not.

Chapter Two

As soon as the lunchtime rush dies down at the bistro where I work, Sylvie is on me like a wolf. "Tell me," she says, dropping to the sofa next to me.

"Nothing to tell."

"Livy, give me a break! You've looked like a bulldog chewing a wasp all morning."

I cast a sideways frown to find my coworker's bright pink lips pressed into an impatient straight line. "A what?"

"Your face is all screwed up in disgust."

"He texted me," I grumble. I'm not telling her the rest. "He texted me to ask how I am."

She scoffs and takes my can of Coke, slurping loudly. "Supercilious moron."

I jump forward without thought. "He's not a moron!" I shout defensively, immediately snapping my mouth shut and retreating back on the sofa when I clock Sylvie's knowing look. "He's not a moron and he's not supercilious," I say calmly. He was loving, attentive, and thoughtful...when he wasn't being a supercilious moron...or London's most notorious male escort. I drop my head on a sigh. Landing myself with one hooker is bad luck. Two? Well, that's just unreasonable of the gods.

She reaches over and squeezes my knee. "I hope you didn't entertain him with a reply."

"I couldn't even if I wanted. Which I don't," I say, pulling myself up.

"Why?"

"My phone's broken." I leave Sylvie on the couch with a wrinkled brow and no further explanation.

All I've told her about my breakup with Miller is that there was another woman. It's just easier that way. The truth is unspeakable.

When I enter the kitchen, Del and Paul are laughing like hyenas, each with a vicious knife in one hand and a cucumber in the other. "What's so funny?" I ask, making them both halt their happy tittering, their faces morphing into a wash of pity as they each assess my weak body and mental state. I stand quietly and allow them to reach the only conclusion there is. I still look whitewashed.

Del's the one to snap back into action, pointing his knife at me, clearly making himself smile. "Livy can judge. She'll be fair."

"Judge what?" I ask, taking a step away from the blade.

Paul pushes Del's hand down on a tsk and smiles at me. "We're having a cucumber-chopping competition. Your silly boss here thinks he can beat me."

I don't mean to, but I laugh. It makes both Paul and Del jump back a little, shocked. I've seen Paul slice a cucumber, or I tried to see. His hand is a blur of motion for a few seconds until the vegetable in splayed out neatly, each slice perfect. "Good luck!"

Del smiles brightly at me. "I don't need luck, Livy, sweetheart." He spreads his legs and lays his cucumber down on the chopping board. "Say when."

Paul rolls his eyes at me and stands back, a wise move judging by the hold Del has on the knife. "Are you ready to time it?" he asks, handing me a stopwatch.

"Is this a regular thing?" I take it and reset the display.

"Yep," Del answers, focusing on the cucumber. "He's beat me on a pepper, onion, and lettuce, but the cucumber's mine."

"When!" Paul shouts, and I immediately press down to start the timer as Del flies into action, bringing the knife down repeatedly and savagely on the poor cucumber.

"Done!" he yells, out of breath, looking over at me. He's broken out in a sweat. "What did I get?"

I look down. "Ten seconds."

"Pow!" He jumps into the air, and Paul immediately confiscates the knife from him. "Beat that, Mr. Master Chef!"

"Piece of cake," Paul claims, taking up position by the chopping board and scraping away the dismembered cucumber before setting his own down. "Say when."

I quickly reset the timer, just in time for Del's, "When!"

Paul, as I knew he would, sails through the cucumber with finesse and control, as opposed to Del's heavy-handed massacre. "Done," he declares calmly, no sweat and no heavy breathing, which defies his overweight frame.

Looking down at the stopwatch, I mentally smile. "Six seconds."

"Get out of town!" Del shouts, marching over to me and snatching the watch from my hand. "You must've cocked up."

"I did not!" I actually laugh. "And, anyway, Paul sliced, you hacked."

He gasps and Paul laughs with me, giving me an endearing wink. "So now I have the pepper, the onion, the lettuce, *and* the cucumber." Paul takes a marker pen and puts a big tick through a basic picture of a cucumber on the wall.

"Bullshit," Del grumbles. "If it wasn't for the Tuna Crunch, you'd be history, buster." Del's moodiness only increases our laughter, both of us chuckling as our boss stomps off. "Clean up!" he shouts back to us.

"Boys," I muse.

Paul smiles fondly. "It's good to see some spirit, darling." He gives me an affectionate rub of the arm, not making too big a deal of it, before strolling off and shaking a pan of something on the stove. Watching him whistle happily to himself, I realize my earlier bubbling anger has completely subsided. Distraction. I need distraction.

* * *

It's the longest afternoon ever, which isn't a good sign of things to come. I'm left to lock up the bistro with Paul, Sylvie having gotten off early to get to her local boozer to nab a front-row seat in time for her favorite band that's playing tonight. She nagged me for a solid half hour, trying to entice me to go, but by the sounds of things, the band is in the heavy metal genre, and my head is banging enough already.

Paul gives my shoulder another friendly rub, the big man clearly uncomfortable with emotional women, before he heads off toward the tube, leaving me to go in the other direction.

"Baby girl!" Gregory's worried call hits me from behind, and I turn to see him jogging toward me in his combats and T-shirt, looking all muddy and grubby.

"Hey." I fight against my body's desire to fold in on itself at the prospect of another pep talk.

He catches me up and we start strolling toward the bus stop together. "I've tried calling you a million times, Livy," he says, worried but annoyed.

"My phone's kaput."

"How?"

"It doesn't matter. You okay?"

"No, I'm not." He scowls down at me. "I'm worried about you."

"Don't be," I mutter, not giving anything else away. Just like Sylvie, he knows nothing of male escorts and hotel rooms, and he doesn't need to. My best friend already hates Miller enough. There's really no need to give him more ammunition. "I'm fine."

"Cocksucker!" he spits.

I don't humor him and instead change the subject. "Have you spoken to Benjamin yet?"

Gregory takes a long, weary breath. "Briefly. He took one of my calls to tell me to stay away. Your cocksucking coffee hater has put the fear of God in him."

"Well, whose fault is that? You said you wouldn't let anything happen to me that night, but when I needed you, you'd skulked off with Benjamin."

"I know," he mutters. "I wasn't thinking, was I?"

"No, you weren't," I confirm, mentally scolding myself for my cheek.

"And now Ben's closed off from me completely," he says.

I look up to Gregory and see a hurt I don't like. He's falling for a man who's pretending to be someone he's not . . . a bit like Miller. Or was he pretending the whole time he was with me? "Completely?" I ask. "No contact?"

Gregory sighs deeply. "He took a woman home that Saturday night and took great delight in telling me so."

"Oh." I breathe. "You never mentioned it before."

He shrugs, playing it easy. "Kinda bruised my ego," he says, his forced indifferent expression turning to mine. "You look a little red-faced."

Still? "I went to the gym this morning." I reach up and feel my brow. I've been hot all day.

"You did?" he asks, surprised. "That's great. What did you do?" He starts dancing around on the pavement. "A bit of circuit training? Some yoga?" He bends into the most obscene pose and looks up at me with a grin. "Downward dog?"

I can't help returning his smile, pulling him back upright. "I punched the crap out of a bag of rocks."

"Rocks?" He laughs. "I think you'll find those leather bags are full of sand."

"Felt like rocks," I grumble, looking down at my knuckles and seeing a row of red blisters on each.

"Shit!" Gregory grabs my hands. "You *did* go to town. Feel better for it?"

"Yes," I admit. "Anyway, don't let Ben mess you around."

He chokes on a laugh. "Olivia, you'll forgive me if I don't take any notice of your advice. What about you? Have you heard from the coffee-hating prick?"

I resist the urge to defend Miller again or to tell Gregory about the text message and gym scene. It'll get me nowhere, except lectured. "No," I lie. "My phone's knackered, so no one can contact me." That thought suddenly thrills me, and it's undoubtedly a good thing should Miller decide to text me again. "This is me." I point at the bus stop.

Gregory dips and kisses my forehead, giving me a sympathetic face. "I'm going to the parents' for dinner tonight. Wanna come?"

"No, thanks." Gregory's parents are lovely people, but keeping up with conversation requires brainpower, and I have none to spare at the moment.

"Tomorrow, then?" he pleads. "Please, let's do something tomorrow."

"Yes, tomorrow." I'll find the enthusiasm for a full-on discussion within the next day, as long as the discussion remains on Gregory's diabolical love life and not mine.

His happy smile makes me smile in return. "Catch ya later, baby girl." He roughs up my hair and jogs off, leaving me to wait for my bus, and as if the gods detect my gloomy mood, they open the heavens and let it pour down on me.

"What?" I exclaim, wriggling out of my jacket and covering my head, thinking it's just typical that my bus stop is one with no damn shelter. And to rub it in, all of my fellow bus waiters have umbrellas and are looking at me like I'm stupid. I *am* stupid—for more reasons than not just carrying an umbrella. "Shit!" I curse, looking around for a doorway, anywhere to escape the pounding rain.

I circle, hunched under my jacket, but I find no place that'll protect me. A heavy, defeated sigh falls from my mouth while I stand hopelessly in the pouring rain, thinking that the day couldn't possibly get any longer or worse.

I'm proven wrong. I suddenly can't feel the rain pelting my body, and the loud pounding of it beating the pavement dulls out, leaving my hearing saturated with words. His words.

The black Mercedes slows and pulls up at the bus stop—Miller's Mercedes. In an action based on pure impulse, because I know he won't want to get his perfection wet, I turn and start jogging up the road, the chaos of London rush hour attacking my chaotic mind.

"Livy!" I barely hear him in the distance, over the pounding rain. "Livy, wait!"

When I reach a road, I'm forced to stop, the traffic zooming through the green light, leaving me among many other pedestrians waiting to cross, all with umbrellas. I frown when the people on both sides of me jump back, but by the time I've realized why, it's too late. A great big truck zooms past, straight through a lake of a puddle by the roadside, kicking oceans of water up my body.

"No!" I drop my jacket on a shocked gasp as the freezing cold water drenches me. "Shit!" The lights change and everyone else starts to cross, leaving me looking like a drowned rat on the curbside, shivering and brimming with tears.

"Livy." Miller's voice is quieter, but I'm not sure if it's because he's far away or the rain is drowning him out. His warm touch on my wet arm soon tells me it's the latter, leaving me surprised that he's ventured out of his car, given the dreadful weather and the effect it'll have on his expensive suit.

I shrug him off. "Leave me alone." I bend to collect my saturated jacket from the ground, fighting the growing lump in my throat and the familiar internal sparks that his touch on my cold, wet skin has instigated.

"Olivia."

"How do you know William Anderson?" I blurt, swinging my eyes to him, finding he's standing beneath the safety and dryness of a giant golf umbrella. I should've known. I've surprised myself with my question, and obviously Miller, too, judging by his slight recoil. There are many questions I should be asking, yet my mind has centered on this one alone.

"It's of no importance." He's being dismissive, making me more persistent.

"I beg to differ," I spit. He knew. All that time he knew. I may have only mentioned William's first name when I spilled my heart, released everything from my conscience about my mother to Miller, but he knew exactly who I was referring to, and now I'm certain that *that* was the cause for the majority of his violent reaction and shock.

He must see the unyielding determination on my face because his impassive expression wavers slightly into a scowl. "You know Anderson, and you know me." His jaw tenses. He means I know what they both do. "Our paths have crossed over the years."

From the bitterness rolling off of him in waves, I determine something quite quickly. "He doesn't like you."

"And I don't like him."

"Why?"

"Because he pokes his nose in where it isn't wanted."

I inwardly laugh, thinking how much I agree, and my eyes drop to the ground, seeing raindrops splashing the pavement. Miller's confirmation only reinforces my previous fear. I'm delusional if I believe for a moment that William will disappear to where he came from without digging for information on my connection with Miller. I learned many things about William Anderson, and one of those things was his desire to be in the know about *everything.* I don't want to explain to anyone, least of all my mother's ex-pimp. And anyway, I don't owe him any explanation.

I'm snapped from my worries when I see Miller's tan brogues appear in my line of sight. "How are you, Olivia?"

I refuse to look at him now, his question restoking my anger. "How do you think I am, Miller?"

"I don't know. That's why I've been trying to contact you."

"You really have no idea?" I look up at him, surprised. His perfect features hurt my eyes, making me instantly drop my gaze, like if I look at him for too long, I might never forget him.

Too late.

"I have an inkling," he murmurs. "I did tell you to take me for who I am, Livy."

"But I didn't know who you were." I grind the words out, keeping my eyes on the bouncing raindrops at my feet, incensed that he would use such a feeble excuse to wriggle out of this. "The only thing that I've accepted is that you're different, with your obsession to have everything painfully perfect and your uptight manners. It can be annoying as hell, but I've accepted it and even started to find it lovable." I should have used any other word—appealing, charming, endearing—but not lovable.

"I'm not that bad," he argues weakly.

"Yes!" I look at him now. His face is straight. It's nothing new. "Look!" I run my finger up and down his dry, suited body. "You're standing here with an umbrella that could keep half of London dry, just so you don't get your perfect hair and expensive suit wet."

He looks a little sulky as he casts his eyes down his suit and slowly back up to me. Then he chucks the umbrella to the pavement, and the rain instantly soaks him, waves of hair falling all over his face, water running down his cheeks, and his expensive suit starting to stick to him. "Happy?"

"You think getting yourself a little wet might fix this? You fuck women for a living, Miller! And you fucked me! You made me one of them!" I stagger back, dizzy from both my fury and the flashbacks of our time in the hotel room.

The water pouring down his face is shimmering. "You don't need to be so crass, Olivia."

I recoil, trying desperately to gather myself. "Fuck you and your bent moral compass!" I shout, making Miller's jaw seize with stiffness. "Are you forgetting what I told you?"

"How could I possibly forget?" Anyone else would think his face utterly impassive, but I see the tic in his cheek, the anger in his eyes—eyes I know how to read. I would say that he's right, that he really is emotionally unavailable, but I've experienced feeling with him—incredible feeling—and now I just feel conned.

I wipe my sopping hair from my face. "Your shock when I confided in you, told you about my history, wasn't because I put myself out there or because of my mother. It was because I'd described your life, with the drink and rich people, taking gifts and money. And. That. You. Knew. William. Anderson." I'm doing a grand job of retaining my emotions. I just want to scream at him, and if he doesn't give me something soon, I might just do that. These are the things that I should have said before. I shouldn't have goaded him into fucking me or put myself in those women's shoes to prove a point—a point I still can't fathom. Anger makes you do stupid things, and I was angry. "Why did you invite me to dinner?"

"I didn't know what else to do."

"There's nothing you *can* do."

"Then why did you come?" he asks.

His straight question catches me off guard. "Because I was angry with you! Flash cars, clubs, and luxury possessions don't make it right!" I yell. "Because you made me fall in love with a man you're not!" I'm freezing cold, but my quivering body is not a result of that. I'm angry—blood-boiling angry.

"You're my habit, Olivia Taylor." His statement is delivered with no emotion. "You belong to me."

"Belong to you?" I ask.

"Yes." He steps forward, prompting me to retreat, keeping the distance between us somewhere near to safe. It's an ambitious endeavor when he's still within sight.

"You must be mistaken." I raise my chin and work hard on keeping my voice even. "The Miller Hart I know has an appreciation for his possessions."

"Don't!" He takes my arm, but I yank it free.

"You wanted to continue with your secret life of fucking woman after woman, and you wanted me to make myself readily available for you to fuck when you got home." I mentally correct myself. He called it destressing, but he can call it what he likes. The principle is still the same.

He freezes me in place with adamant eyes. "I've never fucked you, Livy. I've only ever worshipped you." He steps forward. "I only ever made love to you."

I draw a long, calming breath. "You didn't make love to me in that hotel room."

His eyes clench shut briefly, and when they reopen, I see anguish pouring from them. "I didn't know what I was doing."

"You were doing what Miller Hart does best," I spit, hating the venom in my tone and the mild shock that passes across his heart-stopping face as a result of my statement. Many women may think that that's what London's most notorious male escort does best, but I know different. And deep down, so does Miller.

He watches me for a moment, unspoken words swimming in his gaze. It's right now that understanding slams through me. "You think I'm a hypocrite, don't you?"

"No." He shakes his head mildly... unconvincingly. "I accept what you did when you ran away and gave yourself..." He pulls up. He can't finish. "I accept why you did it. I hate it. It makes me hate Anderson even more. But I accept it. I accept *you*."

Shame eats away at me, and I momentarily lose my fortitude.

He accepts me. And reading between the lines, I think he wants me to accept him. *Take me as I am, Olivia.*

I shouldn't. I *can't.*

When an eternity passes and I've mentally sprinted through every reason to walk away, I hold his gaze and reel off my own version of his words. "I don't want other women to taste you."

His body goes lax on an exhale of defeated breath. "It's not as easy as just quitting."

Those words are like a bullet to my head, and with nothing left to say, I turn and walk away, leaving my perfect Miller Hart, still looking perfect in the pouring rain.

Chapter Three

The week is passing painfully slowly. I've seen my shifts through at the bistro and avoided Gregory, and I've not returned to the gym. I want to, but I can't risk seeing Miller. Every time I seem to edge forward a little, he seems to sense it and materializes from nowhere—mainly in my dreams, a few times in reality—to put me back at square one.

Nan appears at the lounge doorway and takes a few moments to dust the nearby bookshelf before swiping the remote control from my hand. "Hey, I was watching that!" I wasn't watching it at all, and even if I had been utterly engrossed and interested in the documentary on fruit bats, Nan wouldn't give a stuff.

"Hush your mouth and help me decide." She throws the remote onto the couch next to me and runs into the hallway, returning quickly with two dresses on hangers. "I can't choose," she says, holding one up to the front of her body. It's blue with bright yellow flowers scattered all over it. "This one"—she swaps it for the green dress—"or this one?"

I sit up a little and flick my eyes between the two. "I like both."

Her navy eyes roll. "Fat lot of help you are."

"Where are you going?"

"Dinner-dance with George on Friday."

I smile. "Are you going to rock the ballroom?"

"Pfft!" She shakes her head and performs a little jig, making my smile widen. "Olivia, your grandmother rocks just about anything she does."

"True," I admit, scanning the dresses again. "The blue one."

The smile that graces her face replaces some of the lingering coldness that has resided for days, sending a brief shot of warmth to my heart. "I think so, too." She throws the green one aside and holds the favorite up against her. "It's perfect for dancing."

"Is it a competition?"

"Not officially."

"You mean it's just a dance?"

"Oh, Olivia, it's never *just* a dance." She twirls and flicks her gray bob, for what it's worth. "Just call me Ginger."

I chuckle. "And is George your Fred?"

She sighs, exasperated. "God bless him, he tries, but the man has two left feet."

"Give him a break. The poor bloke is in his late seventies!"

"I'm no spring chicken, but I can still bump and grind with the best of 'em."

My brow wrinkles. "Bump and what?"

Her legs bend until she's squatting a little, and then she starts thrusting her old hips forward. "Bump," she says, before changing directions and swiveling her hips around, "and grind."

"Nan!" I laugh, watching as she alternates between thrusting and swiveling. She looks crafty as she increases her pace, leaving me in a helpless fit of giggles on the couch, holding my aching stomach. "Stop it!"

"I might audition for Beyoncé's next music video. Think I'll rock it?" She winks and takes a seat next to me, wrapping me in her arms. I get my laughter under control and sigh into her bosom, embracing her tight clinch. "Nothing gives me greater pleasure than seeing those beautiful eyes sparkle when you laugh, my darling girl."

My amusement subsides and appreciation takes over—appreciation for this wonderful old woman who I'm so lucky to call my grandmother. She's worked tirelessly to fill the gaping hole that my mother left and has succeeded to a certain extent. And now she's adopting the same tactic for the absence of another person in my life. "Thank you," I whisper.

"For what?"

I shrug a little. "Just for being you."

"A nosy old bat?"

"I never mean it when I say that."

"Yes, you do." She laughs and pulls me from her bust, cupping my cheeks in her wrinkled hands and smothering me with her marshmallow lips. "My beautiful, beautiful girl. Dig deep to find that sass, Olivia. Not too much, but just a little. It'll serve you well."

My lips tip. She means not as much as my mother.

"Darling girl, take life by the balls and twist them."

I laugh, and she laughs, too, falling back on the sofa and taking me with her. "I'll try."

"And while you're at it, twist the balls of any arseholes you encounter, too." She hasn't said it directly, but I know who she's talking about. Who else?

The house phone rings, pulling us both up.

"I'll get it," I say, giving Nan a quick kiss on the cheek and heading into the hall, where the cordless device sits in its cradle on the old-fashioned telephone table. In a sad fit of excitement, my eyes light up when I see the bistro's landline number displayed on the screen, and I hope I know why. "Del!" I greet, all cheery and way too enthusiastic.

"Hi, Livy." His strong cockney accent is a pleasure to hear. "I tried your mobile, but it was dead."

"Yeah, it's broken." I need to get a new phone pronto, but I'm also quite enjoying the benefit of seclusion that *not* having one is bringing.

"Oh good. Now, I know you're not keen on evenings..."

"I'll do it!" I blurt, taking the stairs fast. *Distraction, distraction, distraction.*

"Oh?"

"You want me to waitress?" I fall into the bathroom, sadly excited at the thought of a perfect opportunity to escape the risk of falling back into mental torment, now that Nan's antics have expired for the day.

"Yes, at the Pavilion. Damn agency workers are so unreliable."

"No prob—" I halt midsentence and fall against the bathroom door, suddenly thinking of something that could blow my plan of distraction out of the water. "Can I ask what the occasion is?"

I can see Del frown in my mind's eye. "Uh, yeah, annual gala for a bunch of judges and barristers."

My whole being relaxes. Miller is not a judge, nor is he a barrister. I'm safe.

"Should I wear black?" I ask.

"Yes." He sounds confused. "Seven o'clock start."

"Great. I'll see you there." I hang up and throw myself in the shower.

* * *

I hurry into the staff entrance of the Pavilion and immediately find Del and Sylvie pouring champagne. "I'm here!" I shrug off my denim jacket and ditch my satchel. "What should I do?"

Del smiles, then looks to Sylvie, a quiet acknowledgment passing between them at my unusual cheery mood. "Finish pouring, you sweet thing," he says, handing me a bottle and leaving me with Sylvie to finish up.

"You okay?" I ask Sylvie, commencing pouring duties.

Her black bob sways as she shakes her head on a smile. "You look...chirpy."

I swiftly brush off her observation, refusing to let the smile fall from my face. "Life goes on," I say quickly before going for subject change. "How many posh people have we got to feed and water this evening?"

"About three hundred. The reception is from eight until nine before they'll all be pushed into the ballroom for dinner. We'll pick up again at tenish when they're done and the band starts." She places the empty bottle of champagne down. "Done. Let's go."

Despite my enthusiasm to distract myself with work, I don't feel comfortable this evening. I'm gliding through the crowds, delivering canapés and champagne, but I feel uneasy. I don't like it.

When the maître d' announces dinner, the room soon empties, leaving hundreds of cocktail napkins all over the posh marble floor. They might be people of the legal world, but they've littered this stunning room terribly. I rid myself of my tray and start making my way around the room, scooping up the rubbish and stuffing it into a black sack, even finding the remnants of canapés as I go.

"You okay there, Livy?" Del calls across the room.

"Sure. They're a messy bunch," I say, tying my full sack. "Do you mind if I use the toilets?"

He laughs, shaking his head. "What would you do if I said no?"

The question throws me. "Are you going to say no?"

"God love you. Go to the bloody toilet, woman!" My boss disappears back into the kitchen, leaving me to find the washroom.

I take some stairs, following the signs for the ladies, until I'm wandering down a long stretch of corridor, admiring the paintings flanking either side of me. They are all of historical kings and queens, the earliest being Henry VIII. I stop and take in the portly, bearded man in his later years, wondering, stupidly, what would possess a woman to venture there.

"He's not Miller Hart, is he?"

I swing around, coming face-to-face with Miller's "business associate." Cassie. What the hell is she doing here? She's gazing at the picture thoughtfully, arms crossed over the bustier of a stunning silver gown, her glossy black hair tumbling over her shoulders.

"And he may have been a busy boy in the bedroom, but not as busy as Miller." Her sly, hurtful words are like pins shoved viciously into the center of my heart. "Is he as good as everyone claims?" She turns her cocky expression to me, giving me the once-over with eyes full of satisfaction. I crumble a little, yet find a hidden strength to conceal it.

"That depends on how good everyone claims he is," I retort, meeting her stare and matching her confidence. Her question quickly tells me that she's asking because she doesn't know herself, and that satisfies me too much.

"Very good."

"Then they are *very* right."

She barely retains her shock, pushing my confidence further. "I see," she says quietly, nodding mildly.

"But I'll tell you something for free." I step forward, feeling unreasonably superior with the knowledge that I've had him and Cassie hasn't. I don't give her the opportunity to ask what. I'm in my stride. "He makes love even better than he fucks with restraints."

She gasps, backing away from me, and it's in this moment I comprehend the weight of Miller's reputation. It makes me feel nauseous. Somehow, though, I manage to cling on to my sass.

"If your plan was to try to shock me with news of Miller's business, then it's wasted bitchiness. I already know."

"Right," she says slowly, thoughtfully.

"Are we done, or are you going to enlighten me of his rules, too?"

She laughs, but it's a surprised laugh. I've shocked her even more, startled her with my assertiveness, and she wasn't prepared for it, which is now making me smug. "I guess we're done."

"Good," I fire with confidence before finding my way to the toilet and falling apart once I'm safely behind the closed door of the cubicle. I'm not sure why I'm crying when I feel so satisfied with myself. I think I just twisted some balls, and Nan would be so proud . . . if I could tell her.

After spending an eternity pulling myself together, I make my way back to the kitchens and start loading up some trays of champagne in preparation for the return of guests from their meal.

Cassie is one of the first to enter the room, and she is draped all over a mature man, at least thirty years her senior. It's then that the obviousness hits me like a tornado, making my tray of champagne flutes chink as my palm shakes. She's a high-class hooker, too!

"Oh my God," I whisper, watching her giggle and lap up the attention he's showering her with. Why? She has a stake in an exclusive nightclub. She surely doesn't need the cash or gifts. And in this moment, I swiftly realize that I haven't even considered Miller's motive for absorbing himself in that world. He *owns* Ice. He definitely doesn't need the money. I reflect back to our encounter at the restaurant, scanning my mind for some words I vaguely recall.

Enough to buy a nightclub.

I'm buzzing with curiosity, and I hate being curious. It's already got me in too deep and more could see me drowning.

"You gonna stand there all night and daydream?" Sylvie's voice snaps me back into the room, which is now filled with guests and happy chatter. My eyes cast slowly across the gatherings of people, all, as usual, impeccably dressed, and I wonder how many are immersed in a world of high-class prostitution. "Livy?"

I jump, prompting me to steady my tray with my spare hand. "Sorry!"

"What's wrong?" Sylvie asks, looking around the room, and I know it's because of all the other times during these functions that I've had a funny turn.

"Nothing," I blurt. "I'd better get serving."

"Hey, is that the woman..." She pauses and looks at me, her pink lips pursed tight to stop her from completing her question.

I don't answer, instead leaving Sylvie to lose myself in the crowd and let her draw her own conclusion. I've led my friends to believe that Cassie is Miller's girlfriend, and I might have gotten away with it if the slut wasn't parading around blatantly with another man.

Chapter Four

I walk home from work the next evening, taking a few detours to see some of my favorite landmarks on my way. As always, the diversion is welcome, but when I stop at a street vendor to buy a bottle of water, a picture on the front of a newspaper catapults me back to square one. He did this interview weeks ago. Why only now is it in print? My pulse increases as I absorb the photograph of the beautiful male gracing the front page, and then it pumps relentlessly when I read the headline:

London's most eligible bachelor opens London's most exclusive nightclub.

I gingerly pick up the paper and stare down at the words, being bombarded by images of a happy moment, when he had acknowledged his feelings and seemed to have given up trying to hide from them. He'd told that brash journalist to rethink her plan to title the piece with this. She must have been delighted by the news that Miller Hart is, in fact, a bachelor. The hurt is too much and reading the article will only inflame it, so I force myself to throw it back on the pile, forgetting to collect the water I'd originally stopped for.

He's still around every corner. I stare blankly down the pavement, trying to figure out where to head next. In my fog, I step into the road, only to be honked at by an approaching car, but I don't even jump. If that car were to mow me down, I wouldn't feel a thing.

It slows and stops a few feet before me. The Lexus is unfamiliar, but the registration plate isn't. Two letters. Just two.

W.A.

The driver's door opens and an unfamiliar man gets out, tipping his hat to me before briskly walking around the car and opening the rear door, holding it, and gesturing for me to get in. Refusing would be stupid. He'll find me, no matter where I hide, so I tentatively step forward and lower myself into the car, keeping my eyes down, working hard to make my tears recede. I don't need to look to check if I'm alone. I know I'm not. I could feel the power that he wields from outside of the car. Now that I'm within touching distance of him, it's potent.

"Hello, Olivia." William's voice is just how I remember. Soft. Comforting.

I hang my head. I'm not ready for this.

"You could at the very least be courteous enough to look at me and say hello this time. That night at the hotel, you were in an awful hurry."

I slowly turn my eyes and absorb every refined piece of William Anderson, refreshing the distant memories that I've stored at the back of my mind for years and years. "What is it about you types and manners?" I ask shortly, keeping my stare on his shimmering grays. They seem even more sparkly, his full head of gray hair making his eyes seem more like liquid metal.

He smiles and reaches over, clasping my little hand in his big one. "I would have been disappointed had you not fired a little spunk in my direction."

His touch is just as comforting as his handsome face. I don't want it to be, but it is. "And I would hate to disappoint you, William," I sigh. The door next to me shuts and the driver is up front in no time, pulling away from the curb. "Where are you taking me?"

"For dinner, Olivia. It seems we have a lot to talk about." He pulls my hand to his mouth and kisses my knuckles before placing it back in my lap. "The similarities are incredible," he says quietly.

"Don't," I grate, turning to look out the window. "If that's all you want to talk about, then I'll graciously decline your invitation to dinner."

"I wish it really was all there is to talk about," he replies sternly. "But a certain wealthy young gentleman is higher on my list of concerns, Olivia."

My eyes slowly close, and if it were possible, I'd close my ears, too. I don't want to hear what William has to say. "Your concern isn't necessary."

"I'll be the one who decides that. I'm not going to sit back and watch you be dragged into a world where you don't belong. I fought long and hard to keep you from it, Olivia." He reaches over and runs his knuckles down my cheek, watching me closely. "I won't allow it."

"It has nothing to do with you." I'm sick of people thinking they know what's best for me. *I'm the master of my own destiny*, I think like an idiot. I take the handle of the door when the car stops at a red light, ready to jump out and run. But I don't get very far. The door won't budge and William has a firm grip around the top of my arm.

"You're staying in this car, Olivia," he asserts firmly as the car pulls away from the lights. "I'm in no mood for your defiance this evening. You really are your mother through and through."

I shrug him off and rest back in the plush leather. "Please don't speak of her."

"Your hatred hasn't lessened, then?"

I turn cold eyes onto my mother's ex-pimp. "Why would it? She chose your dark world over her daughter."

"You're about to choose a darker world," he says matter-of-factly.

My mouth snaps shut and my heart rate doubles. "I'm choosing nothing," I whisper. "I'm never going to see him again."

He smiles fondly at me on a little shake of his head. "Who are you trying to convince?" he asks, and probably wisely, too. I heard my words. There was no conviction in them. "I'm here to help you, Olivia."

"I don't need your help."

"I assure you, you do. More than you did seven years ago," he says harshly, almost coldly, leaving me *feeling* cold. I remember William's dark world. I can't possibly need his help more now than I did then.

He turns away from me and takes his phone from his inside pocket, punching in a few numbers before holding it to his ear. "Cancel my appointments for the rest of the evening," he orders, and then hangs up, slipping his phone back into his jacket. He keeps his gaze forward for the rest of the journey, leaving me wondering what's about to transpire over dinner. I know I'm about to hear things that I don't want to, and I know there is nothing I can do to stop it.

The driver pulls the Lexus up to a small restaurant and opens the door for me. William nods, a wordless gesture to step out, which I do without a fuss, knowing it will get me nowhere to protest. Smiling at the driver, I wait for William to join me on the pavement and then watch as he buttons his jacket before placing his hand on the small of my back to guide me onward. The doors to the restaurant are opened for us and William greets almost everyone as we pass through. The awareness of his presence by other diners and the staff is powerful. He nods and smiles all the way until we're being seated at a private table at the back, away from prying eyes and ears. A wine menu is handed to me by a smart waiter, and I smile my thanks as I take my seat.

"She'll have water," he orders. "And the usual for me." There's no please or thank you. "I recommend the risotto." William smiles across the table at me.

"I'm not hungry." My stomach's in knots, a mixture of nerves and anger. I couldn't possibly eat.

"You're bordering on emaciated, Olivia. Please let me have the satisfaction of watching you eat a decent meal."

"I have my nan to nag me about my weight. I don't need you nagging, too." I place the menu on the table and take the glass of water that's just been poured.

"How is the formidable Josephine?" he asks, accepting a tumbler of dark liquid from the waiter.

She wasn't so formidable when William sent me back to her. I recall him referring to my grandmother on a few occasions during my reckless spell, but I was too blinkered by my determination back then to delve into the details of their acquaintance. "You knew her?" Now I'm curious again, and I damn well hate being curious.

He laughs, and it's a pleasant sound, all smooth and light. "I'll never forget her. I was her first call each time Gracie performed one of her disappearing acts."

The mention of my mother's name stirs the bile in my stomach, but hearing about my grandmother makes me smile on the inside. She's fearless, not intimidated in the least bit by anyone, and I know William wouldn't have been an exception. His amused tone while talking of Nan is proof. "She's well," I answer.

"Still spunky?" he asks with a slight smile on his lips.

"More than ever," I answer, "but she wasn't too good when you took me home that night seven years ago."

"I know." He nods in understanding. "She needed you."

Regret cripples me, and I crumble within, wishing I could change how I reacted to the discovery of my mother's journal and to my grandmother's grief. "We got through it. She's still spunky."

He smiles. It's a fond smile. "No one ever made me quake in my boots, Olivia. Only your grandmother." The idea of William quaking in his boots is ludicrous. "But she knew deep down that I could no less control Gracie than she or your grandfather could."

William relaxes back in his chair and orders two risottos when the waiter presents himself.

"Why?" I ask once the waiter has scurried away again. This is a question I should have asked all those years ago. There are so many things I should have asked back then.

"Why what?"

"Why was my mother like that? Why couldn't she be controlled?"

William visibly shifts in his seat, clearly uncomfortable by my question, and his gray eyes are avoiding mine. "I tried, Olivia."

I frown across the table at him, finding it strange seeing such a prolific male looking so awkward. "What?"

He sighs and rests his elbows on the table. "I should have sent her away sooner. Like I did you when I discovered who you were."

"Why would you send her away?"

"Because she was in love with me." He watches for my reaction across the table, but he won't find much because I've been stunned into blankness. My mum was in love with her pimp? Then why the hell did she put it about town? Why . . . Realization descends quickly and halts my silent questions.

"You didn't love her," I whisper.

"I loved your mother madly, Olivia."

"Then why—" I sit back in my chair. "She was punishing you."

"Daily," he sighs. "Every fucking day."

This isn't what I expected. I'm totally confused. "If you loved each other, then why weren't you together?"

"She wanted me to do things that I simply couldn't."

"Or wouldn't."

"No, *couldn't.* I had a responsibility. I couldn't walk away from my girls and let them fall into the hands of some immoral bastard."

"So you walked away from my mum."

"And let her fall into the hands of an immoral bastard."

I gasp, my eyes darting around the dimly lit restaurant, trying to comprehend what I'm being told. "You knew. I was looking for answers and you knew all along?"

His lips straighten and his nostrils flare. "You didn't need to know the sordid details. You were a young girl."

"How could you let her go like that?"

"I kept her close for years, Olivia. Letting her loose in my world was disastrous. I stood back and watched her drown men in her beauty and spirit, watched them fall for her. It tore my heart out every fucking day, and she knew it. I couldn't take it anymore."

"So you banished her."

"And I wish to every god that I hadn't."

I gulp back the lump forming in my throat. Everything William has told me might fill a massive hole in my history, but it doesn't fill the hole in my heart. Despite his tale of tortured love though, she still abandoned her daughter. There's nothing he could tell me to make that right. I glimpse across the table at the mature, handsome man whom my mother was in love with, and crazily, I can appreciate it. And even crazier was that I went to find my mother, tried to fathom her mentality. I took her journal and tracked down those men she wrote about, desperate to figure out what she found so appealing. But instead I found comfort in her pimp. My short time with William when I was seventeen showed me a compassionate, caring man, a man who I fast became fond of, a man who cared for me. There was no desire, nor was there any physical attraction, despite his good looks, but I can't deny that I felt a certain sense of love for him.

"How did you not know who I was?" I ask. I survived a whole week before William worked it out. I remember his face, the realization . . . the anger. I know that I look scarily like my mother. How had he not seen it?

He takes a deep, almost frustrated breath. "When you turned up, it had been fifteen years since I'd seen Gracie. The resemblance was uncanny, but I was so blindsided by that alone I didn't stop to consider the possibility. Then I did, but the math didn't add up." His eyebrows jump up accusingly. "Wrong name, wrong age."

I look away, ashamed. I'm humiliated and shattered. Some things are best left dead, and my mother is one of those things. "Thank you," I whisper quietly as our risotto is placed before us.

William lets the waiter fuss for a few moments before flicking his hand, silently ordering him to leave. "For what?"

"For sending me back to Nan." I look up at him and he reaches over and takes my hand. "For helping me and not telling my grandmother." That was what did it. William's threat to pay a visit to Nan terrified me more than anything else because it would have killed her. She was in a terribly dark place. As far as Nan is concerned, I ran away to escape the harsh reality that my mother's journal represented. I couldn't add to her grief. Not after everything she went through with her daughter and then Granddad. "But I read her journal." I let the words tumble from my lips in a moment of confusion. "That's how I found you back then."

"A little black book?" he asks with an edge of resentment to his tone.

"Yes." I'm almost excited that he knows what I'm talking about. "You know of it?"

"Of course I do." William's jaw has noticeably tightened, making me sit farther back in my chair. "She was kind enough to leave it on my desk for a bit of bedtime reading once."

"Oh..." I pick up my fork and start poking at the rice dish that I'm not hungry for—anything to escape the potent bitterness pouring from William.

"Your mother could be a cruel woman, Olivia."

I nod, the purpose of the little black book suddenly very clear. She really did get a thrill from writing all of those passages, describing endless encounters with endless men, all in vivid detail. But it wasn't because she relished doing it. Or maybe she did. Who knows? But the primary reason was to torture William. Her thrill was knowing the hurt and anger she'd cause the man she was in love with.

"Anyway," he sighs, "that's all history..."

I scoff at his insult. "For you, perhaps! For me it's a daily mystery as to why she'd give me up."

"Don't beat yourself up, Olivia."

"Well I do!" I'm outraged that he can pass off my abandonment with such flippancy. Trying to convince myself it was of no consequence that she cleared off was easier than facing the harsh reality. A story of tortured love doesn't make this all better, nor does it make me understand.

"Calm down." William leans across the table and gives my hand a soothing rub, but I snatch it away. I'm furious with so many aspects of my life, and I feel like all of it is out of my control.

"I am calm!" I yell, making William sit back in his chair with a look of exasperation on his handsome face. "I'm calm." I start playing with my risotto again. "Do you think she's alive?"

The harsh pull of breath that stems from the man across the table is full of pain. "I..." He's shifting in his chair again, avoiding my eyes. "I'm..."

"Just tell me," I say evenly, wondering why I care. She's dead to me anyway.

"I don't know." William collects his own fork and pokes at the dish. "Gracie and her ability to make men insane with frustration and lust could have quite possibly driven someone to strangulation, too. Trust me, I know." He drops his fork, the conversation clearly sucking up his appetite. I follow his lead and do exactly the same.

"It sounds like she was a handful," I say, because I don't know what else there is *to* say.

"You have no idea," he sighs, almost on a smile, like he's reflecting. "Anyway, back to the matter at hand." He brushes off the reminiscing quickly and turns all businesslike, and I imagine that's exactly how it was all those years ago with my mother. Even just talking about her exposes vulnerability in this hard-faced, powerful man. "Miller Hart."

"What about him?" I raise my chin cockily, like he's of no importance.

"How do you know him?"

"How do *you* know him?" I'm being conniving, but I'm also even more curious after Miller's vague explanation. All of these warnings and concern. Why?

"He's a ruined man."

"That doesn't answer my question."

William leans forward, and I move back, wary. "That man lives in a dark place, Olivia. Darker than mine. He plays with the devil."

I swallow hard, pain slicing through my heart. No words are coming to me, and even if they did, I wouldn't get them past my thick tongue.

"I know what he does and how he does it," William continues. "He's known as London's most notorious male escort for a reason, Olivia. I worked too hard to keep you from my own business dealings to see you blindly jump into Miller Hart's dark place. I've been in this world for a long, long time. There's not much I don't know, if anything. And I know this..." he pauses, leaving a lingering, unwanted silence hovering between us. "He will break you."

I flinch at his cold claim. I'm desperate to tell him that Miller showed me nothing but tenderness... until that night at the hotel. The night William found me racing away from where Miller had restrained me to a bedpost and treated me like any of his other clients. I still wasn't sure what was worse—his cold impassiveness that night or the way his clever fingers and tongue still made me come in exquisite torture.

"Thanks for the news flash" are the only words I can get out through my pain.

"You're your mother's daughter, Olivia."

"Don't say that!" I yell, making William recoil. He doesn't retaliate, though. He simply takes a sip of his drink and waits for me to calm down. “I’m nothing like my mother. She gave up her daughter for a man who didn’t want her.”

He leans forward, his gray eyes blazing. “A relationship between me and Gracie Taylor would have been impossible. Don’t you dare think for a minute that I wasn’t trying to do what was best for her. Or for you.”

I’m slightly taken aback by William’s unusual show of anger. I’ve never seen him anything less than perfectly composed.

He takes another sip of his drink before continuing. “And a relationship between you and Miller Hart would be as equally impossible.”

“I know,” I whisper, feeling those damn tears pinching the backs of my eyes. “I already know that.”

“I’m glad, but knowing something is bad for you doesn’t stop you from wanting it. Pursuing it. I was bad for Gracie, yet she wouldn’t give up.”

“Will you stop comparing me to my mother, William?” I shake my head, not prepared to listen to the cold, hard truth any longer. “I really should get home. Nan will be worrying.”

“Then call her.” He nods to my bag. “I’m enjoying the company and we have dessert and coffee to order yet.”

“My phone’s broken.” It’s the perfect excuse to escape. I make to stand, collecting my satchel from the floor beside me. “Thank you for dinner.”

“I sense no appreciation in your tone, Olivia. How am I supposed to get hold of you?”

His question worries me. “Why would you want to?”

“To ensure your safety.”

“From what?”

“Miller Hart.”

I roll my eyes, forgetting, again, who I’m dealing with. “I’ve survived just fine without your supervision, William. I think I’m good.” I turn and walk away from him, praying it’s the last I see of him. This dinner, although enlightening, has only brought back too much hurt, which on top of my already searing pain might be the final nail in the coffin.

"You won't survive with Miller Hart in your life, Olivia."

I skid to a stop on my Converse, his declaration freezing my veins. I dare not look at him for fear of what facial expression I might find. *He's not in my life*, I say to myself, hearing the movement of a chair and slow footsteps, but I keep my eyes forward until William has rounded me and is looking down at my pathetic form.

"I know a woman captured by a man when I see one, Olivia. I saw it in your mother and I can see it in you." He takes my dropped chin and lifts. There's an element of knowing in his gray gaze. "I can see you're hurt and angry, and those two emotions can make you do silly things. His business conduct is questionable at best. And you should know that he's in Madrid for a few days." William flashes me a telling look, daring me to inquire further. I don't need to. He's with a client.

"I'm a sensible girl," I murmur meagerly. I can hear the uncertainty in my tone. I don't believe in my strength any more than William does, despite knowing everything he says is the cold, hard truth. He's right to be concerned. "I can take care of myself."

He drops his lips to my forehead and sighs through his delicate kiss. "You need more than words, Olivia." William takes my satchel from my shoulder and starts to guide me from the restaurant. "I'll take you home."

"I want to walk," I argue, breaking free of his hold.

"Be sensible, Olivia. It's late and dark." He reclaims me, tighter than before. "Anyway, we'll stop by a store and replace your phone."

"I can buy my own phone," I grate.

"Maybe so, but I'd like to buy you one as a gift." He raises cautionary eyebrows and his gray eyes darken when I open my mouth to object. "A gift that you *will* accept."

I don't argue further. I just want to go home and try to process what William has and hasn't told me, so I let him lead me from the restaurant and put me in his car, not saying a word.

After stopping by a store and loading me with the latest iPhone, William's driver drops me home, accepting my request to stop around the corner so Nan doesn't spot the strange car and me getting out of it.

"Make sure you charge this up," he orders, putting the lid back on the box. "I have the number and I've stored mine."

"For what purpose?" I ask, pissed off at his intrusion on my life.

"Simple peace of mind." He hands me the box and nods to the door for me to get out. "I would tell you to send Josephine my kindest regards, but I doubt it would be appreciated."

"*Without* doubt." I slide from the car and turn to shut the door. The window lowers and I bend to get William back into my field of vision. His gray eyes are shining, his big body reclined, putting emphasis on his torso. He's incredibly fit for a man in his mid-forties. "She would probably take a baseball bat to your posh car."

He throws his head back on a laugh, making me smile a little. "I can just picture it. I'm sincerely glad she's back to her old ways." He maintains his smile for a few moments before it slowly falls away, prompting mine to fall with it. "Just remember one thing, Olivia."

I almost don't want to ask what, and I don't need to because he draws breath to go on, obviously seeing my hesitance. He's going to tell me, whether I want to hear or not.

"Your body instinctively knows danger. If you feel the hair on the back of your neck rise, a prickly sensation between your shoulder blades, or just overall bad vibes—you run." The window starts closing and William's serious face disappears from sight, leaving me still bent on the pavement with the lingering effect of those cold words.

Chapter Five

Nan slides the plate toward me and hands me a fork. The giant lump of cake makes my stomach turn, but I resist pushing it away and break a corner off while she watches. Nan's eyes are not the only set studying me so closely. Gregory has joined us for supper, along with George, and they are all quiet and watching me as I bring a small piece of cake to my lips. It tastes like rat poison, and it has nothing to do with my grandmother's baking skills. Everything tastes rancid, my taste buds probably punishing me for neglecting them.

"Beautiful." Gregory breaks the uncomfortable silence, performing a little finger-licking session. "You should open a cake shop."

"Pah!" Nan scoffs. "Perhaps twenty years ago." She laughs, turning to the sink and running the tap. I'm thankful for the letup of scrutiny.

George's chubby finger delves straight onto the side of the cake plate, scooping off some stray lemon drizzle, and as if Nan has sensed something untoward is going down, she swings around from the sink.

"George!" She whips at him with her dishcloth. "Where are your manners?"

"Sorry, Josephine." He sits up like a naughty schoolboy and places his hands in his lap, his face straight.

Gregory kicks me under the table, nodding at Nan, and I look to see her shaking her head at the old boy. We're both suppressing our laughs, and then George winks cheekily at us and we both lose the battle to restrain ourselves. We titter together, earning a reproachful look from Nan before she turns back to the sink, and another wink from George.

"Are you ready to help Nan rock the ballroom, George?" I ask, reining in my chuckles before I get a thorough telling off. Old George is looking most dapper in a brown suit, although his mustard tie is questionable.

"Josephine needs no help to rock anything," he replies, looking over to my nan's back. "She does a damn fine job of rocking, as you call it, all by herself." Nan doesn't respond or turn around, but she's smiling down into the sink, I know she is.

"She's going to show you how to bump and grind." I snigger, kicking Gregory under the table but quickly hauling my leg back when Nan swings around from the washing up, making her lovely dress swoosh like it most certainly will be on the dance floor later. She glares at me as she dries her hands on her apron, her gray eyebrows raised.

"You look beautiful, Nan," I say.

Her scornful face drops in an instant and she glances down on a smile. "Thank you, sweetheart."

"Whatever is bumping and grinding?" George asks, totally perplexed, looking to Nan. I'm delighting in the faint blush that rises in her cheeks.

"It's dancing, George." She flicks me a warning look, but it softens the moment she registers my mild grin. "Modern dancing. I'll teach you."

I nearly fall off my chair when mental images of George and Nan getting down and dirty spring into my mind.

"What's so funny?" George asks, throwing frowns around the kitchen. "I knew that." He huffs, plunging his finger back into the lemon cake in a strop. Nan doesn't scorn him this time. She's too busy howling across the kitchen.

"I might wear my hot pants." She giggles, sending Gregory and me delirious with laughter.

"Oh, those little short thingies?" George's eyes sparkle. "Yes, please!"

"George!" Nan shrieks.

"Oh, please stop!" Gregory grabs me for support, falling all over the place, taking me with him. We're crying, shaking with hysterics. "Will they be sparkly?"

"No, leather." She grins. "And crotchless."

I choke on nothing, coughing all over the dinner table, and George looks like he's about to have a seizure. He gathers himself and picks up his newspaper, using it to fan his face. "You have a wicked mind, Josephine Taylor."

"She does." Gregory chuckles, giving me a little wink.

Everyone pulls themselves together and I sigh, starting to poke at my cake again. Then I worry because I hear Nan draw breath—the long kind, the kind that means I'm not going to like what she says. "Why don't you let Gregory take you out?"

I sink into my chair, feeling three sets of eyes all on me again. The misery returns, too.

"Yeah, come on, Livy," my friend interjects, giving me a light knock on my arm with his fist. "We'll go to a straight bar."

"See!" Nan chirps. "How kind. He's even willing to sacrifice a night of passion for your benefit."

I gasp. Gregory laughs and George snorts. He loves Gregory, but he refuses to acknowledge his sexual preference. I think it's an age thing, not that it bothers Gregory. In fact, he plays on it too much, and when he takes a deep inhale of air, I know immediately that he's about to do just that.

"Yes"—he leans back in his chair—"I'll pass up the opportunity to roll around with a naked, sweaty man if it means you'll come out."

I bite my lip, stopping myself from laughing out loud at the awkward fidgeting coming from George's direction. Nan doesn't, though. No, she's in pieces, her body jiggling with laughter as George continues to shift and mutter under his breath.

"You're all wicked," he grumbles. "Wicked minds."

"How very good of you, Gregory." Nan titters. "Now that's a good friend."

George's old face frowns at Gregory across the table. "I thought you were bisexual."

"Oh"—Gregory grins—"I'll be whatever they want me to be, George."

Nan's companion fails to prevent his disgusted snort and Nan fails to prevent her continued amusement.

This is good. The diversion in conversation to Gregory's sexual antics has saved me from further pressure to go out and my struggle to appear fine. I study him for a few moments, watching his shoulders jump up and down as he continues to wind up poor George, and Nan eggs him on with hoots of glee. Their happy banter suddenly only seems to remind me that I'm not happy and no amount of pretending or distraction will remedy it. Things can divert me momentarily, but it soon returns, seeming more painful when it does, like it's making up for its brief absence every time I break a smile.

My chews slow and so do my swallows. My turning stomach is fast, though, executing a fast spin that sends me dashing from the kitchen to the bathroom, where I retch over the toilet for no purpose at all. There's nothing to bring up except acidy bile, making the taste in my mouth even worse.

Hopeless.

The soft knock at the door forces me to lift my head and look blankly at the wood. "Baby girl?" Gregory pushes the door open and slips in, not bothering to warn me first in case I'm on the toilet. His handsome face tries to smile some ease into me but fails miserably. I know he feels as hopeless as I do. He pops a Polo Mint past my lips and pulls me to my feet before brushing my hair from my face and scanning me worriedly.

"Livy, you're wasting away." His eyes drop to my skinnier-than-usual body. "Come on."

Pulling me across the landing to my bedroom, he shuts the door softly behind us and guides me to the bed, tugging me next to him and slipping his arm around me. I snuggle into his side but get no comfort from his embrace. This isn't the *thing* I had with Miller. This isn't warming me to the core or sending my mind into a blissful peace. There's no humming or gentle lips pushing into the top of my head now and then.

We lie for an age in silence until I feel Gregory's chest rise, drawing air, prepared to speak. "Are you ready to give me the full story yet? You're not fine, and don't bother trying to fob me off with the 'other woman' story because you kinda had your suspicions before. It didn't stop you then."

I shake my head no into his chest, but I'm not sure whether I'm declining his offer to explain or if I'm telling him that no, it's not the supposed other woman. The former I don't need to confirm. It's glaringly obvious, but the latter isn't. I could never share the real reason why my life is over. And William? No, no, I couldn't.

"Okay," he sighs above me, squeezing me tighter, but then his phone starts ringing and he eases up a little to dig through his pocket. I definitely don't imagine the increased speed of his heart rate under my ear. Pulling from his chest, I find him staring down at the screen, looking completely defeated. His expression reminds me that while I've been wallowing in self-pity, my best friend has been suffering, too. I feel incredibly guilty, which, even more selfishly, feels so much better than my constant aching heart.

"Are you going to answer it?" I ask quietly, while he continues to stare down at the screen. I'm not sure why he looks so upset. Surely he should be happy that Ben is calling. Or am I missing something? Probably. I don't recall much from the past two weeks at all, but I distinctly remember he'd spoken to Ben briefly and it wasn't good. Or did I imagine that?

He lifts his eyes and smiles, but it's a sad smile. "I guess I should. I've been expecting it."

I frown a little as he connects the call, but he doesn't speak. He just holds the phone to his ear and it's mere seconds before I hear Ben's angry shouts, plain and clear. Gregory winces as his ex-lover hurls abuse down the line, ranting about calling and harassing him. I'm stunned, even more so when Gregory apologizes quietly. He's got nothing to be sorry about. He's not the one pretending to be someone he isn't. He's not hiding from the truth. Familiar anger bubbles but for a whole other reason, and in a moment centered on pure protective instinct, I snatch the phone from my friend's limp hand and let out two weeks' worth of fury. I'm raging.

"Who the hell do you think you are?" I shout, jumping up from the bed when Gregory tries to regain possession of his mobile. I pace doggedly around my bedroom, quaking with rage.

"Who's this?" Ben's voice has quieted. He sounds shocked.

"It doesn't matter who it is. You're nothing more than a fraud! You're a spineless coward!"

Ben is now silent but breathing heavily as I continue to attack him. "You deserve to be miserable! I hope you wallow in misery for the rest of your life, you pathetic, gutless arse!" I'm hyperventilating, physically shaking. "You don't deserve the affection or time Gregory has given you, and you'll soon realize that. And by then it'll be too late! He'll be over you!" I smash the Disconnect button and throw Gregory's phone on the bed, while my friend looks at me in shock, his eyes wide, his mouth agape.

Trying to cool down my boiling blood and rein in my quaking

body, I watch in silence as Gregory attempts to spit some words out. He's stuttering, totally stunned, a bit like me. It wasn't my place to do that. I had no right to interfere, especially as I've chastised my friend when he's tried to step in on my diabolical relationship with a certain man disguised as a gentleman.

"I'm sorry," I pant, failing to stabilize my erratic breathing. "I didn't—"

"Sassy," he says simply, and once again I fall apart, my anger making way for my depression to return full force. My chin drops to my chest, my arms hang limply by my sides, and I sob uncontrollably, my pathetic form now shaking for different reasons. I feel no better after my tirade.

Hearing a heavy sigh of frustration emanate from the bed, I'm pulled down to Gregory's chest and wrapped in his arms. "Shhhh," he soothes, rocking me back and forth, stroking my hair. "I get the feeling those words weren't meant for Ben."

I nod and he tightens his squeeze. They were appropriate for Ben, but I wish I were delivering them to another man. And I also wish I could reap what I sow.

"What a pair we are." He sighs. "How did we get ourselves in this mess?"

I don't know, so I shake my head, sobbing and sniveling uncontrollably.

"Hey." He pulls me out of my hiding place and holds my face gently as he gazes down at me, sympathy gushing from his eyes. "What are we going to do with each other, baby girl?"

"I don't know," I choke out, letting Gregory stroke the trail of tears away from my wet cheek. "I feel hopeless."

"Me too," he agrees softly as our eyes hold each other. "Me too."

There's an unexpected shift in the atmosphere, the two friends comforting each other suddenly looking longingly into each other's eyes, misery and desolation seeming to make way for something else.

Something strange.

Something forbidden.

I'm confused by it, and when my friend's lips part, his eyes flicking down to my mouth and his face coming slowly closer, my head starts spinning wildly. There are plenty of reasons to halt what is about to happen, but I can't think of them at the moment. I can't think of anything, except that this could be exactly what I need.

I start inching closer, too, until our lips meet and my heart starts thudding in my chest. The unusual feeling of my best friend's lips on mine doesn't deter me. I shift my position, throwing my leg over Gregory's reclined body and settling myself across his hips, keeping our mouths joined, letting our tongues dance madly. The sensation of his hands running all over my back and his mouth pressed hard to mine brings me a strange comfort, even if it's alien and not what I'm used to. It doesn't matter. I need different.

"Livy." He breaks our kiss, panting in my face. "We shouldn't. This is wrong."

I don't let him try to talk us out of this. I smash my lips back on his and start working him desperately, feeling his strong arms and smoothing down his tight muscles. He groans, the evidence of his hardness beneath me pushing me on.

"Livy," he argues weakly, making no attempt to push me off.

"We'll help each other," I gasp, pulling at the hem of his T-shirt. He doesn't stop me. He shifts, making my task easier, and is soon rid of it, leaving his chest exposed to my roaming hands. It's not long before I feel my top being pulled off, and I release his lips to sit up, letting my best friend in the whole world strip me. With a lack of a bra covering my modest breasts, I'm left in just my small pajama shorts with Gregory's eyes focused on my tight nipples that are within licking distance.

"Oh fucking hell," he mumbles, looking up at me as I wheeze

in his face. "Oh fucking, fucking hell." He takes the tops of my arms and pushes me to my back, taking my mouth again urgently as he pushes my shorts and knickers down my legs. He's hard and wedged up against my thigh, pulsing incessantly, and I find myself fumbling at the fly of his jeans. He helps me, lifting his hips slightly so I can rid him of the denim, until we're both naked, rubbing up against each other, rolling around the bed, kissing and feeling.

"Fucking hell," he curses again, working his mouth across my cheek while I pant up at the ceiling. "We should stop."

"No," I breathe.

"We shouldn't be doing this." He makes no attempt to halt, finding my mouth again and plunging his tongue in urgently. We're matching each other in the frenzied stakes. Hands and lips are everywhere as we explore unknown territory. We're both consumed with desperation to eradicate our woes, neither one of us seeming prepared to stop this. We should halt it. This won't help.

"Oh God!" I yelp, throwing my head back when Gregory cups my breast. I'm squirming beneath him, my whole being tingling with fevered shots of desperate pleasure. Our mouths quickly find each other again and my hand starts venturing downward until I have his hard, hot length in my grasp.

"Holy shit!" he barks, his hips bucking forward, prompting a full stroke down his shaft. "Oooooh shit."

Pleasure-filled noises are drowning the room. We're lost. Gregory pulls back and gazes down at me, his brow shimmering in sweat, his breath spreading across my heated face.

"Do that again," he breathes, pushing his hips forward.

I pull an even swipe of my palm down his hardness and he draws an uneven breath. His head drops briefly, only for a second, before he lifts again and falls back to my lips, swirling his tongue through my mouth. It shouldn't, but this feels nice. I'm focused only on my best friend kissing me, his hands feeling me, and his body pushed against mine.

"You taste like strawberries," he whispers hoarsely.

Strawberries.

The word hits me like a sledgehammer, and I'm suddenly dropping him from my grasp and wriggling beneath him. "Greg, stop!"

He freezes, pulling back to look down at me. "Are you okay?"

"No! We should stop." I scramble up and pull the sheets over me, covering my naked body, feeling ashamed... guilty. "What are we thinking?"

Gregory sits up and rubs his palms frantically over his face, groaning, but now it's in regret. "I don't know," he admits. "I wasn't thinking, Livy."

"Me neither." I meet his eyes, pulling the protective sheeting closer, while Gregory remains uncovered and quite unbothered by it. He's still... ready... and I try to divert my eyes anywhere except at the hard length of muscle jutting from his lap. It's difficult. It's like a magnet to my eyes. I've never allowed myself to look at my gay friend like this, but when he's totally exposed and looking so ripped, it's impossible. He's everything a man could ask for, and a woman could, for that matter. He's hot, so kind, and totally genuine. But he's my best friend. I can't lose him to the awkwardness that will descend if we continue—if it's not too late already. But that isn't the only reason. No man could ever fill the gaping hole in my heart, nor could they sate my desire. Only one man can do that.

"I'm sorry," I say quietly, guilt consuming me. I don't know why. I have nothing to feel remorseful for, except for jeopardizing my friendship with Gregory. "I'm so sorry."

"Hey"—he pulls me onto his lap and squeezes me—"I'm sorry, too. I think we both got a little carried away."

I snuggle deep, searching for the comfort I need. It's nowhere to be found. "It was my fault."

"No, I instigated that. It's my fault."

"I beg to differ," I whisper, letting him attempt to rub some life back into me.

The rise and fall of his chest under me indicates his heavy sigh. "What a pair," he muses. "A couple of sad-arse losers pining after something we can't have."

I nod my agreement. "You won't go off and screw another woman, will you?" I ask, knowing it's what generally happens when he's dumped by a bloke and probably why things went too far just now. "I don't want you to do that."

"I'm swearing off men *and* women for a while." He chuckles, making me smile a little.

"Me too."

"So you're basically returning to reclusive, then?" he quips lightly.

"Look where being the alternative has got me."

"Not all men are like that cocksucker." He pulls me from his chest and clenches my cheeks fiercely. "Not every man will shit all over you, baby girl."

"I'm not going to give them the chance."

"I hate seeing you like this."

"I hate seeing *you* like this," I counter, his anguish suddenly very obvious and real, now that the information has filtered through my fuzz of misery. "And I'm stealing 'cocksucker' to use for Ben, because he really is a cocksucker, even if he won't admit it."

Gregory smiles, his eyes twinkling. "That's fine by me."

I nod my approval and let my eyes wander down to Gregory's lap. He starts laughing and quickly snatches the sheet to cover himself, leaving me stark naked. I gasp and yank it back, and so a wrestling match with the sheets begins. We're both laughing, pulling back and forth, our earlier ease as friends fully restored... even if we're now both naked. Not that either of us seem bothered as we battle for possession of the sheets.

But we both freeze when the sound of creaking floorboards

muscles in on the happy laughter, and then Nan's curious voice creeps through the door. "Gregory, Olivia? What's going on in there?"

"Oh shit!" I blurt, jumping up from the bed and sprinting across the room. I flatten my naked front against the door. "Nothing, Nan!"

"It sounds like a herd of elephants are doing the cancan up here."

"We're fine!" I squeak, my forehead hitting the door, my eyes clenching shut as I tense and brace myself for a counterattack.

"Well, you sound like you're coming through the ceiling!"

"Sorry. We're on our way down."

"We're off to the dance now."

"Have a nice time!"

"Are you okay?" she asks more softly.

I smile a little. "I'm fine, Nan."

She doesn't say any more, and then I hear the creaking floorboards, telling me she's on her way back downstairs. I roll over, my back pushed up against the door, and find Gregory's eyes making continuous up and down motions as he sits on the bed with the sheets concealing him.

"Good view." He grins, reminding me that I'm still nude. "But you're far too skinny."

I make a vain attempt to cover my modesty, making Gregory fall back on the bed in laughter. He's helpless, while I'm blushing furiously. "Stop it!"

"I'm sorry!" He chuckles. "Really sorry."

My color increases as I scan my room for the nearest thing to save my dignity, settling on a T-shirt draped over the back of my chair in the corner. I dart over and make quick work of throwing it on, feeling better instantly, like I've regained some self-respect after throwing myself at my best friend. Gregory isn't so concerned by his state of undress, though, and is currently rolling around laughing, tangled among the blankets of my bed. It makes me smile more, my head cocking in admiration, musing at his tight backside, but more at his hysterical, carefree state.

"Come on," he says, pushing himself up and patting the mattress next to him. "I won't grope you, promise."

I roll my eyes and join him on the bed, resting my back against the headboard next to him. I fiddle with my ring, wondering what on earth to say. I really don't know, so I say the only thing that I should—the only thing I'm concerned about. "This won't change things, will it?" I ask. "I can't be without you, Greg. I don't want what happened to change us."

"Aaah, baby girl." He drapes his arm around my shoulders and cuddles me close. "Never, because we won't let it. I guess that twenty percent got the better of me."

I smile. "Thank you."

"No, thank you," he sighs. "Let's make a pact."

"A pact." I frown. "What kind of pact?" I'm suddenly concerned that Gregory is about to propose an arrangement that says we marry each other if we haven't found our soul mate by the time we're thirty.

"We stay strong," he whispers, "for each other."

I look up and see a face pleading with me to help him.

"I'm struggling, too, Livy."

I feel terrible. "I'm sorry." I've been so consumed in my own misery, I've not stopped to truly consider my best friend's turmoil, not seen the extent of his own unhappiness. I've been blindsided by my own pitiful state. "I'm so sorry."

"We can do it together," he continues. "I'll help you and you can help me."

"Does that mean confiscating your phone?" I tease.

"No, but it does mean you can delete his number." He grabs his mobile and shoves it in my hand. "Go on."

I scroll through his contact list, deleting Ben's number before going to his text messages—sent *and* received—and deleting any traces of Ben from there, too. Happy I've extinguished Ben from Gregory's mobile altogether, and hopefully his life, too, I hand it back and watch as my friend raises expectant eyebrows at me. He wants to return the favor.

"I told you, my phone's broken."

"And you've not replaced it?"

"No," I reply, sounding rather proud and feeling it as well. I won't be charging the phone William bought me, or any other phone, in fact. Unobtainable. Anyway, I want Gregory to be able to delete Miller Hart from my brain, not just any phone I might be using.

"So we're both free of cocksuckers."

"Cocksucker is reserved for"—I pause for a moment—"you know who."

"Okay."

"I'm glad we've cleared that up." I wince immediately, and Gregory frowns, clearly wondering what the problem is. I shake my head and settle back into his side, feeling a little better, despite the strangeness of the past half hour and despite familiar words falling from both of our mouths without thought or awareness.

Chapter Six

Gregory and I aren't doing a very good job of helping each other through our turmoil. The next evening and in an attempt to move on with our lives, we've had a quiet Italian meal together, which was lovely, but the wine has taken hold and we're now falling toward the doors of Ice, both giggling, both staggering a little. My drunken mind has become vengeful and is stamping all over the fact that Miller is away and he will likely watch all of the CCTV footage from the club when he returns. And I'm going to give him something interesting to view.

"How do you know he's away?" Gregory asks, taking us to the back of the line, since this time we lack an invite or our names on the guest list.

"Text before my phone broke." I can't tell him about William.

"How did it break?"

"Dropped it." I distract Gregory from the reason for the premature demise of my mobile phone by flashing my membership card to Ice.

He grins and takes it from my hand, giving it a quick inspection. "Not much to it, is there?"

I shrug and snatch it back as we near the front. I get a look from the doorman, but he doesn't refuse me entry when I flash my card. He does, however, call Tony to notify him of my arrival. But I'm feeling brash and brave, probably assisted by the three glasses of wine that I drank throughout dinner. Neither one of us is guilty of forcing the other to Miller's club. We just ended up here after I mentioned my membership card and free entry, and neither of us protested—me, because I'm feeling cruel and this is the only way I know how to hurt him, and Gregory because I know he's silently hoping Ben will be here tonight. How long will we continue to torment ourselves?

Calvin Harris's "Feel So Close" greets us as we enter and we find our way to the bar, ordering champagne automatically once we're there, which is daft. What are we celebrating? Being complete idiots? I ignore the strawberry in my flute and sip while gazing around the bar, expecting Tony to appear from somewhere, but after a few minutes of scanning the club, no Tony.

Gregory doesn't tell me to take it easy, probably because he's hell-bent on dulling down his own hurt with alcohol. This is a dangerous position for us both to be in, for the combination of alcohol and our determination to heal our broken hearts is sure to land us in trouble. I can see cameras everywhere. I can also see men watching me, my eyes like a hawk's trying to attract the attention that I'm usually so uncomfortable receiving. I take a deep breath, push all thoughts of disgrace to the very back of my mind, and lose myself in the crowd of London's elite. I shy away from nothing. I accept drinks, I talk with confidence, and I let men rest their hands on my waist or lower back when they move in to talk over the loud music. My cheek is kissed by countless men, and Gregory, although watchful and a little wary, smiles each time.

He moves in when I step away from a tall preppy-type. "You look comfortable. What's changed?"

"Miller Hart," I say nonchalantly before finishing off my champagne. Gregory hands me another and we make the most of our time alone, taking a few moments to drink in our surroundings.

Heads are thrown back in laughter and continental-style kisses are exchanged everywhere. In reality, Gregory and I really don't fit in among these social elitists.

But Ben does.

And he's here.

I know what I should be doing. I should be dragging Gregory away, but just as I convince my alcohol-drenched brain to do exactly that, Ben spots us and starts making his way over.

Shit, I curse to myself, weighing up my options. My drunken mind isn't allowing me to think quickly enough, so before I can haul my friend away, Ben is standing in front of us and Gregory is shifting awkwardly on the spot. I still feel mad, especially when Ben glances at me with high eyebrows. I gather breath to hit him with another torrent of abuse, but he beats me to it and launches into an apology speech. My mouth snaps shut as I flick my eyes from Ben to Greg, back and forth, wondering how this is going to play out.

"I was a total dick," Ben begins quietly, just loud enough for us to hear over the music. He's still in the closet. "I don't want anyone to know before I'm ready to . . . share."

"When might that be?" Gregory snaps, shocking me. I was certain he'd turn to mush all over the dopey-eyed Ben. I'm pleasantly surprised.

Ben shrugs sheepishly and drops his eyes to the glass of champagne in his grasp. "I need to prepare myself, Greg. This is a huge deal."

"You're making it a bigger deal by pretending and dragging it out." Gregory takes my elbow. "We're done here," he says, pulling me toward the dance floor. I let him take me, and I peer over my shoulder as I'm escorted away, seeing Ben standing lonely and looking a little lost, until an over-the-top woman approaches, throwing her arms over him, and he switches straight back to smiley, people-pleaser Ben. Any ounce of sympathy I had for him diminishes instantly.

"I'm proud of you," I say as we arrive on the dance floor and get a little taster of Jean Jacques Smoothie.

He grins and discards our glasses before taking me in his hold and twirling me out on a spin. "I'm proud of me, too. Let's dance, baby girl."

I don't argue, but as I'm twirled around the floor, I'm mindful that Gregory's massive smile and forced carefree appearance are for the benefit of Ben, who's standing at the edge of the floor talking to a different woman but doing a terrible job of engaging, his eyes nailed to my friend. This is good, as long as Gregory continues to hold his own and doesn't let Ben muscle his way back into his life.

I fulfill my role perfectly, laughing along with Gregory and letting him swing me about and grind into my waist seductively, but then the music cuts abruptly before the track ends, not even mixing into another. Everyone halts dancing, looking around a little bemused. The only sounds now are of confused chatter.

"Is it a power cut?" I ask, but quickly realize the stupidity of my question when I register all of the blue illuminating lights still glowing at every turn.

"I'm not sure," Gregory replies, confused. "Maybe the fire alarm will kick in."

I gaze around the club, seeing motionless forms everywhere, all looking confused by the sudden quiet. Even the doormen have entered from outside to find out what's happening, and when I cast my eyes over to the DJ, I see him shrug at the security guy next to him, who's obviously asking what's going on.

Unease sets in, strangeness settles in my gut, and the hairs at the back of my neck rise. William's words are suddenly all I can hear. I reach over to take Gregory's hand, feeling exposed and vulnerable, yet with no explanation except a silly power cut.

"What's going on?" I ask, casting my eyes around the club, looking for . . . I'm not sure.

"I don't know." Gregory shrugs, not in the least bit concerned.

But then the club is suddenly filled with music again, and everyone seems to sag around me, including Gregory, who starts laughing. "I think the DJ might be getting sacked." He turns toward me, his smile dropping when he registers my blank face and static form. I can't move. "Livy, what's up?"

The words to the track soak through the haze of alcohol, punching me in the stomach... hard. "Enjoy the Silence." My eyes close.

"Livy?" Gregory shakes me a little, prompting my eyes to fly open and shoot around the club. "Olivia?"

"I'm sorry." I force a smile, trying to appear fine, but my heart is crashing against my breastbone, set on fighting its way from my chest. He's here. "I need the ladies'."

"I'll come." He starts leading me off the floor.

"No, honestly. Get the drinks. I'll meet you at the bar."

Gregory relents easily, letting me find my way to the toilets alone while he orders more drinks. But I don't head for the ladies'. I divert once I'm out of Gregory's sight and hurry toward the front of the club, taking the stairs fast, down to the maze of corridors beneath Ice. William told me to run, but I doubt he wanted me moving *toward* the danger. I'm a woman possessed as I follow the passageway, taking too many wrong turns and shouting my frustration when I land in front of a storeroom. I can still hear the music—the words distressing me, reminding me, as I rush back the way I came and try a different route. The sight of the metal keypad outside Miller's office fills me with relief and dread all at once as I charge for it. I have no clue what the code is or what I'll find... or what I'll do if I find anything—if I find him.

I don't need the code. The door is ajar and one tiny push swings it open.

Internal fireworks explode.

He's standing in the middle of the room, suit adorned and expressionless, just watching me as I hover on the threshold of his office. My eyes instantly fill with tears as I breathe erratically and watch him watching me. My knees feel weak. The music is relentless. I drink him in, his dark suit pristine, his hair seeming longer, the soft waves flicking out from below his earlobes. There are no words, just intense eye contact. There's no facial expression or body language to tell me what he's thinking. He doesn't need to tell me what he's thinking, though. His eyes are doing that. And they're angry. He's been watching the club's CCTV footage. He's been watching me being hit on by countless men. I take a worried pull of breath. He's been watching me encourage and accept it.

"Did you let any of them taste you?" He steps forward, and I instinctively step back, wary.

This isn't going to be a happy reunion. He has a nerve to ask such a question after he's been in another country with another woman. My shock from his presence is turning into irritation fast. "That's none of your business." He's jealous again, and this gives me an unreasonable thrill.

His perfect jaw is ticking. "When you're in my club, it's my business."

"It'll never be your business again."

"Wrong."

I shake my head as I step back farther, hating my uncooperative body for staggering slightly. "I'm right."

He runs displeased eyes up and down my tight, short-dressed form. "You're drunk."

I ignore his accusation, remembering something. "Which means you can't fuck me."

"Shut up, Olivia!"

"Because you want me to remember every kiss, every touch, every—"

"Livy!"

"Except I don't want to remember every moment. I want to forget them all."

His neck veins bulge to bursting point. "Don't say things you don't mean."

"I mean it!"

"Shut up!" he roars, sending me back a few more paces, his ferocity stunning me into silence. I gather myself fast, but my wide eyes are undoubtedly displaying all of the shock I'm feeling. Shock that I came here, shock that *he's* here, shock that he's so fuming mad. He has no right to be, despite my provoking him. I knew what I was doing. And he knows that, too.

"You told Tony to let me in if I came, didn't you?" It's suddenly very clear. He anticipated this. "You told Tony to monitor me."

"I have over two hundred cameras in this club to do that."

"How dare you!" I spit, feeling my blood heat with rage, rather than the usual desire when I'm within touching distance of Miller Hart. I thought my presence would shock him, but no. He fully expected it.

He steps forward again, but I keep my distance. I'm now in the corridor, not that it deters him. His long strides have him in front of me in seconds, his hand taking my nape and guiding me to his desk determinedly. I'm pushed down into his office chair, where I'm confronted with image after image of me in his club—all with men hovering around me. While I'm ashamed of myself, I'm also quietly delighted. The whole point was to torture him the only way I know how. And it looks like I've succeeded. The apparently emotionless man is furious. Good. I just didn't expect to be around when he watched the footage.

"There are five dead men on these screens," he seethes, leaning down next to me, smashing a button on his remote control. The images all change, but they're all still me... and men. "There are six on these ones." He proceeds to flick through the footage, adding up the men he's going to be slaughtering. "Does that make you happy?"

"They never tasted me," I say quietly.

"They want to! And you're doing nothing to discourage it!" he yells next to me, making me jump in his chair. I can feel the fury pouring from him. He's right. His temper isn't something I want to toy with. "Where's your fucking self-respect?"

Those words ricochet around my head like a bullet. "My self-respect?" I shout, flying up from the chair, letting my purse tumble to the floor and my fear of his temper tumble away. I feel pretty lethal myself right now. "My self-respect?" My palms collide viciously with his chest, sending his tall frame staggering back. My strength shocks me. "My fucking self-respect!"

His eyes have widened slightly at my tiny fuming body and foul mouth.

"You're a joke!" I shout in his face, resisting the urge to lash his cheek with my palm. But I *do* smack him in the chest again. This time my wrists are seized and I'm swung around, my back crashing to his body and my arms secured tightly. His mouth is at my ear, breathing hot, angry bursts of air. I hate the desire ripping through my anger. I hate it.

"The joke isn't on me, Olivia Taylor." He pushes his lips to my cheek and then bites down, leaving me whimpering in desperation. "The joke is on you. You're the one fighting a battle you cannot win, sweet girl."

"I'm stronger than you give me credit for," I breathe, clenching my eyes shut, knowing my words carry no strength whatsoever.

"I'm banking on it." His teeth clamp down on my earlobe, sending my backside shooting back and colliding with his groin. I cry out. He growls. "I *need* you to be strong for me." I'm spun around and grabbed behind the thighs, then yanked up to straddle his lean hips with one easy pull. He thrusts me up against his office door, one of his hands keeping me secured by the back of my thigh, the other slamming into the wood by my head. I don't even flinch. Nothing will power through the lust attacking every fiber of my being.

His blue eyes search mine for a few moments, taking in every detail of my face, before he crashes our mouths together on a yell. I accept his violent kiss. My hands are a knotted jumble in his mess of waves, my body arching into him as he pushes me up the door on continuous moans and muffled words. While the contact is in one sense soothing me, in another it's frightening me, bringing back too many bad memories of our hotel encounter. I start to wriggle beneath him, pulling at his suit jacket, but he mistakes my actions for equal impatience and fights free of his jacket, not breaking our fused lips.

"Miller." I turn my face, yet he manages to find my lips again within a nanosecond. Things are getting out of hand and panic's beginning to flood me. "Miller!"

"You taste so fucking good."

"Miller, please!"

"Fuck!" he barks, finding the strength he needs to release me, letting me slide down the door before he steps away and wipes his brow with his cuff. He looks dazed. We're both panting and sweating.

"This isn't happening." I run and snatch my purse from the floor, then hurry to the door, thinking I need to calm down before I find Gregory.

"Olivia!"

I swing around, finding him wrestling his jacket on. "No!" I scream. "This is it, Miller!" He didn't just worship me. If I let this go further, there will be no worshipping. There will be only fucking. He's been fighting his instincts all this time, and now he's exhausted, desperate. I take my membership card for Ice from my purse and throw it at him, and then watch as he follows its journey to the floor at his feet. "I said you'd never get to taste me again, and I meant it!"

"I just tasted you, and I want more. I want more hours. A lot fucking more."

"You're ruining my life!"

"You merely existed before." His words are arrogant but his tone soft. "I brought you back to life, Livy."

"Yes, for another man to taste." I get no thrill from the look of horror on his face—none at all. There will be no other man. I'm returning full force to solitary confinement because how I'm feeling right now is total devastation. Empty. Lifeless. No man can fix me, not even Miller.

"Take that back now." He points a warning finger at me. "Take it back!"

I remain silent, watching his body heave before me.

"I know I'm a fuckup, Olivia!" His breathing slows, his arm lowering to his side as he takes a moment to compose himself, pulling gently at his clothes, as if he can smooth his temper the same way he smooths his shirt. "I'm on my way to hell."

My bottom lip starts to quiver as I watch his crystal-clear eyes freeze over, a coldness settling around his office that slows my heart.

He steps forward. "There's only one person who can drag me back."

I choke on a sob, but he's expressionless now. I'm getting nothing, except those chilly eyes. I don't like it. Is he asking me for help? The OCD, the freakish manners and uptight attitude. The women, the debasement, the nasty fucking and belts and rules...

No, I can't see past it all.

"I'm not strong enough to help you," I murmur. William's words are spinning in my head, making me dizzy. Miller really is ruined. "You're too damaged."

I run.

My legs work fast, carrying me away from my distress and a man who I don't think can be helped at all. By anyone. I navigate the corridors well, my terror fueling my determination to escape, until I break free of the underground labyrinth of Miller's club. I'm torn when the exit comes into sight, my head snapping back and forth between that and the openness of the club where Gregory is waiting for me.

I need to find him. I tear through the crowds, bumping and pushing into bewildered revelers, who curse or shout when I send drinks flying and knock bodies back.

I spot Gregory. "Where have you been?" he asks as I come to an abrupt halt in front of him, his confused eyes taking in my pale, sweaty face. Handing me a glass cautiously, his concern soon morphs into anger and the drink is withdrawn, his eyes diverting over my shoulders.

"I need to leave," I wheeze, grabbing his hand. "Please, I need to go."

"What's he doing here?" He discards my drink on the bar and starts pulling me away, making sure he knocks into Miller as we pass, but I'm soon captured by the wrist and being yanked away from Gregory. "Get your fucking hands off her," Gregory growls, his body starting to shake. "Now!"

"I'll ask you to do the same thing," Miller retorts on a menacing whisper, tugging at my arm. "We're not done."

"Yes, we are." I wrench myself free and push Gregory onward, knowing Miller won't give in. Ben approaches looking concerned but soon backs off when he clocks Miller following behind, a cautious look on his face. And then there's Tony, who tries to intercept Miller and gets practically thrown to the side for his trouble.

"Miller, son, this isn't the time or place," Tony seethes, looking nervously around the club.

"Fuck you!" Miller spits.

All I can hear is shouting. Miller is cursing. Tony is cursing. Gregory is cursing. Anger is drenching the happy club atmosphere around me, making my determination to escape stronger.

The doorman gives us a wide berth as we barrel out of the club, his eyes widening when he sees who's coming after us. "Don't let her leave!" Miller roars, prompting the doorman to make chase.

He catches me and tosses me up onto his big shoulder, but I'm too stunned to voice my shock, still hearing men swearing.

Explicit language is being fired everywhere, my hampered view of events surrounding me, leaving me wriggling to free myself from the severe grip of the doorman.

"Give her to me!" Miller's voice is dripping with threat, and I feel hands at my waist trying to pull me down.

"Dave, put her down!" Tony yells.

"I will if you all give me some fucking space!" the doorman bellows, taking me away from the grappling of hands, over to the other side of the road. He lowers me to my feet and gives me the once-over. "Are you okay, darling?"

I halfheartedly pull my dress back into place, feeling disoriented and exposed. "Sure," I murmur, but then I'm seized by the waist again in a fierce clench. Internal lightning bolts strike me hard, and as I look up, I see Gregory a few yards away. Miller has me, and the fear of his touch sends me into a deranged mess of flailing body parts. "Let go of me!"

"Never!"

Gregory's at my side in an instant. I'm being yanked from one direction to the other, both men yelling, both men persistent. This is becoming a battle of the egos now.

"Both of you *stop*!" I scream, my shriek having no effect whatsoever, my body still flying from one man to the other, until Miller curls an arm around my waist and hauls me up to his chest. My face is level with his, and the first thing I notice is the lethal danger in his eyes as he focuses past me. There's no sight of the deep twinkle that always hypnotized me. This is another man. Not the man disguised as a gentleman or the loving, worshipping Miller. This is someone else.

"I'll fucking kill you!" Miller bellows, earning a right hook to his jaw from Gregory, the fist skimming my cheek to find its target. He staggers back, and Gregory takes Miller's momentary daze as an opportunity to reclaim me, pulling me from his hold. But he doesn't hold tight enough, and I fall to the ground in a heap of limp muscle, smacking my head on the curb as I land.

"Shit!" Pain sears through me, making me a little dizzy and even more disoriented. I glance up to see Miller tackle Gregory to the pavement, both men rolling around like animals, fists flying, curses piercing the night air, until Tony and Dave intervene and drag them apart.

And the whole time, I'm crumpled on the ground in a pathetic mess, my head pouring blood, my eyes pouring tears. Both men are so consumed by the determination to win, they've lost sight of what they're fighting for. Now I'm injured, blood's gushing down my face, and I've still not been noticed as they wrestle in the holds of Tony and Dave.

"Stay away from her," Gregory snarls at Miller, letting up on his persistent struggle against Tony.

"Only when I'm fucking dead!"

"Then I'll fucking kill you!" Gregory breaks free and launches himself at Miller, taking him *and* the doorman to the concrete. I wince at the sounds of hard knuckles connecting with flesh, blood spraying, and clothes ripping. But even though Gregory is well built, Miller clearly has the upper hand, showing the fighting skills of someone trained.

I've seen him show this kind of punishment before, except it was a limp bag of sand hanging from the rafters of a gym that was subjected to his brutality. Not my treasured friend. Both of them have forgotten about me, neither noticing that I'm injured and distressed on the pavement. Their rationality has been clouded by caveman behavior and bashing horns.

In my dazed state, I struggle to my feet while the spectacle continues. My steps forward are tentative. I need to stop this, but then my arm is taken and I'm being pulled away. I look up, finding Tony focused forward with purpose, directing me to the road. He flags a taxi down and makes to put me inside.

"Tony, I need to stop them."

"I'll sort it. You're best off out of the way," he snaps harshly, encouraging me into the cab.

"Please stop them," I beg as he slams the door.

He nods, a nod that I find reassuring as he leans into the window and hands the driver a twenty. "Take her to A and E." And then he's gone, stalking away, rampant with fury. As the driver pulls away from the horror scene I've caused, he eyes me in his rear-view mirror, prompting me to reach up and feel the top of my head. I wince, tears continuing to fall, more from despair than pain.

"Are you okay, sweetheart?" the taxi driver asks, looking concerned.

"I'm fine, honestly." I rummage through my purse for a tissue but give up when one's handed through the small hole in the glass. "Thank you."

"No problem. Let's get you to the hospital."

"Thank you," I murmur pitifully, resting back in the seat and watching the blurred lights of London by night zoom past the window.

The driver drops me off at A&E and gives me his mobile number to call him as soon as I'm done. After checking myself in, I sit among the masses of Saturday night drunks, all injured, some ranting, some throwing up.

Four hours later, I'm still sitting in the waiting area, my bottom numb, my head banging. I get up and make my way to the toilet, looking down and seeing my ice blue dress soaked with blood. My reflection in the mirror once I arrive in the ladies' reveals even more of a mess. My hair is matted and my right cheek caked in dried blood. I look as pitiful as I feel. After staring at myself for too long and not bothering to remedy my sorry state, I exit into the waiting area again, just catching the tail end of my name being called. I look across the room to see a nurse scanning the waiting area.

"Here!" I call, hurrying over, thankful my time in the drunk-infested space is up. "I'm Olivia Taylor."

"Let's get you sorted out." She smiles kindly and directs me into a cubicle, swiftly pulling the curtain across and settling me on the bed. "What have you been up to?" she asks, frowning at my blood-coated face.

"I fell," I mutter feebly, which isn't far from the truth.

"Okay, lovey," she says, taking a sterile pad from a packet. "This may sting." I pull in a shocked rush of breath as it connects with my head, and she hushes me like an injured child. "There, there. It looks worse than it is. Some glue will sort it out."

I'm flooded with relief. "Thank you."

"Perhaps better footwear is called for." She smiles, looking down at my heels before continuing to glue me back together.

I sit on the edge of the bed and listen to the nurse chat away, offering the odd agreement or answer to her questions every now and then. My face is cleaned up, but there is nothing that can be done with my hair, so I pile it up gingerly, securing it with a loose tie that I find hiding at the bottom of my bag. My dress looks like it's ready for the trash bin. *I* look like I'm ready for the trash bin.

Once I've been seen to thoroughly and checked for concussion, I'm discharged and left to find my way home. But I don't call the nice taxi man because one pulls up, just as the automatic doors swing open, exposing me to the chill of the early hours. I shiver and wrap my arms around my body, trying to squeeze the shudders away as I hurry to the cab. I hop in, but before I can pull the door shut, there's a body blocking it, hindering my attempts.

Then a palm is resting on my nape and internal sparks begin to fizz. "You're coming with me."

Chapter Seven

Despondency and the look of determination in his eyes prevent me from fighting him. I haven't the energy to fight him, so I let him pull me from the taxi and lead me away.

"Get in," he orders when we arrive at his car parked haphazardly nearby.

I do as I'm told and let him shut me in. He climbs in and shocks me when he starts pulling at his wreck of a suit. "Fucking mess," he mutters, looking out the corner of his eye to me. He's probably taking in my own disheveled state, the fool. On a mild shake of his head, he slams his Merc into gear and pulls away from the hospital way too fast, but I don't say a thing. I'd be stupid to say anything. He looks homicidal, totally deranged. And I'm wary of it.

"Are you okay?" he asks, pulling a sharp left onto the main road.

I don't answer, instead focusing forward. He knows the answer to that question.

"I've asked once."

I remain quiet, absorbing the continued fury emanating from his messy form.

"Damn it, Olivia!" He punches the door window, sending me on a startled jump in the passenger seat. "Where are your fucking manners?"

I chance a cautious glance at him, seeing a sweaty brow and that loose curl jumping across his forehead from his shaking. "I'm fine," I whisper.

He takes a calming pull of breath and glances up to the rearview mirror. "Why is your phone turned off?"

"It's broken."

He looks across to me before flicking his eyes up to the mirror again, then taking another sharp left. "How?"

"I threw it at the wall when you texted me," I don't hesitate telling him. "Because I was mad at you."

His face turns to mine and drinks in my blank face for what seems like forever. Then his hand releases the gearstick and starts to slowly come toward my knee until he gently and cautiously rests it on my bare flesh. I look down at him rubbing lazy circles before I pull my leg away and return my stare forward, leaving his hand dropping to the leather by my leg. He quietly curses, and in my peripheral vision, I see him looking to the rearview mirror once again. My hand shoots out to grab the door when he takes another vicious turn into a dark alley on yet another quiet curse, and I instinctively glance out the back of the car. Does he think someone's following us?

I'm just about to speak when the car screeches to a halt and Miller is out, quickly making his way to my side and opening the door. He offers his hand. "Take it," he demands, and I hesitantly reach forward, sensing an element of urgency to his tone. I'm grasped and pulled from the car before his hold shifts to my neck.

"What are you doing?" I ask, my feet moving fast to keep up with his determined strides. "Miller?"

"I've had too much to drink to be driving." He brushes off my question and heads toward the tube entrance across the street, his eyes darting around constantly. "Now's not the time to be difficult, Olivia."

"Why?" I'm looking around nervously now, too.

"Trust me?"

He's jumpy and it's frightening me. "What have you done to make me do that?"

"Everything," he answers immediately, making me frown up at him as my legs continue to keep up with his fast strides.

We enter the station and I'm released momentarily while Miller clears the turnstiles with an easy leap, not prepared to waste time at the ticket machine. He turns and grabs me, lifting me over with no regard for security or onlookers. Then my neck is reclaimed and we begin descending into the bowels of London, taking the escalators fast and frantically.

"Miller, please," I plead, my feet killing, my head banging.

He halts, turns, and scoops me into his arms. I gasp. "I apologize for making you walk."

I look down at him, the close proximity and sudden artificial light giving me a clear view of his face. His cheek is bruised and his lip grazed. But he's still breathtaking. And my reactions to his beauty and touch are still evident. I'm hypnotized by him, my heart being hijacked by a violent, determined thrum, which has nothing to do with my exertion. I don't like these responses to him. They're dangerous.

The platform is empty and we're no longer on the move, yet he doesn't place me down, choosing to keep me secure against him.

A whistling breaks through the silent air, indicating the arrival of a train, and when the doors slide open, he carries me into the car and rests his backside on one of the raised cushions at the end of the carriage. He finally places me on my feet, spreads his legs, and pulls me face-forward to his body, our chests colliding, the internal sparks firing off wildly. His breathing is strained as he feels the back of my neck and pushes me farther into him, like he's trying to morph us together. The severity of his grip stops me from trying to escape. Do I want to escape? I can feel a familiar ease descending, which is obscene, given Miller's strange behavior, but my subconscious is also working hard to remind me of...everything. Yet in the same breath, Miller is working hard to try to make me forget, and his tactic for doing this is by immersing me in his body and attentiveness. Worshipping me.

"Let me taste you again. I beg you," he murmurs into my neck, starting to kiss his way up to my jaw. The familiarity of his slow-moving lips makes me close my eyes and plead for strength. "Forget the world outside and be with me forever."

"I can't forget," I answer quietly, my face nuzzling into his mouth automatically.

"I can make you forget." He reaches my lips and gently brushes over them, his eyes sinking into mine. "You agreed to let no one else taste you." He doesn't speak with any hint of arrogance as he pulls away slightly, revealing his wayward curl and too many lovely places for my eyes to focus on.

"I didn't know who I was agreeing with."

"You were agreeing with the man who you can't function without." His voice is low and hoarse, his eyes continuously glancing to my lips. There is little point in denying his claim when the words are a mirror of my own, spoken aloud and delivered to him personally. And our separation has only proved it. "We were made to fit together. We fit perfectly together. You must feel it, Olivia." He doesn't allow me time to agree, or maybe disagree. He inches forward slowly, carefully, holding my eyes until our mouths meet and he's humming in contentment. My arms lift and hold him, my body pushes into his, and my eyes close in bliss. We kiss for an age, slowly, delicately, lovingly. I can feel our broken pieces shifting and coming together, the rightness of us fused everywhere canceling out all of the wrongness of our doomed relationship. I'm allowed to kiss him. I'm allowed to touch him.

The train begins to slow until we're at a stop and the doors are sliding open, but a quick peek while maintaining our consuming kiss reveals no one getting off and no one waiting to board. I'm allowed to kiss him. That thought and the sound of the doors snapping into action again yank me from the curious world of Miller Hart and puts me back into a place where everything is… impossible. He's been in Madrid. He's been with clients while he's been with me.

I dive from his arms through the tiny slit of space left to exit, landing on the platform before I can register my sharp movement. Looking back at the carriage, I watch as the train starts to pull away and Miller starts hammering on the door frantically. He's deranged, panicked and shouting, as I stand deathly still and watch him disappear into the tunnel. My last tear-filled vision is of him throwing his head back on a ferocious roar and propelling his fist into the glass.

Time seems to slow. I'm numb and useless and running over every reason for me to remain at a safe distance from Miller Hart, while my fingertips run over my lips, feeling his mouth still there. I can feel his body against mine, too, and the lingering burn his gaze has left on my skin. He has worked his way deep into me and I'm terrified there is no shaking him out.

* * *

The front door swings open before I've even made it halfway up the garden path, and Nan's standing looking petrified in her nightie. "Olivia! Oh my goodness." She rushes down the path to collect me, taking my elbow and leading me into the house. "Oh my word, whatever has happened? Oh my goodness!"

"I'm okay," I mumble, exhaustion taking hold, rendering me incapable of proper speech. I should make the effort, though, because Nan looks truly beside herself, her usually fixed hair in disarray and her face looking older. She needs reassurance.

"I'll make a cup of tea." She pushes me toward the kitchen, but I freeze on the threshold when I feel the hairs on the back of my neck rise.

"Where is he?" I ask, jolting forward a little when Nan bumps into my back.

She doesn't answer, instead overtaking me and pulling me into the kitchen. "Come, I'll make tea," she repeats in an attempt to avoid answering my question.

"Nan, where?" I ask, stopping her from pulling me farther into the room.

"Olivia, he's been out of his mind." She tugs me harder until I stumble into the kitchen and he comes into view. Miller's sitting at the table, looking a mighty mess and really pissed off. Yet his evident displeasure and the irritation it spikes in me doesn't prevent the simmering want from our train kiss to reignite.

Defeated.

He slowly stands, giving me warning eyes. I couldn't care less. He has no scruples, dragging in an old lady as a tool to get his way. She's oblivious to the horror that is our dead relationship and, subsequently, my dead heart. I'm about to scream in his face in a desperate attempt to show him my rage at his underhanded tactics, but before I can muster the energy, a sharp pain stabs at my temple, making me clench my head on a hiss and a stumble of my heels.

"Jesus, Olivia." He's in front of me in a second, stroking my face, putting his lips everywhere and mumbling incoherent words, mostly quiet curses.

I'm too tired to fight him off, so I wait until he's finished smothering me before pulling away. I penetrate him with cold eyes. "Nan, please see Miller out."

"Olivia," she rebukes me gently. "Miller has been terribly worried. I told you, you need to replace your telephone."

"I won't because I don't want to speak to *him*." My voice is as cold as my eyes surely are. "Have you forgotten what the last few weeks have been like, Nan?" I can't believe I've been cornered like this again. He has no morals.

"Of course, but Miller has explained. He's very sorry, said it's all a misunderstanding." She hastily gets three mugs from the cupboard, set on making tea quickly, like it will pacify me. Or maybe the consumption of some good English tea will make everything better.

"A misunderstanding?" I look at him, finding the usual impassive blue gaze. Ironically, it's comforting after the maniac I've encountered tonight. It's familiar, which I conclude to be a bad thing. "Tell me. What out of everything have I misunderstood?"

Miller steps forward, but on instinct I step away again. "Livy." He rakes a frustrated hand through his dark waves and attempts to straighten his wrecked suit. "Can we talk?" he tries, his jaw ticking.

"Come on, Livy. Be reasonable," Nan pipes up. "Give him a chance to explain."

I let slip a little laugh, making Nan frown and Miller's jaw tense further. "Never." I turn away, leaving two despairing souls in the kitchen. No one is more desolate than I am, though. I'm crumbling, disintegrating.

My head is thumping as I take the stairs, my mind crippled with too much to absorb. I've never felt more confused and helpless, or angry and frustrated.

"Livy." His voice halts me halfway up and I muster the strength I need to face my heart's nemesis. His eyes are glazed, his shoulders visibly slumped, but that air of confidence still surrounds him. "You've underestimated my determination to fix us."

"We can't be fixed."

"Wrong."

I take the banister for support. His one-word counter is seething with determination and confidence. "I've already told you, I can't fix you. And I can't risk you breaking me beyond repair..." My voice trails off as I reach the end of my declaration. I'm furious that I can't finish as bravely as I started. I'm already ruined. Not broken, but ruined. Broken is fixable. Ruined is not. Ruined is beyond hope. "Good night."

"You're mistaking me for a man who gives up easily."

"No, I mistook you for a man who I could trust." I find my way to my room and strip down before collapsing onto my bed and hiding under the sheets. While I know I'm being sensible, the willpower to maintain my strength is crushing me. *He's* crushing me.

Sleep finds me easily, mainly because the agony of thinking makes my brain retreat into protective mode, shutting down and giving me a few hours of peace before I face another black day.

* * *

I'm surrounded by warmth—I'm too hot. But I can't move to free myself from the covers. Then I notice breathing, and it's not mine. I also notice something hard wedged up against my back, but there's material between my naked body and the solid muscle pushing into me. And it feels like expensive material. Suit material. Bespoke suit material.

If I could, I'd move, but he has me in a vise grip, like he's afraid I might escape while he's snoozing. "Miller." I nudge him, and he groans a little, squeezing me harder. "Miller!"

"Thing," he mumbles sleepily, nuzzling into my neck. "Hold that thought."

He feels amazing, completely surrounding me, but my waking brain is quickly registering this to be a bad thing. "Miller, please!"

He releases me fast and retreats, giving me space to sit up and brush my hair from my face. I immediately flinch on a quiet hiss when I brush harshly over my cut, the pain quickly reminding me of my injury.

"Olivia." He's in front of me quickly, holding my arms to keep me in place, but I shrug him off. "Does it hurt?" he asks softly, giving me the space I'm demanding.

I allow my gaze to lift to his face, knowing it'll be a bad move, but his magnet eyes are far too powerful. He still looks beautiful, despite his tired face and mess of waves. His eyes are dull, his fully suited body is creased beyond creased, and his lightly tanned skin looks sallow. "Not as much as *you've* hurt me," I half sob, trying to combat the tears from falling. "Get out!"

He drops his eyes, and I get off the bed, escaping to the shower. I can't look at him. I'll cave.

The water feels like stabbing blades on my sore head as I tentatively lather up with shampoo, then smooth some conditioner through the ends, all the while reminding myself of everything William has said to me. I take my time, in no hurry to start my day, and by the time I'm done, I expect Miller to be gone, but as I walk into the bedroom wrapped in a towel, he's sitting on the edge of my bed, still disheveled. And he has a cup of tea in his hand.

"Does Nan know you're here?"

"Yes."

Of course she does, I think. Who else produces tea like it's going out of fashion? "You had no right to invade my bed." I slam the door behind me for effect, not that it has an effect. He remains deadpan, completely unruffled.

"I needed you in my arms. You would never allow it while you were conscious, so I used my initiative." He shows no remorse for his sly stunt, taking a slow sip of his tea while I look on, stunned, struggling against my body's instinct to react to those lips in action.

"Are you going to break in every night and violate my privacy?"

"If I have to."

I'm on dangerous ground. I've been on the receiving end of his determination on more than one occasion. I need to stay strong. Memories of the loving, worshipping Miller I remember between the emotional retard are slipping farther away. "Why are you still here?" I make my way over to my chair and negotiate the towel so I can slip some underwear and a T-shirt on.

"Why are *you* all bashful?"

I swing around and find his roving eyes dragging up and down my legs. He looks conceited and victorious, and that makes me feel... defeated. "I'd like you to leave."

"I'd like you to give me the opportunity to talk. But we don't all get what we want, do we?" He stands and makes his way over.

"I'll slap you if you come any closer!" I snap, feeling panic descending as I back away. Damn it, he's going to have me up against the wall and at his mercy, but to my utter shock, he drops to his knees in front of me and looks up, the arrogance disappearing and genuine regret replacing it.

"I'm on my knees, Olivia." His hands slowly lift and slide cautiously under my T-shirt to my bum, like he's expecting me to shout at him to stop. I would if I could find my tongue. Blue eyes watch me as he reaches forward with his lips and rests them on the material covering my tummy. "Let me put right what I've broken."

"That's me," I choke. "You've broken *me*."

"I can fix you, Olivia. And I need you to fix me, too."

My chin starts to tremble at his earnest words. "It's your entire fault," I sob, resisting feeling his wayward hair, knowing it'll offer me comfort that I shouldn't be seeking from him.

"I accept full responsibility." He kisses my stomach again and glides his palms over my bottom. "We're more broken if we don't have each other. Let me put us back together again. I need you, Olivia. Desperately. You're making my world light."

The word I want to say nearly slips past my lips, but there's so much that needs to be spoken about. Too much I fear for any of this to ever be right. I'm pulled down to my knees and smothered by his lush, soft lips. The familiar comfort saturates my senses. "Miller." I break away and hold him at arm's length. "You think it's that easy?"

His stunning brow furrows deeply as he scans my face. "Overthinking."

I can't stop my eyes from rolling at his feeble retort. "We should talk."

"Okay. Let's talk now," he pushes.

I feel frustration starting to take hold again. "I need time to think."

"People overthink things, Livy. I've told you that before."

He must realize what he's saying. He's a smart man. "And make big deals of small deals?" I ask, a light edge of sarcasm lacing my tone.

"There's no need for insolence."

I sigh. "I've told you before, Miller Hart. With you there is."

"How much time?" He has no counter for that.

"I don't know. I've never been in a relationship, and I wanted one with you. Then I found out you fuck women for a living!"

"Livy!" he yells. "Please, don't be so crass!"

"I'm sorry. Did I hurt your feelings?"

I expect a scowl but get an even tone and straight face. "What the hell has happened to my sweet girl?" His eyebrows rise, raising *my* hackles. "Getting drunk, offering yourself to other men."

"You happened!" Yes, I got drunk, but only to dull the pain that *he's* caused.

"I don't want anyone else to taste you."

"I feel the same!" I yell, making him jump before he snarls. His lack of retort should surprise me but it doesn't. It worries me. But something springs to mind. "I saw the newspaper."

His hostility is sucked up in a second. Now he looks downright uncomfortable, and he isn't jumping to his defense, confirming my suspicions. Diana Low didn't take it upon herself to change that headline. Miller told her to.

The sound of pots and pans clanging downstairs distracts me, making my head drop back on a moan of frustration. "What have you told Nan?" I need to clarify this because she's going to be on me like a vulture the second Miller leaves.

"Just that we had words, that you misunderstood a woman I had a meeting with as more than the business associate she was." A sharp crack spikes in my neck when my head snaps back up. He shrugs and drops his arse to his heels. "What else should I have said?"

No answer to that is coming to me. I should be grateful for his quick thinking, but the audacity of his lie to my dear grandmother halts any gratitude. "I'll call you," I breathe.

"What do you mean, you'll call me?" His displeasure is obvious. "And you have no phone!"

"You've been in another country with another woman." I drag myself to my feet, feeling more exhausted than ever before.

"Livy, I didn't sleep with her. I've not slept with anyone since I met you, I swear."

I should be relieved, but I'm not. I'm completely shocked. "No one?"

"No, no one."

"Not a soul?" He's an escort. I've seen him with women. He's been away . . .

His eyes are smiling. "No matter how you ask, the answer will still be no. Not a soul."

"So what were you doing in Madrid? And that woman at Quaglino's?"

"Come sit." He stands and starts pulling me toward the bed, but I doggedly shake him off.

"No." I walk over to my bedroom door and pull it open. Nothing he can say will fix this mess, and even if he finds any soothing words, he will still be an escort with some awful tactics. I need to listen to William.

He makes no attempt to leave my bedroom, his beautiful mind obviously racing. "I'll take you for dinner, and you can't refuse because it's rude to decline a gentleman on an offer to wine and dine you." He nods his approval at his own words. "Ask your grandmother."

"Next week," I suggest in an attempt to get him out before I cave, wondering if I'll ever be ready to take him on. I don't know where he's found the idea that I hold the strength I need to help him.

His eyes widen slightly, but he maintains his composure. "Next week? No, I'm afraid not. Tonight. I'm taking you to dinner tonight."

"Tomorrow," I fire back unconsciously, stunning myself.

"Tomorrow?" he asks, clearly mentally calculating how many hours that is before sighing heavily. "Promise." His lips move slowly. "Promise me."

"I promise," I whisper, drawn to his mouth, thinking it can make everything better.

"Thank you." His tall, crumpled form approaches me and stops at the doorway. "Can I kiss you?" His manners shock me. He doesn't usually care for them in situations like this.

I shake my head, knowing I'll be blindsided and undoubtedly end up on the bed beneath him.

"As you wish." He's full to the brim with aggravation. "For now I'll respect your request, but I won't for much longer," he warns, moodily stomping on his expensive shoes down the hallway. "Tomorrow," he affirms as he disappears down the stairs.

I shut the door, feeling relieved, lost, and proud all at once.

But I still want Miller Hart.

Chapter Eight

With the absence of a certain gentleman at the dinner table, supper has returned to dishes that I'm familiar with and at the kitchen table, rather than at Nan's fancy dining room table. George's top button is undone, and no one is being chastised for their manners. There's no wine, no Sunday best frocks, and there's no pineapple upside-down cake.

But there are three pairs of inquisitive eyes on me, all watching me closely as I force-feed myself. My silence speaks volumes, and Gregory is beside himself, having received the rundown from Nan before I made it downstairs to the dinner table. I heard the hushed whispers, the shocked gasp, and I also heard Nan pacifying a rankled Gregory with excuses of misunderstandings and business associates not being who I thought. Gregory won't buy it, so remaining at the table for as long as possible to avoid his pressing questions is paramount. He has a black eye and a swollen hand. It can't be ignored, and I'm wondering what he's told Nan.

When Nan starts clearing the dinner table, Gregory cocks his head to the side, signaling me to follow him out of the kitchen. I know my time evading him is up. I thank Nan, rub George on the shoulder affectionately, and follow my best friend into the hallway.

But I get in first. "What were you thinking?!" I hiss, looking back to the door and then yanking him up the stairs. "I didn't need you flexing your muscles and bashing horns with him!"

We reach the top of the stairs and I turn to see his mouth dropped open in shock at my tirade. "I was protecting you!"

"At first, yes, but it soon turned into a battle of the biggest ego! You threw the first punch!"

"He was manhandling you!"

Both of our heads snap to the side when we hear Nan. "What's going on up there?"

"Nothing!" I call, pulling Gregory into my room and slamming the door. "*You* pried me from him and dumped me on the pavement before tackling him to the floor!" I bend and point at my head. "I spent hours in A and E being glued together while you wrestled in the middle of the street!"

"You just disappeared!" he shouts, pointing his finger in my face. "And you have no fucking phone!" He throws his hands up in the air in frustration.

I pull up a moment, thinking about something that I really never wanted to think about again. "It's affecting us," I say quietly.

His neck retracts on his shoulders. "Yes, he is."

"I don't mean Miller."

"Then what—" His mouth snaps shut, his eyes wide. "Oh no! Don't blame this on that little thing we had." He waves toward the bed, laughing sarcastically. "This shit between us is down to that fucking prick you've fallen in love with!"

"He's not a prick!" I shout, searching deep for the strength to calm myself down.

"I swear to God, Livy, if you see him again, then we're done!"

"Don't talk stupid!" I'm horrified he would say such a thing. I've helped him through endless shitty breakups, and I've *never* made such a threat.

"I'm not," he says more calmly. "I mean it, Olivia. You know as well as me that *that* cocksucker is trouble. And I know you're not telling me everything."

"I am!" I defend myself far too hastily.

"Don't insult me!"

"At least he cared enough to search for me!"

Gregory recoils in disgust. "He's ruining you." Biting his lip, he watches me closely for a few long seconds. I don't like the look on his face, and I know I'm not going to like his next words. He's thinking too hard about them. "I can't see you if he's in your life."

I gasp as he turns and leaves, making a point of slamming the door behind him, leaving me struck dumb in the middle of my bedroom. I'm speechless, hurt, and mad. He can't slap conditions on our friendship when it suits him. I never have.

I throw myself in bed on an annoyed curse and hide under the sheets. Once again, my mind is grateful for the letup in painful thinking, and I'm soon dreaming of hard warmth pushed up against my back and soft humming in my ear. I'm only dreaming, but the sharp edges under the bespoke suit and the familiar feeling of smooth hands stroking my bare tummy are comforting, even if they aren't real. It's far more welcome than the usual nightmare.

* * *

I don't welcome Monday with any more enthusiasm than I have every other morning since I fled that hotel. On top of my muddled thoughts about a certain man, I now have Gregory to worry about. The calamity that is my life at the moment is certainly making up for all the boring that's come before.

Half of me is wondering why I suggested dinner with Miller today when I was desperate to be swallowed up by him yesterday, and half of me is wondering why I suggested *any* day at all. He hasn't slept with anyone? I need to make a list of questions. If I'm stupid enough to meet him.

I pull my bedcovers back and immediately frown down at my semi-naked body. I have my knickers on, but everything else is gone. Glancing up, I see all of my clothes folded neatly and placed in a pile on my chair. I'm not totally losing my mind. I fell into bed in my clothes after Gregory stormed out; I know I did. I consider the possibility of Nan stripping me down in my sleep, but that pile of precisely folded and placed clothes tells me otherwise.

Still frowning, I untangle my body from the bedcovers and make my way across the room, opening the door quietly and listening out for Nan. There are the sounds of happy singing and clanking dishes, but no talking. Casting my eyes back to the offending pile of clothes, I think hard, trying to remember if it's my doing, but I'm blank. Nothing is coming to me. Maybe I'm walking in my sleep, or maybe I'm tidying in my sleep.

A quick look at my clock tells me I haven't got time to ponder this mystery anymore, so I make quick work of showering and dressing for work, throwing on some jeans and my white Converse, like I want my feet to dictate my mood: lifeless... blank.

There are cornflakes in my bowl before I even sit at the table, and Nan is looking at me with an edge of delight mixed with curiosity. We're alone for the first time since yesterday morning, which means she finally has the opportunity to pick at me for answers. Quickly searching my brain for the best words before she hits me with her own, I *very* quickly come up with... something.

"How was the dance?" I ask.

"We rocked it." She brushes me off, even though I'm certain she has many tales to tell from her night as Ginger Rogers. "And it was two nights ago."

I wince. "Sorry."

"No matter," she insists, and I know why. "Miller looked mighty sad when he left yesterday." She putters around with her tea towel while watching for my reaction. "And I didn't like the sound of you and Gregory arguing."

I sigh, letting my backside fall to the chair, and pour some milk over my cornflakes as Nan loads my tea with too much sugar. "It's complicated, Nan."

"Oh..." Her rounded rump hits the chair next to me, her old navy eyes way too curious. "I can deal with complicated. In fact, I bet I have the answer."

I smile fondly and rest my hand over hers. "This is for me to fix."

"I get the impression that Gregory doesn't like Miller," she says cautiously.

"You've got the right impression, but can we leave it there?"

Her thin lips purse slightly, annoyed that I won't confide in her. I'm not exposing her to the hideousness of my complications, so she'll just have to be annoyed and accept the lie that Miller has fed her. I can't risk sending her into that horrific dark place again. "I might be able to help," she persists, squeezing my hand.

"I'm a big girl, Nan." I raise my eyebrows, making hers fall into a scowl.

"I suppose you are," she relents, still scowling, "but remember one thing, Olivia."

"What?"

"Life's too short to hang around waiting for answers that can only be found by getting off your skinny arse and finding them." She gets up and viciously plunges her wrinkled hands into the dishwater, then proceeds to dump dish after dish onto the drainer heavy-handedly.

* * *

It's a quiet afternoon at the bistro—until Miller Hart walks through the door. He immediately has a hold of everyone's attention in the place. And the bastard knows it.

"Are you free to leave?" he asks politely, but I expect there is only one correct answer to this question, and behind his impassive façade, he's just daring me to give the wrong one.

"Uh..." I can't form words. Del hands me my satchel and denim jacket with a wary nod, but it takes Miller to physically collect me from behind the counter to get my feet moving. He takes my nape gently and starts guiding me from the bistro, massaging my neck as he does, leaving me with no option but to keep up with his pushing pace. The black Mercedes is parked on double-yellow lines, and it's only when he opens the door to guide me to the seat that I speak up.

"What are you doing?" I ask, looking up at him.

My question doesn't make him falter in his attempts to put me in his car. "You promised me dinner. Get in the car."

"That was before you just humiliated me." I twist out of his grip and step back. I definitely notice the semblance of a scowl at my rejection, but Miller's smidgen of emotion isn't the only thing that has my attention.

He leans down, quite a way, so his eyes are level with mine. They are soft and reassuring. They have me. "Why do you keep denying me?"

I rip my stare from his gaze before I can lose myself in it, and walk away from him, my stride quick but completely pointless, too. I'm going nowhere.

He's behind me, his expensive shoes pacing evenly. "I don't like repeating myself." He catches me and turns me in his arms. Then he straightens me out and places my hair neatly over my shoulders before stepping back. "I'll make an exception this time. Why do you keep denying me?"

His audacity sets my emotions in gear. My lips start trembling, my eyes welling. The anger is restoking, too, the hurt magnifying, the confusion tripling. "Because..." I close my eyes briefly, feeling my strength slipping away, despite his arrogance. "Everything." I know William is right. I shouldn't be getting myself caught up in Miller's web of pleasure. I might not like William's interference, and he might not have a right to enforce his demands, but I can't deny that he knows what he's talking about. Everything I now know has been confirmed by William. I should listen to him. He's wise and familiar with *this world*.

Miller's luscious lips purse and his eyes drop, prompting that soft curl to fall forward, but I don't remind him of his rule of looking at someone when they are speaking to you. "You don't desire me?" he asks quietly.

My face bunches in confusion. What kind of question is that at a time like this? "Of course I do." I realize my error immediately when his eyes lift and drown me in…desire. My own desire is reflecting back at me through the never-ending depths of his blue eyes.

"And I you," he whispers. "More than my body desires water to survive or my lungs air to breathe."

I fight for breath. "I'm also frightened of you," I confess.

"And I you."

"I don't trust you."

That statement makes him falter slightly, but he quickly pulls it back. "I trust you with my life." His hand lifts, his thumb stroking over my eyebrow. The skin-on-skin contact puts me in my comfort zone and the sparks fire off within. "I trust you to help me." His finger drifts down my cheek, my jaw, until he's stroking my bottom lip. My eyes close on a quiet hitch of breath. "Let me taste you."

My nod of agreement is automatic. I can feel bursts of life within.

"Thank you," he murmurs quietly, his breath feathering against my cheek before his lips come down on my mouth softly. He's gentle, almost cautious, as he caresses my tongue with his, slowly breaking me down. "Hold me."

"If I do that, I'm yours again." I force myself to step away from him, leaving him still bent with eyes searching mine.

"I've made reservations for dinner." He straightens up. "Will you do me the honor of joining me?"

I'm a mess of conflicting thoughts, struggling to figure out if Miller is my destiny. But as his palm gingerly slides around my back and his heated touch burns through the material of my T-shirt, I think of something. "Where were you last night?"

I don't imagine the slight stiffness on his palm against me and the edge of guilt in those eyes. "Come to dinner with me."

He did. He broke into my house. That's... creepy! I feel violated. "You undressed me?" I can't believe I didn't wake. "I wasn't dreaming, was I?"

"I hope so. And when you're not dreaming of me, I hope you're constantly thinking of me."

"I'm thinking you have a problem!"

"I did," he replies quickly, deadly serious. "My world was fading into blackness again and the only thing that can keep it light keeps running away!"

I flinch at the genuine irritation in his voice. "I have questions."

He nods mildly and takes a deep breath, gathering some calm. "I'm ready to answer anything you'd like to ask me."

My relief is immense, but so is my dread. I'm not sure I want to hear his answers. "Over dinner," I assert. We need to be on neutral ground. No bed in sight. "Just dinner." This will be done my way. I may have laid my cards before, but they can still be turned back over. Actually, they absolutely can't, but Miller doesn't need to know that.

"Just dinner," he agrees, but I can tell it's a reluctant agreement.

"You don't get to taste me or touch me." I don't know why I'm saying such a stupid thing. I'm desperate for the comfort he offers me.

The dash of annoyance that passes over his perfect face makes me all the more determined. He can turn on his arrogant, gentlemanly charm and have me just as quick as the soft, attentive lover. "Now you're just being silly."

I shake my head. "I won't come if you're planning on winning me over by worshipping me." It'll be game-over. I'm still taken by him, even with my growing wariness and knowledge.

"Fine. As you wish," he mutters.

I nod and gather myself. "Where should I meet you?"

"Meet me?" His forehead furrows.

"I'll meet you at the restaurant." Miller picking me up is too familiar, and I can't allow Nan to think all is well when it isn't.

That declaration gains me a flash of irritation, but he contains it coolly. Delving back into solace with Miller is dangerous, but I fear I have no other choice and not just because Miller doesn't appear to be giving me one. He's back in my life, and I really want him to be. I need his comfort, his *thing,* his words. I need it all. Nothing has ever made me feel so protected but at the same time so utterly vulnerable. And nothing has made me feel so strong, yet so incredibly weak. There has to be a middle ground.

"Fine." He exhales a mixture of frustration and annoyance. "When did you become so difficult?"

"The second you touched me," I reply quietly, finding the sass that has become paramount since I fell into the curious world of Miller Hart. I won't survive without it. I won't survive *him* without it.

His palm lifts slowly and cups my cheek, stroking slow circles. "The second I *looked* at you, I saw light through my constant darkness." He moves in, his mouth getting closer, my eyes focused only there. "I saw bright, hopeful light reflecting back at me through those beautiful sapphire eyes." He doesn't kiss me; he just keeps our mouths close, his breath spreading across my face, enhancing the sense of warmth coursing through me. My eyes close. "I'll respect your request for this evening. But remember, you are my possession, Olivia. You're my habit, and I'm not going down without a fight." He releases me, leaving me breathless, dizzy, and feeling abandoned. I open my lids to face torturous beauty. "And I won't lose no matter who takes me on. Even you."

"Where shall I meet you?" I breathe, not caring to challenge him on his confident claim. I've seen him in action, fists flying, and I've also felt him in action... worshipping action. All challengers are doomed. Including me.

"Seven o'clock here." He takes a pen from his inside pocket and scribbles an address on an old receipt from his wallet before handing it to me. "I'll be waiting."

I nod as he starts to back away, smoothing down his suit before sliding his hands into his pockets. Our eyes lock. I see hope there. I see confidence. I see fear. And I see caution. But I'm not sure if that caution is for him or for me. Probably both.

Miller breaks the eye connection, then turns away from me and strolls off toward his car.

My palms hit my cheeks and rub some life back into them. I feel hot, my mind a jumbled mess of contradicting thoughts, worries... fear. I'm frightened of him, but he makes me feel unbelievably safe. I'm worried about him, but I'm worried about me, too. I can't even fathom my thought process, which is jumping from surrendering to fighting harder against him. Nothing is making sense.

I'm in a world of my own, trying to figure out too much, when I find my palm stroking my nape. The hairs are dancing wildly under my touch, tingling, making my skin buzz.

"This is exactly what I was afraid of." The velvet voice pulls my body around slowly, warily, and my heart sprints up to my throat.

Chapter Nine

I'm not sure whether I should be relieved or worried by what I find. William is leaning against his Lexus, arms crossed, ankles crossed. He doesn't look happy, his typically sparkling gray eyes fractious and his soft features cut with annoyance.

"You're following me?" My question spills on a guilty gasp—the guilt for my weakness where Miller's concerned, the gasp for my shock at finding William here.

"I've been trying to call you." He pushes his body away from the car and strolls over casually until his hulking frame is towering over me. "Where's the phone I bought you?"

"I haven't charged it." I divert my eyes downward, for what reason I don't know. He might be right about Miller, but I'm not answerable to him. London's most notorious male escort may have resided in a dark place, but I'm making it light. He wants to change for me. I have to make my own decisions. I'm the master of my own destiny.

"Then you will," he orders. "Tell me why you were at his club."

I look up, shocked. "You *have* been following me?"

"I told you before. I make it my business to know what happens in this world. When I heard of an incident at Ice involving Miller Hart and a pretty little blonde, it didn't take long to figure out who the pretty little blonde was." He cups my jaw and lifts my chin. "Walk away."

I shake my head, my eyes beginning to well with tears. "I've tried. I've tried dozens of times and I can't."

"Try harder, Olivia. You're falling into his darkness and there's no getting out once you land. You have no idea what you're truly getting into."

"I love him," I sob, admitting aloud for the first time that I'm still in love with the confounding man, who is even more of a mystery now than he ever was before some of his secrets were revealed. I can't fall into his darkness if I'm keeping it light. "It's painful love."

He winces at my confession, and I know it's because he identifies with how that feels. "The pain will subside, Olivia."

"Has it for you?" I ask.

"I don't..." He frowns and drops my chin from his hold. I've surprised him with my question.

I don't give him a chance to pull himself together. "You're crippled by agony every day. You let your Gracie go."

"I had no—"

"No," I cut him off, and he doesn't chastise me for it. The formidable William Anderson snaps his stubbled jaw shut without a word. "Don't tell me it gets easier."

His smart-suited shoulders sag and I sidestep him, making my way to the tube, my words spoken to William strengthening my reasons to take Miller on. Years after walking away from Gracie, William Anderson is still in agony. He hasn't gotten over her, and he doesn't look like he ever will. If William Anderson has felt like I do right now for all these years, then I think I'd rather take death.

"Get in the car," William calls from the inside as it slows alongside me.

"No, thank you."

"Damn you, Olivia!" he yells, halting my determined march. "Don't make me manhandle you."

I'm stunned into silence and stillness by his threat, the coolness of this well-respected, well-contained man heated to the boiling point. "You're just going to nag me," I splutter, not knowing what else to say.

He actually rolls his eyes, stunning me further. "I'm not your father."

"Then stop acting like it," I spit, that word enhancing the absence of a male confidant in my life. I haven't needed one for twenty-four years. But then again, I've not encountered a Miller Hart during that time. Until now.

"Would you kindly get in and allow me to drive you home?"

"Are you going to chew my ear off?"

He refrains from laughing, leaning over and opening the door. "I've done some questionable things in my time, Olivia, but I'm not guilty of chewing any ears."

I narrow my eyes suspiciously until he gives me an expectant look. I've no doubt William would manhandle me, so to save a public spectacle, I cautiously slide into the Lexus and shut the door gently.

"Thank you," he says, relaxing back in his seat. The driver pulls away and I rest my bag on my lap, fiddling with the buckles for something to do other than wait for him to speak. "Will nothing I say convince you that he's a bad idea?"

I sigh, exasperated, and flop back against my seat. "You said you weren't going to chew my ear."

"No, I said I never had before. There's a first time for everything."

"Cute," I mutter. "I'm meeting him for dinner this evening."

"Why?"

"To talk."

"About what?"

"I think you know."

"What happened in that hotel?"

"Nothing." I grind the words through my tight jaw. I was delusional to ever think he would let that go. I'm not telling him, despite the fact that I suspect he knows all too well. And, anyway, I'd never be able to utter the words. Thinking them is hard enough.

"Nothing," he muses. "So you looked like a frightened kitten because nothing happened?"

"Yes," I spit, despising that he clearly has his suspicions. I'm not confirming them.

"Of course," he sighs. "What's worrying is that you're going back for more."

"More what?"

"More of Miller Hart."

I have to fight to stop myself from screaming, *"That wasn't Miller Hart!"*

"Where are you meeting?" he continues after observing me closely for a few moments.

"I don't know. He gave me an address for a restaurant."

"Let me see."

Losing a bit of patience, I fish through my satchel and pull the receipt out, thrusting it across the backseat without looking at William. "There."

It's taken from my grasp, and I hear him hum thoughtfully. "Nice place. I'll take you."

"Oh no!" I laugh, swinging disbelieving eyes his way. "I'll get myself there." I don't want William interfering. Enough people are already, even if they're unaware of the whole horrid story. And their determined effort to stop me from seeing Miller only spells out how much more resistance I'll be facing should they know.

"I'll simply drop you off."

"It's not necessary."

"Either you accept my ride, or you don't go." He's deadly serious.

"Why are you doing this?" I ask, but then his reasons are too clear. "Is this an attempt to ease your guilt?"

"What?" He's all defensive, spiking my curiosity *and* my annoyance.

"Gracie. You failed her, so you're trying to redeem yourself by helping me?"

"That's nonsense!" He laughs, looking away from me.

It's not nonsense at all. It's *perfect* sense.

"I don't need your help, William. I am not my mother!"

His handsome face slowly turns back to mine. All previous amusement has disappeared as if it was never there. He looks grave. "Then why were you at his club?"

My mouth snaps shut momentarily. "I..."

His gray eyebrows lift slightly, his question and look making me retreat in my seat. I open my mouth to speak, but nothing materializes, prompting William to come closer. "Punishing him, were you?"

I'm immobilized by realization, crippled by the cold, hard truth. "I'm not..." I can't finish.

William slowly pulls back and settles his eyes on my hand, where I'm fiddling with my ring. "You are more like your mother than you realize, Olivia." He gently clasps my hand and takes over the twirling of my ring. "Don't mistake that as a bad thing. She was a beautiful, passionate woman with an addictive spirit."

A lump the size of London has jumped into my throat, and I turn away from him to gaze out the window so he doesn't see my tears. I don't want to be like her. Selfish. Reckless. Naive. I want to be none of those things.

The ring on my finger is silently twirled by William while I have my tears. He says no more, and neither do I.

* * *

Much to my relief, Nan isn't home. She's left a pot of stew, along with a note to let me know that she's gone out with George. After finding my new phone, I tag on a message to hers saying I've gone out with Sylvie, leaving my new number for her. Then I spend an hour slowly getting myself ready, but more time is spent mentally preparing, rather than making myself look presentable.

At six-thirty, I wander down the garden path to the Lexus awaiting me. The driver opens the door; I slip in quietly and immediately feel his gray eyes on me.

"You look lovely," William says genuinely, and I look over to find him taking in my short black dress, one of only three evening dresses I have.

"Thank—" I'm interrupted by the unfamiliar sound of a phone chime, but William doesn't go to retrieve his mobile and after it rings for a few seconds, I realize it's coming from my purse. I rummage through, locate my new iPhone on a frown, and glance down at the screen. Then I look to William.

"Just checking." He smiles, his hand appearing and cutting the call from his own phone.

"Haven't you got better things to do than ferry me around?" I ask, slipping my phone back into my purse.

"I have plenty to do, and doing my best to stop you from free-falling into his world is one of the most important."

"You're a hypocrite," I accuse, fairly or not; I don't care anymore. "Your world, his world. It's more or less the same damn thing. How can you claim to know him so well?"

"Our worlds collide every now and then," he answers swiftly, and devoid of feeling.

"Collide?" I question, a little confused and also cautious with the use of the word *collide* in that statement. Collide hints at crashing. He didn't use *meet* or *pass*.

He leans toward me and speaks on a mere whisper. "I have morals, Olivia. Miller Hart does not. It's caused friction between *our worlds.* I don't agree with how he conducts business and I'm not afraid to tell him, despite that lethal temper of his."

I recoil, unable to argue with him. I've seen how Miller conducts business and I've seen that temper. "He can change," I murmur, knowing I've failed to inject any confidence into my tone. William's sardonic huff of laughter tells me he's just as doubtful. "I'd like you to drop me around the corner," I say confidently, knowing that Miller isn't likely to appreciate me being dropped off by another man, especially William and especially knowing that their worlds *collide* every now and then. I don't want tonight to be one of those *every now and thens.*

"Of course."

"Thank you."

"Tell me," he begins, "how such a stable, sweet young woman could fall in love with a man like Miller Hart."

Like Miller Hart? Stable and sweet? I rack my brain for an answer to that question. And I find nothing, so I utilize Nan's words. "We don't choose who we fall for."

"You might be right."

"I know I'm right," I say to myself. I'm living proof.

"And knowing what you know, you still feel the same?"

"I know he hasn't been with another woman since he met me."

"He's had dates, Olivia, and please don't try to tell me otherwise. Don't forget, there's nothing I don't know."

"Then you'll know that he hasn't slept with any of them," I grate, feeling my patience wearing thin.

"And I'd love to know how he avoided it," William muses. I don't reply to that, quietly pleased that he hasn't challenged my claim. "I have a question. Probably the most important question."

"What's that?"

"Does he love you?"

I wilt on the inside at William's perfectly reasonable inquiry.

Nothing less than a yes should be good enough here. William knows it. I know it. I shouldn't even entertain the idea of exposing my fallen heart to more hurt without that confirmation. "He's fascinated by me." I turn to look out the window, feeling young and stupid.

"Does fascinate equal love?"

"I don't know," I murmur, barely audibly, but I know he's heard me when his palm rests on my knee and squeezes gently.

"Do your talking," he says quietly. "Then do your thinking."

I nod in acceptance and feel strangely comforted by William's affectionate touch. I'll talk and I'll think, but I don't actually *think* anything Miller could tell me will lessen or diminish my fascination with London's most notorious male escort. I want it to, but I'm being real. I'm caught up in his confounding, dark world, and I have no faith that anything can free me from it, not even William, no matter how hard he tries.

* * *

The driver doesn't drop me off around the corner as agreed. He pulls up right outside the restaurant, and William doesn't point out his error. I start to voice the mistake, but then I spot Miller standing on the pavement waiting, and the wary look he's giving the Lexus tells me he knows the car. But he doesn't know I'm in it.

"Please"—I turn to William, panicked—"ask your driver to pull into the next street."

"There's no need." He dismisses my concern and exits the car swiftly and confidently and with the utmost superiority. I want to crawl under the seat and hide. I haven't looked out to see Miller's reaction to William's appearance. I don't need to. I can feel the air freeze around me, and he hasn't even seen *me* yet. "Hart," I hear William say tightly. Then my door is opening and William is looking down at me and extending his hand for me to take. I want to scream at him for his underhandedness. He's being threatening and I've seen Miller under threat. It's frightening.

Closing my eyes and taking a deep breath of confidence, I reject William's offering and step out, slowly straightening my body until I'm engulfed in the glacial air that has nothing to do with the poor weather conditions. Then I turn and face him. Blue eyes have slightly widened and his shadowed jaw is tense, but he remains quiet as William escorts me to him. Miller, as ever, looks unfathomably stunning in a dark gray three-piece suit, pale blue shirt—tie perfectly knotted—and tan brogues. His eyes, although shocked, are shimmering as I approach, his dark hair a tousled array of waves and his tall body striking. As I near, he flicks William a cold look before returning his eyes to mine and sliding his palm around my nape, tugging me forward. The icy air is still rife, but now it's mixed with a delicious warmth being injected into me from our joining. Dipping slowly, he gets his face level with mine and gives me a hint of a smile. It reminds me that Miller Hart has the most beautiful beam and it's been too long since I've seen it.

He blinks slowly, another of his lovely traits, and gently rests his lips on mine. I know William is twitching behind me, but nothing will prevent me from absorbing Miller. Not even me. "You put perfection to shame, my gorgeous girl." He pecks my lips and pulls back to get my eyes. "Thank you for coming."

I feel utterly stupid with William playing minder behind me, so I turn and find him watching us closely. "You can leave now." I feel Miller's arm snake around my waist and pull me into his chest. He has completely ignored my request of no touching and tasting, and I've done nothing to stop him. He's staking his claim, marking his territory.

The tall, mature, gray-haired male steps away slowly, not taking his eyes from Miller until he's at his car. "I know morals are something you struggle with, Hart, but I'm asking you nicely to do the right thing now." William may be asking nicely, but his tone is drenched in threat.

"Don't question my morals when it comes to Olivia Taylor, Mr. Anderson." Miller's grip on me increases. "Never do that."

The animosity bouncing between these two powerful men is intoxicating. My head is awash with questions of associations and worlds colliding, and that's on top of the list I have ready for Miller.

"Do the right thing," William says before turning grays onto me. "You'll call me." He slides effortlessly into the car without waiting for my agreement and pulls away fast, leaving me on the pavement, tense and bracing myself for a round of questions from Miller.

It's a few silent moments before he speaks, and when he does, it's not at all the reaction I've been bracing myself for. "Well that was a surprise," he muses quietly, making me frown. "How did you come to keep company with William Anderson?"

I'm totally perplexed. "He was my mother's pimp," I remind him, holding back on the information that I've recently been enlightened on. And I know Miller won't appreciate the reminder of my encounter with William during my reckless spell, so I omit that, too. "And while we're on the subject," I fire, turning in his arms and stepping away from him, "how did I come to be keeping company with you?"

He looks at me a little bemused. "You've already defaulted on your no touching and tasting rule." Stooping down, he lands me with a cheeky peck on my lips. Damn me, I don't shy away from it. "It would be silly to reinstate it now." His eyes are sparkling wildly, his face full of unseen victory. Silly because it was a given that I'd fail, or silly because of where I might end up should I give in, which is ultimately in Miller's bed being worshipped.

"It wouldn't be silly at all," I counter with grit. While Miller-style worshipping is the ultimate escape from my troubles, I need to maintain my strength, no matter how much I want him to indulge me and swallow me up in his mind-blowing world of pleasure. "Are we having dinner?"

"Yes." He gestures across the road, and when I glance over, I see his car. "After you."

My brow puckers, but I turn toward the restaurant instead. I don't get very far.

"Wrong way," he says simply, taking my nape and guiding me in the direction of his car with a little twist of his hand on my neck.

"Dinner and a talk," I remind him. "You agreed to meet me for dinner and a talk."

"Yes, I agreed to meet you at the restaurant. You never specified that the eating and talking should happen there."

I laugh nervously, wondering where he plans on doing the eating and talking. "You can't twist my words."

"I've not twisted anything." He guides me across the road with ease and places me in his car. "We're having dinner at my apartment." The door shuts on me and the locks click into place.

Now I'm freaking out. Being at Miller's is a bad, *bad* idea. I try the door, for no purpose whatsoever. I heard the locks. Then I hear them again and I try the handle once more but get nowhere. He slides in beside me. "This is kidnapping!" I protest. "I don't want to go to your apartment."

"Why?" he asks, starting the engine and pulling his seat belt on.

"Because . . . I . . . because . . . it will . . ."

"Be natural for us to make love?" He slowly turns his eyes to me. Serious eyes.

The words alone send my pulse into overdrive. I'm feeling hot, lustful, and helpless, and that's a dangerous situation to be in with Miller Hart. "Talk," I murmur weakly.

He shifts in his seat and rests his forearm on the wheel. He can see my wanton condition. I'm breathless. "I've always promised that I'd never make you do anything I know you don't want to. Haven't I?"

I nod.

He smiles a little and reaches over to rearrange my wild blond hair. "Do you know how hard it is to refrain from touching you, especially when I know that you want me to?"

"I want to talk," I affirm, finding my very last scrap of strength to utter my demand, leaving me defenseless should he choose to ignore my request.

"And I want to explain, but I'd like to do it in the comfort of my own home." He says no more and returns his attention to the road, pulling away from the curb. There's no speaking or even any glances across the car to me. The only thing I have to focus on, except my racing mind, are the words of Portishead's "Glory Box" that echo in the enclosed air around us.

They sink into my mind, making it spin, and then I hear Miller utter two words to himself, so quietly I barely hear. "I will."

Chapter Ten

I'm regretting insisting on the no tasting and touching rule. I'm close to collapsing by floor nine as we climb up to his penthouse, and Miller's knowing look is a clear sign that he can detect my regret. But my hot face and aching calves also remind me of the first question I'd like to ask.

He unlocks his black shiny door and stands to the side, holding it open for me and revealing the inside of his palatial apartment. The urge to run overwhelms me.

"I'm not allowed to physically restrain you, so I beg you don't run away from me."

I turn my face up to his and find blue eyes full of pleading. He's being that respectful, loving man, the one I love most of his split personalities. "I won't run," I promise, stepping over the threshold and tentatively rounding the table in the entrance hall. The front door shuts behind me and Miller's fancy shoes click on the marble as he approaches.

"Would you like some wine?" he asks, removing his jacket and draping it neatly over the back of a chair.

"Water, please." I'm dehydrated after my marathon stair climb, and I need a clear head.

"As you wish," he says, disappearing into the kitchen and

quickly returning with a bottle of spring water and a glass. He walks over to his drinks cabinet, pours two fingers of scotch, and then turning to face me, he brings the glass to his lips slowly, making me avert my eyes to avoid the pleasurable sight. He knows what those lips do to me, and he's brandishing them unethically. "Don't deprive me of your face, Olivia."

"Don't deprive me of your respect," I retort calmly.

He has nothing to say to that, so instead he says, "Sit," as he makes his way over with my water.

"I thought we were having dinner?"

He falters midstride. "We are."

"In the lounge?" I ask, my voice loaded with sarcasm. I know Miller Hart and his obsessive world of perfection, and there is not a chance in hell he would eat off his lap.

"There's no need—"

"Yes, there is," I sigh. "I assume we're eating in the kitchen." I take the water being offered and leave Miller to head for the kitchen, coming to an abrupt halt at the doorway on a little gasp.

"You didn't give me a chance to add the finishing touches," he murmurs from behind me. "Candles, music."

The smell of something delicious permeates the room and the table is laid Miller-perfect. I could have wandered into The Ritz by mistake. "It's . . . perfect," I breathe.

"It's not perfect at all," he says quietly, inching past me. He sets his drink down, tweaks its position, then lights the candles running up the center of the table. Moving across the kitchen, he puts his iPhone in the docking station before playing with a few buttons. I just stare at him as Ellie Goulding's "Explosions" seeps from the speakers and he slowly turns to face me. "It's still not perfect," he says, wandering slowly over. He lifts his hand hesitantly and looks to me for permission. I nod, letting him gently take my hand, and follow his steps across the kitchen. The chair at one end is pulled out and he releases me, indicating for me to take a seat. I follow his request and let him tuck me neatly under. "Now it's perfect," he whispers in my ear, stealing a nip of my lobe and throwing me into desire desolation. I'm tense everywhere, and he knows it. After ensuring I get a few unbearably gratifying moments of his heated breath in my ear, he takes his time ripping his bended body from my seated frame. "Wine?" he asks.

I close my eyes briefly to gather some abandoned strength. "No, thank you."

"Being free from alcohol won't sate your desire for me, Olivia."

He places a cloth napkin across my lap before taking the chair at the other end. He's right, of course, but avoiding alcohol might help me think clearer.

"The distance is acceptable?" he asks, indicating between us with a sway of his hand.

No, it's not; he seems so far away, but it would be foolish to tell him so. Not that I need to tell him a thing. He knows very well. I nod and scan the table before me, my usual nerves present whenever I'm presented with a table set by Miller. "What are you feeding me?"

He restrains a grin and pours some red wine into one of the larger wineglasses. "I can't feed you anything from over here."

I bite my lip and resist the urge to fiddle with the fork at my place setting, knowing I'll never replace it accurately.

"Do you like me feeding you?" he asks, pulling my eyes from the perfect table to his perfect face.

"You know the answer to that question." Images of strawberries and puddles of dark chocolate jump all over my mind.

"I do," he agrees. "And I don't need to tell you how much I enjoy nourishing you."

I nod in silent acknowledgment, remembering the satisfaction on his face.

"And worshipping you."

I squirm in my chair, fighting off the throb threatening to

attack me between my thighs. No matter what persona he takes on, he has me every time. "We're supposed to be talking," I point out, eager to steer away from thoughts of worshipping, strawberries dipped in warm chocolate, and Miller's general magnetism.

"We *are* talking."

"Why are you so terrified of elevators?" I go for the jugular but feel immediately guilty when his face drops just a tiny bit. He quickly gathers himself, though.

"I have a phobia of enclosed spaces." He swirls his wine thoughtfully while he watches me. "Which is why you'll never convince me to hide in a closet."

My guilt is increased by his confession and my unwitting demand in my bedroom that time. "I didn't know," I whisper, also reminded of his terrified face when I refused to get out of the elevator. I'd worked it out as I fled the hotel and I used it against him.

"Of course you didn't. I didn't tell you."

"Where does it stem from?"

His shoulders jump up a little and he looks away, evading my eyes. "I don't know. Many people have phobias of certain things with no explanation."

"You have an explanation, though, don't you?" I press.

He won't look at me.

"It's polite to look at me when I'm talking to you, and it's polite to answer someone when they ask you a question."

Blue eyes filled with irritation slowly find mine. "Overthinking, Olivia. I have a phobia of enclosed spaces, and that line of conversation will finish right there."

"What about your freakish tidiness?"

"I have an appreciation for my possessions. That doesn't make me a freak."

"You have more than that," I reply. "You have obsessive-compulsive disorder."

Miller's mouth drops open a little. "Because I like things a certain way, I have a disorder?"

I exhale a wary breath and stop my elbows from hitting the table just in time. He won't acknowledge his freakish obsessiveness, and it's clear I'm getting nothing on the claustrophobia front, either. But these are trivial issues in the grand scheme of things. There are more important things to address. "The newspaper. Why was the title changed?"

"I realize how that looks, but it was for your benefit."

"How?"

His lips fix in a straight line. "To protect you. Trust me."

"Trust you?" I fight off the urge to laugh in his face. "I trusted you with everything! How long have you been London's most notorious male escort?" The words feel like acid burning my tongue as I spit them from my mouth.

"Are you sure you wouldn't like some wine?" He lifts the bottle from the table and looks at me hopefully. It's a pathetic attempt to shirk my question.

"No, thank you. An answer would be nice, though."

"How about some appetizers?" He stands and strides over to the fridge, without waiting for my answer. I can't eat with my stomach in such knots and my brain a fuzz of unanswered questions, and I doubt my appetite will appear once I finally squeeze the answers from him.

He opens the huge mirrored fridge and pulls out a platter of something. Then he shuts the door but doesn't return to the table, instead messing with whatever's on the tray, poking and shifting things around. He's trying to buy time, and when he glances cautiously up to the mirror, he catches me watching him in the reflection. He knows I know his game.

"You said you're ready to answer my questions," I remind him, keeping my determined stare on him in the mirror.

His eyes drop to the tray briefly, and then he slowly turns on a deep breath and makes his way back to the table, pushing that dark lock of hair off his forehead en route. I nearly choke when the platter is placed with utter accuracy, revealing a pile of oysters.

"Help yourself." He gestures to the silver dish, then sits.

I ignore his offer, annoyed by his choice for starters, and ask my question once again. "How long?"

Lifting his plate, he takes three oysters and sets them neatly down. "I've been an escort for ten years," he says, choosing not to look at me as he delivers his answer.

I want to gasp in shock, but I resist, instead taking my water to moisten my suddenly parched mouth. "Why notorious?"

"Because I'm unforgiving."

Now I *do* gasp, and I hate myself for it. This shouldn't be news to me. I've experienced him being unforgiving.

He sees me struggling but continues. "Because in the bedroom, I'm wicked, unloving, unfeeling, and unbothered by it. The women can't get enough of me and the men can't work out why that is."

"They pay for you—"

"To be the best fuck of their life," he finishes for me. "And they pay obscene amounts for the privilege."

"I don't get it." I shake my head, my eyes darting all over his flawless table. "You don't let them kiss you or touch you."

"When I'm naked, no. When we're intimate, no. I'm a perfect gentleman on dates, Olivia. They can feel me over my clothes, work themselves up, and enjoy my attention. But that's as far as their control goes. I'm the perfect mix of man for them. Arrogant... attentive... talented."

I inwardly wince. "Do *you* get anything from it?"

"Yes," he admits. "I'm in full control in the bedroom and I come every time."

I flinch at his earnest words, looking away, feeling sick and wounded. "Right."

"Show me that face," he demands harshly, and my head lifts automatically, finding soft eyes replacing the hard ice. "But nothing will ever come close to the pleasure I gain from worshipping you."

"I'm struggling to see that man now," I say, making the softness of his expression drift into misery. "I so wish you'd never made me one of them."

"Never more than me," he whispers, slumping back in his chair. "Tell me there's hope."

All I can see is Miller in that hotel room. My desire and need for him are still there, but our short conversation has brought the harsh reality of his life crashing down around me. I'm not equipped with enough strength to deal with him. If I let him in again, then I'm facing a lifetime of torture and possibly regret. Nothing will make me forget the unforgiving lover. All I'll see when he takes me is a red mist of misery. My life has been difficult enough as it is. I can't make it harder.

"I asked you a question," he says quietly. The tone of his voice tells me he's slipping into that clipped, arrogant mode, probably because he can see my sudden despondency, and with a flick of my eyes to his, I *see* that arrogance, too. He won't go down easily.

"The woman in Madrid?"

"I didn't sleep with her."

"Then why did you go?"

"Prior obligation." He's impassive and sharp, yet strangely I believe him. But it's not making any of this easier to deal with.

"May I use your bathroom?" I ask, standing from the table, his gaze rising with me.

"Once you've answered my question. Is there hope?"

"I don't have an answer yet," I lie, placing my napkin on my chair.

"Might you have once you've visited the restroom?"

"I don't know."

"Don't overthink, Olivia."

"I'd say that was impossible after what you've presented me with, wouldn't you agree?" I'm being yanked in two directions, wanting to listen to William because I know he's definitely right and wanting to trust my heart because maybe, just maybe, I can help Miller. But a *definitely* should always win over a *maybe.* The confliction is too much. It's tearing me apart.

He watches me carefully. Nervously. "You're leaving, aren't you?"

"I've asked my questions. I never said I'd stay once you answered them. And I never said I'd like or accept the answers." The *definitely* wins. William wins. I leave the kitchen hastily to escape the intensity that he's exuding.

"Olivia!"

Swinging the front door open, I dash from his apartment, knowing he'll never allow me to leave without a fight. My troubled mind only just allows me to register my safest route from his building. I head straight for the elevator. My heart is thumping chaotically, my breathing panicked and frenzied as I bash the Call button for the elevator.

"Olivia, don't get in that elevator, please!" His charging footsteps have me repeatedly smacking the metal button and cursing while I wait for what seems like decades for the doors to slide open. "Fuck! Olivia!"

I dive in, smack the button for the ground floor, and push myself up against the far wall. I'm being cruel, but desperation is overriding any guilt I'm feeling for using this weakness against him.

I knew he'd make it in time, but I still jump when his arm appears and crashes against the doors, pulling them open. His brow is a sheen of sweat, his eyes wide with fear. "Get out!" he yells, his broad shoulders heaving.

I shake my head. "No."

His jaw looks set to shatter from tenseness. "Get out of the fucking elevator!"

I keep quiet, pushing myself farther into the wall. He's fuming mad, frighteningly so.

"How could you do this?" he pants, yanking the door open when it tries to close again. "How?"

"I can't be with you, Miller." My voice is barely audible over his labored breathing and my clattering heart.

"Livy, I beg you, don't do this to me again." He's beginning to shake, his eyes darting continuously from me to the inside of the elevator.

"I can't forget that man." I reach out and press the button again.

"Fuck!" He releases the doors and they start to close. "I refuse to give up, Olivia." Blue eyes glaze over, his expression straightening. "I won't lose."

"You've already lost," I murmur as his face disappears.

Chapter Eleven

I don't know how I've ended up here. Probably to reinforce my decision. Seeing the four-poster bed, the regal room, and the images of me restrained is helping steel my resolve. But it's also magnifying the pain. I'm standing in the middle of the hotel room, gazing around, torturing myself further and praying for some strength to see me through. Run away. Disappear forever. I can see no other way. My skin is prickling and cold. My eyes are sore with tears. The plans I started to make so many times need to be completed and fulfilled now. I need to go away for a while, put space between us and hope the saying "out of sight, out of mind" is true. For both of us.

"Why did you come here?" The question filters through the rush of blood that's distorting my hearing, dragging me back into the chilly room.

"To help convince myself that I'm doing the right thing."

"Does it feel right?"

"No," I admit. Nothing feels right. It's all so very wrong. I hear the door click shut, snapping me from my daydream, and I swing around to find a mess of a man, his hair wild, his suit crumpled. But his blue eyes are relieved.

"I won't lose," he says, resting his hands in his pocket. "I *can't* lose, Olivia."

Tears begin to trickle down my cheeks as I stand before him, defeated.

Conquered.

His back hits the door, his own eyes glazing over as his body sags into the wood. The sight of Miller Hart fighting to prevent his tears from falling rips my heart from my chest and makes my knees buckle, sending my body folding to the floor. My chin hits my chest, and my hair tumbles over my shoulders. And I cry. The broken man before me has always made my eyes hurt, but this time it's not with pleasure at his beauty. This time it's seeing him looking so tormented. Desperate. Ruined.

I'm engulfed by him in a nanosecond, his warm arms wrapped tightly around me, my face pushed into his chest. "Don't cry," he whispers, pulling me onto his lap. "I need you to be strong for me."

I'm scooped up and carried to the bed. "It ends here," he says, laying me down gently and spreading his body over me, burying his face in my neck. I don't fight. I let his body melt into mine, let his strength seep into me, holding on to him like my life depends on it. He does the same. Each of us is squeezing tightly, both of our hearts pounding a strong, steady thrum. I can hear the beats. We're both coming back to life.

His head lifts slowly until I'm staring into blue eyes filled with anguish. "I'm so sorry." He wipes my eyes. "I know I've run away, too, but I accept it now." He dips and kisses me gently, his soft lips wanted and terribly needed. "I need you to do the same." He sits up and pulls me onto his lap with ease, swamping me with his arms and kissing my face repeatedly. "What we have is beautiful, Olivia. I can't give it up." He grasps my dress by the hem but doesn't set about removing it. "May I?"

I answer by pushing his suit jacket from his shoulders, and he drops my dress to allow me to rid him of it. I need his naked skin on mine.

"Thank you," he breathes, removing my dress and casting it aside. His lips find mine and begin a delicate caress, his tongue tentative and soft as it slips into my mouth. My mind blanks, but my body responds instinctively. I accept his kiss, returning his soft, lazy pace, soaking up the emotion pouring from his entire being. His warm hands are all over me, touching and feeling everywhere, reminding me of the lack of skin beneath my palms. I start unbuttoning his waistcoat, then his shirt, until my hands are diving inside of the material, feeling him everywhere for too short a time before I'm pushing the garments from his body, refusing to release his lips, not even to take in his perfect torso. Once his arms are free again, he unhooks the clasp of my bra and slowly pulls it from my body, exposing my tight, tingling nipples. He breaks our kiss, and I whimper in protest, reaching down to unfasten his trousers.

That hypnotizing mouth is parted, allowing breathy pants to escape, and his eyes are focused on my modest breasts. I pull at his trousers once they're undone, impatient for him to be naked.

He rips his eyes from my chest and looks up at me. "Taste me."

I waste no time, but I seek out his neck rather than his mouth, nibbling on his throat and taking a long inhale of his manly scent. I'm all over him, making him moan and mumble in gratification.

"My mouth," he groans, and I divert immediately to his lips with his plea. "Oh Jesus, Olivia." Big palms find my cheeks and hold my head securely while we kiss, soft and slow. "I can't imagine anything could feel better than kissing you," he says against my lips. "Tell me you're mine."

I nod against him and meet his swirling tongue as he takes me down to the bed, letting me quickly push his trousers down his long legs. He abandons me momentarily, producing a condom from nowhere and slipping it on, hissing and clenching his eyes shut before falling back down to my body. I whimper when he settles between my thighs and I feel the broad head of his erection nudging at my entrance.

"Say it." He bites at my bottom lip, rearing back. "Don't deny me."

"Yours." There's no question.

He rests his forehead on mine and pushes into me on a controlled surge of breath. "Thank you."

"Miller," I sigh, feeling the pieces of my fallen heart merging back together. My eyes close on a satisfied exhale, a peace settling over me, and he begins a lazy sway of his hips. With my hands free, I can touch him, and I make the most of it, slowly sliding my palms everywhere, feeling every inch of him. Our tongues are dancing sweetly, his hips are rolling gently, and reverence is pouring from him. He's fully redeemed, his attentiveness extinguishing the horror scene of this hotel, this perfect moment reminding me of the sweet, gentle man he is when he's worshipping me—the man I need him to be. The man he wants to be. For me.

"I'm never freeing your lips," he declares, our sweaty bodies slipping languidly. "Never." I'm rolled from beneath him so I'm straddling his lap, still full to the maximum, the movement sending him so incredibly deep.

"Oh God!" My palms slap into his abs and brace, my chin hitting my chest.

"Fuck!" Miller curses, grinding up into me, his hands gripping the tops of my thighs. "Olivia Taylor," he whispers. "My most precious possession."

"You're never freeing my lips," I choke through the desire, then gasp as his palm is quickly secured on my nape and yanking me down to his face. He thrusts up again. I cry out.

Then he sends me out of my mind with a kiss so full of hunger, I struggle to remember my name.

"Move." He nips my tongue and encourages me by smoothing his hands around to my bottom and tugging up. I feel him slip from my passage, instigating a delicious friction that prompts me to fly up on a yell. My hands delve into my hair. "That's it, Livy!"

The pleasure contorting his face injects some fortitude into me. I lift and fall onto his lap uncontrolled. "Like that?" I ask, not waiting for his answer. His clenched eyes tell me, so I repeat, gripping my blond masses of hair harshly. "Miller, tell me!"

"Yes!" His eyes fly open, his jaw clenched. "You can do whatever the fucking hell you want to me, Olivia. I'll take it all."

I pause, breathing heavily, feeling him throb incessantly within me, my muscles stroking every pulse. "Me too."

He moves quickly, taking me to my back and slipping back into me with ease. Then his fingertip makes a lazy trail down my hot cheek before he claims my mouth again. "I wish you were in my bed," he murmurs around my lips, circling his hips, beginning another excruciating pattern of steady circles and deep plunges. "Please say I can take you back to my bed and cuddle you all night."

His request triggers a question, making me break our kiss so I can ask, "How can cuddling be your thing?" I don't allow him time to answer. I'm missing his mouth terribly already, so I waste no time sealing my lips to his and dipping my tongue in his mouth as he continues to rock lazily into me.

"It's only a *thing* with you." He nibbles on my lip and plants feathery kisses from one corner of my mouth to another. "I just want to squeeze you to death."

I smile up at him and nearly burst into tears when he blasts me back with his rare but beautiful smile, his blue eyes twinkling wildly. He really has redeemed himself, the brutal Miller long forgotten. I want his lips on mine again, but I also want to look at his face when it's smiling the brightest I've ever seen. "I love your smile," I declare on a breathy gasp, just as he blesses me with a smooth rotation of his groin, catching me just perfectly on my front wall. "Oh God!"

"I only smile for you." He pecks my lips and pushes his torso up so he's braced on his long, lean arms. "I love your breasts." He flicks his eyes to them and licks his lips provocatively.

"I don't have much." I almost want to cover my lack of assets with my palms but my hands have other ideas and are feeling out his forearms.

"I beg to differ." He gasps a little and slowly closes his eyes as he delivers the ultimate, deep, precise grind. My muscles stiffen, and I push against his rooted arms.

"Oh my goodness," I gasp, feeling the head of a delicious orgasm brimming.

"Are you going to come, sweet girl?"

"Yes," I moan, my back bowing, my legs curling around his waist. The hot rush of pressure in my groin is descending swiftly.

Dropping his head, he slowly peels his eyes open and falls to his forearms. "Give me your lips," he groans as he plunges, retreats, and inches carefully back into me. The crippling pleasure that he's inflicting on me is sending me dizzy. "Livy, I've asked once."

He puts his face closer to mine so with a slight lift of my head, our tongues meet and begin dueling delicately, but when I start shaking as my climax takes hold, he pushes farther into me, kissing me ardently and moaning loudly. My hands find his hair and dive into his wet waves, pushing into the back of his head.

"I'm coming," I groan. "Miller, I'm coming." I start to contract around him and try to harden my kiss as I'm attacked by waves of pleasure, but he doesn't allow me to. He just pulls away ever so slightly for a few seconds before brushing our lips together, silently guiding me.

Hot sparks of pleasure seem to attack me from every direction. I can't breathe through the overwhelming sensations. I scream. I explode. My flesh pulses and my eyes become heavy as he continues to worship my mouth and thrust lazily into me. I can feel the shattered pieces of me pulling back together again under his adoring attention. We can do this. As long as we have each other, we can battle through the challenges before us. My fortitude has never been so strong.

"Thank you," I sigh on a smile, letting my arms flop above my head.

"Never thank me."

Through my blissed out state, I vaguely register the absence of him softening within me. "You haven't come," I wheeze.

He slowly pulls out of me and starts to kiss his way down my body until his head is between my thighs and he's sending me delirious with a tickling flick of his tongue over my quivering flesh, followed by a firm lash straight up my center. I writher under him, trying to control the pulsing twinges as he crawls back up my body and sinks his tongue back into my mouth.

"I worship *you*." He drops a kiss lightly on my forehead and circles our noses. "Give me my *thing*."

"My arms don't work."

"Give me my *thing*, Livy." He raises cautionary eyebrows at me, making me smile more. "Now."

It doesn't take much effort at all to fulfill his demand. My arms circle his shoulders and crush him to me. "I want to be in your bed," I mumble into his hair, wishing I were there already.

"Then you will be." He rolls over, taking me with him, and then pushes me up so I'm astride his stomach. He studies me quietly.

"What are you thinking?" I ask.

"I'm thinking I've never been shocked in my life," he says, reaching up and circling my nipples until they're bullets, tingling and sensitive, "but when you threw that money on the table in Langan's, I had to resist coughing up my wine."

I blush a little at my own brashness, wholeheartedly wishing I never had. "I won't be doing it again."

"Neither will I," he whispers, transferring a hand to my wrist and stroking over the area where the sores have now faded to nothing. "I'm so sorry. I was so consumed with desperation to—"

I pull my arm from his grip and shut him up by dropping my body to his and my lips to his mouth. "Please don't feel guilty."

"I appreciate your compassion, but nothing you can say will ease my remorse."

"I pushed you."

"It's no excuse." He sits up and shifts us to the edge of the bed, placing me on my feet. "I'm going to make it up to you, Olivia Taylor," he vows, standing and cupping my cheeks in his palms. "I'll make you forget that man." His lips meet mine, reinforcing his words, and I nod my acceptance against him. "He's not the man I want to be for you."

I let him drown me in his mouth and remorse, let him push me up the wall desperately, let him feel me everywhere. "Take me to your bed," I plead, needing the comfort and security that being in Miller's arms and bed brings—something that I'm not wholly feeling here in this hotel room, where the four-poster bed is a constant reminder of a wholly different Miller.

"I'll do anything you want me to," he breathes, letting up a little on his apology kiss and pecking continuously at my lips. "Anything you want. Please try to erase what's happened."

"Then take me away from here," I insist. "Get me out of this room."

He starts to panic a little, pulling away when he realizes the extent of my desperation to escape the reminders. It's made him desperate, too. He shakes himself into action, removing the condom and getting dressed at lightning speed, not caring for a straight tie or a crease-free suit. He leaves his shirt half unbuttoned and hanging out of his trousers, his waistcoat is thrown on haphazardly and his jacket equally so, before he's snatching up my dress and quickly getting me into it.

After grasping my hand, he leads me away from the coldness of the extravagant hotel room. We take the stairs, and he looks back every few steps to check up on me. "Am I going too fast?" he asks while keeping up his determined stride.

"No," I answer, my legs struggling to keep up but wanting to go faster. Nothing will get me out of this place quick enough.

We hit the palatial foyer of the hotel, both of us catching the eye of the posh clientele in our disheveled state. I'm not concerned by the looks and neither is Miller. He practically throws the room's key card over the desk to the lady at the reception. He's as desperate to get out of here as I am.

The car park feels like miles away, when it is only around the corner. The journey feels like hours when it's probably only minutes. The stairs to Miller's apartment feel like thousands, but there are probably only a few hundred. And as soon as the door is shut behind us, my dress is pulled impatiently from my body, my underwear discarded, and I'm lifted up to his carelessly dressed physique and carried across his apartment, while he indulges me in his mouth the whole way, except we don't enter his bedroom. He takes me to his studio and places me on the sofa, where I sit awkwardly and a little bewildered by his mounting desperation as he hurries out of his clothes, leaving them a pile of expensive material on the floor. Bringing his body down over mine, he engulfs me completely and pins me to the old worn sofa beneath me. His face is in my neck, taking a long inhale of my hair, and then his mouth is on mine, working through delicately with his tongue, humming and moaning as his kiss gets harder, completely defeating the whole purpose of our reunion. It is always me driving things forward and Miller insisting on calm, and now I know why. But worry is getting the better of him.

I try to slow our kiss, bring it down a few levels, but he's blinded by purpose to make me forget. It's not incredibly hard, not at all, yet it's not what I want or need. "Slow down," I gasp, breaking away from his lips, but he homes in on my neck, resuming the force there. "Miller, please!"

At my short plea, he bolts upright in shock, his hands delving into his waves. The fear in his eyes is more than I can cope with, and it's in this moment I realize he's two entirely different people—physically *and* emotionally. At least he is now that I'm in his life. I suspect before me he was simply the man disguised as a gentleman and the punishing lover—or escort.

"Are you okay?" I ask, inching myself up into a sitting position.

"I apologize." He stands and walks to the huge window. His naked back in the night glow looks almost ethereal. I feel the overwhelming need to be close to him, but he's lost in thought and I should let him have those thoughts. For so long, I've thought it was just me who's the damaged half of this relationship. I was so wrong. Miller's more broken. I've seen the result of this lifestyle. I saw the effect it had on my mother and the lifelong impact it's had on my grandmother. And on me, too. I've done some stupid things. Except Miller has no family to effect. There's only him, no matter how I ask the question. And he isn't on his way to hell. I've pulled him back, but that sobering claim strengthens my hope. Miller has spent too many years doing something he didn't want to.

"Miller?"

He slowly turns, and I don't like what I see.

Defeatism.

Sorrow.

Sadness.

His head drops. "I'm fucked up, Olivia. I'm sorry."

"You've apologized enough. Stop saying you're sorry." I can feel the panic flaring in me. "Please, come here."

"I don't know what I'll do if you choose to, but you really should run a mile, sweet girl."

"No!" I snap, worried by his change in approach to our reunion. "Come here." I'm about to physically fetch him myself when he starts to make his way over. He sits at the other end of the couch, too far away. "Don't say things like that," I warn, lying down on my back and resting my head in his naked lap so I'm looking up at him.

He drops his head so his eyes meet mine, his hands stroking through my hair. "I'm sorry."

"If you say that one more time," I warn, reaching up to feel his neck out. I pull him down, forcing him to bend so we're forehead to forehead. "I'll..."

"You'll what?"

"I don't know," I admit, "but I'll do something." So I kiss him, because that is all there is left to do. And he lets me. It is me setting the delicate pace, me who's guiding Miller. I'm the strong one right now. Me. It doesn't matter what has come before me. What matters is that we have both found each other and finally accepted each other. I feel it's like the blind leading the blind, but my determination is now fierce. I've let him break down my barriers, and in the process, I've innocently bashed down his, too. This feeling of his lips isn't something I'm prepared to surrender. This sense of belonging isn't going to be given up. This is where I'm supposed to be. I'm not prepared to fight against this anymore. I have the strength to help him. He gives me that strength.

He halts our kiss abruptly and breathes heavily in my face, making a deliberate show of stroking my cheeks and hair so very tenderly. "Was that you telling me off?" he asks seriously, dropping a light peck on my nose. "Because if so, then I'm sorry."

"Stop it."

"I'm sorry."

"You're being silly."

"I'm sorry."

"I'll do something," I warn, pulling a little on his hair.

He shifts my head from his lap and lays himself down, repositioning me so I'm spread all over him, my face level with his. "Please do," he whispers, putting his lips close to mine and blinking teasingly slowly.

"You want me to kiss you?" I ask quietly, keeping the distance between our mouths minimal and resisting the urge to capture the temptation within licking distance.

"I'm sorry."

"Don't be."

"I'm sorry." He brushes our lips, and I lose all resistance, the enticement of him impossible to fight off. "I'm so sorry."

My tongue plunges relentlessly but softly, working smoothly and with complete reverence. We're back to where we belong. My world is right again. Everything can be forgiven, except now there is so much more to forgive. His rules, the ones that prevented me from touching him and kissing him, are being blown out of the water now. I'm feeling him everywhere, kissing him like I'll never have the pleasure again. It's loving, meaningful, and completely mind-blanking. It's perfect.

"I love your punishments," he mumbles, twisting onto his side and pulling me closer to his chest, still kissing me and still feeling me everywhere. "Stay with me tonight."

I'm the one who severs the contact, my lips stinging and swollen. His dark stubble is always so prickly and coarse, but familiar and comforting. I run my palm down his cheek and watch his lips as they part when my thumb drags across them. "I don't want to stay just one night," I murmur. My eyes reluctantly climb his nose until I'm staring into blue circles of understanding.

"I want you to stay forever," he replies softly, following up his words with a hard push of his lips on mine. "I need to put you in my bed." He untangles us from the sofa and picks me up, resuming his kiss as I lie across his arms and he carries me to his bedroom.

"Do you know how you make me feel?" he asks, placing me gently down and encouraging me to turn onto my front.

"Yes." I turn my face into the pillow when he begins a slow, delicate flick of his tongue up the column of my spine, finishing with a soft kiss on my shoulder blade.

The hard head of his erection teases my opening, making my arse lift fractionally to urge him on. "Thank God I have you again." He sinks into me on a harsh pull of breath, then holds still, trying to regain control of his breathing. I bite at the pillow, moaning quietly. The hardness of his torso is pressing into my back, pushing me into the mattress, and my fists are balling into the sheets. "You've taken the only resilient part of me and annihilated it, Livy," he whispers hoarsely, performing an easy grind of his hips.

I turn my heated face back outward when I feel his lips at my ear and find dark lashes framing sparkling blue eyes. "I don't want to take anything. I want you to give it to me."

He retreats slowly and pushes forward firmly, again and again, drawing constant moans of pleasure each and every time. "What do you want me to give you?"

"What's the most resilient part of you?" I groan the words through an excruciatingly deep thrust.

"My heart, Livy. My heart is the most resilient part of me." He loses control momentarily and bucks forward on a bark.

My chest swells at his admission. "Let me see you." I wriggle under his body. "Please, I need to see you properly."

"Fucking hell," he curses, and quickly slips out of me, allowing me to spin over and grab at his shoulders before he quickly reenters me, pounding forward uncontrolled. "Livy!" he shouts, pushing his torso up on his arms. He holds still, panting and staring down at me. "I'm petrified of you."

I tilt my hips up, making him drop his chin to his chest, his waves falling forward as he does. "I'm scared of you, too," I whisper. "Terrified."

He lifts his eyes and circles his hips. "I'm an emotion virgin, Livy. You're my first."

"What are you saying?" I ask quietly.

He goes to speak, then seems to think better of it, his eyes darting all over my face. "I've fallen, Olivia Taylor," he whispers.

I bite down on my bottom lip to prevent a sob slipping free. That's the only thing that matters. "You fascinate me," I counter. I'm reaffirming my feeling, making it known that nothing has changed. I've wasted too much precious time pushing him away—time that I could have been helping him and making myself stronger.

He drops to his forearms and starts pumping his hips slowly, carrying me farther into rapture. "Please don't drop me," he breathes.

I shake my head and feel the back of his head out, meeting each one of his advances with matching thrusts of my hips. I don't know what's happening, but I do know that my feelings are profound. And now they've only been strengthened.

"I've been saved by a gorgeous, sweet girl," he whispers, gazing down at me. "She makes my heart quicken and my senses slow."

I close my eyes, letting him drive on, the perfection of this moment tearing at my soul.

"I'm going to come," he gasps, "Olivia!"

My eyes snap open, by body squirming under his hard physique. His pace has advanced, along with my pleasure. Our bodies are locked together, as are our eyes, and the connection remains intact until we both whimper as our climaxes take hold in unison and both of us go rigid, gasping into each other's faces. A strange sensation floods me. Literally. My insides are warm, feeling good. Too good.

"You're not wearing a condom," I say quietly.

Recognition dawns on his perfect face, his gentle drives halting too abruptly. He thinks hard for a few moments before he eventually speaks. "I guess I'm not the gentleman I claim to be."

I shouldn't smile, given the serious situation, but I do. Miller's unusual show of humor, even if it's inappropriate, makes it impossible not to. "You have a dry humor."

He pushes into me, deep and high, his semi-hard-on stroking

me, reminding me of the rightness of his bareness. "There's nothing dry about our current condition."

I laugh. Miller Hart never ceases to amaze me. "That's terrible!"

"It feels pretty damn good to me." He flashes me a boyish grin and dips to bite my cheek. He's right, it feels incredible, but that doesn't make it a good thing.

"I'll need to visit my doctor." I push my face to his mouth and muster the strength required to hold him tightly.

"I'll take you. I accept full responsibility." Pulling back, he studies me closely. "It felt better than I ever imagined. It'll be difficult to return to condoms."

I comprehend something immediately. "You knew, didn't you? The whole time you were aware."

"It felt too good to stop." He kisses my startled face chastely. "Besides, we can ask the doctor to prescribe you the pill while we're there."

"We can?"

"Yes," he answers surely. "Now I've had you with nothing between us, I'm greedy for more."

I have nothing to say to that.

"Would you mind if we slept on the sofa in my studio?" he asks.

"Why?"

"It soothes me, and with you in my *thing*, too, I'm going to sleep extremely well."

"I'd love to."

"Good, not that you had a choice." He scoops me up and transports me back to his art studio, where I'm placed neatly on the old squidgy sofa before he mirrors me, pulling me back to his chest and resting his head on mine so we both have the stunning view in sight. The silence surrounding us gives me an opportunity to consider some of the answers I'm still to learn.

"Why wouldn't you let me kiss you?" I whisper.

I feel him stiffen behind me, and I don't like it. "I'm reluctant to answer any more of your questions, Livy. I don't want you to run away again."

I find his hand and bring it to my mouth, kissing it sweetly. "I won't run."

"Promise me."

"I promise."

"Thank you." He tugs at me, helping me to turn around and face him. He wants eye contact while we're conversing. "Kissing is a very intimate act," he says, pulling my face to his and giving me a long, slow, languid one, both of us humming contentedly.

"So is sex."

"You're wrong." He pulls away and scans my confused face. "There is only intimacy if there is feeling."

I absorb his words in an instant. "We have feeling."

He smiles and makes an elaborate gesture of *feeling* by coating my face in wet kisses. I don't stop him. I let him stifle me completely. I drown in his affection until he decides that my face has been given enough intimacy. The knowledge of Miller's rules, the no kissing or touching, sends a warm feeling of satisfaction deep into the very center of me, alleviating the anguish that's crippled me since my discovery. He allows me to kiss him and he allows me to touch and feel him. Those women missed out on something obscenely gratifying.

"You haven't slept with a woman since you met me?"

He shakes his head.

"Yet you've had"—I pause, thinking what word I should use—"bookings?"

"Dates," he corrects me. "Yes, I've had dates."

William's curiosity gets the better of me. He wondered how Miller managed to uphold his dates without having sex with those women. If I hate my own curiosity, then I despise William's. "If they pay to get the best fuck of their life, then how did you avoid giving it to them?"

"It wasn't without its difficulties." He brushes my hair from my face. "I'm not a fan of small talk."

"You talked?" I ask, shocked.

"I might have said the odd word when I was paying attention. Most of the time I was thinking of you."

"Oh."

"Are we done?" he asks, clearly uncomfortable with the conversation, yet I'm not. I should be. I should be satisfied with his offered information, glad he's opened up and enlightened me, glad there are no feelings involved. But I'm not. I'm too confused.

"I don't understand why those women want you like that." Good Lord, if they experienced what I have with Miller Hart, if they were worshipped, then I'm certain they would be bashing down the door to get to him.

"I make them orgasm."

"Women pay thousands for an orgasm?" I blurt. "That's..." I'm about to say *obscene*, but then I recall each of my own orgasms and Miller's hint of a smile tells me he knows what I'm thinking. I deflate. "You make all women feel as good as I do when you have me in bed."

He nods.

"So there's nothing special about me." I sound hurt. I *am* hurt.

"I beg to differ," he argues, and I'm about to challenge him, but he hushes me with his glorious lips, sweeping his tongue through my mouth slowly. My senses scramble and I completely forget what I was going to say. "There's something very special about you, Olivia."

"What?" I ask, relishing in his attention.

"You make me feel as good as I know I make you feel—something that no one else has ever done or ever will. I had sex with women. Nothing about any of those encounters made my heart race."

"You said it was pleasurable," I remind him, keeping myself

attached to him. "I didn't get any pleasure when you took me like that. Did you?" I definitely remember him climaxing.

"I felt nothing but disgrace before, during, and after."

"Why?"

"Because I swore on my own life that I'd never tarnish you with my dirty brush."

"Then why didn't you stop?"

"I blacked out." He drops my lips and shifts uncomfortably. "When that switch flicks, I don't register anything except my own aim."

"How do these women get any satisfaction from it?"

"They desire me. But I'm unobtainable. Everyone wants what they can't have." He watches me closely, almost apprehensively.

I sever our eye contact, trying to process all of this, but Miller interrupts my train of thought.

"Do you know the statistics when it comes to women climaxing during penetrative sex?"

My gaze lifts. "No."

"It's incredibly rare. Every woman I fuck comes when I'm inside of her. I don't even have to try. That kind of makes me talented. And in demand."

I'm stunned into silence, astounded by his frankness. He's explaining like it's a burden. It might be. And exhausting. My poor, innocent mind is racing, and it homes right in on a little detail. My orgasm in the hotel room. I didn't try for that one. I was shut off from my body. It came all by itself... but then my spiraling thoughts register something else. "You had to help me once," I breathe, remembering feeling so useless and frustrated. "You used your fingers."

He frowns. "That makes you even more special."

"I've buggered up your flawless track record."

He smiles at me, pulling one from me, too. It's ridiculous that I'm mirroring his amusement, but the alternative is wretchedness. "Arrogance is a really ugly emotion," he whispers.

My eyes widen. "Says you?" I choke.

He shrugs.

"I might sell my story," I announce seriously, watching as his mild smile spreads into the rare, full-blown one I cherish seeing. "London's most notorious male escort loses his touch." I remain serious, watching his eyes continue to twinkle and his mouth twitching.

"What will it cost me for your silence?" he asks.

I look up to the ceiling and pout, feigning thinking hard about his question when I know exactly what I'm going to say, and I knew the moment he posed the question to me. I return my eyes to his. "A lifetime of worshipping."

"I hope you mean from me." Our lips reattach.

"Exclusively. You owe me a thousand pounds," I mumble against his mouth, making him pull away on a puckered brow. "I paid for goods that I wasn't satisfied with. I want my money back."

"You want a refund?" He smiles, but it falls away in a second, being replaced with worry. "I left your money on the table."

"Oh." I sit up and straddle his lap, not matching his concern at all. I don't want that money any more than I want the thousands that are stashed in the bank accounts where it came from. "I bought you dinner." I shrug.

"Livy, oysters and wine do not cost a thousand pounds."

"Then I bought you dinner and left a very generous tip."

His lips press into a straight line in an obvious attempt to restrain his amusement. "Now you're just being silly."

"And you are being uptight."

"I beg your pardon!"

"Oh, lighten up!" I collapse onto his chest and nuzzle into him.

He scoffs at my insult but cuddles me fiercely. "Your request has been noted, Miss Taylor."

I grin into his skin, feeling an overwhelming sense of happiness. "Jolly good, Mr. Hart."

"Cheeky."

"You love my sassy streak."

He sighs deeply and rests the side of his head on mine. "I do," he whispers. "If you're sassy with me, I love it, most of the time."

His indirect declaration cements it for me. I'm utterly and completely in love with Miller Hart. He turns me away from his body and pulls my back into his chest. My head rests on his forearm and my hand finds his, our fingers intertwining in a silent message.

Never let go.

"Unobtainable," I whisper on a sigh.

"I'm perfectly obtainable to you, Olivia Taylor." He constricts me, inhaling deeply before tenderly kissing the back of my head. "I've never made love to a woman in my life." I barely hear his words. "Only you."

His sobering confession sinks into my mind, shocking me. "Why me?" I ask quietly, refraining from spinning over to see his eyes. I shouldn't make a big deal of it, even though it's a huge deal.

He sinks his nose into my hair and breathes me into him. "Because when I look into those bottomless sparkling sapphires, I see freedom."

My body relaxes on a contented sigh. I would not have thought I could take my eyes from the stunning outlook of Miller's squidgy sofa, but when he follows up his heartfelt words with his signature hum, I'm proven wrong. London slowly disappears before my eyes, and the horrid images I've fought and failed to remove from my mind's eye for so long disappear with it.

Chapter Twelve

I come awake slowly, feeling safe and content, the hardness of Miller's torso pushed into my back, his arms wrapped tightly around my waist and his face buried snugly in my neck. Smiling, I melt farther into him, closing any space there may have been, gripping his hand on my tummy with mine. It's early, the rising sun offering a hazy glow through the window, and I'm warm and cozy, but I'm also thirsty. Completely parched.

Breaking away from Miller's firm clench is close to unthinkable, but I can quickly find my place again once I've quenched my thirst. So I tentatively peel my body from his, detaching his arms from around my midriff and shifting toward the edge of the sofa, being sure not to disturb him. Then I quietly stand and study him for a while. His hair is everywhere, his dark lashes spread and his full lips slightly parted. He looks angelic, beautifully tangled up among the blankets. My emotionally impaired part-time gentleman.

I could remain here motionless for an eternity, just watching him sleeping serenely. He looks peaceful. I feel peaceful. The air surrounding us is so peaceful.

On a contented exhale, I take my naked self out to the corridor and follow my feet until I'm standing before one of Miller's paintings. London Bridge. I cock my head, pouting while I ponder his perception of the landmark, the blur of paints sending my eyes crossed after a few moments of staring, making me see the bridge perfectly. Then I frown, uncrossing my eyes, making the painting a perfect mess of oil paints again. He's taken a beautiful London landmark and made it almost unappealing—like he wants people to be averse to its actual beauty, and it's in this moment I wonder if Miller Hart sees everything in his life as distorted and unclear. Does he see the whole world in this tainted manner? My neck retracts as another speculating moment descends on me abruptly. Does he see *himself* in this tainted manner? At a distance, the painting looks perfect, but get up close and beneath the surface, you find a wreck. A mess of color—something ugly and confusing. I think he does see himself like this, and I think he goes all out to blur people's perception of him, too. The sobering thought is paining but equally maddening. He's beautiful inside and out. But I may be the only person on this planet who knows that for sure.

A distant chiming sends me on a startled jump and yanks me from my pondering, my hand flying up to my chest to put some pressure on my suddenly pumping heart. "Jesus!" I blurt, following the sound until I'm rummaging through my bag for my new phone. A glance at the screen tells me it's five-fifteen and Nan's calling. "Oh shit!" I answer immediately. "Nan!"

"Olivia! Oh my goodness, where are you?" She sounds beside herself, and my face screws up guiltily, mixed with a little dread. "I woke to use the toilet and checked your room. You're not in bed!"

"Well obviously." I wince and drop my bare bum to a chair, hiding from no one by burying my face in my spare palm. I hear a little gasp through the phone. It's a gasp of realization. It's a happy gasp.

"Olivia, sweetheart, are you with Miller?" She's silently begging the answer is yes, I know she is.

My naked shoulders rise and brush my earlobes. "Yes," I squeak, my face screwing up farther. I should be apologizing for causing her such worry, but I'm too busy clamping down on my bottom lip in anticipation of her reaction to this news.

Nan coughs, clearly trying to restrain her squeal of delight. "I see." She's failing terribly to sound nonchalant. "Well, um, in that case, uh, I'm sorry for disturbing you." She coughs again. "Yes, I'll be going, then."

"Nan." I roll my eyes, my face heating with embarrassment. "I'm sorry, I should have called you to—"

"On no!" she screeches, piercing my eardrum. "It's fine! So, so fine!"

I knew it would be. "I'll be home to get ready for work."

"Okay!" She must be waking the whole street. "George is taking me shopping early. I might not be here."

"I'll see you after work, then."

"Ooooh, with Miller? I'll do dinner! Beef Wellington! He said it was the best he'd tasted!"

I rub my forehead and flop back in the chair. I should have expected this. "Maybe another time."

"Oh, well, I can't organize my life around you two." She can and she would. "Inquire as to what day would suit him."

"I will. See you later."

"Yes, you will." She sounds slighted, and her tone is threatening. I'm going to be grilled later.

"Bye." I go to disconnect the call.

"Oh, Livy?"

"Yes?"

"Give his buns a little squeeze from me."

"Nan!" I gasp, hearing her giggling as she hangs up on me, leaving me gaping at her crude comment. The filthy minx! I'm about to throw my phone down on the table in disgust, but the text icon catches my eye, telling me I have a message. And I know who it's from. I open it, despite wanting to throw this phone at the wall, too.

> I would appreciate being enlightened on this evening's events.
> William.

He wants me to check in? I scowl at my phone, then toss it on the table. I'm not telling him anything, no matter how terse the demand. Nor am I going to let him talk me out of this. Or *force* me out of this. Never. Resolute and confident, I stand, suddenly eager to join Miller back on the sofa. I hurry over to the cupboard, grab a glass, and fill it from the tap, not prepared to delay myself further by fussing with bottled spring water. I glug it all down, put the glass accurately in the dishwasher, and then make my way back to Miller's studio, pulling to a sudden halt when I spot my dress strewn across the floor. Or *still* strewn across the floor. He's not picked it up, folded it neatly, and placed it deftly in his bottom drawer? I frown at the offending garment, not being able to resist scooping it up and shaking it out before folding it. Then I stand thoughtfully for a few moments and before I know it, I'm standing in Miller's studio staring at all of his clothes scattered everywhere. I know his painting space is typically a royal mess, but his suit doesn't belong in here on the floor. It's all wrong.

I hurry and gather up his clothes, shoving them under my arm and doing my best to smooth and fold while I take myself to his room. I wander through to his wardrobe, making sure everything is put in its rightful place—his jacket, trousers, and waistcoat hung up; his shirt, socks, and boxers in the laundry basket; and his tie on his tie rack. Then I make sure my dress and shoes land in the bottom drawer of his dresser in the bedroom. I start to leave and notice the bed is a huge mess, too, so I spend a good ten minutes messing with the sheets, attempting to restore it to its former glory. He's slept through the night, with no tormenting thoughts or dreams of items in the wrong place. I don't want him diving up in a panic to fix that. Creeping quietly back to the studio, I slip under the blankets, shift cautiously so I don't disturb him . . . and squeal when I'm seized by the waist and yanked onto his body. I don't get a moment to gather myself. I'm hauled up and carried to his bedroom where he throws me on the bed with no consideration that I've just perfected it. Or probably *not* perfected it by Miller's standards.

"Miller!" I'm pinned by my wrists beneath him, all disoriented, with his dark locks tickling my nose. "What are you doing?" I'm too stunned by his uncharacteristic act to laugh.

"Hold that thought," he mumbles into my neck, nudging my thighs apart so he can make himself comfy. The skin of my neck is suddenly hot and wet, his tongue the source of heat. "How are you feeling this morning?" He bites and licks my throat, sending me rigid, my thighs clamping onto his hips.

"Perfect," I reply quietly, because I really am. My arms find their way around his shoulders when he releases me and hold him tightly while he spends an age worshipping my neck. I don't want to go to work. I want to do what Miller suggested one time and lock the doors, stay here forever with him. He's in an exceptionally good mood, no traces of the clipped man in sight. I'm exactly where I'm supposed to be and Miller is, too, in body *and* in mind.

His face appears close to mine, those eyes sending me deeper into my contented bliss as he studies me for a few moments. "I'm glad you're here." He pecks my lips. "I'm glad I found you, I'm glad you're my habit, and I'm glad we're irrevocably fascinated with each other."

"Me too," I whisper.

His eyes twinkle, his lips twitch, that lovely dimple showing signs of an appearance. "It's a good job because you really don't have a choice."

"I don't want a choice."

"Then this is a pointless conversation, wouldn't you agree?"

"Yes," I answer decisively on a nod, making Miller's lips twitch more. I want to see that full-blown, beautiful smile and dimple, so I slowly skate my palms down his back, feeling every smooth piece of him while he watches me with interest until I'm at his lovely arse. His eyebrow cocks curiously, and I cock mine right back.

"What are you up to?" he asks, blatantly restraining his lips from tipping farther.

I pout a little on a tiny shrug. "Nothing."

"I beg to differ."

On a little grin, I sink my nails into the solid flesh of his bum. His brow furrows. "That's from Nan."

"Pardon!" He coughs, pushing up onto his forearms.

I'm really grinning now. "She said to give your buns a little squeeze." My nails dig in again, and Miller chokes on a laugh. A proper laugh. His dimple is deep on his cheek and my smile falls away in an instant as I watch his head drop, his hair flopping forward and his shoulders jumping up. I know I wanted a smile, but I wasn't prepared for this. I'm not sure how to handle it. He's in bits, and with a lack of a natural reaction coming to me, I can do nothing more than lie here, trapped beneath his jerking body, and wait for him to pull it together. But he doesn't look anywhere near to composure. "You okay?" I ask, still stunned, still frowning.

"Olivia Taylor, your grandmother is a treasure." He chuckles, pressing his lips hard to mine. "An eighteen-carat-gold treasure."

"She's a pain in the royal arse, that's what she is."

"Don't speak of a loved one in such a way." He pulls back to reveal that familiar straight face, all laughter and happiness gone like it was never there. The sudden change in mood makes me appreciate how insensitive my words were. Miller has no one. Not a soul.

"I'm sorry." I feel thoughtless and guilty under his accusing gaze. "I wasn't thinking."

"She's special, Olivia."

"I know she is," I retort quietly. I was joking, although I'd do well to remember that Miller Hart isn't the joking kind. "I didn't mean it."

He slips into thought, flicking his blues around my face before settling back on my eyes. His shining orbs soften. "I overreacted. I apologize."

"No, there's no need." I shake my head on a sigh, keeping myself lost in the softness of his puddles of blue. "You have a someone, Miller."

"A someone?" His beautiful brow furrows.

"Yes," I begin enthusiastically. "Me."

"You?"

"I'm your someone. Everyone has a someone, and I'm yours, like you are mine."

"You're my someone?"

"Yes." I nod sharply, watching as he thinks about my declaration.

"And I'm your someone?"

"Correct."

Miller's head bobs mildly on an agreeable nod. "Olivia Taylor is my someone?"

I shrug. "Or habit."

His nodding stops in a heartbeat and I watch delightedly as his lips begin to twitch again. "Both?"

"Of course," I agree. I'll be whatever he wants me to be.

"You don't have a choice." The twitching transforms into his lovely smile, nearly blinding me.

"I don't want one."

"Then this—"

"Is a pointless discussion, yes, I agree." I yank him down to my body and secure my legs around his waist, my arms over his shoulders. And then something in this moment makes me say it loud and clear—no code or words with actions. "I love your bones, Miller Hart."

He pauses with his sucking on my neck and pulls back slowly to gaze down at me. I brace myself, for what I don't know. He knows how I feel. He thinks for a moment before drawing breath. "I'm going to take an educated guess and suggest you mean that you love me deeply."

"Correct." I laugh, pushing into his mouth when his head dips to lock back onto my neck.

"Excellent." He kisses me chastely and works his way up my jaw, across my cheek, and onto my lips. "I'm deeply fascinated by you, too."

I'm reduced to mush beneath him. That's all I need. That's his way. That's Miller Hart, the emotionally deprived fraudulent gentleman expressing his feelings with words—funny words, but I understand them. I understand him.

I let him kiss me, let his scratchy stubble rub against my face, and I relish every sweet second, grumbling my annoyance when he pulls away.

"I'm going to the gym before work this morning." He rises to his knees and pulls me up to his lap. "Would you like to come?"

"Oh?" I'm not sure that I need to now. All my anger and stress has completely disintegrated, thanks to Miller and his worshipping ways. Punching a bag of sand to death isn't necessary anymore. "I don't have membership to any gyms," I lie, thinking it's also not necessary for me to observe Miller beating a bag of sand to death. The scenes from the studio at the gym and outside of Ice are not events I relish or want to relive.

"You'll be my guest." He lands me with a quick kiss and lifts me from the bed. "Get dressed."

"I need a shower," I say, watching his back disappear into his wardrobe. The scent of sex is heavy and clinging all over me. "I'll be two minutes." I make my way toward his bathroom but gasp when I'm intercepted and swiped from my feet.

"Wrong," he says matter-of-factly, carting me back to the bed across his arms. "There's no time."

"But I feel all... sticky." I cringe as I'm placed on my feet, finding Miller semi-clothed in only his shorts, his bare chest being waved like a red flag to a bull. I can't rip my eyes away as it gets closer and closer until my nose is almost touching it.

"Earth to Olivia." His silky voice yanks me out of my trance and I step back, lifting my eyes to find a sanctimonious grin.

I grin back. "God paid extra special attention when crafting you."

His eyebrows arch and his grin stretches farther across his face. "And he created *you* for me."

"Correct."

"I'm glad we've cleared that up." He cocks his head toward the bed. "Want to help me make my bed?"

"No!" I blurt the word without thought, thinking I've already wasted too much energy on fussing over his beloved bed, and also remembering the last time I made a masterpiece of it. He could barely contain his compulsion to rip off all of the sheets and fix it. And he eventually did. "You do it." He'll only put it all right again, so it'll be a total waste of my time.

"As you wish," he says on an agreeable nod. "Get dressed."

I don't argue, leaving Miller to fix his bed while I retrieve my clothes from the bottom drawer. "I don't have any gym clothes."

"I'll take you home." He flaps the quilt onto the bed artfully, and it lands pretty perfectly, but he still makes his way around, pulling and tweaking corners. "Then I'll take you to work. What time do you need to be there?"

"Nine."

"Excellent. We have three-point-five hours." He positions the pillows and steps back to assess his handiwork before turning and catching me watching him. "Chop-chop."

Smiling, I shimmy into my dress and slip my heels on. "Teeth?" I can hold off on the shower if he insists, but I need to freshen up my mouth.

"We'll do it together." He sweeps his arm out in a gesture for me to lead on, which I do with a smile on my face. He's still predominantly uptight, but there's an air of peace surrounding him, and I know the source of that harmony is me.

Chapter Thirteen

The health club is heaving. After finding a small space on one of the benches in the ladies' changing rooms, I hurry into my gym kit and shove my bag in a locker before escaping the happy morning chatter of many gym buddies and falling into the corridor, feeling exhausted already. I make a quick scan of the corridor, but I can't see Miller, so I pace toward the end of the building where I remember the gym to be, passing the many glass-paned doors and spotting the various classes under way. Stopping at the last door, I watch as dozens of women prance around in front of a huge mirror, each looking super fit and toned, each, although showing exertion, displaying perfect makeup-adorned faces. My hand lifts and feels the knotted bun on my head, and my face in the reflection catches my attention. I've not a scrap of makeup on, nor do I look like a regular. It seems the gym isn't an excuse to skimp on personal appearance.

"Oh!" I gasp when I feel hot breath at my ear.

"Wrong way," he whispers, snaking his forearm around my waist and lifting me from my feet. "We're in this room." I'm transported back the way I came with no complaint, until Miller is entering the very room where I spied on him. The door is closed behind us with my back still secured against his chest, and he soon spins me around and pushes me up against it. My first thoughts are of disappointment when I find him wearing a T-shirt, but they are soon hijacked when I'm hoisted up to his lips and blind-sided by the wonderful talents of his mouth. This is a workout of another kind.

"You could have kept me in bed and tasted me," I mumble, feeling him smile against my lips. All of these smiles and his relaxed persona, especially out of the bedroom, are throwing me all off-kilter. I love it, but it's all so very new.

"I can taste you wherever I like." He lets me slide down the door to my feet and steps back, leaving me resentful of the sudden space between us.

So I close it and circle his waist with my arms, burying my nose in the material of his T-shirt. "Let's just have our *thing*."

"We're here to work up a sweat." He has humor in his tone as he collects my wrists from behind his back and disconnects me from him.

"There are too many things I could say to that," I grumble.

"Is my sweet girl exposing her sassy streak?" His eyebrow cocks as he grasps the hem of his T-shirt and slowly pulls it up over his torso, revealing ripple after ripple until I'm cross-eyed with delight.

"You're being childish," I accuse with slightly narrowed eyes. "Why would you do that?"

"What?"

"That." I wave my arm up and down his chest, and he looks down, that wayward curl falling loose. "Put your T-shirt back on."

"But I'll get hot."

"I won't be able to focus, Miller." I'm very swiftly feeling the need to punch a bag of sand, but my frustration is of another kind. My finicky, obsessive Miller Hart is playing games and although it's so very lovely to see him at ease, his tactics are irritating the hell out of me.

"Tough luck." He folds his T-shirt and places it neatly to the side, and then takes my hand, leading me to the huge padded mat where the bag of sand is swaying from the rafters. "And your focus will be fine, trust me." Looking down at my feet, he frowns. "What are you wearing?"

I follow his line of sight and wriggle my toes in my Converse, noticing he's barefoot. Even his feet and toes are perfect. "Shoes."

"Take them off," he orders, sounding totally exasperated.

"Why?"

"You'll go barefoot. Those things have no support." He gives them a disgusted look and points to them, reinforcing his order. "Off."

I grumble under my breath as I kick them off, so I now have bare feet to match Miller. "Aren't you putting your T-shirt on?" Bare feet, bare chest. This will be torture.

"No." He wanders over to a bench, takes his iPhone from his pocket, and then crouches, placing it in a docking station. He spends an age scrolling before declaring, "Perfect," as Florence and the Machine's "Rabbit Heart" fills the huge studio.

I cock my head a little in surprise as he makes his way back, a face full of purpose, and let him place me where he wants me. I'm mentally cursing his perfect arse to hell and avoiding letting my eyes feast too much. Impossible. "What are we doing?" I ask, watching him collect a long length of material and smooth it through his fingers, folding and arranging it just so.

"We're going to spar." He takes my hand in his and begins neatly wrapping it in the material while I frown up at his focused face. "You're going to hit me."

"What?" I pull my hand away fast, horrified. "I don't want to hit you!"

"Yes, you do." He almost laughs as he takes my hand back and continues with the wrapping.

"No, I don't," I affirm, not laughing at all. "I don't want to hurt you."

"You can't hurt me, Olivia." He releases my hand and collects the other. "Well, you can, but not with your fists."

"What do you mean?"

"I mean," he sighs, like I should already know, while he keeps up his wrapping task, "the only physical pain you can cause me is to my heart."

My confusion transforms into satisfaction in an instant. "But it's too resilient."

"Not where you're concerned." His blue eyes flick briefly to mine. "But you already know that, don't you?"

I hide my satisfied smile and flex my fists beneath the bandaging. "I have a vicious swipe," I remind him, rightly or wrongly. I don't particularly relish the reminder of that night, but his cockiness is annoying me. I did well on the punch bag before. I worked up a sweat, and I had the achy arms to prove it.

"I concur," Miller agrees with a hint of sarcasm, grabbing some gloves from a hook and negotiating my hands into them.

"Why all the wrapping?"

"Mainly for support, but it'll also prevent blisters from developing on your knuckles."

The heat rises in my cheeks. I really am an amateur. "Okay."

"You're done." He hits the tops of the gloves with his balled fists, sending my arms jolting down. "Resistance, Olivia."

"You caught me off guard!"

"Always be on your guard. It's rule number one."

"I'm *always* on my guard where you're concerned."

He bashes the tops of the gloves again, sending them downward… again. Then he smirks. "Really?"

"Point taken," I mutter, trying in vain to brush a stray hair from my face and getting nowhere.

"Here, allow me."

I let him tuck the wayward strand behind my ear and try my very hardest not to rub my cheek onto his hand…or cast my eyes to his chest...or smell him...or... "Can we get on with this, please?" I shake him off and bring my gloves to my chin, ready to strike.

"As you wish." He's smug.

"So you just want me to crack you one?"

"You mean hit me?"

"Knock you out."

His face twists in amusement. "You will not knock me out, Olivia."

"I might." I'm sounding cocky now, and deep down I know I'll regret it.

"I love your sass," he says on a shake of his head. "Take your best shot."

"As you wish." I quickly draw back my arm and throw it out, aiming straight for his jaw, but he pulls back stealthily, sending me on an uncontrolled spin on the spot, and before I know where I am, he has my back locked against his chest.

"Good try, sweet girl." He bites at my ear and pushes his groin into my lower back, making me choke on a breath mixed with shock and desire. I heave against him, all disoriented; then I'm spun back around and released from his secure grasp. "Better luck next time."

His cocky demeanor injects me with irritation and I immediately thrash out again, hoping to catch him off guard...and fail. "Oh!" I cry, finding myself back in the hardness of his chest with his groin pushed into me, his stubbled cheek against mine.

"Oh dear." His breath tickles my ear, and my eyes clench shut while I look for the poise I need to take him on. "You're being driven by frustration. It's the wrong fuel."

Fuel? "What do you mean?" I puff.

Releasing me, he places me back in position and brings my fists up to my face. "Frustration will make you lose control. Always maintain control."

My eyes widen at his statement. I don't remember seeing any

element of control all of the times I've seen Miller's fists flying, and judging by the fleeting look that passes over his face, he's just considered that, too.

"*You* don't help," he says quietly, holding his hands out to the sides. "Again."

Mulling over his words, I try to find some calming thoughts and my inner control, but it's hidden deep and before I can locate it, my arm rockets forward again on impulse, doing nothing more than sending me into a physical tailspin, as well as a mental one. "Damn it!" I curse, pushing my bum back when I feel his hips brush up against me again. There's nothing controlled about this, either, my body naturally reacting to the contact. "I can do it!" I yell, annoyed, wriggling free of his grasp before I give in to temptation and turn to rip his shorts off. "Give me a minute." Taking some deep, calming breaths, I raise my fists to my face and my eyes to his. He's regarding me thoughtfully. "What?" I ask shortly.

"I'm just thinking how lovely you look in boxing gloves, all sweaty and exasperated."

"I'm not exasperated."

"I beg to differ," he deadpans, widening his stance. "Ready when you are."

His coolness is heating my annoyance. "Why are we doing this?" I ask, thinking I desperately need to expel some of this pent-up frustration before I explode. My solo gym session was far more satisfying, even if I didn't have Miller's sharp physique to focus on.

"I told you, because I love seeing you all exasperated by me."

"You always make me feel exasperated," I mutter, extending my arm fast and ending up, yet again, in the heated hardness of Miller's chest. "Damn it!"

"Frustrated, Olivia?" he whispers, running his tongue up the edge of my ear. My eyes close, my breathing slowing to breathless gasps that have nothing to do with my exertion. His teeth bite lightly at my ear and shots of desire stab harshly in my groin, making my thighs clench.

"What's the point of this?" I breathe.

"You're my possession and I have an appreciation for my possessions, which includes doing anything I can to protect them."

The words are quite impersonal, but it's my emotionally wrecked male who's delivering them, and although it's a peculiar way of communicating his feelings, I accept that it's *his* way. "Does this help you?" I ask, just locating the ability to voice my question through my fevered state that's fast being diluted by anxiety. He has anger issues.

"Immensely," he confirms, but doesn't elaborate and instead escalates my fever by lifting me and carrying me across to a wall. I frown, not because I'd like an explanation, even though he's confirmed my suspicions, but because I'm looking at dozens of colored, plastic molded lumps protruding sporadically from the surface of the wall—starting from the base and staggering up to the ceiling.

"What are they?" I ask as he pushes me into a part of the wall that's free from strange lumpy bits.

"This"—he reaches around me and takes my hands, removes the gloves, and slowly unravels the bandages—"is a climbing wall. Hold on." My hands are placed on two of the plastic molds. I grip hard, and then I gulp as he gently takes my hips and pulls back. "Comfortable?"

I can't speak. All previous pent-up, workout-related stress has made way for anticipation. So I nod.

"It's polite to answer someone when they ask you a question, Livy. You know that." He pulls my shorts aside, along with my knickers.

"Miller," I gasp, slightly concerned by our location, feeling his fingers skimming my sex. "We can't, not here."

"This room is booked out to me daily from six to eight. No one will disturb us."

"But the glass..."

"We're out of sight." His finger pushes forward and my forehead meets the wall on a deep inhale of shaky breath. "I've asked once."

"I'm comfortable," I answer reluctantly. I'm comfortable in my position, but not in my location.

"I beg to differ." He circles deep, enticing a deep moan from us both. "You're tense."

Thrust!

"Oh God."

"Loosen up." He eases gently into me, this time with two fingers, and his tender movement reduces my tenseness, softening my whole body. "Better."

It *is* better. The continued slipping of his fingers into me is pushing me into a rapturous state, my mind no longer concerned by our location. I'm too lust-fueled. I'm quivering. I'm... I'm... I'm... "Miller!"

"Shhhh." He hushes me gently and withdraws his fingers, taking a firm but gentle hold of my hips. The loss of friction pushes me to insanity and I release one of the grips and bash the side of my fist into the wall.

"No, please!"

"Didn't I tell you that I'd drive you crazy with desire on a daily basis?"

"Yes!"

"And am I?"

"Yes!"

"And you know it delights me, right?"

"Fucking hell! Yes!"

He groans his approval and slips the head of his cock across my flesh. Then he eases into me on a drawn out hiss. My knees buckle.

"Oooh." My body liquefies, depending on Miller to hold me up.

"Steady," he breathes, coiling his arm around my waist to

support my limp body. My chin drops lifelessly to my chest. "It would appear we've steered off course." His hips ease forward, each fraction deeper that he plunges sending me giddier until he's fit snuggly within me and holding still. In my darkness, I see nothing, but the loss of sense is of no consequence. I can smell him, hear his fitful breaths, feel him, and when his hand slides up my front until his fingers are resting on my lips, I can lick him and taste him, too. "Would you like me to move?" he asks, his voice rough and full of searing hot craving.

My mouth is busy lapping at his fingers, so I find some strength to stabilize my legs and use it to push my bottom into his groin. He inhales sharply. I bite down on his finger.

"Olivia?" He wants an answer.

I relax my bite and find my voice. "Move. Please move."

"Oh Jesus." His hand is in my hair, yanking my hair tie out, before strong fingers are combing through it, sending my waves tumbling freely. Then his palm encases my throat and tugs until the back of my head meets his shoulder. My lips part and I keep my eyes shut tight, my face pointing up to the ceiling. He's still unmoving, yet my flesh is quivering incessantly with a tidal wave of crippling sensations that are getting set to send me delirious with pleasure the moment he begins to pump into me. I'm tinkering on the edge already, Miller's steady, pulsing cock sending my internal muscles into spasm. Heavy breathing invades my ears. "I'm so happy that you're my someone, Olivia Taylor."

"And I'm so happy that I am your habit," I murmur, finding it easy to utter those words amid my mind-numbing bliss.

"I'm glad we've cleared that up." His face falls into my neck and he begins a lazy pump of his hips, making all air leave my lungs on a satisfied rush of quiet breath.

I smile through my pleasure and I feel him smile against my neck as he kisses me delicately while maintaining his precise pace, keeping his palm spread across my throat.

"You taste divine," he whispers hoarsely.

"You *feel* divine."

"You're tightening around me, sweet girl."

"I'm close." I can feel all of the present signs intensify—the tenseness, the pulsing, the heaviness. "Oh God!"

"Shhhh, Livy," he chokes, his hips taking on a mind of their own, bucking briefly before he locks his teeth on my neck and takes some steadying breaths. He stops moving.

Sweat beads spring onto my forehead. The heat of his mouth on my flesh is spreading through my clammy body, burning deep into my very center.

"How close?" he asks on a strangled gasp. "How close are you, Livy?"

"Close!"

His hips seem to start vibrating, a clear sign of his fight to refrain from bucking wildly.

"Shit!" I cry when he advances quickly but carefully, my knuckles turning white from my despairing grip. Out he draws again before striking intently. My lungs drain of air and my surging heart rate escalates to dangerous levels. I feel faint. "Miller," I gulp, making my arms rigid against the wall. I'm buzzing, feeling out of control, the heights of pleasure sending my mind spiraling into meltdown. I don't know what to do to cope with him. Nothing changes and I hope it never does. "Miller, please, please, please." I'm on the cusp of tumbling over the edge, but he's holding me there, teasing me. He knows exactly what he's doing.

"Beg," he grunts, hitting me calmly with another burst forward of his hips. "Beg me for it."

"You're doing it on purpose!" I yell, thrusting back onto him in an attempt to catch the rush of pressure and let it explode, earning a bark from Miller and a shocked yelp from me. My face is yanked to his and I'm eaten alive, our kiss spurring on my imminent climax.

"Beg," he repeats against my lips. "Beg me to devote the rest of my life to you, Olivia. Make me see that you want *us* as much as I do."

"I do."

"Beg." He bites my lip and lets it drag through his teeth gently before his blue eyes are burning into me, searing my soul. "Don't deny me."

"I beg you." My eyes hold his and absorb the need seeping from them. Need for me. It's reassuring. We're in desperate need of each other.

"And I beg you." A delicious swiveling of his hips begins, reminding me of my previous explosive state. He pecks my lips and finds his rhythm again, plunging deep and retreating slowly, crippling me with his expert worshipping. "I beg you to love me forever."

My face falls into his neck and nuzzles. "You don't need to beg me," I murmur. "There's nothing more natural to me than loving you, Miller Hart."

"Thank you."

"Can you stop driving me crazy now?" My climax is still being held in limbo. It's screaming for release.

"God, yes." He drives into me firmly and holds himself deep, grinding his hips. I rocket on a cry and the built-up pressure gushes from my being, sending me dizzy and useless in his arms. "Fuck, fuck, fuck!"

"Don't drop me!" My body is quivering, my head shaking from side to side.

"Never."

"Oh . . . ," I breathe, the twinges showing no sign of receding as I relax into him. My world is a haze of distorted sounds and blurred images as I fight my way through the intensity of my orgasm. I can't feel my limbs, only Miller biting lightly on my cheek and his erection pulsing within me. Vivid images are flashing through my mind, each one of Miller and me, some past, some very much present, and some of our future together. I've found my someone—a damaged someone, a someone who displays his emotions in the most unusual fashion and conducts himself in a way to mostly repel affection. But he's *my* damaged someone. I understand him. I know how to ease him, handle him, and most importantly, I know how to love him. Despite his lifelong mission to reject the potential of feeling and caring, he's let me fight my way past his harsh, cold exterior—helped me do it to a certain extent—and I've allowed him to have the same effect on me. How I'm feeling right now, safe, cherished, loved, was worth every modicum of heartache we've both endured to this point. He accepts me and my history. We're worlds apart but utterly perfect for each other. He's beautiful from afar, and he's equally beautiful up close. And beneath that external beauty, he's even more beautiful. It goes deep, and the deeper I look, that beauty only strengthens. I'm the only person who sees it, and that's because I'm the only person who Miller has allowed to see it. Just me. He's mine. All of him. Every beautiful piece.

Miller's teeth sinking into my shoulder and his pulsing length still buried within me brings me back down to Earth, where I'm staring at the ceiling and my fingers are numb and set in place from my fierce grip of the wall's gripper things. I'm exhausted but energized, weak at the knees but strong within. "I watched you once," I whisper. I'm not sure why I'm compelled to tell him this.

He sucks my flesh into his mouth and pecks his bite mark lightly before sweeping my hair into his fist and turning my face into him. "I know you did."

He doesn't ask what I mean or where I watched him. He knows. "How?"

"My skin tingled."

My smile is one of confusion as I search his eyes, looking for anything more than those three confounding words. I see sincerity, total belief in his statement. "Your skin tingled?"

"Yes, like subtle fireworks exploding under my skin." His face remains straight.

"Fireworks?"

His lips meet my forehead and his hips retreat, his semi-arousal slipping free. My knickers and shorts also slip back into place, leaving me resentful and bitter for my loss. I'm gently turned in his arms, my hair arranged neatly down one side and my arms draped over his naked shoulders. He's damp and warm, and his skin is glistening under the harsh artificial light of the studio. My affronted body and lack of Miller inside of me is forgotten when my eyes and mind are met by the hard planes of his torso—tight nipples, smooth skin, and chiseled muscles. It's truly a sight to behold.

I watch him scan the wall behind me before edging me a fraction to the left, and then that masterpiece of a physique moves in and barricades me against the coolness behind me, every inch of his semi-nakedness coating my gym-clad body. His forefinger rests under my chin and directs my face up to his. "Up here." He smiles and kisses my cheek tenderly. "Share with me your tell."

"My tell?" The confusion in my voice isn't concealable. I have no idea what he's talking about. "I'm not sure I know what you mean."

He gives me a dimple smile, cute and almost shy. "When you're near, even out of touching distance, my skin lights up. Like fireworks. Every inch of my flesh tingles deliciously. That's my tell." His palm cups my cheek, his thumb ghosting over the surface of my lips. "That's how I know you're close by. I don't need to be able to see you. I feel you, and when we physically touch"—he blinks lazily and pulls a long, steadying breath—"those fireworks explode. They make me dizzy. They're beautiful, bright, and consuming." Leaning in, he kisses the tip of my nose. "They represent you."

My lips part, my hold moving to the back of his head. I spend a few silent moments absorbing his gaze and his body pressed hard to mine. I also absorb his words. There's nothing confounding about that statement. I know just what he's talking about now, except my tell is a little different.

"I have fireworks, too." I kiss the pad of his finger, and his side-to-side drag across my bottom lip stops as he regards me quietly. "Except mine implode."

"That sounds dangerous," he murmurs, dropping his gaze to my mouth. I disregard William's caution of rising neck hair, certain my mind was working overtime, probably because of my messed-up mind and loss of Miller. Or it could be part of my tell.

"It *is* dangerous," I confess.

"How?"

"Because every time I look at you, feel you, or even sense you, those fireworks shoot straight for my heart." I feel emotion grip me from every direction as I watch his eyes drag up my face until they're locked with mine. "I fall in love with you a little bit more each time that happens."

He slowly nods his acknowledgment. It's almost undetectable. "We're going to see and touch each other a lot," he murmurs. "You're going to be incredibly in love with me."

"Already am." I close my eyes when his thumb moves and his lips replace it. And I fall that little bit more. Our mouths move gingerly together, purposely slow, our wild abandon of a few moments ago being replaced with cautious motions and complete aching tenderness. He's speaking with this kiss. He's acknowledging his understanding. He feels that way, too, except he calls it fascination.

"To my bones?" he asks into my mouth, making me smile.

"Deeper than that."

"And I'll pray for that continued love every day."

"It's a given."

"Nothing in this world is a given, Olivia."

"That's not true," I argue, detaching myself from his mouth, my contentment of a view moments ago vanishing. I'm under his close scrutiny as I form my next words in my mind. I'm not sure what other way I can say it. "Why won't you accept it?"

"It's hard to accept something that shouldn't be." His palm works its way to the back of my head and nestles into my hair. "I'm not worthy of your love."

"Yes, you are." I can feel heated anger rising into my cheeks, replacing my postorgasm flush.

"We'll agree to disagree."

"No, we won't." My body reacts to his blindness, my hands shifting to his chest and shoving him gently back. "I want you to accept it. Not just tell me you do to keep me happy, but really accept it."

"Okay." He doesn't hesitate to agree, but there's no conviction.

My shoulders sag, defeated, all of the dazzling hope that's shone since our reunion dulling too fast. "What's made you so negative?"

"Reality." His tone is flat and lifeless, and my mouth snaps shut. I have no counter for that—no words or sense of encouragement. At least not off the cuff. Given a few moments, I'll think of something and I'll make sure it's valid and logical. But my sprinting mind is interrupted in mid-construction when the door to the studio swings open.

Both of our heads snap to the side, and my hackles instantly rise.

"Time's up." Cassie's silken voice riles me further, her perfect figure laden in Lycra not helping in the least bit. Her eyes are full of resentment, with a little alarm mixed in for good measure. She's shocked to see me and that pleases me too much.

"We're just leaving," Miller retorts curtly, taking my nape and leading me to collect his phone before directing me toward the door.

I watch with narrowed eyes as she struts across the room and shamelessly reaches down to touch her toes, stretching before sliding down into the splits on a conniving smirk. The diamond cross that always graces her lovely neck skims the floor. "Pilates," she purrs. "Does wonders for flexibility. Isn't that right, Miller?"

I look up at him with wide eyes, hoping I'm not interpreting those words correctly. He doesn't humor me with confirmation or even a reassuring look. "Rein it in, Cassie," he spits, opening the door and gently pushing me through.

"Have a great day!" she sings on a laugh.

As soon as the door slams behind us, I fight my way from Miller's hold and swing to face him, my hair whipping my face. "What's she doing here?"

"She has the studio from eight to ten."

I bristle. "Have you slept with her?"

"No." His answer is swift and decisive. "Never."

"Then what's her bendy arse harping on about?"

"Bendy arse?" One corner of his mouth tips in concealed humor. It doesn't improve my mood.

"I know she's a hooker, Miller. I saw her at a function with some old, fat, rich man."

Any signs of amusement slip away from his face in an instant. "I see," he says simply, like it's of no importance.

"You see?"

"What else would you like me to say? She's an escort."

My sass shrivels. I don't know what I want him to say. "I need to get to work." I pivot, making for the ladies' changing rooms, feeling hot wetness trickling down my thighs. Damn it!

"Olivia."

I ignore him and push my way through the door. The possessiveness coursing through my fire-filled veins is a little shocking, my returning sass transforming into…something else. I've not quite identified it yet, but it's dangerous. I know that much. My backside plummets to a slatted bench and my head falls into my hands. She's going nowhere. She's bold and obviously possesses a hatred for me. Can I handle that?

"Hey." Warm palms skate up my thighs and I peek through my parted fingers to find Miller kneeling in front of me. A brief scan of the changing room quickly tells me that we're not alone. There are two towel-clad women at the other end, watching with interest, but neither seem concerned by their lack of clothing.

"Miller, what are you doing?" I return my eyes to his crouched form, seeing an expressionless face but sympathy in his eyes.

"I'm doing what a man does when he sees the woman he adores in pieces."

Adores? Not fascinated? Even now, when I'm struggling to locate any sense, that simple word thrills me. "I don't like her."

"Neither do I sometimes."

"Just sometimes?"

"She's misunderstood."

"I don't think I'm misunderstanding her. She doesn't like me."

"That's because *I* like *you*. Very much so."

Fascinated. Adores. Like. "Does she want you?"

"She wants to make things difficult."

"Why?"

He sighs, low and drawn out, and clamps his palms on either side of my cheeks, getting nose to nose with me. "She can't see past what she knows."

She can't see past sex and glamour? I shake my head, a little confused but more frustrated. So she expects Miller to follow the same theory? "I want to run away," I whisper, my legs twitching already, eager to carry me from the stark truth of Miller and his history. Everything everywhere is a constant reminder. I'm not sure if I can get past it. "With you," I clarify when a wave of trepidation floats across his face. "Will any of these people let us be?"

"Sweet girl, I'm prepared to annihilate anything that blocks my path to freedom." He leans in and kisses my forehead—an act so tender but bursting with reassurance. Or supposed to be. Uncertainty was pouring from his eyes before his lids closed and concealed it. "I beg you don't let the demeaning words of others interfere."

"It's hard." I let him press his lips over every part of my face until he's pulling away. He's got the uncertainty under control. Now his blues are beseeching. He thinks I'll allow these people—Cassie and whoever else there is, because I know there will be more—to scare me away. They won't. Nothing will. "I love you."

He smiles and pulls me to my feet. "I accept your love."

"You're just saying that."

"Will I ever win this argument?" he asks, his hairline pulling back from the sudden height of his eyebrows.

I consider his question for a moment. "No," I state, short and exact, because he can't. I'll never really know if he truly accepts it. His words will never convince me.

"Get showered and changed." He clasps my shoulders and turns me away from him. "We'll be late."

A cheeky tap of my bottom sends me on my way, but the uncertainty that I found in Miller's eyes seems to have rooted itself deep within me. If he can't ease my trepidation, then no one can.

Chapter Fourteen

We're a few streets away from the bistro, caught up in a traffic jam. I can feel him studying me, so I cast a sideways glance on a tiny smirk. He leans over and kisses me sweetly. "Your hair's a little wild."

I frown while he makes a haphazard job of tucking it behind my ears. Then I smile. "I didn't have any conditioner." Reaching forward, I smooth my hand through Miller's perfect dark waves. "I should have asked to borrow yours."

He freezes mid-arranging of my hair and flicks amused eyes to mine. My smile widens. "You're perfect." He untucks my hair. "This is perfect. Never cut it off."

"I won't."

"Good."

"I'll jump out here. You can slip up that side street and avoid the traffic."

"No, I'm in no rush." He brushes me off and proceeds to join the other horn-happy drivers, smacking his palm into the center of the wheel.

"That'll get you nowhere." I laugh. "And, anyway, I *am* in a rush. I can't be late." I peck his lips and jump out of his Mercedes.

"Olivia!" he shouts after me.

I turn and bend to get him in my line of sight. "It's a couple of streets away. I'll be there in two minutes." I smile at his scowling face and shut the door, hurrying to the pavement.

I lose myself amid the sea of people, all scurrying to their places of work. It's familiar to me, comforting, but the strange sensation I'm feeling as I scamper like an ant with my fellow Londoners isn't. I reach up to my shoulder and brush away a tingle, shivering when it immediately jumps back onto my skin. Something tells me to look behind me, so I do, but I only note a mass of bobbing bodies following the flow of foot traffic. My Converse speed up without any prompt from my brain, and I start overtaking people, uneasy but with no explanation. As I round a corner, I look back again, a familiar chill resonating through me, the hairs on my nape rising.

"Oh!"

"Watch where you're going!"

I stagger, taking the man's briefcase with me, the expensive leather getting tangled between my clumsy legs. "I'm sorry!" I yelp, catching the side of the brick wall to steady myself.

"You've scuffed my case, you stupid woman!" He snatches up his property and brushes it down, grumbling and huffing his aggravation.

"I'm sorry," I repeat, straightening myself out, bracing myself for a further verbal bashing.

"Fucking imbecile," he grunts, stomping off into the crowd, leaving me being sidestepped by more impatient pedestrians.

My eyes dart everywhere, scanning faces coming toward me and the backs marching away from me, my internal alarm screaming. Reaching up, I run my palm over my nape, smoothing down the hairs. I feel a stupid sense of relief when they remain flush with my skin once I remove my hand. But my stomach is turning, anxiety gripping me. I'm circling on the spot, unease lingering deep and fretfulness plaguing me.

I turn and hurry across the road to Del's, constantly looking over my shoulder.

The bistro is the last place on earth I want to be right now. I feel nauseous, and my dread at facing my colleagues is only amplified when three sets of cautious eyes monitor my walk from the door to the kitchen. I feel judged. I *am* being judged. They all think I'm daft, but they haven't experienced Miller when he's not armored up in one of his fine three-piece suits. They have drawn their conclusions on the little information they know, and I'm past the point of feeling the need to justify my relationship with London's most notorious ex-escort, to Sylvie, Del, Gregory, or anyone for that matter. It's exhausting enough trying to justify it to Miller, and he's the only one who really matters. God help me and my ears if any one of these people were to discover Miller's history. To them, he is simply an uptight arsehole who's played me. And it'll stay that way.

"Morning." Sylvie's tone is lacking its usual chirpiness, her hands redundant on the filter handle of the coffee machine.

"Hi." I flash a small smile. "Oh, I have a new phone. I'll text you the number."

"Okay." She nods as I pass her, entering the kitchen and immediately getting into my apron.

Paul follows me in and takes up position behind the stove, lifting and tossing a pan full of onions. "You have a good evening?" he asks. I detect genuine interest and look up to find an expression displaying indifference.

"I did, thank you, Paul. You?"

"Sure," he grunts as he slides two plates across the counter. "Tuna crunches for table seven. Let's have some service around here."

I swing into action and grab the plates, bypassing Sylvie and Del on my way out, my boss remaining tight-lipped, my friend's lips remaining pursed. "Tuna crunches?" I ask, sliding them onto the table.

"Ta, darlin'," a potbellied man sings, all happy, almost dribbling as he pulls both plates toward him while licking his lips. His big mouth wraps straight around one corner and he looks up at me, smiling, soggy bread spilling from his chops. I grimace. "Fill this up, will ya?" He pushes his coffee mug into my hand and my stomach turns when a lump of tuna slips past his lips and splatters on the floor at his feet. I follow his finger as it swoops down and mops it up. Then I watch with horror when he takes the half-chewed food and laps it off his pudgy finger with a tongue lathered in Paul's secret recipe. I gag, my palm slapping across my mouth as I sprint across the bistro, thinking Miller would have a seizure if he witnessed the display of such caveman manners.

"You okay?" Sylvie asks with alarm as I fly toward her.

"Refill. Table seven." I thrust the mug at her and dart past, trying desperately to stop the bile stirring. I clatter past tables, bump into chairs, and smack my shoulder into the wall as I round a corner. "Bollocks!" I curse, way too loud and in front of a table of two old dears who are enjoying tea and cakes in the quieter part of the bistro. I wince and rub my arm, then turn to apologize.

And throw up all over them.

"Goodness gracious!" One old lady shoots up from her chair, rather fast for an old-timer. "Oh! Doris, your hat!" She swats her friend's head with a napkin, trying to brush away the lumps of vomit that I've sprayed all over the poor old lady. I swipe up a napkin and hold it over my mouth.

"Oh, Edna, is it ruined?" Her friend's hand goes straight for her head and sinks into the sick-coated fur of her hat. I heave violently again.

"I fear it might be. Oh what a shame! Don't touch it!"

"I'm so sorry," I splutter through the napkin, watching the two old biddies fussing over each other. I can feel eyes punching holes into me from everywhere, and a quick glimpse over my shoulder reveals a bistro full of silent observers. Even the filthy-mannered fatty who's the cause of my vomiting episode is looking at me with disgust. "I..." I can't finish. Sweat has jumped onto my forehead and heat has jumped onto my cheeks. I'm mortified. And I feel terrible—sick, embarrassed, and stupid. I let the corridor that leads to the ladies' room swallow me up, and I flop over the sink, running the tap and splashing my face before rinsing my mouth. Looking up, I'm greeted by the reflection of a pale, meek-looking creature. Me. I feel rotten.

Which reminds me. Once I wash and dry my hands, I take my phone from my pocket and spend five minutes cringing down the line, explaining to my doctor's receptionist why I need an emergency appointment. "Eleven?" I ask, pulling my phone from my ear to see the time. My shift finishes at five. "Have you anything later?" I try, already running over a plausible excuse for me to escape work for an hour or two. My shoulders sag when she gives me no other option, then points out hastily that I only have a seventy-two-hour window if the morning after pill is going to work. Damn. "I'll take eleven," I say, giving my name before hanging up.

"Livy?"

Sylvie is peeking around the door. "Hey." I pop my phone back in my pocket and snatch a paper towel to dab at my wet face. "Am I fired?"

She smiles, her pink lips wide, and joins me by the sink. "Don't be silly. Del's worried about you."

"He shouldn't be."

"Well, he is. And so am I."

"Neither of you should be worried about me. I'm fine." I turn back to the mirror, not prepared to suffer another lecture about my relationship with Miller.

"Sure you are." She laughs, making me frown at her in the mirror. She's belittling me. "I assume things didn't go so well after he abducted you from the bistro yesterday."

"You're wrong," I seethe, turning to face her. The smile has dropped and shock has replaced it. She assumes because I'm a little off color that things had gone all wrong last night. That Miller is responsible. "I feel a little under the weather, Sylvie. Don't presume that Miller is the catalyst for everything." I dump the used towel in the bin harshly. "Miller and I are fine."

"But—"

"No!" I cut her off. I'm not standing for it anymore. Not from Sylvie, not from Gregory, not from William. No one! "A disgusting man just spat his tuna crunch all over the floor and scooped it up with a filthy finger. Then he ate it!"

"Eww!" Sylvie recoils, her hand going to her midriff and circling slowly, like sickness has just jumped up and bit her on the arse. She should have seen it.

"Yes, exactly." I tuck a wayward strand of hair behind my ear and straighten my shoulders. "*That* is why I threw up, and I'm fucking miserable because I'm sick of hearing people griping about me and Miller, and even sicker of receiving sympathetic fucking looks!"

Her eyes widen while I bubble with anger before her, my chest pulsing with labored breaths. "Okay," she squeaks.

I nod sharply, determinedly. "Good. I have to get back to work." I slip past a startled Sylvie and bump into Del in the corridor. "I'm fine!" I snap petulantly.

His head seems to sink into his neck. "Clearly. But the two old birds in there aren't."

I cringe. "I'm sorry."

"Go home, Livy," he sighs.

I admit defeat easily on a slump of my shoulders, grateful for not having to make an excuse to escape for my appointment, and follow through on my boss's sharp order. I take my drained body down the corridor and into the kitchen, slipping quietly past the two old ladies who I've just spewed all over. They're distracted with fresh cakes and a new steaming pot of tea.

Weaving my way through the tables of customers, my need

to escape the confines of the bistro becomes urgent under the repulsed looks of the clientele. I burst out the door and land on the pavement, my head falling back on my shoulders and looking to the heavens. The fresh air hits my lungs, and I close my eyes and expel it on a heavy, frustrated sigh, relieved to be in open air.

"The signs aren't good." William's rich tone sucks all of that relief out of me, my head dropping down slowly, my expression tired. "I assume you know how to operate the iPhone that I bought for you."

"Yes," I grate. It's not even ten o'clock and I've poked up with far too much already today. Now William, too. He's leaning up against the Lexus, arms crossed over his chest in authority. He looks formidable. And cross.

"Then I'm going to assume there's a perfectly good explanation for you ignoring my message."

"I was busy." I throw my satchel across my body and square my shoulders.

"Doing what?"

"None of your business."

"Being blindsided by a handsome man who has seduction down to a fine art? Is that what you mean?"

I bristle, my teeth clenching. "I am not answerable to you."

He laughs lightly, a splash of recognition invading his face. I'm behaving like my mother, and I hate myself for it. But for the first time in forever, I'm thinking hard about her own battle against the people who obstructed her mission to win William. The man before me included. If this is how she felt, then I'm beginning to relate, and that's something I never dreamed I'd do. But I'm feeling pretty reckless. Determined. I've been there before and I'd probably go there again, if I didn't now have the support of my someone. Gracie never did, and I can fully comprehend how that impacted her. "Tell me how my mother came to love you so much."

My abrupt question wipes the amusement from William's face

in an instant. He's fallen into that uncomfortable mode again, shifting and diverting his liquid gray stare from mine. "I've told you."

"No, you haven't. You've told me nothing, only that she was in love with you. You haven't explained how that came to be. Or how you fell in love with her." I'm dying to ask him where his manners are, too, but I refrain, waiting patiently for him to piece together his story instead. I need to know. I need to hear how William and my mother came upon each other. One thing I remember vividly is William saying loud and clear that she put herself in his world for him. But how did they meet?

He coughs, keeping his eyes off me, and opens the rear door of his Lexus. "I'll take you home."

I huff my displeasure at his evasion and leave him waiting for me to get in his car, making tracks toward the bus stop.

"Olivia!" he shouts, and I hear the car door slam harshly. It startles me, making my shoulders hit my earlobes, but I disregard his evident annoyance and pick up my pace. "It was instant!" he yells, pulling me to a rapid halt. The unsure tone of his words and rushed delivery of them is proof of the pain they're causing him. I slowly turn to assess exactly how much pain I'm dealing with, and when his face comes into my view, I see a sadness that deflects right off William and punches a hole in my gut. "She was seventeen years old." He laughs a nervous laugh, almost embarrassed. "It was wrong of me to look at her the way I did, but when those sapphire eyes turned to me and she smiled, my world exploded into a million shards of sparkling glass. Your mother knocked me on my arse, Olivia. I saw a freedom that I knew I couldn't have."

My heart slows, a crevice cracking wide open and exposing a horrid reality. I don't like what I'm hearing. My brain is failing to locate any words of comfort for William, but it's jumping all over his admission. "Why are you trying to sabotage our love?" I ask.

It's a perfectly reasonable question, especially in light of this information. It's not jealousy or resentment. William could've had that freedom, just like Miller can. Except Miller is more determined to get it. Miller isn't prepared to let me slip through his fingers. Miller will fight for us—even if, maddeningly, he questions his worthiness.

William's eyes close slowly, reminding me of my part-time gentleman's lazy blink. It makes me want to dash to Miller without delay, let him immerse me in his sanctuary and *thing*. "Please, allow me to take you home." He steps back and opens the car door again, gesturing with pleading eyes for me to get in.

"I'd rather walk," I tell him. I still feel ill and the fresh air will do me good. Plus, I need to get to my doctor and I can't ask William to drop me there. The thought makes me shudder on the spot.

My petulance is irritating him, but I stand firm, not prepared to be bossed into his car again. "Then at least give me five minutes." He indicates across the road to the square where Miller once sat me—the time I finally gave in and let him have his one night.

I nod, silently pleased he isn't demanding me into his car. He needs to know I can assert some control, too. We start to wander across together, William giving his driver a mild nod as we leave. My stomach is churning, a mixture of sadness and compassion. I feel like I'm falling into an abyss of knowledge. I don't want to continue my descent because I know it'll be a bumpy landing—one that's going to shred the unforgiving resentment I hold for my mother and replace it with overwhelming guilt. Each minute I spend with William Anderson is weakening the band circling the hardened part of my heart that I've reserved for holding utter contempt for Gracie Taylor. It's going to snap soon and let the cynical fragments merge with the soft, fallen part. I'm not sure whether I can cope with more heartache, not after I've barely recovered and can feel light filling the darkness. But curiosity and the overpowering need to validate what Miller and I have is overriding my reluctance.

We both lower to a bench and I remain quiet, watching William's stiff body trying to relax next to me. And failing on every level. He places his hands on his lap and removes them. He reaches for his phone, checks it, and replaces it in his inside pocket. He crosses his legs, then uncrosses them, and his elbow rests on the bench's arm. He's uncomfortable, which is making me uncomfortable, too. Although I continue to study his string of awkward motions.

"You've never told anyone your story, have you?" I ask, surprising myself when my palm lands on his knee and squeezes in a gesture of comfort. It's obscene for me to be offering my empathy. He sent my mother away and lost her forever, for both of us. But he sent me away, too. And saved me.

The distinguished gentleman stops shifting and drops his gaze to my hand. Then he lays his big palm over mine and holds it. He sighs. "I was in training, if you will. Being ordained to take over for my uncle. I was twenty-one, a nasty little fucker, and fearless to boot. Nothing and no one fazed me. I was the perfect successor."

My eyes drop to our hands and I watch closely as he fiddles with my ring thoughtfully before drawing breath. "Gracie had landed in my uncle's club by accident. She was with friends, tipsy and bold. She hadn't the first idea of what she'd stepped into, and I should've sent her on her way the second I clocked her, but I was rendered immobile by her spirit. It emanated from her entire being, right from her soul, and it held me in its claws. I tried to walk away, but they dug in farther. They held me there."

He reaches up with his spare hand and rubs at his eyes on a long, drawn-out sigh. "She laughed." William gazes ahead thoughtfully. "Tipped martinis down her beautiful throat and carried her stunning body onto the dance floor. I was rapt. Hypnotized. Among the corrupted, sinful best of London was my Gracie. She was mine. Or going to be. When my duty was to lead her away from the seedy underworld that I was destined to run, I was instead luring her in."

The particles holding that contempt for my mother and the considerable part of my heart that holds pure, raw love for Miller begin to blend. I'm beginning to lose the ability to distinguish between the two…just as I suspected and feared. William looks up at me and smiles wistfully, his handsome face pained and remorseful. "I bought her champagne. She'd never tasted it. Watching her eyes sparkle in newfound delight lifted a layer from my hard heart. Not once did she stop smiling and not once did my doubt waver that I had to make this young woman mine. I knew I was swimming murky waters, but I was blinded."

"You wish you had," I suggest, knowing I'm right. "You wish you had seen her out and forgotten about her."

He laughs a little. It's condescending. "There wasn't a hope of me forgetting Gracie Taylor. Sounds ridiculous, I know. I snatched a measly hour with her, stole a kiss when she resisted, and told her I'd be taking her out the following evening. Somewhere off the beaten track. Somewhere private, where no one knew me. She said no but didn't stop me when I helped myself to her purse and found some identity to confirm her name and address." His smile broadens in an obvious moment of reflection. "Gracie Taylor." The sound of my mother's name pleases him, and I can't prevent a fond smile from developing on my own lips. The blossoming feelings between Gracie and William are picture perfect. Novel material. Consuming and irrational. Then it all went horribly wrong.

I can totally relate to my mother. Despite William and Miller clearly despising each other, they have many similar qualities. She must have been just as blinded by William Anderson as he claimed to be by her. And as I am by Miller Hart.

"Your obligation to your uncle ruined everything."

"Obliterated it," he corrects sardonically. "My uncle was planning to retire, but a freak accident sent his body to the bottom of the Thames before we got to give him his timepiece."

My brow crumples. "Timepiece?"

He smiles and lifts my hand to his lips, kissing it sweetly. "It's commonly recognized as a good retirement gift."

"It is?"

"Yes, funny, don't you think? Someone who no longer has to clock-watch is given a watch."

I chuckle with William, feeling a bond between us budding. "It's quite ironic."

"Very much so."

What's also ironic is that we're laughing about this when he's just informed me that his uncle died so tragically. "I'm sorry about your uncle."

William huffs a sarcastic puff of breath. "Don't be. He got what he deserved. Live by the sword, die by it. Isn't that what they say?"

I don't know. Do they? I'm being fed information that is way too vivid and complex for my poor mind to process.

I stammer all over my words, but the comprehension seems to bite me on the arse. "Was your uncle an immoral bastard?"

"Yes." He chuckles again, wiping under his eyes. "He was *the* immoral bastard. Things changed once I took over. I might have been a nasty bastard when I needed to be, but I wasn't unfair. I implemented new rules, sorted the girls out, and weeded out the arseholes on the client list as best I could. I was young, fresh, and it worked. Earned me far more respect than my uncle ever gained. The ones who wanted to stick around and do things my way stayed. The ones who didn't like the changes went and continued to be immoral bastards. I earned myself a lot of enemies, but even at that age I was not to be taken lightly."

"Have you killed anyone?" I blurt the question without thought, and startled grays flip to mine fast. I almost let an apology slip for asking such a thing, but the wary glaze that descends over William's clear eyes tells me it's not such a stupid inquiry. He has.

"That's irrelevant, don't you think?"

No, I don't, but his cautionary glare prevents me from saying so. Had he not taken someone's life, then I'm certain he'd be quick to put me right. "I'm sorry."

"Don't be." He reaches over and skims his knuckles over my cheek. "Your beautiful mind doesn't need to be tarnished with ugliness."

"Too late," I whisper, making William's delicate touch falter. "But we're not talking about me and my decisions. What happened then?"

Shifting in his seated position, William takes both of my hands and turns to me. "We courted."

"Dated?"

"Yes, if you will."

I smile, remembering Nan using the very same word. "And?"

"And it was intense. Gracie, although young and lacking in experience, had passion built in and ready to unleash. And she unleashed it on me. It sparked an undiscovered hunger in me. A hunger for her."

"You fell in love."

"I think that happened immediately." Sadness washes over his features again, his eyes dropping to his lap. "I spent only a month swallowed up in your mother's fiery desire. Then reality hit, and Gracie and I were suddenly an impossible combination."

I know exactly how he must have felt, and whatever bond we share just got a little stronger. "What happened?"

"My eye was off the ball and one of my girls paid for it."

I gasp and reclaim a hand.

He rubs his forehead, reliving the pain. "Damage control was something else. My enemies would have been pigs in shit over it."

"So you broke things off with her."

"Tried to. For a long, long time. Gracie was addictive and the thought of facing a day without immersing myself in her was unthinkable. And anyway, she knew how to render me stupid, how to brandish her sass and body unfairly. I was screwed." William relaxes back on the bench and gazes across the square, drifting off somewhere distant and troubled. "I kept us on the down-low. She would have been a target."

"It wasn't just your obligation to the girls that stopped you being together, was it?" I don't need confirmation.

"No, it wasn't. If I allowed my feelings for that woman to be known, she would have been a red flag. I may as well have served her on a fucking plate."

"But that happened anyway," I remind him. He sent her away, let her fall into the hands of an immoral bastard.

"After a few traumatic years, yes, it did. I always hoped you would be enough to pull her around."

I scoff, pissed off at being reminded of my lack of incentive to my mother. "We all know how that worked out for you," I snipe. "Sorry I let you down."

"Enough!"

"How did she become pregnant with another man's child?" I ask, ignoring his irritation at my candidness. "She was nineteen when she had me. That's not long after you met."

"She punished me, Olivia. I already told you that. I don't need to remind you of the book. Remember reading much of me in there?"

"No," I admit, feeling almost sorry for William.

"She became pregnant with another man's child. It deflected any suspicion there may have been about your mother and me."

"Who was he?"

William scoffs. "Who the hell knows? Gracie certainly didn't."

Resentment pours from him and he releases a calming rush of breath. Speaking of this makes him angry. And it just makes me hate my mother more. "You were probably the best thing that could have happened."

"I'm glad someone thinks so," I scathe.

"Olivia!"

"I'm glad I served a purpose." I laugh wickedly. "And here's me thinking no one wanted me, yet it turns out that I did my mother's pimp a favor. My purpose in life is making me so proud."

"You saved your mother's life, Livy."

"What?" I snap. He's not going to suggest that my purpose was to deter the enemy, to deflect from Gracie and William's relationship? "Just so she could abandon me later?" I ask. "For all we know, she's dead, William! My purpose stands for shit because despite everything, she still ended up fucking dead! I still have no mother and you have no Gracie!" I heave violently next to him, blinking back tears of fury. The compassion has been sucked up, the merging parts of my heart severed in the blink of an eye... or the delivery of a thoughtless sentence. He was doing so well. The history of their relationship momentarily made me forget about the matter at hand. Miller. And me. Us. We're not destined to follow the same destructive path of tortured love and irreparable heartache. We were on our way, but we saved each other.

I stand and swing toward him. He's regarding me carefully. "Miller won't let me down like you did Gracie." I turn and storm away, hearing him hiss on a wince. I half expect to be seized before I make it out of the square, but I'm allowed to remove myself from William and his revelations without intervention.

* * *

I don't mean to, but when I finally make it home, I slam the front door shut, still reeling after my time with William and exhausted after my time at the doctors. I don't recall much of my time sitting opposite my GP's desk. I blurted my predicament, was interrogated before being prescribed the morning-after pill and contraceptive pill, and left, taking myself across the road to the pharmacy. And it was all done in a cloud of hopelessness.

The harsh clatter of the door crashing within the frame prompts Nan to scuttle from the kitchen in alarm. "Livy, whatever's the matter?" She glances down at her old watch. "It's not even midday."

I don't bother trying to compose myself—I'm still too wound up—so I utilize my only other option, which is fine because it's part true. "Del sent me home."

"Are you ill?" Her steps increase in pace as she wipes her hands on the tea towel, until she's standing before me feeling my forehead. "You have a temperature."

Yes, I do. I'm burning with blinding rage. Sagging against the front door, I let my grandmother fuss over me, grateful for the sight of her friendly face, even if it's etched in worry right now. "I'm okay."

"Pa!" she scoffs. "Don't piss down my back and tell me it's raining!" She brushes some damp tendrils from my face. "The faster you learn that I'm not doo-lally-tap the better." Her old sapphire eyes drill holes into my pathetic form. "I'll make tea." She's off up the hallway. "Come."

"Because tea makes everything in the world right," I mutter, pushing myself off the door and following her.

"What?"

"Nothing." I land in a chair and retrieve my phone from my satchel when it chimes.

"A call?" Nan asks, flicking the kettle on.

"A text."

She turns genuine curiosity my way. "How do you know the difference?"

"Well, because a call…" I halt midsentence as I unlock my shiny new device. "Are you ever going to have a mobile phone?"

She laughs and returns to tea-making duties. "I'd rather get a back massage by Edward Scissorhands! Why at my age would I need one of those silly things?"

"Then it doesn't matter what sound signals a text, call, or e-mail, does it?"

"E-mail?" she screeches. "You can send e-mails?"

"Yes. And you can use the Internet, do your shopping, and delve into social media."

"What's social media?"

I laugh, flopping back in my chair. "You won't live long enough for me to explain, Nan."

"Oh." She shows complete indifference as she pours boiling water into the teapot, and then milk into a tiny jug. "There will be little point for people to leave their homes if technology continues at this rate. Texts and e-mails. Whatever happened to having a face-to-face conversation with someone, hmmm? Or even a nice chat on the phone. Don't ever send me a text."

"I can't—you don't have a mobile."

"An e-mail, then. Never send me an e-mail."

I smirk. "You don't have an e-mail account, so I can't send you an e-mail, either."

"Well, that's a relief."

I titter to myself and direct my eyes to the screen of my phone as Nan brings the tea to the table and pours, loading mine with sugar.

"Need fattening up," she grumbles, but I ignore her because William's name is glowing at me, telling me he's sent me a message—one I know I won't want to read. It doesn't stop me from pushing the Open button, though.

This can't end well.

My teeth grit and I delete the message, damning myself for reading it.

"I haven't seen Gregory in a while." Nan's statement is laced with forced nonchalance. She knows he and I aren't speaking. I can't bring myself to call him, not after his rant. He was furious and undeniably serious in his threat.

"He's been busy." I toss my phone in my bag and swipe up my cup of tea, blowing the steam from the surface while I watch Nan stir hers slowly.

"He's never been too busy before."

No valid reason for Gregory's absence is dawning on me. She knows Miller and Gregory don't see eye to eye. It would be easier to tell her that he's slapped conditions on our friendship, but I just can't be bothered. "I'm going to lie down." I scoop my satchel up and stand, giving my grandmother's pouting face a peck. She hates it when I keep things from her, but with my spunky Nan being the only person on the planet, other than Miller and me, encouraging our reunion, I've concluded that everything should be on a need-to-know basis. And she doesn't need to know.

I drag myself upstairs and collapse to my arse on the familiar, messy sheets of my bed as I rummage through my satchel and pull out a paper bag. Flicking through the boxes, I find the ultimate pack and open it, popping out the pill before placing it on my tongue and closing my mouth. I just sit there, the tiny tablet feeling like lead on my tongue. Closing my eyes, I eventually swallow it down and chuck the boxes in the top drawer of my bedside table. Then I fall to my back. There's no darkness to be found, even if I were to pull the curtains across, so I yank a pillow close and roll into it, nuzzling my face deep and clenching my eyes shut. I'm only a fraction through the day and all of the elation I felt on waking this morning has been killed stone-cold dead.

Chapter Fifteen

Fireworks implode, a soft crackling rousing me from a peaceful slumber. It's dusk and I'm safe. He's here. I smile and shift in his hold until I'm lost in beautiful, soft blue eyes. My hands disappear beneath his suit jacket, around his back, and I pull myself closer until his warm breath is coating my cheeks. Circling our noses, he shifts his palm to the back of my thigh, tugging it up to his hip. "I was worried about you," he whispers. "What happened?"

"I threw up on a pair of grannies."

His eyes sparkle mischievously. "I heard."

"Then William showed up." I'm not surprised when the sparkle dulls and Miller stiffens in my hold.

"What did he want?"

"To irritate me," I mutter, snuggling into his chest, my cheek resting over his heart. It's beating a strong steady thrum and the sound settles me completely. "Tell me you'll never abandon me."

"I promise." He doesn't falter, like he's had a warning that I'd make this request, like he knows why William is hounding me.

It's enough, because Miller Hart doesn't make promises that he can't keep. "Thank you."

"Don't thank me, Olivia. Never thank me. Come here, let me see you." He wrestles me from the sanctuary of his body and props himself up against my headboard, arranging me on his lap just so. I can feel his erection wedged between our bodies, long and hard, but by the look on Miller's face, I'm on my own in the lust department. I frown and take a sneaky grind as he clasps my hands and entwines our fingers. Then he cocks a knowing eyebrow at me. "Why do you work at the bistro?"

His odd question halts my tempting tactics in their tracks. "To earn money." That's not strictly true. I have a bank account bursting at the seams with cash.

"I have plenty of money. You slaving away in a London café isn't necessary."

I bite my bottom lip, worrying it back and forth as I comprehend what he's saying. His Adam's apple is bobbing in his throat from his constant swallows. He's nervous of my reaction, and he should be. "I don't need any man's money," I state quite calmly, even though his hint has zapped my serenity of a few moments ago.

"I'm not just *any man*, Olivia." His palms slide to my upper arms and pull me close to the stubbled shadow of his jaw. Blue eyes scorch me with heated annoyance, but he's still gentle with me, and his tone is soft. "Don't upset yourself."

"I'm not. I just want to earn my own money."

"I know you have more ambition than making coffee." Miller's tone is patronizing, and while I could point out that his ambitions were a lot less commendable, I'm not up for another confrontation today.

"I'm tired." I cop out from the line of conversation with that pathetic statement and fall onto his suit-covered chest, pushing my face into his neck and filling my nose with his manly scent.

"Tired." He sighs and envelopes me in his arms. "It's six-thirty in the evening and I believe you have been in this bed since noon."

I ignore his observation and reach up to play with his ear, rubbing his lobe through my index finger and thumb. "How was your day?"

"Long. What did Anderson want?"

"I told you, to irritate me."

"Elaborate."

"No."

"I've asked once."

"You can ask as many times as you like," I whisper. "I don't want to talk about it."

I'm moving before I can stiffen my muscles to hinder him. He pushes me up so I'm straddling his lap and clamps down on my thighs, impatience hazy in his gaze. "Tough luck."

"For you," I mutter indignantly. I'm pushing his buttons, but I have no desire to share my recent revelations with Miller right now—probably never will. I was a baby of convenience, and not of the regular kind. I served one purpose and one purpose alone, and that failed miserably, anyway.

I'm under close scrutiny. He's waiting for my elaboration, which will never come, yet Miller's expectant pose doesn't block more unpleasant thoughts from creeping through the barriers of my mind. How must William have felt knowing Gracie got pregnant by another man when he loved her so deeply? She was punishing him by sleeping with other men, that's now clear, but did she mean to get herself knocked up? Was one of my purposes to cripple William with hurt, too? And would William have made my mother terminate me had I not been of use in diverting the enemy? I was a pawn, that's all. An object used to William's advantage.

"Olivia?" Miller's gentle, encouraging mention of my name sucks my dejected mind back into the room where I'm faced with someone who *does* want me. Not because I serve a purpose, but because I am *their* purpose.

"William used me," I murmur, the words causing me physical pain. I was over this. I was past the hurt of being abandoned, but now I'm facing a new kind of hurt. "My mother got herself pregnant by another man to punish William." I wince at my own cold words and clench my eyes shut. "They were in love. William and my mother were hopelessly in love and couldn't be together because of William's world. If the wrong people found out about his relationship with Gracie, they would have used her against him." I'm suddenly considering the possibility of William keeping Gracie close by, not only to fuel his need to see her, but also as another deterrent. He never got involved with his girls. It was common knowledge.

My eyes remain locked tightly shut until I feel movement beneath me and Miller's warm mouth on mine. "Shhh," he hushes me, despite the fact that I've stopped speaking. I have nothing more to say and I hope Miller doesn't push for more. Every tiny snippet of information that William fed me this morning, all of the intensity and passion between him and my mother that he spoke of, was annihilated with his final enlightenment.

You saved your mother's life.

No, I didn't, and my current state of mind won't allow me to feel remorseful about it. "How long have you known William?" I ask quietly as he rains gentle pecks on my cheeks and lips.

"Ten years." His answer carries an air of finality and his mouth continues to seduce mine, his tongue slipping past my lips and sweeping reverently in circles. I feel distracted, so I pull away from his busy mouth and study him for a moment, pushing his misbehaving wave from his brow. He's not happy about my withdrawal, which only increases my suspicion.

"When you found out I knew William, you knew he'd have something to say about us, didn't you? He doesn't agree with how you conduct business."

"Correct."

"That's it?"

He shrugs a little, displaying indifference. "Anderson has a lot to say about a lot of things, me included."

"He said you're immoral," I whisper, dropping my gaze to our laps, almost ashamed of sharing William's thoughts, which is ridiculous when I've heard William tell Miller this to his face.

"Look at me." The pad of his finger slips under my chin and raises my face to his. I'm immediately consumed with blazing eyes and soft parted lips. "Never with you," he says slowly, quietly, holding my eyes like magnets.

I knew that. Our horrid hotel encounter needs to be forgotten. That wasn't my Miller. "I love you," I tell him on a quiet gush of air, slipping my arms under his and melding into his torso, my cheek lying on his shoulder. He responds with an almost undetectable groan and takes me to my back, the length of his body pinning me to the bed. "You'll be all crumpled," I muse, ruffling his hair and trying to push my rendezvous with William away. All of those years I wished for an explanation, went to epic lengths to find it, and now I've stumbled upon it and I wholeheartedly wish I hadn't.

"It could be worse." He nips at my neck, the hot pressure of his mouth sending me on a little writhe.

"How?" Miller's obsession with his appearance is definitely lessening, and while it should please me immensely that some of his uptight, picky ways are evidently easing up, I can't figure out why I seem to be more bothered by his waning care than he does.

"We could be scheduled to eat out."

My brow furrows, but he continues before I can ask what on earth he's talking about.

"Luckily, your lovely grandmother has offered to feed us." He pushes up on his forearms and looks down at me, a cunning glint in his eyes. I know what he's looking for and I won't disappoint him. I roll my eyes.

"Did she pin you down until you agreed?"

"Not necessary." Miller drops a lazy kiss on my lips and rises, the shift pushing his hips into my lower stomach. My eyes widen and moisture bombards my center. Now that I have emptied my mind of unwanted burdens, there's room for something else. Something appealing.

Desire.

Nibbling my bottom lip, I reach up to his shoulders and smooth down the sleeves of his suit jacket, the feel of tight muscle beneath only heightening my growing wanton state. He shakes his head slowly, definitely, unwaveringly, and I deflate on an annoyed huff of breath. "Control yourself, then." I tip my hips up and spike a sharp inhale of breath from him, followed up with a poor attempt to scowl at me. I grin and repeat. Of course, this only teases me further, too, but Miller's struggle to contain himself ignites a childish rebellion in me. I flip up again and watch on a laugh as he jumps off the bed and starts brushing himself down and pulling at his jacket.

"Really, Olivia?"

I sit up, a wicked grin on my face. "It's always on your terms," I state, resting my chin in my palm and my elbow on my knee. He's still busy rearranging himself, choosing to answer without looking at me.

"It's a good job, wouldn't you agree?"

"It's polite to look at someone when they're talking to you."

Frantic hands halt in their fussing and an impassive face slowly rises to mine. "It's a good job, wouldn't you agree?"

"No, I wouldn't." Images of a gym, a paint studio, and cars jump all over my mind. At least there's a bed here. And it's *my* bedroom. I slide off the mattress and pace slowly and purposely over to him. He watches me, standing silently, almost cautiously, until my chest is pushed into his. I lift my eyes to his mouth. Hot, lusty air streams from parted lips, fueling my hunger, swelling my confidence. "I won't make it through dinner," I warn, flicking my eyes to his.

"I won't disrespect your grandmother, Olivia."

My eyes narrow and a conniving hand stretches forward and brushes over his groin. He jumps back. I move forward. "Don't be so uptight."

Strong hands circle my upper arms and a face full of frustration lowers to mine. "No," he says simply.

"Yes," I retort, struggling out of his hold and cupping him over his trousers. "You're the one who's unleashed this need, so you're under obligation to remedy it."

"Fucking hell!"

I inwardly cheer, knowing I have him. He can't make me endure another dinner at Nan's table when I'm in this condition. I'll spontaneously combust. "Loosen up."

"Give me strength, Olivia." He knocks my hand away from his groin and tackles me to the bed, the frame squeaking, the headboard smacking the wall behind. My victory fills me with unreasonable pride. My lips press together and my eyes clench shut as he circles deliciously into me, the friction having me trying to shift my legs beneath him to alleviate the pressure building between my thighs. My actions earn me more restraint. He nails my wrists to the mattress. "You want me?" he breathes in my face, gently thrusting forward, pushing the bated breath from my lungs. I cry out, my eyes flying open. Dark lashes greet me, framing intoxicating blues. "Don't make me ask you again."

"Yes!" I yelp at the delivery of another calculated thrust, feeling him solid beneath the material of his trousers. Dizziness overwhelms me and the room starts spinning wildly, yet Miller's perfect face is still perfectly clear before me. "Miller," I pant, loving and hating his control over my body all at once.

Smug satisfaction plagues his features. And then he pushes himself off me and sets about sorting his suit out again. "Come. Your grandmother has gone to a lot of trouble."

My mouth falls open in utter disbelief. "You're not..."

"Oh, I am." He collects me from the bed and begins to make

me look presentable while I stand unequivocally dumbstruck by his underhanded game. He's solid. It must be painful, because I know that I'm suffering. He brushes my wild hair over each shoulder, looking satisfied with the result. "Your cheeks are flushed," he says, his voice loaded with smugness.

"How—" His finger meets my lips to hush me before he replaces it with his lips, escalating my sexed-up condition. "Just think how much more you'll enjoy me later when I can take my time with you."

"You're unbelievably cruel," I whimper, throwing my arms around his neck and tackling his wonderful mouth, desperate to get all I can before he wrestles me off him.

He doesn't pry me away, instead lifting me from my feet and carrying me to the door while returning my kiss, accepting my tongue dancing wildly in his mouth and moaning his appreciation as he does. In an attempt to trap him further, I curl my thighs around his tight hips and arch my spine, sealing our chests and balling my fists in his hair. I hum, I whimper, I sigh. My head tilts, my mouth tracks the lines of his lips, and my teeth bite down in between plunges of my tongue. This isn't improving my thirst, but if it's all I'm getting for the time being, then I'm making the most of it. My eyes are closed and Miller's palms are cupping my bottom, squeezing, massaging, and smoothing as he takes the stairs down to the hallway. My time's running out.

"Olivia," he pants, breaking our mouth contact.

"Nuh-uh," I moan, pushing into the back of his head, reattaching my lips to his.

"Jesus, you're ruining me."

Through my dizziness, I register the stupidity of such a statement. "Take me to your place," I beg, knowing I'm pleading in vain. Miller's far too polite to stand my grandmother up. I can smell a hearty meal, something stodgy simmering upon the stove, and I hear Nan singing chirpily in the kitchen.

"She's gone to too much trouble." He peels me away from his suit and sets me on my feet, tugging my top into place. "Aren't you hungry?" His eyes drop to my too-flat stomach.

"Not really," I concede. There's no room in my brain to register hunger.

"We need to resolve this appetite issue," he quips curtly, "before you disappear before my eyes."

"There's no issue." I reach up and take Miller's tie, jiggling with the dislodged knot for a short time before I'm happy that it's straight and tidy. "I eat when I'm hungry."

"Which is when?" He throws me an expectant look as he removes his jacket and hangs it on the coat hooks before he turns into the mirror and undoes what I've just spent thirty seconds of my time perfecting. His back broadens with the position of his hands at his neck, the material of his waistcoat pulling taut. I sigh my appreciation. "We need to get you to the doctors."

His statement yanks me back to the here and now, having me look up to a serious face. "I've been," I whisper.

He can't hide his shock. I love that I can spike all of these emotions from him, but not now. "You went without me?"

My shoulders jump up a little, displaying detachment. "The receptionist said it's best to take the morning-after pill as soon as possible, and they only had an available appointment this morning."

"Oh." He drops his hands from his tie, looking uncomfortable. "I didn't want you to have to do it alone, Olivia."

"I swallowed a pill." I smile, trying to lighten him up. He feels guilty.

"And birth control?"

"Done."

"Have you started?"

"On the first day of my next period." I definitely remember that part, but not much else.

"Which is when?"

I mentally sprint through my cycle, frowning to myself. "Three weeks." This won't please him. I only just had a period while Miller was . . . absent.

"Excellent," he says, all formal, like he's just secured a profitable business deal. I roll my eyes and ignore his inquisitive look.

"And before you ask, yes, there's a need for insolence."

His lips purse and his blistering blue eyes narrow slightly. "Sass," he whispers, making me smile. "I would have come."

"I'm a big girl." I brush off his concern with ease, despite it being entirely his fault that I wound up in that position. It won't happen again. "And, anyway, you did come." I grin, trying to ease his guilt. "Inside me."

He matches my grin. "Double sass."

Footsteps interrupt us and Nan appears, her jolly face jollier than normal, and I know it's because Miller is here and he's agreed to let her feed him. "Hot pot!" she sings, delighted. "I didn't have time for anything more extravagant."

Miller rips his eyes from mine and pivots on his expensive shoes. Nan's delight increases, even if she's lost the lovely view of Miller's buns. "I'm sure that whatever you've decided on, it'll be just perfect, Mrs. Taylor."

She flaps a tea towel at Miller, all bashful and giggly. "I've laid the table in the kitchen."

"Had I known we'd be eating together, I would have brought something," Miller says, taking my nape and encouraging me to follow Nan toward the kitchen.

"Nonsense!" Nan laughs. "Besides, I still have the champagne and the caviar."

"With hot pot?" I ask on a frown.

"No, but I doubt Miller would have brought a barrel of cheap ale to slurp." Nan flips her hand, indicating a chair. "Sit."

My chair is pulled out for me and tucked back under once I've taken my seat. His mouth meets my ear. "How fast can you eat hot pot?"

I ignore him and concentrate on soaking up the heat of his breath in my ear, probably a stupid thing to do, but it doesn't matter how fast I can eat because Miller's manners prevent him from scoffing down food.

He takes his seat next to me and gives me a salacious smirk, just as a huge pot of Nan's hot pot lands in the center of the table. I inhale the smell of meat, veggies, and potatoes. And grimace. I'm not in the least bit hungry, only for the infuriating male seated next to me.

"Where has George got to?" Nan gripes, looking impatiently down at her watch. "He's five minutes late."

"George is joining us?" Miller asks, nodding at the steaming pot, his instruction for me to dive in. "It'll be nice to see him again."

"Hmmm, it's not like him to be late."

She's right. He's usually sitting at the table armed with his knife and fork in plenty of time to be the first into the pot. Unfortunately, I get the pleasure today. I take the serving spoon with as much enthusiasm as I feel and plunge it into the middle, wafting the smell into the air surrounding us.

"Smells delicious," Miller informs Nan, keeping his eyes on me. I'm not sure how much I can stomach, but with Nan *and* Miller both taking a vested interest in my eating habits, I'm destined to struggle my way through a whole bowl.

The chime of the doorbell saves me. "I'll get it." I drop the spoon and lift my bum from the chair, only to be pushed back down.

"Allow me," Miller interjects, taking the serving spoon and transferring a heaped spoonful into my dish before he makes off down the hallway.

"Thank you, Miller," Nan croons, smiling brightly. "Such a gentleman."

"Some of the time," I mutter under my breath, collecting the serving spoon and piling Miller's bowl high until it's near to overflowing.

"Is he hungry?" Nan asks, her old eyes following the spoon traveling back and forth from the pot to Miller's dish.

"Starving," I declare, silently smug.

"Save some for George. He'll blow a gasket if he doesn't get at least two helpings." She peeks into the pot, noting the remaining contents.

"There's plenty."

"Good. Tuck in." She waves her finger at my bowl, and I wonder where the table etiquette has disappeared to—the one where we wait for everyone to start together. Nan glances down the hallway on a wrinkle of her brow. "Do you think he got lost?"

"I'll go." I jump up, anything to delay eating, hoping by some miracle I'll find my appetite while I'm finding Miller and George. Showing no urgency, I stroll down the hallway, catching a glimpse of Miller's back as the door closes behind him.

"What do you want?" I hear him spit on an attempted hush. It's a mega fail.

It takes me only a split second to figure that whoever rang the doorbell wasn't George. They would be back at the table by now, and Miller wouldn't be asking that question in such a vicious tone. My pace quickens and so does my heart. I take the door handle and pull, but it shifts only millimeters, the resistance increasing slightly under my tug. I don't want to shout at him and attract Nan's attention, so I wait a few moments until I feel the resistance ease up; then I throw all of my might into yanking it open. It works. I catch Miller stagger slightly from his unexpected loss of grip, his hair falling onto his brow, his shocked blues darting to me.

"Olivia." He hardly contains his sigh of exasperation as he steps toward me and slides a palm onto my nape. Then he shifts to the side, revealing the mystery guest.

"Gregory," I breathe, delighted and cautious all at once. This isn't ideal. I would never have chosen to try to repair our friendship with Miller around, but he's here now and there's nothing I can do about it. Gregory's ticking jaw isn't a good sign that his tolerance of Miller has improved, and Miller's buzzing form touching mine indicates the same response to my friend.

"Nice and cozy," Gregory grinds out with scathing eyes roaming from Miller to me.

"Don't be like that," I say softly, attempting to move toward him and getting nowhere. Miller isn't releasing me, not come hell or high water. "Miller, please." I twist out of his hold and get growled at for my trouble.

"Forget it, Olivia." He reclaims me and I glance up, seeing murder etched all over his face. I don't need this. "What do you want?" Miller's tone is soaked in threat.

"I want to speak to Olivia." Gregory states his request on a snarl, matching Miller's fieriness. They're like two wolves in a staring standoff, heaving and gnashing jaws, each one getting ready to attack, except I'm not sure which one will lose their control first. Gregory's bravado is commendable.

"Then speak."

"Alone."

Miller's head shakes mildly, confidently, supremacy oozing from every pore of his refined physique. "No," he says on a whisper, but the near-silent word is loaded with determination—no raised volume necessary.

Gregory rips his brown eyes from Miller and they land on me with a contemptuous bang. "Fine, you can stay," he relents, the vein in his neck throbbing.

"That's not up for negotiation," Miller clarifies.

My best friend doesn't bless Miller with a disdainful look, instead keeping cold eyes on me. "I'm sorry," he says, with zero sincerity, his face holding the look of indifference that's been apparent since I clapped eyes on him. He doesn't appear or sound sorry in the slightest, yet I'm willing him to be. I want to apologize, too, but for what I don't know. I don't think I have anything to be remorseful for. Nevertheless, I'll willingly offer up an apology if it means I'll get Gregory back. I may have been distracted since our altercation, but he's not been around and it's been gnawing on my conscience. I've missed him terribly.

"I'm sorry, too," I whisper, ignoring Miller's increased breathing and twitching beside me. "I hate this."

I watch as his face drops to match his broad shoulders. He slips a hand into his jeans pocket, his work boots scuffing the pathway beneath. "Baby girl, I hate this, too, but I'm here for you." He lifts tortured eyes to mine. "You need to know that."

Happiness floods me, the hugest weight lifting from my tired shoulders. "Thank you."

"You're welcome," he replies, and then removes something from his pocket. His arm extends toward me with something gripped between his fingers. Confusion replaces the relief, and I definitely don't imagine Miller turning stone cold next to me. "Take it," Gregory prompts, waving his arm forward.

A shimmer of silver catches the porch light, seeming to blind me like low, winter sunlight. Then I notice the perfect scrolled font. Miller's "business" card. My heart beats up to my throat and wedges itself there.

Miller's hand flies out and snatches the card. "Where the fuck did you get this?"

"It doesn't matter," Gregory says calmly, in total control, while I lose control completely, my body vibrating violently with shakes.

"It fucking matters," Miller growls, balling his fist, folding his business card in on itself until it's out of sight. "Where?"

"Fuck you."

Miller's gone from my side in a heartbeat. "Miller!" I scream, but he's fallen into a zone of rage and nothing will pull him back.

Gregory manages to dodge the first blow, but it's not long before both men are crashing to the concrete on a thunderous bang. "Miller!" My frantic screams are hopeless and so are my frozen limbs, which I vaguely appreciate through my fog of panic. Getting between these two would be foolish, but I hate feeling so useless. "Please stop," I cry quietly. The tears building in my eyes swell and release, streaming down my cheeks, blurring the painful sight before me.

"You should've kept your fucking nose out!" Miller roars, yanking Gregory up by his shirt and landing a sickening punch to his jaw, sending my friend's head snapping to the side. "Why the *fuck* does everyone think they have some god-given right to interfere?"

Smack!

Another punishing blow splits Gregory's lip and blood bursts from the wound, coating Miller's knuckles. "Leave us the fuck alone!"

"Miller, stop!" I shout, attempting to step forward, but my legs turn to jelly, making grasping the wall essential if I'm to stay on my feet. "Miller!"

He's straddling Gregory on the ground, his whole body heaving, sweat streaming down his face. This is the worst I've seen him. He's completely out of control. He yanks Gregory's torso up by the scruff of his collar bunched in each fist. "I'll rip out the spine of anyone who tries to take her away from me. You're no exception." He shoves Gregory to his back and stands, all the while keeping wild eyes on my friend. "You'll keep this to yourself."

"Miller," I cry on a sniffle, struggling to gain a steadying breath through my choked sobbing.

He turns slowly toward me and I don't like what I see. Irrationality. Unruliness. Lunacy. This side of him, the violent, crazy, reckless part, I don't like at all. It frightens me, not only because of the damage that he can so easily inflict, but also because he seems so unaware while he's in this destructive mode. Our eyes hold for the longest time, me trying to bring him back around before he does further damage, him heaving uncontrollably before me. Gregory's in a bad way, struggling to get to his feet behind Miller, clenching his stomach and hissing in pain. He didn't deserve that.

"She needs to know," Gregory mumbles, standing half bent, clearly in tremendous pain. His barely decipherable words register loud and clear. He thinks I don't know. He thought he was coming here to share some information on the man he hates that would see me throwing him out of my life. He thinks that's why Miller has lost the plot, not simply because of his interference and risk of exposure to Nan, which I know now is a massive concern to him. My poor heart is still in overdrive, pounding in my chest, and this realization has just flipped it up another gear.

"I already knew," I say on a breathy gasp, keeping my eyes on Miller's. "I know what he was and what he did." And I know this news will cripple Gregory. He thought he had the perfect reason for me to leave Miller, and he thought he'd be able to comfort me as I dealt with the horrid revelation. He was hoping for that the most. But he's wrong, and I'm fully aware that this could equal the final blow to our friendship. He'll never understand why I'm still with Miller, and I doubt my ability to make him see why or the strength required to do it.

"You knew?" His tone is now dripping with pure shock. "You know that this piece of shit is a fucking gigolo?"

"An escort," I correct. "And *was*." I allow my eyes to travel over Miller's pulsing shoulders to Gregory's folded body. He's starting to straighten up.

The disbelief on his face spikes unwanted and unwarranted shame to attack me. "What the fuck has happened to you?" His look of hatred slices right through me, and I clamp my lips together to prevent a sob from ripping past them, knowing it'll trigger Miller's insanity again.

I don't register the door swinging open behind me, but I do

register Nan's age-worn voice. "Dinner's getting cold!" she snaps, and then silence falls for the briefest of moments while she takes in the scene she's happened upon. "What the devil?"

I don't get the chance to even think of what explanation can be given to my grandmother. Gregory springs to life and charges at Miller, throwing himself at his midsection and taking them tumbling down the path onto the street. "You bastard!" he yells, pulling back his fist and sending it catapulting forward on an angry bellow, but Miller's head dodges it, sending Gregory's balled fist into the concrete beside his head. "Fuck!"

Miller's up and dragging Gregory with him, pinning him to the low wall at the end of our front garden.

"Goodness gracious!" Nan flies past me and throws herself into the middle of the two men, her notorious spunk rearing its ugly head. There's no display of fear on her old face, just sheer determination. "Pack it in!" she yells, muscling between them and pushing them apart on a shout. "That's enough!" Both men heave on each side of her, sweating and glaring over her head. She's brave, but my fear for her is rife as I absorb potent anger firing off from both men, showing no sign of receding. She's far from frail, but she's an old lady nonetheless. She shouldn't be intervening between these two men, especially not Miller. He's frenzied, unable to rationalize. "I'm giving you one chance!" she warns. "Cut it out or deal with me!"

Her words put the fear of God in me, but I doubt they'll have any effect on these two. So imagine my shock when both men relax and break the staring deadlock in unison. Then I remember William's light quip.

No woman made me quake in my boots, Olivia. Only your grandmother.

"That's more like it." She releases her palms from each man's chest slowly, ensuring they'll remain in place. Her face screws up in disgust as she flicks eyes heated with anger between Miller and

Gregory. "Don't you dare make me pull you apart again. Do you hear me?"

I'm staggered when Miller nods short and sharp and Gregory sniffs an agreement, wiping his bleeding nose.

"Good." She points to the front door. "Get in the house before the neighbors start talking."

I remain a quiet, stunned observer as Nan takes the reins and regains control of the horrid situation, pushing both men toward the house when neither moves fast enough for her liking. Miller's head is dropped, and I know it's in shame at having my dear grandmother, a woman who he respects, bear witness to this aggression. I'm only thankful that she didn't appear moments earlier when she would've caught Miller in full psycho action.

Gregory passes me first, then Nan, and when Miller approaches my motionless form, he slowly drags disturbed eyes to my traumatized ones and stops in front of me. He's a disheveled wreck, his shirt and waistcoat all askew and ripped at the shoulder, his hair wild and tangled.

"I apologize," he says quietly, and then turns and strides down the pathway, his long legs eating up the distance to his car in no time.

"Miller!" I shout, panicked as I go in pursuit of him. My unsteady legs are of no assistance and tires screech away from the curb before I make it to the end of the path. My hand instinctively reaches for my chest, like a bit of pressure might calm the erratic thumping. It doesn't and I'm not sure there is anything that will.

"Livy?" George's low husk brings my eyes away from Miller's disappearing Mercedes to his confused form approaching the house. "Sweetheart, what's going on?"

I give in to my emotions again and fall apart, letting him wrap me in a bear hug and hold my weak body up. "It's all gone horribly wrong," I cry into his cable-knit jumper, letting his squidgy chest mould around my diminutive frame.

"Oh dearie me," he soothes, rubbing calming circles into my back. "Let's get you inside."

George takes a firm hold of my shoulders and guides me up the path, shutting the door gently behind us. Then he steers me toward the kitchen, where we find Nan dabbing Gregory's nose with a damp compress. I can smell the TCP and hear Gregory's continued hisses, proof that it's Nan's treatment of choice. "Hold still," she chastises him, annoyance still rife in her tone.

Gregory eyes me as George pushes me into a chair and hands me his clean hanky, and Nan swings around, clocking the loss of one person and the gain of another. "You're late!" she yells at a poor, innocent George. "Dinner's ruined and I've had a wrestling match in my front garden!"

"Now hold on one minute, Josephine Taylor!" George's back straightens and mine tenses. She's in no mood to take any back chat, and George should note this from the annoyance pouring from her short, plump body. It doesn't deter him, though. "I've just arrived and I can see that dinner being ruined is the least of our worries, so why don't you put a lid on it and let me help sort out these two sorry states."

She slaps the compress over Gregory's lip harshly on a few stutters of shock. "Where's Miller?" she blurts, her fury now directed at me.

"He left," I admit, wiping at my eyes with the hanky and stealing a risky glance at Gregory. His eyes are narrowed and it isn't because they're closing up from the swelling. He's going to have a shiner on one eye for sure, the opposite eye to the one Miller blackened during their last clash.

My battered friend grumbles something on a sardonic laugh, but I don't ask him to repeat himself because I know for certain I won't want to hear whatever he's said, and neither will Nan or George.

"What's happened?" George asks, taking up the seat next to me.

"Damned if I know." Nan covers Gregory's split lip with a padded plaster and presses around the edges to ensure it's stuck tight, ignoring the hisses of protest coming from her patient. "All I know is that Gregory and Miller seem to dislike each other, yet no one is willing to enlighten me as to why." She turns her expectant eyes toward me, making me drop my gaze to the table, evading her.

Truth is, Miller and Gregory hated each other before Gregory found out about Miller's tainted past. Now I can only surmise that they categorically despise each other. There's nothing that'll fix this. I can have one man or the other. Guilt rips through me as I watch my oldest friend, my *only* friend, being taped up—guilt for being the root cause of his pain and injuries, and guilt because I know that I won't pick him.

I stand and pull every set of eyes in the room to me, each body stilling to gauge my next move.

Rounding the table calmly, I lean down to kiss Gregory's cheek. "When you love someone, you love them because of who they are and how they came to be that person," I whisper into his ear, and immediately appreciate that Nan's acute hearing might have caught my declaration. I pray Gregory keeps this information to himself—not for me or Miller, but for Nan. It'll stir too many ghosts. "I didn't give up on him and I'm not about to now." I straighten up and walk calmly out of the kitchen, leaving my family behind to go and comfort my someone.

Chapter Sixteen

The masses of sparkling mirrors lining the lobby of Miller's apartment block bounce my reflection everywhere, the image of me, tear-stained and hopeless, unavoidable. The doorman tips his hat politely, and I force a meager smile in return, choosing to ride up to Miller's in the elevator rather than take the few hundred stairs that I've almost become unaffected by. I keep my eyes forward when the doors meet and I'm confronted with more mirrors, looking through myself and avoiding the direct ugly sight of the waiflike woman that I'm faced with.

Once I've been in the elevator for what seems like forever, the doors slide open and I force my legs to carry me to the shiny black front door. It takes even more mental encouragement to knock. I would question whether he's even here...if it weren't for the heavy air surrounding me. Miller's anger is lingering in the space, closing me in and suffocating me. I can feel it spreading over my skin and settling deep.

I jump back when the door flies open on a harsh yank and I'm met by Miller, looking no better than he did when he stalked away nearly an hour ago. There's been no attempt to restore his perfect self, his hair still mussed, his shirt and waistcoat still ripped, and his eyes still reflecting rage. A glass of whisky sits in his hand, his fingers coated in Gregory's blood. White fingertips indicate the unforgiving grip he has of the glass as he brings it to his mouth and tips the rest of the contents down his throat, keeping steely eyes on me. I'm fidgeting, my eyes now darting across the floor at my feet, but they fly up when I catch an almost undetectable shift of his shoes. Or stagger. He's drunk, and when I look harder, focus on those eyes that never fail to capture my attention, I see something more—something unfamiliar—and it catapults my unease to a place beyond anything I've ever experienced while in Miller's presence. I've felt vulnerable before, hopeless and helpless, but always on an unsure level. I've never felt frightened like this, not even during his psychotic displays of madness. This is a different fear. It's snaking up my spine and wrapping itself around my neck, making words impossible and breathing challenging. It's my nightmare. The one where he leaves me.

"Go home, Livy." His tongue is heavy in his mouth, making his words slur slowly, but it's not his usual, purposeful lazy rasp. The door slams in my face, echoing around me, and I jump back, startled at his maliciousness. I'm pounding the wood with my fist before I can decide if it's a wise move, fear sailing through me.

"Open the door, Miller!" I yell, not relenting with my hammering of the black, shiny wood, ignoring the fast numbing sensation spreading across the side of my balled hand. "Open!"

Bang, bang, bang!

I'm going nowhere. I'll hammer all night long if I have to. He doesn't get to shut me out of his apartment *or* his life.

Bang, bang, bang!

"Miller!"

I'm suddenly attempting to hit thin air, and it sends me on a few disoriented staggers forward. I just manage to steady my flailing body before it collides with Miller's. "I said go home." He's restocked on dark liquid, the tumbler near to overflowing.

"No." I raise my chin in a brave act of defiance.

"I don't want you to see me like this." He steps forward hostilely, an attempt to make me retreat, but I stand firm, unwilling to be frightened off. We're closer because of my tenacity, nearly chest to chest, and he's breathing liquor vapors all over my heated cheeks. "I won't ask again."

I inwardly wither on the spot, yet sheer determination is refusing to allow him to see it. "No," I fire simply and confidently. He's trying to repel me. "Why are you doing this?"

In obvious uncertainty, he polishes off the tumbler of dark liquid, a slight wince and gasp spilling from his mouth that's accompanied by potent liquor fumes. They make my nose wrinkle in distaste, both at the sight of Miller and the smell of the alcohol.

"I *won't* ask again." I push the words through my clenched jaw, playing him at his own game.

He looks me up and down, musing quietly, mumbling incoherent words under his breath as he does. Then his heavy gaze lazily climbs back up the length of my body, appearing to be its usual effort, but drunkenness is the cause this time, not Miller's customary sultry way. He begins to sway. "I'm fucked up."

"I know." I don't disagree with him. He's speaking the cold, hard truth.

"I'm dangerous."

"I know."

"But not to you."

My heart shows signs of life again. I knew that. Deep down, I knew that. "I know."

His head performs something between a nod of satisfaction and an uncontrolled bob upon his wide shoulders. "Good." He turns and wobbles through his apartment, leaving me to shut the door and follow behind. I know where he's headed before he momentarily stops and changes course, going to the drinks cabinet. He's drunk enough, at least to me. However, Miller has other ideas.

He clangs the bottle against the glass and tips more on the cabinet than into his glass. "Bollocks!" he curses, dropping the empty bottle haphazardly between the masses of other bottles, causing a loud clattering of glass. "Fucking mess!"

On an exasperated sigh, I wander up behind him and set about rearranging the bottles and wiping down the mess he's made, hoping that restoring part of his perfect world might inject some peace into him.

"Thank you," he murmurs, so quietly I almost don't hear.

"You're welcome." I can feel his stare burning through my profile as I mess with the bottles, taking my time... or biding it.

Bang!

I fly around quickly toward the sound, Miller a little slower.

Bang, bang, bang!

My previously settling heart rate ramps up a few gears, and I look to Miller, who's staring in the direction of the door, too. But he doesn't seem in a rush to go and find out what the commotion is, so I make toward the entrance hall and circle the table, just as another harsh knock rings out through Miller's apartment.

"Wait," Miller snaps, grabbing my upper arm and pulling me to a stop. "Stay here." He passes me, his usually easy strides challenged by alcohol. I remain still, my mind racing as I watch him glance through the peephole. I can virtually see his hackles rise, and it prompts me to step forward, cautious but too curious to stop myself. He pulls the door open a fraction and makes to step out into the corridor, but his obvious plan to hide our visitor is totally defeated when they push their way into the apartment with ease, no doubt due to Miller's less-than-stable frame.

Now my hackles jump up, too, and my jaw instantly tightens when William presents himself to me, his body oozing authority. He regards me closely for a few moments before dragging his gray gaze over to Miller's wrecked form. This isn't ideal. Miller looks shocking, and now William is going to want to know why.

"What have you been up to?" William asks, flat and even, like it's no surprise and maybe he already knows.

"That's not your concern," Miller slurs, slamming the door. "You're not welcome here."

I feel the need to back Miller up, but that curious part of me has multiplied, as has the caution. So I remain with my lips sealed, soaking up the animosity batting back and forth between these two men.

"And you're not welcome in Olivia's life," William retorts, turning to me. He must see the disbelief on my face, not that he seems in the least bit perturbed by it. "You're coming with me."

I cough my objection, noting Miller behind William twitching slightly, but not nearly enough for me to be sure that he'll intervene. *Please don't tell me he's going to back William up!*

"No, I'm not," I reply surely, squaring my shoulders. I'm staggered by Miller's lack of input thus far, especially after his violent reaction to Gregory's interference only an hour ago.

"Olivia," William sighs, "you really are trying my patience."

I brace myself for another comment on my mother, worrying about the anger simmering within me just at the thought of William making reference to her. If he comes out and says what I know he's thinking, then I might be giving Miller a run for his money in the crazy department. "You are trying mine!"

William disguises his recoil well, and I know it's because he doesn't want to show a scrap of compassion in front of Miller. No, now he'll uphold that powerful reputation... which means it could get very ugly, very quickly. "I've told you, you don't belong here with him."

My breath catches slightly, remembering William saying a version of those words to me when I was seventeen. I was sitting in his office, drunk. I didn't belong with William. I don't belong with Miller. "Where do I belong?" I ask, making William eye me cautiously. "It seems you don't think I belong anywhere. So tell me, where the fucking hell do I belong?"

"Oliv—" Miller pipes up, stepping forward, but I cut him straight off, not liking the potential of him agreeing with William.

"No!" I yell. "Everyone thinks they know what's best for me. What about me? What about what I know?"

"Calm down." Miller's by my side, unsteady, trying to soothe me by taking my nape and kneading gently. It won't work. Not now.

"I know I'm supposed to be here!" I yell, making myself shake with my building frustration. "I've been stumbling through my life since you sent me away." I point an accusing finger in William's direction. It makes him withdraw slightly. "Now I have him." I throw my arm around Miller's waist and plant myself to his side. "The only way you'll stop me from being with him is if you put me six feet under!"

William's speechless, Miller is stiff beside me, and I'm convulsing with anger, searching deep for the focus I need to take some steadying breaths and calm down. I gulp back air. I feel like I'm having a panic attack.

"Shhh." Miller pulls me in closer and drops a kiss on the top of my head. It's not a full-on *thing*, but it's working to a degree. I turn into him and hide, and his lips meet the top of my head, pecking and humming as I clench my eyes shut.

It's a long, long time before someone speaks. "How do you feel about her?" William asks, reluctance and caution rife in his tone.

I stay where I am, dreading what Miller might say. Fascination just won't cut it. I can feel his heart pounding, can almost hear it, too.

"She's the blood in my veins." He speaks clearly and softly. "She's the air in my lungs." There's a slight pause, and I'm sure I hear William inhale a shocked breath. "She's the bright, hopeful light in my tortured darkness. I'm warning you, Anderson. Don't try to take her away from me."

I blink back my tears and burrow deeper into his chest, grateful he's backed me up. That silence falls again. It's eerily quiet, and then I hear breath being drawn and I know whose it is. "I couldn't care less what happens to you," William says. "But the second I get a whiff that Olivia is in danger, I'll be coming for you, Hart."

And with that, the door slams shut and we're alone. Miller's hold loosens on me, the vibrations of his body receding, and he releases me when I really want him to hold me tighter. He paces on unsteady legs to his drinks cabinet and clumsily restocks on whisky, knocking it back fast and gasping. I remain still and silent, then after what seems like centuries, he sighs. "Why are you still in my life, sweet girl?"

"Because you fought to keep me in it," I remind him without hesitance, forcing myself to sound sure. "You've threatened to rip the spine out of anyone who tries to take me away from you. Are you regretting that?"

I steel myself for an unwanted reply as he faces me, but his gaze is dropped. "I regret dragging you into my world."

"Don't," I snap, not liking his loss of fortitude now that William has gone. "I came willingly and I'm staying willingly." I choose to ignore the referral to *my world.* I'm getting sick of hearing the words *my world*, yet hardly anything about it.

More whisky is tipped down his neck. "I meant it." He makes an attempt to focus on my eyes but gives up, turning and wandering off across the lounge instead.

"Meant what?"

"My threat." His arse meets the low coffee table and he places his glass accurately to the side, despite his drunkenness. He even swivels it before releasing it, now happy with its placing. His curl is present and clearly tickling his forehead because he flicks it away and then drops his face into his palms, elbows braced on his knees. "My temper has always been a burden, Olivia, but I frighten myself when it comes to my overprotectiveness with you."

"Possessiveness."

His head lifts and a frown wriggles its way onto his forehead. "Pardon?"

A diminutive smile pulls at the corners of my mouth at his show of manners when he's so intoxicated and we're in such a wretched place. I walk across to him and kneel between his feet, and he looks down at me, watching as I remove his elbows from his knees and hold his hands in mine. "Possessiveness," I repeat.

"I want to protect you."

"From what?"

"Interferers." He drifts into thought, his eyes looking past me for a few moments before returning to me. "I'll wind up killing someone." His admission should shock me, yet his acknowledgment of his unreasonable flaw strangely settles me. I'm about to suggest counseling, anger management, anything to get this under control, but something stops me.

"William is interfering," I blurt.

"William and I have an understanding." Miller stumbles over his words. "Although you were never in the equation before. He's walking a thin line." The abhorrence in his drunken tone is palpable.

"What understanding?" I don't like the sound of this. They both have terrible tempers. My guess is that both men know what damage they can do to each other.

He shakes his head on a frustrated curse. "He wants to protect you, as do I. You're probably the safest woman in London."

My eyes widen at the inaccuracy of his comment and my hands drop his. I disagree. I feel like the most *exposed* woman in London. But I don't tell him so. I fight off my urge to continue the

William-Miller debate. William hates Miller, and the feeling is totally mutual. I know why, so I should just get used to it. "Do you want the good news or the bad news?" I ask as I stand and offer my hand. My unease subsides slightly when I catch a brief twinkle in Miller's eyes. It's familiar and needed.

"Bad." He rests his hand in mine and studies our joining as I secure my grip and give a little tug, encouraging him to stand, which he does with too much effort.

"The bad news is you're going to have a bitch of a hangover." I mirror his tiny smile and start leading him to his bedroom. "The good news is I'll be here to nurse you when you're feeling sorry for yourself."

"You'll let me worship you. That'll make me feel better."

I raise doubtful eyebrows over my shoulder as we enter his bedroom. "Will you be in any fit state?"

He drops his arse to the bed when I give him a little shove in the shoulder. "Don't question my ability to satisfy you, sweet girl." His palms slide around to my bum and apply pressure, pulling me between his spread thighs. He's looking up at me with a carnal stare that's leading to one thing.

I shake my head. "I'm not sleeping with you when you're drunk."

"I beg to differ," he counters, his hands working their way to my front and sliding under my top. His eyes are challenging me to stop him, and although I have just been flung into desire overload, I'm not budging. It takes every molecule of strength that I possess, but I locate it fast before I'm tossed into surrender mode. I don't want to be worshipped by a drunken Miller. I remove his hands on another shake of my head.

"Don't deny me," he breathes, pulling me forward onto his lap and arranging my legs across him. I have no choice but to curl an arm around his shoulder, bringing me closer to his face. The alcohol fumes only increase my willpower.

"Stop it," I warn, not prepared to fall victim to his tactics. "You're in no fit state and if I kiss you, then I'll probably end up as drunk as you are."

"I'm fine and perfectly capable." His hips push into my bottom. "I need destressing."

He has a nerve! I'm the one who needs destressing, but if I'm honest with myself, then Miller taking me under the influence of alcohol makes me nervous. I know he fights to maintain control during our encounters and a belly full of whisky won't aid him.

"What?" he asks, regarding me with suspicion, obviously perceiving my wandering thoughts. "Tell me."

"It's nothing." I brush off his concern and attempt to remove my body from his lap. And get nowhere.

"Olivia?"

"Let me give you your *thing*."

"No, tell me what's troubling that beautiful mind of yours." He's insistent, firming up his hold of me. "I won't ask again."

"You're drunk," I blurt quietly, ashamed for doubting the care he takes with me. "Alcohol makes people lose reason and control." Now I'm cringing. Miller doesn't need whisky to lose control, and both scrapes with Gregory are evidence of that. And the hotel encounter…

I remain on his lap and let him process my worries while I twist my ring nervously around and around, wishing I could retract my words. He's rigid beneath me, every hard plane of his body seeming to bruise my flesh. Then he takes hold of my face, squeezing my cheeks gently, and brings it to confront him. He looks remorseful, which increases my guilt *and* my shame. "My self-hatred claws at my dark soul daily." He seems to have rapidly gathered something close to soberness, maybe my omission feeding it. His blue eyes seem stronger and his mouth is now forming clear, exact words. "Never fear me, I beg you. I could be of no harm to you, Olivia." His somber statement takes the edge off my despondency, but only a little. Miller fails to comprehend the destruction he can cause by hurting me emotionally. That's what I fear the most. Losing him. I can recover from physical injuries in time, if unintentionally caught up in one of his psychotic outbursts, but no amount of time will fix the mental injuries he can inflict upon me. And that terrifies me.

"It's like you take leave of your senses," I begin cautiously, choosing my words wisely.

"I do," he mutters before nodding for me to continue.

"I'm not frightened for me; I'm scared for your victim and *you*."

"My victim?" He coughs. He's not happy with my choice of word. "Livy, I don't prey on innocent people. And please don't worry about me."

"I *do* worry about you, Miller. You'll be thrown into jail if someone presses charges, and I don't like seeing you hurt." I reach up and brush over a faint blemish on his bristly cheek.

"That won't happen," he sighs, pulling me into his chest and attempting to rub some comfort into me. Weirdly, it works, and I melt into his relaxed body, matching his tired sigh. He sounds confident. Too confident. "Gorgeous girl, I've said it once before and on this occasion I have no problem repeating myself." He falls to his back, taking me with him, and tussles with me until I'm cuddled into his side and he has access to my face. Feathery kisses trail from one cheek to the other and back again. "The only thing in this world that can cause me pain is currently being held in my arms." He lifts my chin so my lips are level with his and the lingering stench of whisky invades my nose. I find it easy to disregard. He's gazing at me like I'm the only thing that exists in his world, those eyes easing my remaining anxiety from this long day. His lips move in and I brace myself, my hand slipping onto his chest to feel him. "May I?" he whispers, pausing mere millimeters from my mouth.

"You're asking?"

"I'm aware that I smell like a distillery," he murmurs, making me smile. "And I'm sure I won't taste much better."

"I beg to differ." All of my reluctance to let him have me in these circumstances diminishes under his tenderness, and I close the small gap between us, our mouths clashing more forcefully than I intended. I don't care. Disinclination has been hijacked by an urgent need to reinstate my serenity and Miller's recently relaxing disposition. I can taste the whisky, but Miller's essence dominates the alcohol, drowning my senses with pure yearning. It's making me light-headed. The only instructions I can find in my suddenly lust-filled mind are ones telling me to let him worship me. That *that* will chase away my woes. *That* will make the world right again. That will calm him. Our passion collides and everything else is of no importance. It's perfect in these moments, but hard to hold on to when faced with endless resistance.

Miller rolls to his back, keeping our mouths fused, and locks one palm on my nape and his other under my bottom, ensuring I'm secure in his clutch. "Savored," he mumbles against my lips, that one familiar word making me see past my consuming desperation for him and follow his demand to slow things down. My fear was unwarranted. I'm the one being told to rein it in, Miller appearing to have full control and lucidity, despite the obscene amount of whisky that must have passed his lips. "Better," he praises, molding at my neck. "So much better."

"Hmmm." I'm not prepared to release him to speak my agreement, choosing to hum it instead. I feel his lips spread into a smile through our kiss and that *does* make me pull away, and pull away fast. Catching a glimpse of one of Miller's rare smiles will send me delirious with happiness. I'm sitting up fast, wiping my hair from my eyes, and when my view is clear, I see it. It's something else, a no-holds-barred, megawatt smile that sends me giddy. He's always devastating, even when he looks downright miserable, but right now he's surpassed perfect. He's ruffled, tatty, and messy, but utterly beautiful, and when I should be returning his smile, matching his ease and cherishing the rare sight, I start crying instead. All of the crap that today has dealt me seems to come collectively together and pour from my eyes in silent, uncontrollable sobs. I feel silly, overwrought, and weak, and in an attempt to hide it, I bury my face in my palms and blindly remove my body from his.

The only sound in the peaceful air encompassing us is my shallow sobs as Miller silently shifts, seeming to take forever to find my shuddering body—probably because his usually stealth movements are hampered by too much alcohol. But he eventually makes it to me and embraces me, sighing heavily into my neck and delicately rubbing calming circles into my back. "Don't cry," he whispers, his voice like sandpaper, rough and low. "We'll survive. Please don't cry." His tenderness and barely spoken understanding only escalate my emotions, making clinging to him tightly my only purpose.

"Why can't people leave us alone?" I ask, my words disjointed.

"I don't know," he admits. "Come here." He collects my hands from the back of his neck and holds them between us, fiddling with my ring unconsciously as he watches me fight my tears away. "I wish I could be perfect for you."

His admission cripples me. "You *are* perfect," I argue, however wrong I know I am deep down. There's nothing perfect about Miller Hart, except for his visual appeal and incessant obsession to have everything surrounding him precise. "You're perfect to me."

"I appreciate your unrelenting belief, especially since I'm drunk right now and have shamed myself in front of your grandmother." He shakes his head on a frustrated exhale and reaches for his head, holding it for a few moments as if the consequences of his actions have just registered, or maybe a hangover has.

"She was pissy," I tell him, seeing no reason to try to make him feel better. He'll need to face her wrath eventually.

"I gathered that when she manhandled me up the garden path."

"You deserved it."

"I concur," he accepts willingly. "I'll call her. No, I'll visit." His lips straighten and he appears to think hard about something before refocusing his attention on me. "Do you think I can win her over by offering a bite of my buns?"

My lips press together as he raises his eyebrows, looking for a serious answer. Then he loses the battle to maintain his serious face, his twitching lip lifting a smidgen. "Ha!" I laugh, shocked by his comedy streak, all sadness sucked up by humor. I lose control. My head falls back and I fall apart atop him, shoulders jumping, stomach aching, and tears now springing from amusement, which is so much more appealing than the despair of a few moments ago.

"Much better," I hear Miller conclude, gathering me into his arms and striding across his room to the bathroom. I'm not sure if the staggers and sways are a result of Miller's drunkenness or my persistent jerks in his arms. He places me with accuracy onto the vanity unit and leaves me to collect my hysteria while he unbuttons his waistcoat, regarding me with a dash of humor on his heart-stopping face.

"I'm sorry." I chuckle, concentrating on breathing deeply to dampen down the shakes.

"Don't be. Nothing gives me greater pleasure than seeing you so happy." He shrugs out of his waistcoat and I'm stupidly delighted when I see him fold it neatly before slipping it deftly into the washing basket. "Well, something else does, but your happiness comes a close second." He starts on his shirt, the first button revealing a slither of taut, tempting flesh.

I stop laughing immediately. "You should laugh more. It—"

"Makes me less intimidating," he finishes for me. "Yes, you've told me. But I think I—"

"Express yourself just fine." I reach forward and assist his fumbling fingers with the tiny buttons, then help him slide the white cotton from his shoulders. "Perfect," I sigh, sitting back to relish in my stunning view, watching with lusty eyes as every muscle of his super-perfect torso undulates while he folds his shirt. He places it skillfully in the washing basket and he's back before me, arms draped limply at his sides, chin dropped, eyes heavy. I soak up his concentrated stare and lift my hands to catch a feel of the harsh stubble that's darkening his face. I'm allowed to take my time feeling him, my fingers tracing the planes of his jaw, drifting up to the corners of his eyes, and tenderly smoothing over his lids when they close for me. I cherish every part of him with my eyes and touch until I'm working my fingertips down his arms and onto his hands. "Let me fix this," I say, turning over his hand, revealing knuckles reddened with blood and a little blemishing.

His eyes open and fall to my fingers threading through his, and his hand flexes in my hold, but he doesn't wince or hiss with pain. "In the shower." He shakes me away and takes the hem of my top, working it up my body, forcing me to lift my arms so he can rid me of the material. Then my bra is slowly removed, exposing my modest breasts that feel swollen and heavy under his appreciative, if a little drunken, gaze. My nipples harden to pebbles, tingling sweetly as the pad of his thumb brushes gently over each in turn. "Perfect," he says, leaning in and planting a chaste kiss on my parted lips. "Jump down."

I follow through on his soft order and slide from the counter to my feet, kicking my Converse off and taking the initiative to begin on his trousers while he, too, removes his shoes. There's no rush, each of us happy to take our time undressing the other until we're both naked. I watch him collect a foil packet from the cupboard, his fingers fiddling clumsily as he slides the condom out, so I step forward and take it from him. I feel comfortable as I sheathe him, feeling his blues burning into my face, and once I'm done, he's swiftly lifting me to his body with ease. My limbs respond on impulse and coil around him. We're nothing but skin on skin, heart on heart, need on need. He keeps us to the side of the shower spray while it warms up, and once he's happy that it's at a comfortable temperature, he takes us under and stands silently holding me while water rains down and washes away the dirt, the tension, the doubt, the pain.

"Are you comfortable?" he asks.

"Perfect." It's the only word I can think to use. I smile into his shoulder and pull back, getting his perfect face, all wet and dazzling, into my sight. "Can I stay with you tonight?"

"Of course."

"Thank you." I show my appreciation by nibbling at his rough chin.

"It wasn't really up for discussion," he informs me, taking me to the wall and encouraging me to rest my back against it. "Too cold?"

I suck in a shocked breath as the coolness of the mosaic tiles spreads across my back. "A little." He goes to peel me away but I stiffen, stopping him. "No, I'm used to it now."

He eyes me doubtfully but doesn't challenge my little white lie. "You're all slippery and wet," he muses, widening his stance and moving his palms to the rear of my thighs. His intentions are clear and longed for, and my hitching breath tells him so. "I want to slide myself into your core and bathe in the fulfillment that you reward me with."

I wheeze shallow breaths of anticipation. "Fulfillment by worshipping."

"By acceptance," he corrects me, rearing back and taking a hold of his arousal. "You give me the greatest pleasure by accepting me in my entirety, not just by accepting me into this beautiful body."

I'm at serious risk of breaking down on him again, his reverent words immobilizing me. "There's nothing more natural to me."

"My gorgeous, sweet girl." He takes my lips as he slips past my swelling folds, pushing deep and high on a strangled groan.

The instant sensation of his thickness submerged to capacity within me pulls my back straight and I whimper, trying to meet the steady rhythm of his tongue as it seduces my mouth while he holds himself inside me, unmoving, twitching, and groaning.

"Am I hurting you?"

"No." I'm adamant, regardless of the fact that there's mild discomfort.

"Still scope for breaking in?"

It will determine whether I fuck you hard immediately, or break you in first.

"Always." I smile and pull away, resting the back of my head against the wall to lose myself in Miller and his wondrous eyes, rather than savor the attention of his addictive mouth.

On a subtle nod, he withdraws slowly, making my eyes flutter and my stomach furl, too many gratifying elements attacking me at once—the feel of him, his worshipping, the sight of him, his smell, his attentiveness, and my favorite wayward curl—all giving me glorious, inexorable pleasure. I brace myself for his advance and when it happens, exact and expertly, a shallow cry of gratification gushes past my lips. I pant, refusing to shut my eyes and miss a moment of his face contorting with heady craving. It sharpens his features. I could pass out just at the sight of him.

"How does that feel?" He chokes the words out and retreats again, slipping out almost all the way before tilting his hips up, sending him plunging on a shaky exhale of breath.

"Good." I grasp his shoulders and clench my teeth, soaking up each delicious drive. He's into his stride now, pumping his hips continuously, each thrust as controlled and measured as the last.

"Just good?"

"Amazing!" I yelp, catching a dash of friction on my clitoris that sends me wild. "Shit!"

"That's more like it," he muses to himself, repeating the move that had me cursing a second before.

"Oh God! Oh shit! Miller!"

"Again?" he teases, not waiting for the answer he knows I'm going to give, delivering hastily instead.

I'm out of my mind. His rigorous flow is crippling me, but he's as controlled as ever, watching me fall apart against him. "I need to come," I breathe, feeling desperation setting in. I need to release all of the day's stress and trauma on a satisfied moan, maybe even a scream, as I climax.

I bore down onto him when his momentum remains slow and defined, bunching his sodden hair in my fingers. The onslaught of pressure is becoming too much to handle, and Miller's expanding and throbbing length buried deep is a massive relief. He's close, too.

"It feels too good, Olivia." His eyes clench shut and his hips judder forward, pushing me a little closer. I'm tinkering on the edge, half my body dangling, waiting for the rest to follow and send me into an abyss of exploding stars.

"Please," I plead, as always never opposed to begging during these moments. "Please, please, please!"

"Bollocks!" His curse signals his surrender and he pulls back, takes a long, disciplined breath, then fixes me in place with darkening eyes as he surges forward on a severe shout. "Jesus, Olivia!"

My eyes close as my orgasm takes hold, my head going lax but my body rigid as it strives to cope with the flashes of pressure stabbing harshly at the very tip of my sex. I'm pinned against the tiles, our bodies compressed together, vibrating and slipping, and fitful breathing sings around my fuzzy mind. He's stealing nibbles and sucks of my throat as I pant up to the ceiling, and my arms refuse to play ball any longer, dropping to my sides, my palms slapping against the wall. The only thing holding me in place is Miller's body. My world has clicked back into place and is turning steadily on its axis, and an intoxicating cocktail of sweat, sex, and alcohol is rife, reminding me that he's still drunk.

"You okay?" I wheeze, letting my head drop to bury my nose in his sopping hair. That's the only action I can muster, leaving my arms hanging lifelessly by my sides.

He shifts and straightens a little, the movement causing his softening length to stroke my inner wall deliciously. "How could I not be?" Pulling his face from my neck, he takes both of my hands and brings them to his lips, pressing them firmly against my knuckles and keeping me pinned to the wall by his body. "How could I be anything but blissful when I have you safe in my arms?"

My sated smile of contentment doesn't encourage one from Miller. He's content, too, but I don't need to hear it. I can see it. "I love your drunken bones, Miller Hart."

"And my drunken bones are deeply fascinated by you, Olivia Taylor." He indulges in my mouth for a few blissful moments before gently easing me away from the wall. "I didn't hurt you, did I?" His lovely face is etched with genuine concern as his wobbly gaze travels all over my wet face.

I'm quick to reassure him. "You were the perfect gentleman."

His grin is immediate.

"What?"

"I was just thinking how lovely you look in my shower."

"You think I look lovely everywhere."

"Best of all in my bed. Can you stand?"

I nod and let my legs slide down his body, but my mind starts venturing off in another direction. My hands meet his pecs and I drift down his body while keeping my eyes on him as he watches me. I want to taste him, but my tempting tactics are halted when the tops of my arms are seized and I'm tugged back up to his lips. "I get to taste *you*," he mumbles quietly, lavishing me with his lips. My wayward thoughts scatter all over the shower. "And you taste out of this world." He takes my neck once the wall isn't supporting us any longer, almost certainly using me for assistance.

Then I'm gently guided toward the shower's exit as he slides the condom off. "I need to wash my hair."

He pushes onward, unconcerned by my concern. "We'll do it in the morning."

"But it'll look like I've shoved my finger in a plug socket." It's wild enough with the backing of a good conditioner...which reminds me. "You have very untamed hair, too."

"So we'll be untamed together." He disposes of the condom and collects a towel, then slowly drags it all over me before taking care of himself.

"How's your head?"

I'm gently pushed on, into the bedroom. "Fine and dandy," he mutters, and I laugh, earning a frown as we reach the bed. "Please share what's got you all giggly."

"You!" What else?

"What about me?"

"You saying you're fine and dandy when you're clearly not. Headache?"

"Early signs, yes," he concedes on a huff, releasing his clasp of me to clench his head instead.

I smile and set about removing all of the fancy cushions from his bed and placing them neatly in the designated storage compartment. Then I pull the covers back. "Hop in." I drag my greedy gaze from his eyes, all the way down the perfection of his lean physique to his perfect feet. They start to pace the carpet toward me, prompting my eyes to climb back up the length of him, reaching those blues as he reaches me. "Please," I whisper.

"Please what?"

I've forgotten what I'm asking of him. I search my empty head under the observation of knowing, salacious blue eyes and find nothing. "I can't remember," I admit.

Bright white teeth blind me. "I believe my sweet girl was bossing me into bed."

My lips purse. "I wasn't bossing."

"I beg to differ." He chuckles. "I quite like it. After you." His arm sweeps in direction toward the bed, his gentlemanly manners taking over.

"I should call Nan."

His smile drops in an instant. I hate that I can draw those rare beams but just as quickly wipe them away. The result as if they were never there and they might not ever return. He's thoughtful for a long moment, struggling to keep his eyes on me. He's ashamed. "Would you be kind enough to inquire if she might be home tomorrow morning?"

I nod my answer. "Get in. I'll be back as soon as I've pacified her."

He slips into the sheets and onto his side, his back away from me. I shouldn't feel compassion, but his remorse is strong and so is my hope that Nan will accept what I know will be a sincere apology.

Finding my top, I wriggle it on and go in search of my bag, finding my phone and seeing endless missed calls from her already. My guilt surges and I don't delay calling her right back.

"Olivia! Damn you, child!"

"Nan," I breathe, letting my naked bottom hit the chair. My eyes close as I prepare for the rant that I know is coming.

"Are you okay?" she asks softly.

I snap my eyes wide open in shock. "Yeah." The word rolls off my tongue slowly, uncertainty plaguing me. There has to be more than that.

"Is Miller okay?"

This question stuns me further, my naked bum starting to shift nervously on the chair. "He's okay."

"I'm glad."

"Me too." It's all I can think to say. No rant? No prying questions? No demand to walk away? I hear her breathe thoughtfully down the line, a lingering, empty space of unspoken words stretching between us.

"Olivia?"

"I'm here."

"Sweetheart, those words you whispered to Gregory."

I swallow hard. I knew she'd heard but hoped she hadn't. There's nothing aged about my grandmother's acute hearing. Humming my acknowledgment, I sit back in my chair and lay my palm across my forehead, ready to ease the pounding head that's about to ensue. It's already working up to a light thudding, just at the thought of explaining those words. "What about them?"

"You're right."

My hand drops and I gaze ahead at nothing in particular, confusion replacing the threatening headache. "I'm right?"

"Yes," she sighs. "I've told you before, we don't choose who we fall in love with. Falling in love is special. Holding on to that love, despite circumstances that could destroy it, is even more special. I hope Miller realizes how lucky he is to have you, my darling girl."

My bottom lip begins to tremble, my throat closing off any words that I'd like to say in return—the most important words being *thank you. Thank you for supporting me—for supporting us, when it feels like the whole of London is on a mission to sabotage what we have. Thank you for accepting Miller. Thank you for understanding, even if you don't know the full truth.* Gregory knows what this could do to her. "I love you, Nan." I swallow hard around my words and the puddles of tears in my eyes start to tumble down my cheeks.

"I love you, too, darling." Her voice is even and strong, yet soaked in emotion. "Are you staying with Miller tonight?"

I nod and sniff, just spitting out a "yes" in response.

"Okay. Sleep tight."

I smile through my tears and use the sound of her loving tone and her words to gather myself and speak. "I won't let the bedbugs bite."

She chuckles, joining me in my fond memories of one of Granddad's favorite bedtime lines. "Get yourself off up those apples and pears," she says, reminding me of another.

"Miller lives in an apartment. There are no stairs to the bedroom."

"Oh, okay." She falls silent for a while. "Are you cream crackered?"

"Exhausted," I confirm on a laugh. "I'm going to bed now."

"Good. Nighty-night."

"Night, Nan." I smile as I cut the call and immediately consider calling back to ask how Gregory is, but stop myself. The ball's in his court. He knows the deal; he knows I'm going nowhere, and he knows that nothing he can say will change that, especially not now. There's nothing more I can say and there's no guarantee he'll listen. It kills me, but I'm not putting myself in the firing line again. If he wants to talk, then he'll call. Satisfied with my decision, I make to leave the kitchen but pause at the doorway, my mind wandering to silly places.

Like the top drawer where I know Miller's date book to be.

I try to disregard my bout of irritating curiosity, I really do, but my damn feet take on a mind of their own and I'm standing looking at the drawer before I can convince myself that it's so very wrong to snoop. It's not that I don't trust him, I wholeheartedly do, but I just feel in the dark, unaware and ignorant, and while that's undoubtedly a good thing, I can't help the raging inquisitiveness from getting the better of me.

Curiosity killed the cat. Curiosity killed the cat. Damn curiosity killed the fucking cat.

I open the drawer, and it's looking up at me, teasing me... tempting me. It's like a magnet to my hand, drawing me in, pulling me closer, and before I know what's happened, the leather book is lying in my palms, feeling like a forbidden spell book. Now I just need the pages to miraculously start flapping open, but after staring at it for way too long, it's still closed. And it should probably stay that way—sealed forever, never to be looked upon again. History closed.

But that would be in a world where curiosity doesn't exist.

I shift the book in my palms and slowly pull the front cover open, but my eyes don't home in on the first page. They drift down to the floor, following a square of paper that's slipped from the inside cover, until it comes to rest by my naked feet. Closing the book on a frown, I scoot down and collect the wayward piece and immediately note the paper to be thick and glossy. Photograph paper. The chill that sneaks up my backbone confounds me. I can't see the photo, it's still facedown in my hand, but the presence of it unsettles me. I glance to the doorway, trying to think, and then return my curious eyes to the mystery picture. He has said there's just him. No one else, no matter how many ways I ask the question. Just Miller—no family, nothing—and while I was shocked and curious, I never pressed too hard on the matter. There were too many other Miller revelations that came about to be dealt with.

Drawing a deep breath, I slowly turn it over, knowing that a piece of Miller's history is about to be revealed. I'm chewing my lip nervously, my eyes closed to slits in preparation for what I might be confronted with, and when the full picture comes into view . . . I relax. My shoulders loosen and my head cocks to the side as I study the image, placing Miller's organizer back in the drawer without looking.

Boys.

Lots of little boys—laughing, some with cowboy hats on and some with Indian feathers protruding from their happy heads. I count fourteen in total and guess an age range of five to fifteen. They're in the overgrown garden of an old Victorian terraced house—a tatty-looking house, with what look like rags hanging at the windows. A quick assessment of the boys' clothing tells me this picture was taken in the late eighties, maybe early nineties, and I smile fondly as my eyes travel across the photograph, feeling the elation of the boys' happiness, mentally hearing them shout their delight as they chase each other with bows and arrows and pistols. But my smile is short-lived, dropping away the moment my gaze creeps onto a lone little boy standing to the side, looking on at the shenanigans of the other boys.

"Miller," I whisper, my fingertip meeting the picture, stroking across the image like I could rub some life into his little body. It's him; I have no doubt whatsoever. There are too many of the traits I've come to know and love—his wavy hair, looking wilder than ever, his wayward curl present and correct, his impassive, emotionless face and his piercing blue eyes. They look haunted... dead. Yet this child is inconceivably beautiful. I can't pull my eyes off him, can't even blink. He must be around seven or eight. His jeans are ripped, his T-shirt far too small, and his trainers are wrecked. He looks neglected, and that thought, plus this image of him looking despondent and lost, cripples me with unrelenting sadness. I don't realize that I'm sobbing, not until a tear splashes onto the glossy surface of the photograph, blurring the painful sight of Miller as a boy. I want to leave it that way, blurry and masked. I want to pretend that I never saw it.

Impossible.

My heart is breaking for the lost boy. If I could, I'd reach into this picture and cuddle the child—hold him, comfort him. But I can't. I look toward the kitchen doorway in a haze of sorrow and suddenly wonder why I'm still standing here when I can cuddle, hold, and comfort the man who that child has become. I rush to wipe my tears away, from the picture *and* my face, then slip the photo back into Miller's organizer and shut the drawer. Shut it away. Forever. Then I virtually sprint back to his bedroom, at the same time pulling my top off, and slip between the sheets behind him, snuggling as close as I can get and breathing him into me. My comfort is restored quickly.

"Where have you been?" He takes my hand from his stomach and pulls it to his mouth, kissing it sweetly.

"Nan." I give one word, knowing my simple reply will halt further questions. But it doesn't halt him from turning over to find my eyes.

"Is she okay?" He's timid. It magnifies the pain in my chest and swells the lump in my throat. I don't want him to see my sadness, so I hum my answer, hoping the restricted light is hindering his vision of me. "Then why are you sad?"

"I'm okay." I try for a reassuring tone but manage only an unconvincing whisper. I won't ask him about the picture because I already know that anything he tells me will be agonizing.

His face is dubious, but he doesn't pressure me. He uses the last of his drunken energy to pull me into his chest and envelope me completely in his strong arms. I'm home. "I have a request," he murmurs into my hair, squeezing me farther into him.

"Anything."

We're briefly bathed in a peaceful silence while he sprinkles kisses in my hair before he softly whispers his wish. "Never stop loving me, Olivia Taylor."

His plea requires no thought. "Never."

Chapter Seventeen

Morning greets me a split second later, or that's what it feels like. It also feels like I'm restrained, and a quick assessment of the position of my limbs confirms that I actually *am* restrained. Tightly. Shifting a little, I monitor his peaceful face, watching for any sign of disturbing him. There's none, and the heavy odor of stale whisky tells me why. My nose crinkles and I hold my breath, edging my way out of his hold until he rolls onto his back with a grumble. He'll need coffee and aspirin on waking. I check the clock, seeing it's only seven, then quickly throw my clothes on and hurry for the front door. I won't even bother attempting to make him a coffee to his liking. There's a Costa Coffee around the corner. They can make it for me.

Taking Miller's keys from the table, I leave him in bed and automatically head for the stairs, hoping I can return before he wakes and serve him coffee in bed. Aspirin, too. Echoes ring around the concrete walls of the stairwell as I dance down the steps, flashbacks of a lost little boy jumping all over my mind, dragging me back to sorrow. It doesn't matter how hard I try to kick them to the back of my brain; the memory of Miller's face in that picture is too vivid. But the thought of being able to make up for lost cuddles—lost things—fills me with purpose.

I crash through the exit door into the lobby and wave a hand over my shoulder to the doorman when he greets me, breaking into the fresh morning air feeling breathless. I don't let my labored breathing hold me back, though, and jog down the street, landing in the bustling coffeehouse in no time at all.

"Medium Americano, four shots, two sugars, and topped up halfway," I gasp to the young guy behind the counter, slapping my purse down. "Please."

"Sure thing," he replies, a little alarmed by my flustered form. "Drinking in?"

"Takeout."

"And four shots?"

"Yes, topped up halfway," I reiterate. If I knew how it should taste by Miller's standards, then I'd take a slurp to test it, but I can only imagine that it tastes like coffee beans have been grinded to a pulp and that it resembles something close to tar.

He gets straight to work at the coffee machine, and I find myself counting the shots as they are added to the takeout cup. He isn't going fast enough, but my manners prevent me from chivvying him along, so I shuffle impatiently instead, glancing over my shoulder on a frown when that strange sensation settles over me. I feel like I'm being watched again, but when I scan the coffeehouse, I find only businessmen and women with their faces in laptops, slurping and tapping, so I shrug off the strange feeling and return my attention to the dithering server. Now he's taking his time wiping the steam pipe, whistling as he does.

"Would you..." I pause, halted by the return sense of being observed, but this time I have the cold chill across my shoulders and raised neck hair to accompany it. A shiver reverberates through me, gliding slowly down my spine.

"What did ya say?"

I look blankly at the guy, who has turned from his task and is looking at me expectantly. What did I say? "Nothing," I breathe, reaching up to run my palm over my nape, unease settling over me like a blanket. I shake my head mildly and he shrugs, returning to the coffee machine.

I look around but only find other customers waiting impatiently, nothing out of the ordinary, yet my body's screaming that something isn't right.

"Three-twenty, please."

I drag my wary eyes to the counter, finding Miller's coffee and a hand being held out. "Sorry." I shake myself back to life and fumble for my purse, taking forever to locate a fiver before shoving it into his hand. Scooping up the takeout cup, I slowly turn, my eyes darting everywhere looking for *something*, but I haven't the first idea what. I feel stifled by anxiety. Claustrophobic. My steps are careful as I make for the exit, my eyes measuring every person I pass. None of them return my gaze. No one seems interested in me. I'd brush off my discomfort as paranoia, if my internal alarm bells weren't still ringing like crackers.

"Miss, your change!"

The muffled yell of the server doesn't make my steps falter. My legs have switched to automatic and seem hell-bent on carrying me away from the source of my distress, even if it's not obvious what that source is. I break free of the confines of the coffeehouse, hoping my freedom will restore some rationality and calmness. It doesn't. My legs take off down the street at a steady jog, and I glance over my shoulder repeatedly, every time finding absolutely nothing. I'm frustrated with myself but can't seem to convince my legs to slow, and I'm not sure whether I should be grateful or frightened by this. The increasing coldness of my skin tells me frightened. My strides quicken, my breath instantly drained as I weave through the passersby, stupidly careful not to spill or drop Miller's coffee as I do. My relief is immense when Miller's apartment block comes into view and a quick check over my shoulder reveals... something.

A man. A hooded man chasing me.

And that confirmation registers in the part of my brain that's feeding the instructions to my legs. My pace rockets, and I return my focus forward, my mind oblivious to my surroundings. The vision of someone hooded bursting through the crowds behind me is all I can see. The pounding of my heart is all I can feel.

I rush into the lobby and head for the elevator, autopilot not taking me to the stairs this time. Now autopilot is desperately trying to get me away from my cloaked shadow.

"Elevator's broken," the doorman calls, pulling me to a sharp halt. "Engineer's on his way." He shrugs before returning to his desk.

I growl my frustration and dart toward the stairwell, trying to gather some levelheadedness. The door bashes against the wall behind me and I hit the concrete stairs, sprinting up them two at a time. The combination of my heavy breathing and pounding feet combine, ricocheting loudly off the walls around me.

Then a loud crash from below brings me to an abrupt halt on the sixth floor.

I freeze, my legs now refusing to work at all, and listen as the echo of that crash travels up the shaft of the stairwell, eventually fading to nothing above my head. I hold my breath, listening carefully. Silence. My lungs are screaming for some air, but I refuse them, concentrating on the stillness around me and the continued anxiety coursing through my cold veins. Long seconds pass before I brave a step forward, craning my neck to peer down the shaft, seeing nothing but steps, stair rails, and cold, gray concrete.

I roll my eyes to myself, thinking I'm being ridiculous. It could have been a runner. There are hundreds on the streets of London. Get a grip! Allowing some air into my burning lungs, I bring my body farther forward, almost laughing at my silliness. What the hell is wrong with me?

Feeling foolish, I begin to pull back from the rail, but when I see a hand grip one of the stair rails a few floors below, I turn to stone. Then I watch in silent terror as it glides silently upward, getting closer, but there's no evidence of feet hitting the steps, like whatever's heading toward me has no feet...or they don't want me to know they're there.

My head is screaming instructions to run, that I need to get away, yet none of my muscles are listening. I'm frustrated, mentally screaming back at my mind's torrent of urgent instructions, but the deafening shrill of a mobile phone breaking through my mental argument brings me crashing back into the stairwell. It takes me a few confused seconds to register that it isn't mine. Then I hear thundering footsteps coming closer. I can't move. I've never been so terrified.

Nothing is working—my legs, my brain, my voice, nothing, but when I hear another crash of a door from below, energy seems to surge through me, snapping me into action and sending me sprinting up the remaining flights of stairs. The other set of footsteps increases its pace, which only catapults my fear *and*, subsequently, my speed.

Relief nearly knocks me to my arse when I reach the tenth floor, and I fall through the door into the corridor that'll take me to safety, the sight of Miller's shiny black door probably the most welcome vision ever—the most welcome until the door swings open and I'm powering toward a semi-naked, alarmed-looking Miller.

"Miller!"

"Livy?" He starts toward me, his sleepy eyes widening by the second the closer we become, until it's quite apparent that he's wide awake and wondering what the hell is going on.

I drop the coffee and my purse as I reach him and launch myself into his arms, my panic now subsiding, making way for emotion. "Oh God," I gasp, letting him lift me from my feet and pin my full length to him, securing me to his bare chest with a firm hold at my neck and lower back. "Someone's following me."

"What?" He doesn't ease up on his fierce clench.

"They're in the stairwell." My words are strained through my breathing, but I fight to spit it all out of my exhausted lungs. I wasn't imagining it before. Someone's been following me.

He's suddenly prying my numb limbs from his naked body, fighting to free himself. "Livy."

I shake my head into his neck, not willing to let him go. I know where he'll head. "Please don't," I beg.

"Livy, please!" he shouts, pulling impatiently at my body. "Let go!" His anger doesn't deter me, and I grapple at his body, my fear rocketing, but my tenacity is flattened by an irate yell and a fast shift in movement that detaches me from his body. I'm being held at arm's length in a heartbeat. My eyes are full of terror, his full of anger. "Stay," he orders, releasing me slowly to ensure I do as I'm bid. Overpowering fear prevents me from doing anything else.

The loss of his hold leaves me unsteady, and I watch through my haze of tears as he stalks toward the stairwell. His dignity is concealed only by his boxer shorts, but his lack of cover only enhances the fury emanating from his lean, naked physique. He's quaking with anger, the muscles of his back rolling in waves, appearing to be flexing in preparation for what he might find beyond that door. He shoves it open with no caution or care, and passes the threshold, disappearing from my sight quickly. I attempt to get my breathing under control so I can listen, but I can't hear a thing.

Then life seems to stop as a high-pitched ding rings out in the corridor air.

The elevator.

The broken elevator.

My heartbeat begins to pulse in my ears as I remain frozen, my eyes casting slowly over to the elevator. The doors begin to slide open. I start to back away, terrified.

Then I gasp, my back hitting the wall as a man falls out of the elevator. It seems to take an age for his boiler suit and tool belt to register in my distraught mind.

"Sorry, love. Didn't mean to startle you."

I sag, my palm pressing into my chest as I exhale my held breath and watch him disappear back into the elevator.

"Nothing." Miller appears, pacing toward me, looking no less angry than when he left. He takes my nape, guiding me into his apartment, and I hear the door slam, making me wince. He's buzzing with anger. "Sit," he instructs, releasing me and indicating the couch.

"I saw someone this time," I say, lowering myself to the sofa.

"This time?" He recoils. "Why haven't you said anything? You should have said something!"

My hands meet in my lap, my gaze dropping to them as I thumb my ring. "I thought I was being silly," I confess, now realizing that my inner alarm bells are working and they're working well.

Miller is standing above me, twitching. I can't look at him. I know he's right, and now I'm feeling more foolish than ever.

Firm hands land on my thighs and I force my eyes to lift a fraction in an attempt to gauge his expression. He's crouched before me, his hands have begun a soothing caress, and he's reinstated his impassive demeanor. All of these things restore my lost comfort. "Tell me when," he encourages me with an easy, gentle tone.

"On my way to work the other day when you dropped me off. In the club." I'm watching Miller, and I'm not liking what I'm seeing. "Do you know who it could be?"

"I'm not sure," he replies, replacing my returned comfort with a little disbelief.

"You must have some idea. Who would want to follow me, Miller?"

His eyes drop, hiding from my questioning glare.

"Miller, who?" I'm not letting this drop. "Am I in danger?"

When fear should be slicing me, I find anger brimming instead. If I'm at risk, then I should know about it. Be prepared.

"You're in no danger when you're with me, Olivia." He keeps his eyes down, refusing to face me.

"But I'm not always with you."

"I've told you"—he grates the words slowly—"you're probably the safest woman in London."

"I beg to differ!" I blurt, shocked. "I'm mixed up with you and William Anderson. I think I'm intelligent enough to figure out that *that* probably places me in the high-risk category." Good God, I dread to think of the enemies these two men have between them.

"You're wrong," Miller says quietly but insistently. "Anderson and I may not like each other, but we have one key interest."

"Me," I answer for him, but I don't see how that makes me safe.

"Yes, you, and with Anderson and I being on, let's say, rival teams, it places you in safe hands."

"Then who the hell has been following me?" I yell, yanking Miller's startled face up. "I don't feel safe. I feel very *un*safe!"

"You don't need to worry."

I can see the strength it's taking for him to remain calm. I'm past that. I'm pissed off and annoyed that he's attempting to brush off my warranted fear with excuses of being in safe hands.

I stand abruptly, forcing Miller back on his heels. His steel-blue gaze regards me closely as I try to pull a valid claim together, something to put *his* claim to shame. It's quite easy. "I didn't feel very safe when I was being chased down out there," I yell, throwing my arm out to the side to point at the door.

"You shouldn't have left without me." He stands and holds my hips, keeping me in place, then hunkers down, unleashing his curl and sinking into my angry eyes with worried blue ones. "Promise you'll never go anywhere alone."

"Why?"

"Just promise me, Olivia. Please don't hit me with your sass."

My sass is the only thing holding me up right now. I'm angry but frightened. I feel safe but exposed. "Please tell me why."

His eyes close, clearly trying to gather some patience. "An interferer," he whispers on a sigh, his whole body deflating but his grip of my hips firming up to steady me when I wobble on a gulp. "Now promise."

My eyes are wide and I'm frightened, no words coming to me.

"Olivia, please, I beg you."

"Why? Who's the interferer and why are they following me?"

He holds my eyes, speaking to me through the intensity of his gaze as well as his words. "I don't know, but whoever it is can obviously predict my next move."

His next move? Realization sucker punches me in the gut. "You haven't stopped?" I gasp.

It's not as easy as just quitting.

His clients. They've all had him at the drop of a hat and a few thousand quid. Not anymore, and it's obvious that some won't give him up easily. Everyone wants what they can't have, and now because of me, he's even more unobtainable.

"I've not officially quit, Olivia. I know the upset this will cause. I need to do this right."

It's abruptly very clear. "They'll hate me." Cassie hates me, and she's not even a client.

He huffs an agreeable puff of sarcastic air. Then he sinks into me with reassuring eyes. "I'm not sleeping with anyone else." He articulates the words slowly and precisely, a desperate attempt to make himself clear, and I don't doubt for a moment that he's telling me the truth. "Olivia, I've not tasted anyone or let anyone taste me. Tell me you believe me."

"I believe you." I don't hesitate. My faith is profound, despite my muddle, with no evidence except Miller's say-so. I have no explanation for why this might be, but something deep and powerful is guiding me. It's instinct, and instinct has served me well up to this point. I'm sticking with it. "I believe you," I affirm again.

"Thank you." He takes me in his arms and hugs me with the most incredible amount of relief. I'm confused and shocked. Women scorned and following me? They can predict his next move. They know he's going to quit and they don't want him to.

"I have a request," he breathes into my neck, his hands skating every inch of my back.

"What?"

"Never stop loving me."

I shake my head, wondering if he recalls making that request last night when alcohol and tiredness were consuming him, and that makes me wonder whether he recalls my reply. "Never." My confirmation is as equally resolute as it was before sleep took us last night, despite my short delay in delivering it.

Chapter Eighteen

Nan's waiting on the doorstep when we pull up outside the house, arms crossed over her bosom and guarded sapphire eyes set firmly on Miller. I check for a tapping slipper as she follows our path to the house, anything to avoid the risk of meeting her gaze. She may have been understanding and compassionate on the telephone last night, but I don't mistake that as being the end of it. We're face-to-face now. There's no escaping. She'll be pouncing on Miller, and judging by his quiet thoughtfulness since we left his apartment, he's fully expecting it.

His warm palm slides onto my neck as we approach and begins massaging gently, his attempt to rub the nerves out of me. He's wasting his time. "Mrs. Taylor," Miller says formally, bringing us to a stop.

"Hmmm," she hums, not relenting on her threatening glare. "It's past nine." She's speaking to me now but still holding Miller in place with suspicious eyes. "You'll be late."

"I'm—"

"Olivia isn't going to work today," Miller cuts me off. "Her boss has agreed to give her the day off."

"Oh, really?" Nan asks, gray eyebrows high in surprise. I feel like I should be the one explaining, but instead I'm a spare part between these two while Miller continues to speak.

"Yes, I'm taking her out for the day. A bit of respite and quality time together."

I find it easy to suck back the condescending laugh that's threatening. Miller insisted that I needed a break, and the opportunity to spend a whole day with him is rare and should be seized with both hands. But I'm not naive enough to believe that that's the only reason.

Miller looks down at me with a little reassurance in his gaze. "Go take a shower."

"Okay," I say reluctantly, knowing there's no avoiding leaving Miller to handle Nan on his own. His insistence that I didn't have time to shower at his apartment this morning now makes sense. It gives him the perfect opportunity to speak with Nan while I'm out of the way.

"Go," he encourages me softly. "I'll be here."

I nod, nibbling on my lip, not in any rush to part company with them. In fact, I'd like to turn, run, and take Miller with me. Nan subtly cocks her head, her way of saying *scoot*. There's no avoiding the inevitable, but if it wasn't for Miller's desire to apologize, then I wouldn't now be taking the stairs slowly and leaving them behind to *talk*. I've given Miller the lowdown on my conversation with my grandmother last night, and he smiled fondly when I relayed what Nan had told me about special love. But Nan doesn't know the gruesome details, and it *has* to remain that way.

I glance over my shoulder when I reach the top of the stairs, finding them watching me, neither prepared to speak until I'm out of earshot. Nan is radiating authority and my finicky, fine Miller is oozing respect. It's an amusing sight. "Chop-chop," Miller calls on a mild grin. He finds my worry amusing? Rolling my eyes on an exasperated sigh, I resign myself to the fact there's nothing I can do.

I take myself into the bathroom and shower in record time. The water is cool, but I'm not prepared to wait until it's more tolerable, and the conditioner barely touches my hair before I'm rinsing it off. My mind has plenty of things to focus on, all unpleasant and worrying, but it's hijacked by images of Nan's finger waving in Miller's face and her asking prying questions that I hope to God he can wriggle out of answering.

Flinging a towel around my cold, sopping body, I dart across the landing to get dressed, listening briefly for heated words—Nan's mainly—before I charge into my bedroom and throw my towel to the side.

"Well, hello."

I jump back against the door, my hand clenching my heart. "Jesus!"

Miller's sitting on my bed, phone to his ear, with a devilish grin on his perfect face. He doesn't look like he's just been verbally terrorized. "Apologies," he says into the phone, eyes on me. "Something's just come up." Clicking to end the call, he lets his phone slide to the center of his palm while he taps his knee pensively with his fingertips. "Cold?"

His one-word question and the area that his twinkling eyes are focused on pulls my eyes downward. Yes, I am, and it's plain to see, but my chilly nipples start to tingle with something other than coldness as I remain under his examination. "A little," I concede, cupping my boobs, hiding them from view. "Where's Nan?"

"Downstairs."

"Are you okay?"

"Why wouldn't I be?" He's calm and collected, not displaying any signs of unease after dealing with my protective grandmother.

"Well, because... it's just...," I stutter and stammer all over my words, stupidly uncomfortable. This is ridiculous. I roll my eyes and drop my hands. "What did she say?"

"You mean while she was tapping her biggest carving knife on the table?"

"She wasn't," I laugh, but halt my nervous giggling when Miller remains completely serious. "Was she?"

He tucks his phone into the inside pocket of his jacket and stands, resting his hands in his trouser pockets. "Olivia, I'm not prepared to go any further with this line of conversation while you're wet and naked." He shakes his head, like he's shaking away wicked thoughts. He probably is. "Either get dressed or shimmy that gorgeous little body over here so I can taste it."

My spine lengthens and I fight off the shots of desire that fire like bullets across the room, from Miller to me. "You wouldn't disrespect my nan," I stupidly remind him.

"That was before she threatened to remove my manhood."

I laugh. He's serious and there's no question that Nan was, too. "So now the rule doesn't apply?"

He pouts, a wicked glint in his stunning eyes. "I've assessed and mitigated the risks associated with worshipping you in your nan's home."

"You have?"

"Yes, and the best thing is that you can put measures in place to lower a risk." He's talking like he's negotiating a business transaction again.

"Like what?"

Miller's lovely lips press into a straight line as he considers my question; then he wanders over to my chair and picks it up. "Excuse me," he says, waiting for me to move from the door, which I do without complaint, watching in amusement as he wedges the top of the backrest under the handle. "I believe we may be close to a risk-free worshipping session." A huge smile spreads across my face as I watch him checking the stability of the chair before he jiggles the handle. "Yes," he concludes on a satisfied nod of his handsome head. "I believe I've covered every eventuality." He turns toward me and spends a few moments burning my naked skin with his scorching gaze. "Now I get to taste you."

My libido responds fast. I'm in full-on responsive mode, and I'm delighted to see Miller is, too. I can see the evidence through his trousers.

"Olivia!" Nan's screech slices straight through the sexual tension and kills it dead. "Olivia, I'm putting on a white wash. You have any?" The creaking floorboards indicate her close proximity.

"Fucking perfect," Miller grumbles with one hundred percent frustration. "Just . . . fucking . . . perfect."

I grin and dip to retrieve my towel. "You missed a risk," I muse, wrapping myself up.

Adjusting his groin area, he drills holes into me, unmistakably unamused. "I didn't anticipate a white wash day." He removes the chair from the door and pulls it open, revealing Nan with her arms full of white material. Miller plasters an insincere smile on his face, but it's still a smile and it's still relatively rare, even if it's fake. Not that Nan would know. "You should have someone to do that for you, Mrs. Taylor."

"Pfft! You rich people!" She shoos him out of the way and stalks around my room, collecting anything white on her travels. "I'm not scared of hard work."

"Neither is Miller," I pipe up. "He cleans and cooks."

Nan halts, shuffling the masses of white material between her arms. "Oh, so it's just my age that suggests I should have some help, then, hmmm?"

I smirk when I see Nan hit Miller with a contemptuous look, making him shift awkwardly on his expensive shoes. "Not at all," he says, flicking pleading eyes to mine. I'm smug. Now he's getting the gist. She can be a pain in the royal arse and I'll remind him of this little scene when he chastises me for saying it as it is. "I didn't mean to—"

"Save it, mister," she spits, marching past him and giving me a devious wink. Then she stops in front of me and runs old eyes up and down my *white* towel. The one that's covering my dignity. "I'm doing whites," she muses, holding back an impish grin.

"Well this can go in the next load." I pull my towel in, narrowing my eyes in warning.

"But this doesn't make a full load." She gestures to the pile of washing in her arms with a minuscule nod of her head. "It'll be a terrible waste of water and energy. I should fill the machine."

My lips purse and hers curve. "You should fill your mouth so you can't speak," I retort, making her grin widen. She's incorrigible, the old minx.

"Miller!" she gasps. "Do you hear how she speaks to an old lady?"

"I do, Mrs. Taylor," he replies speedily, rounding her short, plump body until he's standing behind me, looking at Nan's now serious face over my shoulder. She's a bugger, playing the old, sweet lady. I know better, and I'll make sure Miller does, too. He bends and rests his chin next to my ear, his arm curling around my waist so his hand is splayed on my towel-covered tummy. "I have an apple in the car that'll fit your mouth perfectly. Should do the trick."

"Ha!" I laugh.

She gasps in horror, her face contorting in irritation. "Well!"

"*Well* what?" I ask. "Quit the defenseless old bird act, Nan. It's past its sell-by date."

She huffs and puffs on the spot, looking back and forth to me and Miller, whose chin is still settled on my bare shoulder. I take his hand on my tummy and squeeze, craning my head to get his delicious face in eyeshot. He smiles brightly and kisses me hard on the lips.

"Respect!" Nan squawks, snapping us out of our moment. "Give me that!" She yanks the towel from my body.

"Nan!"

She starts laughing menacingly as she bunches it up with the existing pile. "That'll teach ya!"

"Shit!" I grab the first available thing in sight to cover my modesty . . . which happens to be Miller's hands.

"Oh!" Nan bends over, chuckling uncontrollably as I slap Miller's palms over my breasts.

"Well hello again," he rasps in my ear, giving a little squeeze.

"Miller!"

"You put them there!" He chuckles, making the most of my panic-induced error.

"Bloody hell!" I shrug him off and rush over to the bed, yanking at the covers until I'm concealed again. My face is flaming, Nan is in bits, and Miller isn't helping, chuckling to himself. It's the most beautiful sight, but my embarrassment and irritation won't allow me to appreciate it for long. "Don't egg her on!" This is wrong on so many levels!

"Sorry." He attempts to compose himself, pulling at his suit and brushing down his front, his shoulders still jiggling.

"Nan, get out!"

"I'm going, I'm going," she breathes tiredly as she trots toward the door. I know she's just winked cheekily at Miller because he quickly diverts his straying eyes from her, and his lips have straightened. He's also still rearranging his perfect suit, which isn't unusual, but the frantic hand movements and tense shoulders are giving away what would be a normal undertaking as diversion. I'm thoroughly unamused by the time she leaves, highly smug and tittering her way down the landing.

Fighting with the mass of material surrounding me, I march to the door and slam it behind her, sending Miller on a startled jump. He fails to hold back on his delight any longer.

"You're supposed to be on my side," I snap, pulling the material tangled at my feet.

"I am." He laughs. "Honest, I am."

I eye him moodily as he saunters over to me and whips the bedding away before he scoops me into his arms. "She's a treasure."

"She's a pain in the arse," I counter, and I don't care if I get scorned for it. "What did she say?"

"I told you, my manhood is at risk."

"That doesn't mean you get to back her up for fear of losing it."

"I wasn't backing her up."

"Yes, you were."

"If your grandmother is happy to expose your gorgeous naked body in my presence, then I'm not going to complain about it." He carries me to the bed and settles on the edge with me spread across his lap. "In fact, I'll be highly grateful for it."

"Don't show your gratitude so willingly," I grumble. "And I love it when you laugh, but not at my expense."

"Would you prefer I showed *you* my gratitude?"

"Yes." My reply is decisive and haughty. "Just me."

"Your request has been noted, Miss Taylor."

"Jolly good, Mr. Hart."

He grins, restoring my contentment, and lavishes me with one of his mind-blanking kisses. Not for long enough, though. "The day is passing quickly and we haven't even made it to breakfast yet."

"We'll do brunch." I don't allow him to break our kiss, reaching to his neck and pulling him in.

"You need to eat."

"I'm not hungry."

"Olivia," he warns, "please. I'd like to feed you and I'd like you to accept."

"Strawberries?" I try. "British for the sweetness and dipped in yummy dark chocolate."

"I don't think we'll get away with that in public."

"Then let's go back to your place."

"You're insatiable."

"It's you."

"Agreed. I've awakened this unquenchable desire in you and I'm the only man who'll ever get to sate it."

"Agreed."

"I'm glad we've cleared that up, not—"

"That I have a choice, I know." I bite his lip and drag it through my teeth. "I don't want a choice."

"Good job." He places me on my feet and looks up at me with soft eyes, a hint of a smile gracing his lovely lips.

"What?" I ask, mirroring his mild beam.

Smooth hands slide around to my bum and pull me between his spread thighs. Then he plants a light kiss on my tummy. "I was just thinking how lovely you look standing naked before me." His chin rests on my navel and he gazes up at me, his divine blues bursting with contentment. "What would you like to do today?"

"Oh..." My brain kicks into gear, running over all of the fun stuff we could do together. I bet Miller's never partaken in fun stuff. "Roam, meander, wander." I'd love to ramble the streets of London with Miller, point out my favorite buildings, and give him a rundown on their histories. Mind you, he's hardly dressed for wandering. My eyes flick over his perfectly precise three-piece suit on a frown.

"You mean walk?" he asks, a little taken aback, pulling my eyes back to his. He doesn't seem impressed.

"Nice walking."

"Where?"

I shrug, a little saddened that Miller doesn't appear to find my idea of fun very appealing. "What do you suggest, then?"

He ponders my question for a few moments before he speaks. "I have lots to do at Ice. You could come and tidy my office."

I recoil in disgust. His office is clinical. It doesn't need tidying, and no amount of enthusiasm injected into his tone will convince me that going to work with Miller will be fun. "You said quality time."

"You can sit on my lap while I work."

"Don't be daft."

"I'm not."

I feared he was serious. "I'm not taking a day off work just to go to work with you." I stand back and fold my arms across my chest, hoping he comprehends just how adamant I am. The smile that graces his yummy lips makes my resolve waver. He's dishing out smiles left, right, and center, and it's delightful and maddening all at once. "What?" I ask, thinking I should stop questioning his reasons for his obvious joy and simply accept it without a word. But this exasperating man piques my curiosity constantly.

"I was just thinking how lovely you look with your arms pushing your breasts up." His eyes gleam relentlessly, and I look down, sizing up my lack of chest.

"There's nothing there." I push into my boobs a little more, not being able to fathom what he can see that I can't.

"They're perfect." He snatches me up quickly, and I squeal as I'm tossed onto the bed and covered in his suit-clad body. "I request that they remain exactly how they are."

"Okay," I agree, just before his mouth swamps me, smothering my lips delicately but purposely. I'm blindsided, totally swallowed up, loving Miller's relaxed condition. All uptight behavior is lost.

Well, almost.

"My suit," he murmurs, pecking a path to my ear. "My appearance has never been so questionable since you invaded my life, sweet girl."

"You look perfect."

Snorting his disagreement, he lifts from my desire-drenched nakedness and stands to rearrange his suit, finishing by fiddling with the knot of his tie as I watch him. "Get dressed."

I sigh and shift to the edge of the bed as he meanders over to my mirror so he can see what he's doing. Even though I'm now used to Miller and his fussy ways, my fascination remains strong. Everything about him, everything that he does is always undertaken with the utmost care and attention, and it has fast become endearing...except when his temper is unleashed. Kicking that thought away, I leave Miller playing with his tie and get myself ready, throwing on a floral tea dress and some flip-flops before blasting my hair dry and messing with it for a good few minutes, cursing myself for not allowing the conditioner to work its magic before I rinsed. I tie it up, pull it back down, ruffle it a few times, and finally exhale my exasperation at my untamed locks, pulling it into a loose ponytail over my shoulder.

"Cute," Miller concludes when I turn to present myself to him, his eyes taking a leisurely jaunt up and down my frame, still messing with his tie. "No Converse today?"

I look down at my pink toenails and wriggle my feet. "Don't you like them?" I bet Miller's feet have never seen a pair of flip-flops in their life. In fact, I bet Miller's feet have been nothing but spoiled with handmade, top-quality fancy leather shoes. He doesn't even wear trainers at the gym, going barefoot instead.

"Olivia, you could wear a rag and look like a princess."

I smile and collect my satchel, throwing it across my body, allowing myself a few riveting moments to regard Miller's preciseness. "People must think we're a strange match."

His face contorts with a frown as he approaches and takes my nape, leading me out of the bedroom. "Why?"

"Well, you all suited and booted and me"—I look down, searching for the right word—"cutesy." I can't think of a better one.

"Enough of that," he scolds me quietly as we take the stairs. "Say good-bye to your grandmother."

"Bye, Nan!" I call, not being given the opportunity to find her. I'm led straight to the door.

"Have fun!" she calls from the kitchen.

"I'll deliver Olivia home later," Miller says, back to formal, just as the front door shuts behind us. I glance up at him with tired eyes and ignore his questioning look when he catches it. "Get in." He opens the door of his Mercedes for me, and I slip into the soft leather of the passenger seat.

The door is shut gently and he's beside me, starting the car and pulling off before I have a chance to put my seat belt on. "So what are we doing?" I inquire again as I pull my belt across my body.

"You tell me."

I look across at him, surprised, but don't delay my answer. "Park up near Mayfair."

"Mayfair?"

"Yes, we'll wander." I return my stare forward, noticing the dual temperature display glowing the digits "16," just as they were last time, except now it's far warmer. I suddenly feel stifled, but not wanting to upset Miller's perfect world, I open the window a touch instead.

"Wander," he muses thoughtfully, like it worries him. It probably does, but I ignore the concern in his tone and remain quiet in my seat. "Wander," he says to himself again, starting to tap the steering wheel. I can feel the uncertainty rolling off of him in waves. "She wants to wander."

I smile on an undetectable shake of my head, then settle farther into my seat when Miller kills the stretching silence by turning the media system on. Kid Mac's "Pursuit of Happiness" fills the car, and my face scrunches up in utter wonder at Miller's continued surprising choices in music. I know for sure he's flicking occasional glances in my direction, but I don't humor him with my curious mind. Instead, I remain silent for the rest of the journey, musing over so many elements of my curious Miller Hart and the curious world that I've come willingly into.

Chapter Nineteen

When Miller slips into a parking space and cuts the engine, I know better than to let myself out of the car. He rounds the front, fastening his jacket, and opens the door for me. "Thank you, sir."

"Most welcome," he replies, with no hint of acknowledging my sarcasm. "Now what?" He glances around at our surroundings briefly, then pulls the sleeve of his jacket up to check the time.

"Are you in a rush?" I ask, immediately irritated by his rude gesture.

His eyes flick to mine and his arm drops. "Not in the least bit." He straightens his suit again, anything to avoid my bitter tone. "What now?" he repeats.

"We wander."

"Where?"

My shoulders droop. This is going to be hard work. "This is supposed to be relaxing. Something leisurely and enjoyable."

"I can think of far more gratifying ways to pass my time, Olivia, and it doesn't involve keeping you in public." He's wholly serious, and my thighs clench as he takes another fill of his surroundings.

"Have you ever wandered?" I ask.

Curious eyes return to mine quickly. "I go from A to B."

"You've never basked in the opulence London has to offer?" I ask, astounded that anyone could live in this beautifully grand city and not immerse themselves in its history. It's a travesty.

"You're one of London's finest opulences, and I'd love to bask in you right now." He studies me thoughtfully, and I know what's coming. The increased beat between my legs is a good sign, and so is the desire pooling in his eyes after executing one of those lazy blinks. "But I can't very well worship you here, can I?"

"No," I answer quickly and decidedly stanch before I'm hauled deeper into those riveting blue eyes. He doesn't want to wander, but *I* do. I'm bubbling everywhere, my desire tangible in the open air around us, but I want to take pleasure from Miller in another way. "What about your paintings?"

"What about them?"

"You must appreciate the beauty of the things you paint or you wouldn't bother painting them." I disregard the fact that they could be even more beautiful if they were clearer.

He shrugs nonchalantly, again looking around us. It's *really* irritating me now. "I see something I admire, I take a picture and I paint it."

"Just like that?"

"Yes." He doesn't give me his eyes.

"Don't you think it would be far more rewarding if you painted it in the flesh?"

"I don't see why."

On a tired exhale of breath, I toss my bag over my shoulder. I still don't fully get him, despite constantly telling myself that I do. I'm kidding myself. "Ready?"

He answers by taking my nape and pushing onward, but I halt and wriggle free of his hold. Then I hit him with a contemptuous look as he stares down at me, puzzlement obvious on his lovely face. "What's the matter?"

"You're not guiding me around London by my neck."

"Why ever not?" He's truly flummoxed. "I like having you that close. I assumed you like it."

"I do," I admit. The warmth of his palm spread across my nape is always an appreciated comfort. But not while wandering around London. "Hold my hand." I can't imagine that Miller has ever held a woman's hand casually, and I also can't picture it. He's led me by my hand on a few occasions, but it's always been purposeful—to put me somewhere he wants me to be, never relaxed and lovingly.

He spends way too long thinking about my request before he eventually takes my offering on a little pucker of his brow.

"Boo!" I yell on a smirk, making him wince on a little startled jump before he quickly composes himself and slowly lifts unamused blue eyes to mine. I smile. "I don't bite."

He's full to the brim with aggravation, I can tell, but he's giving me nothing but his cool impassiveness. It doesn't affect my smiling face, though. I'm properly grinning. "Sass," he says simply, firming up his grip, refusing to humor me as he takes the lead.

I follow, changing the hold of our joined hands as we wander down the street so our fingers are entwined. I keep the direction of my stare forward, only allowing myself a brief glimpse of Miller. I don't need to look, but I do, seeing him gazing down at our hands and feeling the flex of his grip as he gets used to his hold. He really hasn't held a woman's hand like this before, and while the thought delights me, it also tarnishes the immense comforting feeling that I relish in when he holds me by my nape. Is that how he holds all women? Do they get the rush of warmth bolting through their body when he does that? Do their eyes slowly close and their neck flex a little in absorption and satisfaction? These questions have my hand tightening around his and my head turning to gaze up at him, just to get a good fill of the look on his face, just to see how uncomfortable our connection is making him. He's stiff as a board, his hand constantly flexing in my grasp, and his expression is almost mystified.

"You okay?" I ask quietly as we turn onto Bury Street.

The even beats of his expensive shoes hitting the pavement falter very slightly, but he doesn't look down at me. "Fine and dandy," he says, and I laugh, letting my head fall onto his upper arm.

He's far from fine and dandy. He looks awkward and inconvenienced. Miller, despite being dressed in exquisite finery that blends into London-by-day just fine, is exuding an air of unease. I look around as we continue toward Piccadilly, seeing businessmen everywhere, all suited, some on mobile phones, some carrying briefcases, and all look perfectly comfortable. They look full of purpose, probably because they are. They're on their way to brunch or a meeting or maybe to the office. And as I return my eyes to Miller, I realize that he's lacking that purpose right now. He goes from A to B. He doesn't wander, yet he's trying his hardest for me. And failing terribly. My mind dips momentarily into the possibility that Miller looks so out of place because I'm attached to his arm, but I toss that thought out just as quickly. I'm here and I'm staying, and not just because Miller says so. The notion of attempting to continue my life without him in it is unthinkable, and my train of thought alone sends a chilliness coursing through my current contentment, making me shiver into his lean body. My spare arm lifts without instruction and my palm wraps around his upper arm, just below my chin.

"Olivia?" I leave my head and palm exactly where they are, lifting only my eyes to find him looking down at me with mild concern etched on his face. I force a tiny smile through the anxiety that my wayward thoughts have spiked.

"I know and love my sweet girl's look of bliss, and she's trying to fool me now." He stops and turns into me, making releasing him unavoidable and tremendously painful, but I allow myself to be detached from him. Masses of blond ponytail are collected from my shoulder and released to cascade down my back before his palms encase my cheeks. He bends a little, making sure his face is level with mine; then he reinstates a little of my contentment by blinking so incredibly lazily, I think he might not ever open his eyes again. But he does, and I'm blasted back by unreserved comfort that's pouring relentlessly from every fiber of his beautiful being. He knows. "Share with me your burden."

I smile on the inside and try to mentally pull it together. "I'm fine," I assure him, taking one of his hands from my cheek and kissing his palm gently.

"Overthinking, Olivia. How many times do we need to go over this?" He seems cross, although continuing to be super gentle.

"I'm okay," I insist, diverting my eyes from the intensity of his questioning stare, letting them fall down the length of his body to his posh brogues. My mind captures every fine thread of his attire and the outstanding quality of his shoes. And then I think of something and look across the street. "Come with me," I say, taking his hand and tugging him into the road.

He follows obediently, with not a murmur of protest, to the end of Bury Street and a little way down Jermyn Street until we're standing outside a men's clothes store—a boutique-style one, all stuffy and proper, but I see something I like the look of.

"What are you doing?" he questions, looking nervously at the shop window.

"Window-shopping," I answer nonchalantly as I drop his hand and turn to face the window, taking in the solid wooden mannequins dressed in top-quality menswear. I can see mainly suits, but they're not what have my attention.

Miller joins me, slipping his hands into his trouser pockets, and we both just stand there for an age, me pretending to browse, when all I'm thinking is how I'll get him in there, and Miller twitching nervously beside me.

He clears his throat. "I think that's enough window-shopping for now," he declares, taking my neck to lead me away.

I don't budge, not even when his strong fingers increase their pressure a bit. It's hard, but I root myself to the spot, making moving me of the utmost difficulty. "Let's go in and take a look," I suggest.

He stills, halting his attempts to get me shifting. "I'm particular about where I shop."

"You're particular about everything, Miller."

"Yes, and I'd like to keep it that way." He tries to move me again, but I dip from his hold and head hastily for the entrance.

"Come on," I urge.

"Olivia," he calls, his tone laced with warning.

I stop on the shop step and swing around, plastering a huge smile on my face. "Nothing fills you with greater pleasure than seeing me so happy," I remind him, leaning up against the door frame and casually crossing one leg over the other. "And it would make me really happy if you would accompany me into this shop."

Blue eyes twinkle but narrow, as if he's trying to conceal his amusement at my smart-arse comment. His lips are twitching, too, which only broadens my happiness into overwhelming elation. This is just perfect because Miller loves it when I'm happy, and I couldn't be any happier right now. I'm being playful and he's reciprocating . . . nearly.

"You're very hard to resist, Olivia Taylor." He shakes his head wistfully, propelling my happiness further as he takes the few remaining strides toward me. I stay on the shop step, looking down at him, unable to wipe the smile from my face. He keeps his hands to himself and reaches up with his lips, bringing them close to mine. "It's almost impossible," he whispers, engulfing my face with his soft breath and my nose with his manly scent. My resolve wanes, but I quickly snatch it back and disappear into the shop before I'm swallowed up and led away from the store.

On entering, I'm immediately given the once-over by a stout man who appears from the back of the store. He looks like he's just wandered out of an estate in the English countryside. His tweed suit is crisp and neat, and on closer inspection, I notice the knot of his tie is as perfect as Miller's. Stupidly, I think that Miller will approve of this, which will only enhance his good mood, so I pivot to face him, but deflate fast when I find he's disappeared from the door and is now looking through the shop window again, his mask slipped back into place. He's hovering, looking around cautiously . . . dubiously.

"Can I help you?"

I leave Miller contemplating whether he's going to venture into the store and return my attention to the store assistant. Yes, he *can* help me. "You do casual wear?" I ask.

He laughs a pompous laugh before signaling to the back of the store. "Why, of course; however, we are far more renowned for our suits and shirts."

My eyes follow the direction of his pointed finger and find a section to the rear of the store with just a few rails of casual garments. It's quite sparse, but I'm not risking leaving to try to get Miller to a shop with a wider range. It'll give him too long to worm out of it. And on that thought, I swivel again to see if he's braved venturing into the shop. He hasn't.

On a sigh loud enough for him to hear, even from outside, I turn to find the assistant again. "I'll have a look." I go to pass him, but he shifts on an uncomfortable shuffle of his portly body, blocking my path. I frown and throw him a questioning look as he runs disapproving eyes down my floral dress, all the way to my exposed pink toenails.

"Miss," he begins, returning his beady eyes to mine, "you'll find most shops here on Jermyn Street will be of the . . . how should I say?" He hums in thought, but I don't know why. He knows what he wants to say, and I know it, too. "The higher end of the clothing spectrum."

My sass runs and hides. I'm not his typical clientele, and he isn't afraid to voice it. "Right," I whisper, too many unwanted thoughts running through my mind. Like posh people eating posh food and drinking posh champagne... all of which I serve to them from time to time.

He smiles the most insincere smile and starts fiddling with the sleeve of a nearby shirt on a mannequin. "Maybe Oxford Street would be more suitable."

I feel foolish, and this rotten man's reaction to my inquiry has only confirmed my constant worries, and he hasn't even seen Miller. That'll shock him. Me with a finely dressed specimen such as Miller?

"I believe the *young lady* would like to be shown the casual department." Miller's voice creeps over my shoulders and makes them seize up. I've heard that tone. Only a few times before, but I'll never forget or mistake it. He's angry. I note the shop assistant's widened eyes and stunned expression before I chance a very wary glance at Miller as he joins me in the store. To the man *not* trying to help me, I know he'll look perfectly composed, but I can see the brimming fury. He's not happy and I expect Mr. My-Garments-Are-too-Posh-for-You will know about it very soon.

"I'm sorry, sir. Is the young lady with you?" I can see the surprise and it eats away all of the reassurance that Miller constantly fills me with. It's gone. I'll face this daily if I continue to try to immerse myself in Miller's world. I know I'll never leave him—not ever, not a chance—so it should be something that I must either learn to accept or learn to deal with better. I have copious amounts of sass for my uptight, part-time gentleman, but I seem to struggle on some occasions beyond that. Like now.

Miller's arm slips around my waist and pulls me closer. I can feel the tightness of his strung-up muscles, and panic makes me want to remove him from the store before they release and knock this old guy on his plump arse. "Would it matter if she wasn't?" Miller asks tightly.

The man shifts and shuffles in his tweed, laughing nervously. "I thought I was being helpful," he insists.

"You weren't," Miller retorts. "She was shopping for me, not that it should matter."

"Of course!" Stout Man gives Miller a quick appraisal, nodding his approval before carefully pulling down a white shirt. "I believe we have much that you would find appealing, sir."

"Probably." Miller shifts his hand to my neck and starts rubbing that reassurance back into me. He never fails. I'm warm and feeling less exposed to the demeaning words that have been directed at me, despite him being perfectly polite in his insult. Miller steps forward and runs a fingertip over the luxury material of the shirt, humming his approval. I watch him cautiously, still sensing those coiled muscles and knowing for damn sure that *that* hum of approval was entirely fake.

"Wonderful piece," the assistant says proudly.

"I beg to differ." Miller returns to my side. "And it could be made of the finest material money could buy, but I wouldn't buy it from you." I'm turned by a gentle flex of his hold. "Good day, sir." We exit the store, leaving a dumbfounded man with a lovely white shirt hanging from his limp hands. "Fucking prick," Miller spits, pushing me onward.

I keep my mouth shut. I can't even locate the need to be annoyed that I haven't managed to get Miller interested in some casual clothes, and after that scene, my determination should be stronger. But I never want to face another confrontation such as that, not just because it was humiliating, but also because of my lingering worry about Miller's temper. He looked feral, bordering on becoming that frightening creature who takes leave of his senses and doesn't seem able to control himself.

I'm marched down the street, my heart sinking with each step we take when it becomes apparent that we're heading for his car. That's it? Our quality time together consisted of a reality check in a posh clothes store? *Disappointed* doesn't cover it.

We arrive at Miller's Mercedes, where he places me neatly in the passenger seat. I watch silently with careful eyes, not daring to voice my discontent as he steams around the front of the car and throws himself into the driver's side.

I'm nervous.

He's pissed.

I'm silent.

He's breathing erratically.

The anger seems to be intensifying rather than dulling. I'm struck stupid, not knowing what to say or do. He slams the key into the ignition on a hiss, turns it, and revs the engine so hard, I think the car might blow up. Sinking farther into my seat, I start toying with my ring.

"Fuck!" he roars, smashing his fist into the center of the steering wheel. The punch alone startles me, making me fly back in my seat, but the horn sounding off drags out my alarm. That nasty fear bolts through my speeding heart, but I keep my eyes on my lap. I can't look at him. I know what I'll see and Miller's rage isn't a pretty sight.

It seems like forever before the echo of the horn fades to nothing, leaving a ringing in my ears, and it's even longer before I find the courage to glimpse at him. His forehead is resting on the steering wheel, his palms gripping the circle of leather, and his back is rising and falling erratically.

"Miller?" I say quietly as I lean forward a fraction, cautious, but I soon retreat when his palms lift and smash back down on another shout. He flings his body back into the seat, falls silent for a few, long moments, and then he yanks at the handle of the door, getting out and slamming it behind him. "Miller!" I shout as he paces away from the car. "Shit!" He's going back to the shop! I blindly feel for the door handle, watching his long legs eat up the pavement, but then I halt my frenzied grappling when he comes to a sudden standstill and his hands fly into his hair. I'm frozen, weighing up the merits of trying to calm him down. I don't relish the thought. Not at all. My heart continues to clatter in my chest, threatening to break free as I wait for his next move, praying he doesn't push onward because there isn't a chance on earth that I can stop him from doing whatever he intends to do.

My whole being relaxes a tad when I see his arms drop, and a little more when I see his head fall back on his shoulders, looking up to the heavens. He's calming down, letting rationality push through the fuzz of rage. I swallow and follow his steps to a nearby wall, then relax even more on an inward sob when his palms meet the bricks and he braces himself, head dropped and his back rising and falling in a controlled, steady manner. He's taking deep breaths. My hands relax in my lap and my back against the leather seat as I watch quietly, leaving him undisturbed while he gathers himself. It doesn't take as long as I anticipated, and the relief that floods my seated form when he begins to straighten out his suit and hair is beyond comprehension. Enough air to fill a thousand balloons leaves my lungs on a thankful exhale. He's pulled it back, although why he lost it so badly in such a silly situation is beyond me.

After spending a few minutes ensuring he's presentable, Miller makes his way back to the car, opening the door calmly, sliding into the seat like liquid, calmly, and relaxing back in his seat, *very* calmly.

I wait cautiously.

He thinks deeply.

Then he turns to me with tortured blues and takes both of my hands, bringing them to his lips and closing his eyes. "I'm so sorry. Forgive me, please."

A hint of a smile traces the edges of my lips at his plea and at his ability to revert from gentleman to madman to gentleman, all in the space of a few minutes. His temper is a worry that our relationship doesn't need. "Why?" I ask simply, pulling his eyes open and up. "That man wasn't trying to interfere. He wasn't driving a wedge between us or threatening our relationship."

"I beg to differ," Miller counters quietly. My brow wrinkles at his claim, more so when he insists on me joining him on his side of the car by tugging me over. He's crumpled enough after his little flip-out, even though he's spent plenty of time ironing himself out again. I'm positioned on his lap, my knees straddling his thighs, and my hands placed on his shoulders before he circles my waist with his palms. Drawing a deep breath, he firms up his grip of my waist and locks eyes with mine. They have lost their wildness and are now serious. "He most certainly *was* driving a wedge between us, Livy."

I try to hold back my confusion but my face muscles let me down and I'm awash with perplexity before I can retract it. "How?"

"What were you thinking?"

"When?"

He sighs deeply, frustration starting to brim. "When that pri—" He snaps his mouth shut and rethinks his words before continuing. "When that undesirable gentleman was speaking to you, what were you thinking?"

I catch his drift immediately. He really doesn't want to know what I was thinking. It'll make him mad again, so I shrug, dropping my eyes and keeping my mouth firmly sealed. I'm not risking it.

Miller lightly digs into my flesh with a flex of his fingertips. "Don't deprive me of that face, Olivia."

"You know what I was thinking." I refuse to look at him.

"Please look at me when we're talking."

I take my eyes straight to his. "I fucking hate your manners sometimes." I'm cranky because he's nailed me *and* my thought process, and I'm thrilled because his soft lips are batting off the threat of a smile at my sass.

"What were you thinking?"

"Why do you want me to say it?" I ask. "What point are you trying to prove?"

"Okay, I'll say it. I'll explain why I very nearly returned to teach that man some manners."

"Go on, then," I goad.

"Every time someone makes you unhappy or speaks to you in such a way, it makes you overthink. You know how I feel about overthinking." He nudges me again, reinforcing his point.

"Yes, I know."

"And my gorgeous, sweet girl already overthinks too much all on her own."

"Yes, I know."

"So when these people get your lovely little mind racing further, I get mad because you start doubting *us*."

I narrow my eyes on him, but I can't deny it. He's one hundred percent right. "Yes, I know." My teeth are clenched.

His voice drops. "And that heightens the risk of you leaving me. You'll conclude these people are right and leave me. So, yes, they are driving a wedge between us. They are interfering, and when it comes to people poking their noses into our relationship, then I have something to say about it."

"You have more than something to say!"

"I concur."

"Well, that's a relief."

He frowns. "What is?"

"Your agreement." I remove my hands from his shoulders and lean back against the steering wheel, keen to put as much distance between us as possible. It's hardly worth it, in all honesty. "I think you need anger management or therapy or something." I blurt it all before I can chicken out. Then I brace myself for his scoff.

But it doesn't come. In fact, he laughs a little. "Olivia, enough people have intruded on my life. I'm not going to invite a stranger in to interfere some more."

"They won't interfere. They'll help."

"I beg to differ." He gazes at me, all fondly, like I'm naive. "I've been there. I think it was concluded that I'm beyond help."

My heart dies a little. He's already tried therapy? "You're not beyond help."

"You're right," he answers, surprising me and filling me with hope. "All the help I need is sitting on my lap."

My optimism is sucked up in a second. "So you behaved like a loon before you met me?" I ask doubtfully, already knowing that he's never touched rage like he has since I've been in his perfect life. That little line of thought is laughable. Perfect life? No, Miller tries to *make* it perfect by keeping everything surrounding him perfect—namely his appearance and his possessions, and given that it has been established that *I* am also one of Miller's possessions, then that means me, too. And that's the problem. I'm not perfect. I'm not impeccably dressed or impeccably mannered, and it's sending my finicky Miller and his perfectness spiraling into chaos. I'm all the help he needs? He's putting an obscene amount of pressure on my shoulders.

"I'm a loon now?"

"Your temper really isn't something to toy with," I say quietly, remembering Miller delivering those words and now appreciating his warning fully.

His palm slips around my neck and pulls me gently forward until we're forehead to forehead. He's already distracted me from my undesirable thoughts with his touch on my skin and his eyes stuck to mine, but I can tell that I'm about to be distracted further. "I'm madly fascinated by you, Olivia Taylor." He ensures our eyes hold. "You fill my dark world with light and my hollow heart with feelings. I've persistently informed you that I'll never go down easily." Soft lips meld to mine and we share the most incredibly soft, slow kiss. "I'm not prepared to be immersed constantly in that darkness again. You are my habit. Just mine. I need only you."

On an agreeable sigh and a happy skip of my heart, I encase Miller in my hold and spend a few blissful moments expressing my understanding. And he accepts. The fluidity of our joined mouths yanks me from the harsh reality we're faced with and puts me firmly back into Miller's realm, where comfort, anxiety, safety, and danger all conflict with one another. In Miller's eyes, everyone is trying to interfere, and sadly he is probably right. I've taken the day off work under Miller's instruction so we can spend some quality time together after yesterday's diabolical events and this morning's fright. He's trying to repair the mess of the past couple of days, and I need *no one* to interfere—not just today, but ever.

"I'm glad we've cleared that up," Miller mumbles, nibbling at my lips. He pulls his head back and leaves me a worked-up pile of hormones on his lap. Hot. Wanton. Blinded by perfection. "Let's be on our way." My lithe body is transferred to the passenger seat with care before he starts the engine and pulls into the traffic.

"Where are we going?" I ask, the disappointment of our day being cut too short still rife.

He doesn't answer, instead twiddling a few buttons on his steering wheel, prompting the Stone Roses to join us in the car. I smile, rest back in my chair while humming to "Waterfall," and let him take me wherever he likes.

Chapter Twenty

I look up at the posh windows of Harrods, remembering my last visit here with Nan. I remember Cassie. And I remember a pink silk tie cascading down Miller's chest. All are things I'd like to forget, and I groan my annoyance at the reminders. But I'm ignored, and Miller slips from the car and rounds it to collect me. He opens the door and offers his hand, and I let my eyes slowly climb up his body until my exasperated gaze settles on his contented one. He flashes me an expectant look as his hand thrusts forward in prompt. "Chop-chop."

"I've changed my mind," I say coolly, ignoring his demand for my hand. "Let's get something to eat." I may win with this diversion because with all of the palaver at the previous shop, Miller hasn't fulfilled his insistence for me to eat yet. And I can think of nothing worse than assisting Miller in buying more masks.

"We'll eat soon." My hand is claimed and I'm pulled from the car before he transfers his hold to my nape. "I don't plan on this taking long."

Optimism gushes into my unenthusiastic mind as I'm led into the store, where I immediately feel overwhelmed by the hustle and bustle and flurry of activity. "It's so busy," I moan, following

Miller's purposeful strides. My gripe is brushed off as we weave the masses of shoppers, mostly tourists.

"You wanted to shop," Miller reminds me, coming to a stop at the men's fragrance counter.

"Would you like any help, sir?" a painted lady asks, smiling brightly. She's definitely checking him out. It makes me even grumpier.

"Tom Ford, original," Miller orders shortly.

"Certainly." She indicates the shelf behind her. "Would sir like the fifty or the hundred milliliters?"

"Hundred."

"Would you like a tester?"

"No."

"I would." I cut in, moving closer to the counter. "Please." I smile and watch her eyebrows rise in surprise before she spritzes some onto a card and hands it to me. "Thank you."

"Most welcome."

I hold the card to my nose and sniff. And very nearly die of pleasure. It's like Miller has been bottled. "Hmmm." My eyes close and I keep the card to my nose. Heaven.

"Good?" he whispers in my ear, his closeness adding to my delighted sense of smell.

"Out of this world," I say quietly. "It smells just like you."

"Or *I* smell like *that*," Miller corrects me as he hands a credit card to the woman, whose eyes are now bouncing back and forth between us. She runs the transaction through and smiles as she hands the bag over to me. It's a fake smile.

"Thank you." I accept the bag, finally relenting and removing the fragranced card from my nose, popping it in the bag. Then I claim Miller's hand. "Have a good day."

He leads me away to the escalators, Miller choosing to walk the stairs instead of letting them carry us to the top.

We leave the escalator and Miller fights our way through more people, guiding us onto another set of stairs, and then through more people and departments.

I'm all disoriented, the buzz of activity and the twists and turns through the giant store sending me dizzy. I'm just following Miller's lead, gazing around blankly while he strides on with purpose, clearly knowing exactly where he wants to be. This doesn't sit well. If I see a suit, I might rip it up.

"Here we are." He stops on the threshold of an area designated for men and drops my grasp, sliding his hands into his pockets. My eyes widen at the array of clothes before me. Heaps of them. Things are jumping out already, my legs eager to take me off in one direction, but then my eyes spot something else I quite fancy and halt me. There's too much.

And it's predominantly casual.

His breath hits my ear. "I believe this is what you are looking for."

Happiness and exhilaration sail through me and I turn to look up at him, finding a satisfied glimmer in his brilliant blue eyes. "You must be soaring in your second favorite pleasure," I tell him, because I'm beside myself with glee. He's going to let me dress him. He's like a human clotheshorse, every inch of his physique just perfect and ready for me to grace it with something other than a three-piece suit.

"Indeed I am," he confirms, making me want to squeal in excitement when he scrambles my elation further by smiling.

I hold my breath to stop the screech of joy and grab his hand. Then I practically haul him through the department, my eyes darting everywhere, looking for perfect casual pieces to dress my perfect Miller in.

"Livy!" he gasps in alarm as he virtually staggers along behind me. But I don't stop. "Olivia!" He's laughing now, and that does snap me out of my dogged march through Harrods, having me flying around to catch a glimpse of it.

I nearly pass out at the sight...nearly. My wooziness is an improvement on bursting into tears. "Oh shit, Miller," I whisper, my hand gliding across the back of my neck and stroking... soothing...doing what Miller usually does. I'm missing it. I'm like a kid in a candy shop with too many appealing things surrounding me—Miller smiling, Miller laughing, and an abundance of casual wear to dress him in. I'm getting all confused by it, not knowing whether to soak up the pleasure of seeing Miller so animated or drag him into the dressing rooms before he changes his mind.

His face gets closer to mine, his eyes still shimmering and his lips still stretched into a smile. It leaves me with my usual dilemma.

Eyes or mouth.

"Earth to Olivia." He speaks softly, displaying enjoyment at my muddled state. "Do you need my *thing*?" His delicate touch ghosts my pale cheek, and I nod for fear of wailing on him again. I feel emotional, which is stupid. He's making me happy, even if a fraction of the reason why we're here is guilt because of his outburst at the previous store.

Miller holds my eyes with his as he moves in closer until his scent drowns me and his nose is nuzzling my cheek. Then he presses the firmness of his body into me and slowly lifts me from my feet and moves his nuzzle into my neck. I cling on tightly. Very tightly. And so does he.

We remain entwined, lost in each other's embrace, right in the middle of Harrods, and neither of us is bothered by any potential observers. I suddenly don't care so much for trying to strip down Miller's suit-clad façade. I want him to take me home, put me in his bed, and worship me.

"I said I didn't want to be long," he whispers into my neck, still holding on to me securely.

"Hmmm." I muster the strength from somewhere to release him and find my feet. "Thank you." I spend a few seconds brushing down the sleeves of his suit while he watches me.

"Don't ever thank me, Livy."

"I'll always be grateful for you." I finish up with my smoothing hands and step back. He's brought me back to life, even if that life is questionable and stressful. But I have my fastidious part-time gentleman and his perfect, precise world now.

Superb shoes appear in my downcast vision, prompting my eyes to flip up to his. He's still smiling, but it's subsided a little. "You have thirty minutes."

"Right!" I snap from my thoughtfulness and immediately stride off toward a wall of shelves with piles and piles of jeans filling them. Miller in jeans just seems . . . weird, but I'm desperate to see the back of those suits, or at least reduce their appearances. And the potential of his perfect arse encased in perfect denim is far too appealing to resist. I scan the tags that describe the fit of each style and finally snatch down a stonewash pair that claim to be a relaxed fit. Which sounds perfect. "Here." I turn as I shake them out, trying to gauge the size. The legs of these are way too short for Miller's long, lean limbs. I quickly fold them back up and swap them for a longer leg. "There." I hold them up against my front, smiling to myself when I have to raise the waist to the base of my chest just to get the hem of the legs off the floor. "These should fit."

"Would you like to know my size?" he asks, pulling my stare from the blue denim to the blue of his smiling eyes. They're nearly a perfect match.

My lips press together and I make a quick scan of his physique.

"This body should be carved onto that lovely mind of yours, Livy." His voice is low, seductive, and sexy as sin.

"It is"—I shuffle on the spot—"but I couldn't put numbers on it."

"Those are perfect." He takes them from my hands and gives the garment a dubious look. "And what would my gorgeous girl have me wear with them?"

I grin at his willingness to humor me and pivot, spotting a T-shirt across the way. "That." I point and watch from the corner of my eye as Miller follows my gesture.

"That?" he questions, a hint of alarm in his tone.

"Yes." I wander over and unhook the faded, vintage-look T-shirt from the rail. "Plain, casual, laid-back." I hold it up. "Perfect."

He doesn't think it's perfect at all, but he still joins me and takes it from my hand. "Feet?"

I glance around on a frown. "Where's the shoe department?"

A heavy sigh engulfs my hearing. "I'll show you."

It's a strain for him, but I'm utterly stunned by his willingness, not that I'll show it. Right now, I'm in my element. "Lead the way." I swoop my hand out on a grin and immediately follow him when he strides off. My hands are twitching at my sides, desperate to grab a few more items on our travels, but I know this is taking all of his patience and the risk of him running out of it deters me. One step at a time.

I watch Miller with interest as we pass through another department, this one bursting at the seams with suits. They're everywhere, teasing him, and it takes everything in me not to laugh when I catch him having a cheeky peek. "Ralph Lauren does some exquisite suits," he remarks quietly, forcing himself to push on.

"He also does lovely casual wear," I counter, knowing Miller wouldn't know that.

"Miller!" The high-pitched shrill eats away at the flesh on my shoulders and when I turn to see an annoyingly preened woman approaching, a sour expression replaces my happy face. She's glowing, hurrying her steps to make it to him faster. She's near-on perfect, just like the rest of them, all shiny hair, flawless makeup, and expensive clothes. I'm bracing myself for another reality check. I immediately hate her.

"How are you?" she sings at him, not giving me a second

glance. No, her attention is rooted on my perfect Miller. "You look as dashing as always."

"Bethany," Miller greets, flat and cold, all evidence of the ease that was delighting me disappearing in a flash of red lips and perfectly styled hair. "I'm very well, thank you. Yourself?"

She pouts her lips and transfers her weight onto one hip, tilting her body to the side. Her body language is throwing off vibes of attraction left, right, and full-force center. "Always well, you know that."

I roll my eyes and bite my tongue, wilting on the inside. Another one. Now she just needs to spot me and finish me off with one of those looks or the delivery of some mocking words. And if she pulls out one of his cards, I won't be held responsible for my actions.

"Excellent," he replies, short and sharp, despite being perfectly polite. I can sense his restlessness, all of the signs of Miller and his need to repel people surfacing, and it's in this moment that I wonder why these women are so taken by him when he can be so hostile. He's a perfect gentleman on dates—he said so himself—but what's the pull beyond that? How would they respond to him if he were to bless them with his worshipping ways? I inwardly laugh. They'd be like me. Nonfunctioning without him. Doomed. Dead.

Miller clears his throat and shifts the clothes in his hands. "We'll be on our way," he says, sidestepping Bethany, obviously expecting me to follow, but when I feel a pair of inquisitive eyes land on me, I'm unable to convince my legs to move. Here it comes.

"Oh," she breathes, running interested eyes down the full length of me. "Looks like someone beat me to him today." My mouth drops open, and she smiles, clearly unperturbed by my affronted state. "I'm sorry, you are?"

I'm going to tell her exactly who I am. *Accept it or learn to deal with it better.* Those are my options. I have sass, that's been confirmed, and I need to start using it wisely. This woman, just like the rest of them, makes me feel inferior, yet Miller isn't showing signs of anger at the potential of this woman driving a wedge between us or making me doubt my worthiness. "Hi, I'm Oli—"

"Sorry, we're late," Miller cuts me off, just when I've located my sass and am about to unleash it. "Always a pleasure." He nods at Bethany, who now looks *really* interested, and gently pushes into my back rather than take his customary hold of my neck.

"Oh, it is," Bethany purrs. The rigidity that dominates Miller's entire being is instant. "Hope to see you soon."

I'm pushed away fast, both of us silent, the tension palpable. *Always a pleasure.* I bristle on the inside *and* out. We round a corner, arriving at the men's shoe department, and Miller immediately grabs the first pair in sight and presents them to me. I don't look. Bethany has undone all of our progress this morning. "These?" He's desperately trying to divert me. It won't work. The sass I was about to hit that woman with is now bubbling, a bit of anger mixing in for good measure, and there's only one other person to release it on.

I bat the shoes away. "No."

He recoils, eyes wide and perfect lips slightly agape. "I beg your pardon?"

My eyes narrow into angry slits. "Don't start with the begging," I warn. "She was a client. Could she be following me?"

"No." He almost laughs.

"Why didn't you just let me introduce myself? And why didn't you put her straight?"

Miller places the shoe carefully back onto the display stand and even tweaks the damn thing into position before stepping into me thoughtfully. My body's response is irritating and unwanted, but a given. "I've told you before, I don't want anyone interfering, so the fewer people who know, the better." The pad of his index finger brings my tense chin up to his dark stubbled face. I can see annoyance hovering on the edges of his beauty. "When I say there is only *us*—no *me* or *you*—I also mean no *them*."

However tempting an existence with only me and Miller is, it's also impossible. "How many are there?" I ask. I need to know how many of them I have to face. I need a tick sheet, something to mark them all off as I'm confronted with them. How many will predict his next move? How many will follow me?

"It's of no importance"—he slides his palm over my shoulder and starts massaging some calm into me—"because now there is only *my* sweet girl." His sincerity creeps into me, chasing my doubts away.

Leave it.

Gathering myself, I find no words in reply, so I grab a boot from a nearby table. "These," I announce, not giving Miller the chance to refuse and handing them straight to an assistant instead.

She smiles, her back straightening when she captures her first look of Miller. "Yes, madam. Size?" She keeps her greedy eyes on him, unwittingly goading me. I'd love to tell her what size, but I'm devastated to have to turn to Miller to ask.

"Eleven," he says quietly, regarding me closely. I hate the inward gasp of delight that emanates from the sales assistant, and I hate myself for biting to her clear interest.

I step in front of Miller and turn annoyed eyes onto her. "An eleven," I confirm, nodding at the shoe. "And it's true what they say." I'm stunned by my blatant suggestion, and Miller's shocked cough behind me tells me he is, too. But I don't care. Today has been far from quality time, and all the interference is beginning to piss me off.

"Certainly!" The shop assistant jumps at the decibel level of her own voice, avoiding my eyes and fighting a furious blush. "Please, take a seat. I'll be right back." She's off without delay, no swaying arse or coy look over her shoulder in sight. I grin to myself, getting a satisfied thrill from the discomfort I've caused while making a mental promise to maintain this sass.

"I have a request." Miller's whisper in my ear wipes my smugness clean from my face. I don't want to confront him, but I'm given little choice when my shoulders are clasped and I'm turned in his hold. I brace myself, knowing what I'll find. I'm right. He's expressionless with a familiar hint of disapproval in his eyes.

"What?" All satisfaction has been drawn from my body by the condemnation leaking from Miller in droves. I've overstepped the mark.

His hands slide into his pockets. "What's true and who says it?"

My lips stretch to the point of ripping. "You know what and who."

"Elaborate," he orders, not returning my delight.

It makes me grin harder. "In Harrods?"

"Yes."

"Well"—I shift and quickly scan our surroundings, seeing too many shoppers in close proximity to speak of such a thing—"I'll tell you later." He's doing this on purpose. He knows.

"No." He moves in, bringing his chest to mine, breathing down on me. "I'd like to know now. I feel in the dark." If he's struggling to maintain his seriousness, then he's not showing it. He's perfectly composed, even grave.

"You're playing." I step back, but he's having none of it and closes the small space that I've created.

"Tell me."

Damn him. I search deep for my sass and piece together an explanation on an embarrassed whisper. "Feet and a male's"—I cough—"manhood."

"What about them?"

"Miller!" I fidget, feeling my cheeks heat under the pressure.

"Tell me, Livy."

"Fine!" I snap, reaching up on my tiptoes to push my mouth to his ear. "Big feet are said to equal big cocks." My face flames as I feel his head nod thoughtfully against me, his hair tickling my cheek.

"Is that so?" he asks, maintaining all seriousness. The bastard.

"Yes."

"Interesting," he muses, then blows hot breath into my ear. It knocks me even more off kilter and my stability fails me, sending me on a little stagger forward. I collide with his chest on a gasp. "Okay there?" His tone is loaded with conceit.

"Fine and dandy," I mutter, forcing some strength into my weakness and pulling out of his chest.

"Fine and dandy," he muses quietly, a roving eye watching me struggling to compose myself. "Oh look." He nods over my shoulder, prompting me to turn. "Here are my size elevens."

I chuckle to myself, earning a poke in the back by Miller and a puzzled look from the sales assistant. "Elevens!" she sings, making my laughter cross the line into uncontrollable body spasms. "You okay, miss?"

"Yes!" I yell, turning away and picking up the first shoe I can find, anything to distract me from the size elevens. I cough when I look at the size, seeing it stating in big, bold type that the shoe I've chosen to distract myself with is, in fact, a size eleven. I fold over on a titter and shove it back.

"She's fine," Miller confirms. I'm not looking at him, but I know he's staring at my back, appearing expressionless to the assistant, but he'll have that playful twinkle in his eyes. If I could face Miller and the flirty assistant without snorting all over them, then I'd be swiveling fast to catch the wonderful sight. But I can't stop laughing, my shoulders bouncing violently.

Studying the random shoe carefully, grinning like an idiot, I listen to the crumpling of tissue paper as the assistant removes the boots from the box. "Do you need a shoehorn, sir?" she asks.

"Doubt it," Miller grumbles, probably inspecting the boots and mentally complaining about their lack of leather soles. I pull it together and rotate slowly, finding Miller sitting on a suede seat, wrestling his foot into a boot. Observing quietly, as does the assistant, I think how lovely the boots are, all casual in soft, worn brown leather.

"Comfy?" I ask hopefully, bracing myself for his scoff, but he ignores me and stands, looking down at his feet before hastily returning to sitting.

He undoes the laces and places the boot neatly back in the box. I want to scream my excitement when I see him shift it, making the pair as neat as possible amid the tissue paper. He likes them, and I know that for sure because he has an appreciation for his possessions and those boots are now his possession. "They'll do," he says to himself, like he doesn't want to admit it out loud.

My grin is back. He *will* concede, damn him. "Do. You. Like?"

Tying his laces with the utmost care, he turns his face up and studies me. "Yes." He draws the word out with raised brows, daring me to make a big deal of it.

I can't hide my happiness. I know it, Miller knows it, and when I grab the box, then turn and thrust it into the assistant's hand with a huge smile, she knows it, too. "We'll take them, thank you."

"Wonderful, I'll place them behind the counter." She's off with the box, leaving Miller and me alone.

I scoop up the jeans and T-shirt. "Let's try these on." His sigh of tiredness won't make me give in. Nothing will. I'll get him kitted out in a casual outfit if it kills me. "This way." I march off in the direction of the changing rooms, knowing Miller is following because my skin is alight with the signs of his close proximity.

I turn and hand him the clothes, then watch as he takes them without a word of complaint and disappears into the changing room. I take a seat to watch the hustle and bustle of Harrods, spotting every walk of life—the tourists; the people here to treat themselves, like Nan and her fifteen-quid pineapple; and the people who clearly shop here on a regular basis, like Miller and his bespoke suits. The mix is eclectic and so is the stock. There's something for everyone; no one leaves empty-handed, even if it's a simple tin of Harrods biscuits that they'll give as a special gift or save for Christmas. I smile, then whip my head around when I hear a familiar cough.

My smile widens into silly territory at the sight of his expression, stressed and challenged—then falls away when I cop a load of what's below his neck. He's standing barefoot in the doorway, jeans hanging low, a perfect fit, and his T-shirt clinging in all of the right places. I bite my lip to stop my mouth from falling open. Fucking hell, he looks too sexy. His hair is all ruffled from where he's pulled the T-shirt over his head, a flushed look on his cheeks from the stress of it, which is laughable. There's no buttons to neatly fasten or hem to tuck in, no belt to secure or tie to knot, no collar to arrange, making it a stress-free task.

Supposedly.

He looks stressed to breaking point. "You look amazing," I say quietly, taking a quick glimpse over my shoulder, finding what I knew I would: women at every turn staring, mouths agape at the otherworldly man before them. Closing my eyes on a calming suck of air, I leave the sight of the dozens of observers and confront my spectacular part-time gentleman. Miller adorned in the finest of fine suits is a sight to behold, but strip him bare of all of the exquisite cloth and throw him in some worn jeans and a plain T-shirt, then we're bordering unreal.

He fidgets and pulls at the T-shirt and kicks his feet out, uncomfortable with the hems of the jeans. "*You* look amazing, Olivia. *I* look like I've been dragged through a hedge backward."

I restrain my smirk, Miller's agitation giving me the strength to do so. I need to win him over, not irritate him further, so I move in slowly, watching as he notices me nearing. He stops fiddling and follows my path until I'm looking up at him. "I beg to differ," I whisper, my eyes running all over his bristly face.

"Why do you want me in these clothes?"

His question brings our eyes together. I know why, but I can't articulate my answer so he'll understand. He won't get it, and I also run the risk of angering him. "Because... I..." I stumble all over my words under his crowding frame. "I..."

"I'm not wearing these clothes if the reason is simply to make you feel better about us or if you think it'll change me." He slides a palm onto my shoulder and rubs soothing strokes into my tense muscles. "I'm not wearing these clothes if you think it'll stop people interfering... looking... commenting." His other hand rests on my other shoulder, his arms braced, his head dipping to hold our eyes level. "It is me who is the unworthy one, Olivia. And *you* help me. Not the clothes. Why don't you see that?"

"I—"

"I'm not finished," he cuts me off, firming up his grip and drilling into me with warning eyes. I'd be stupid to argue. His suit has gone, but this casual attire hasn't chased away his authority or powerful presence. And I'm glad. I need that. "Olivia, take me as I am."

"I do." Guilt consumes me.

"Then let me put my suit back on." He's begging me with his absorbing blues, and for the first time ever, I realize that Miller's suits aren't just a mask; they are armor, too. He needs them. He feels safe in them. He feels in control in them. His perfect suits are a part of his perfect world and a perfect addition to my perfect Miller. I want him to keep them. I don't think forcing him to wear jeans will lighten him up in the least bit, and I wonder whether I even want him to lose his uptight demeanor. I understand him. It's of no consequence to me how he behaves in public, because for me, he's worshipful. Loving. My finicky fine Miller. It's me who's the issue here. My hang-ups. I need to get a grip.

Nodding, I take the hem of his T-shirt and pull it over his head as he lifts his arms willingly. A mass of lean, cut flesh is revealed, drawing more attention from shoppers nearby, even the men, and I hand the crumpled T-shirt to the assistant, keeping my sorry eyes on Miller. "It's not suitable," I murmur. Miller smiles at me—a grateful smile that yanks painfully at my selfish, fallen heart.

"Thank you," he says softly, taking me in his arms and pressing me against his naked chest. My cheek rests into a pec and I sigh, sliding my hands beneath his upper arms and holding him tightly.

"Don't ever thank me."

"I'll always be thankful for you, Olivia Taylor." He mimics my words and kisses my forehead. "Always."

"And me you."

"I'm glad we've cleared that up. Now, would you like to remove these jeans?"

I let my gaze fall to his thighs, a stupid move because I've just been reminded of how incredible Miller looks in denim. "No, you go." I push him into the changing room, eager to deprive my eyes of the glorious vision, especially since it's quite apparent that I won't be seeing it again. "I'll wait here."

Happy with myself, I take a seat, feeling a million eyes on me. From every direction. But I don't humor any of the onlookers and instead retrieve my phone from my bag . . . to be greeted with two missed calls and a text message from William. My body sags on an almighty groan. Facing interested stares is suddenly very appealing.

> You're maddening, Olivia. I'm sending a car for you this evening. 7 pm. I presume you will be at Josephine's. William.

My neck retracts, as if taking my eyes farther from the screen will change what the message says. It doesn't. Irritation consumes me and my thumb bashes over the touch screen automatically.

I'm busy.

There. He'll send a car? Like hell he will, and I don't plan on being there anyway. Which prompts me to send another message.

I won't be there.

I don't need the curtains twitching and Nan's inquisitive nose pushed up against the glass. She'll fly into meltdown if she sniffs William out. His response is instant.

Don't push me, Olivia. We need to talk about your shadow.

I gasp, recalling his vow when he walked out of Miller's apartment yesterday. How does he know? I spin my phone in my hand, thinking this is the ammo he needs to follow through on his threat. I'm not confirming it, despite my overwhelming need to know how he knows, and just as I reach that decision, my phone starts ringing. I tense and automatically stab at the Reject button before I send him a quick text, telling him I'll call him later, hoping it'll buy me some time. I phone Nan to tell her that my battery is dying and I'll call her from Miller's, earning a rant about pointless mobile telephones. Then I turn my phone off.

"Olivia?"

I look up and feel all irritation and panic evaporate from my body at the sight of Miller restored to his normal, perfect, suit-adorned self. "My phone's died," I tell him, tossing it carelessly into my bag and standing. "Lunch?"

"Yes, let's eat." My neck is grasped and we're on our way without delay, leaving behind a casual outfit that I love but don't care for now and a flurry of women reassessing Miller now that he's changed. They still like what they see, which is a given. "Well, that's half an hour of our lives together that we'll never get back."

I hum my agreement, trying not to let my mind wander too much, yet appreciating that no matter how much I pray, William Anderson isn't going away, especially if he knows about my shadow.

"It's a good thing we're no longer limited to one night."

I gasp and twist my neck in his palm to see him. He's staring blankly forward, not a hint of irony on his face. "I want more hours," I murmur, seeing blues full of recognition flick down to me.

He dips and kisses my nose chastely before straightening and leading on. "My sweet girl, you have a whole lifetime."

Happiness bombards me and I slip my arm around his waist, hugging his side, feeling his forearm rest against the top of my spine so that he can maintain his hold while accommodating my demand for closeness. The chaos of Harrods is no longer registering. Nothing is, except memories of a one-night proposition and all of the events that have led us here. My fallen heart bursts with happiness.

CHAPTER Twenty-ONE

I flap the fleece blanket and let it settle on the grass, visiting each corner to get it as straight as possible in the hopes of reducing any obsessive need that Miller may have to fix it. "Sit." I point on my command.

"Whatever was wrong with a restaurant?" he asks, placing two M&S carrier bags on the grass.

"You can't picnic in a restaurant." I watch him lower awkwardly to the ground, pulling the tails of his suit jacket from beneath his arse when he sits on them. "Take your jacket off."

Blue eyes hit me, awash with shock. "Why?"

"You'll be more comfortable." I drop to my knees and start pushing his jacket from his shoulders, encouraging him to pull his arms out. He doesn't complain or object, but he *does* watch worriedly while I fold it in half and lay it as neatly as possible at one end of the blanket. "Better," I conclude, grabbing the carrier bags. I ignore the slight twitching that Miller's body has developed. It requires no acknowledgment, because within a minute he'll be rearranging his jacket to fit his compulsive need, whether I acknowledge the issue or not. I could iron it into position and it would still be wrong. "Would you like prawn or chicken?" I hold up two containers of salad, just catching him quickly yanking his eyes from his jacket.

He tries his damn hardest to look unbothered and unaffected, flicking an indifferent look at me and then signaling between the bowls with a casual flick of a hand. "I really don't mind."

"I like chicken."

"Then I'll have prawn."

I can see the muscles of his eyes pulling his blues in their sockets toward his jacket as I hand him the prawn salad. "There's a fork in the lid." I pop the lid of my salad and settle on my haunches, watching as he inspects the container.

"It's plastic?"

"Yes, it's plastic!" I laugh, placing my bowl on the blanket and taking Miller's. I remove the lid, snap the fork into one, and plunge it in the array of salad and prawn. "Enjoy."

He takes the bowl and has a little poke before taking a tentative mouthful and chewing slowly. He's like a science project. The need to study him in action is overwhelming. I follow his lead and take my own salad and fork, popping a forkful in my mouth. It's all done absentmindedly, my desire to continue my engrossed examination of Miller too much to resist. I bet Miller Hart has never sat on his arse in Hyde Park. I bet he's never eaten a salad from a plastic container, and I bet he's never entertained the idea of disposable cutlery. It's all very fascinating—always has been, probably always will be.

"I hope you're not overthinking."

I'm pulled so fast from my musing by Miller's declaration that I drop a lump of chicken into my lap. "Shit!" I curse, scooping it up.

"See," Miller says, his tone full of smugness. "That wouldn't happen in a restaurant and you'd have a napkin." He pops a forkful of lettuce in his mouth and chews smugly.

I glare at him, unamused, and reach for the bag, pulling out a pack of disposable napkins and ripping it open. With precision and on a sarcastic hum, I wipe up the mayo smearing my floral dress. "Problem solved." I screw up the paper and toss it to the side.

"And a waiter would be available to clear our litter."

"Miller," I sigh. "Everyone should picnic in Hyde Park."

"Why?"

"Just because!" I point my fork at him. "Stop looking for issues."

He snorts and rids his hands of his salad bowl, then moves stealthily toward his jacket. "I'm not looking. They are quite apparent without the need to search for them." He collects his jacket and refolds it before placing it gently down. "Seasoning?"

"Huh?"

"Seasoning." He takes his place again, and his salad. "What if I required some extra seasoning on this"—he glances down at the bowl doubtfully—"meal."

I drop my bowl and collapse to my back in exasperation. The sky is blue and clear and I'd usually be captured by it, but the pleasant view is being hampered by a mind crammed with frustration. A picnic. That's all.

"What's wrong, sweet girl?" His face appears, hovering above me.

"You!" I accuse. "Quality time, that's what you said, and this could be it if you'd stop being such a snob and enjoy the scenery, food, and company."

"I *love* the company." He drops his mouth to mine and blindsides me with his worshipping, soft lips. "I'm merely pointing out the drawbacks of picnicking, the biggest drawback being unable to worship you."

"You couldn't do that in a restaurant."

"I beg to differ." He cocks a suggestive eyebrow at me.

"For being such a 'gentleman,' sometimes your sexual etiquette is questionable." I wince at my careless words, but Miller doesn't acknowledge them, choosing to nudge my thighs apart and cradle himself between them. I'm stunned. He'll be a crumpled mess.

He clasps my cheeks and his nose meets mine. "For a sweet girl, sometimes your sweetness is questionable. Give me my *thing*."

"You'll be all creased."

"I've asked once."

I smile and waste no time embracing Miller's momentary spontaneity *and* his body. Soaking up the weight of him, I inhale the fresh air that's diluted by his scent. My eyes close and I bliss out completely, finally relishing in the quality time that I've been promised. He's warm and soothing and all mine, and as I start to zone out, the hustle and bustle of Hyde Park fading into a distant hum, thoughts start tickling the edges of my contented mind—tickling for a nanosecond, before something so stupidly obvious wraps around my entire brain, leaving no room for contentment and making my relaxed body solidify beneath Miller. He senses it, because probing eyes are gazing down at me in a heartbeat.

"Share with me," he says simply, smoothing my hair from my face.

I shake my head in his hold, hoping to shake away my uninvited thoughts.

And fail.

Miller's face is close, but all I can see is a grubby, lost little boy. You can't tell me that the child in the photograph ate like a king, and I know for sure there were no expensive threads adorning his young body, more rags instead.

"Olivia?" I detect concern in his tone. "Please, share your burden with me." There's no evading him, even less so when he pushes himself up to his knees and pulls me to mine. We're mirroring each other, our hands clasped and resting in his lap while he rubs gentle circles across my skin with his thumbs. "Olivia?"

I make a point of holding our eyes when I speak, searching for any mild reaction to my question. "Please tell me why everything needs to be so perfect."

There's nothing. No frown, no expression or telling signs in his eyes. He's perfectly composed. "We've had this discussion before, and I'm certain we agreed that we'd exhausted that subject."

"No, you *told* me that the subject was exhausted." It wasn't exhausted at all, and now my horrible thought process is stamping all over my conclusions. He's ashamed of his upbringing. He wants to eradicate it all from his memory. He wants to hide it.

"For good reason." He drops my hands and looks away from me, searching for something to do other than face me and my pressing questions. He settles on messing with his suit jacket, smoothing the already immaculately folded garment.

"And what is that reason?" My heart breaks when he glances at me out of the corner of his eye, caution on his handsome face. "Miller, what is that reason?" I inch toward him slowly, as if approaching a frightened animal, and rest my hand on his forearm. He looks down, frozen in position, clearly in a muddle. I'm patient. I've drawn my conclusion, yet I'm unable to share it with him. He'll know I've snooped, and I want him to volunteer this information about his history. Share it with me.

It's merely seconds, but it feels like an eternity, before he shakes himself back to life and stands, leaving my hand falling to the blanket and my eyes looking up at him. He takes his jacket and slips it on, buttoning it fast before pulling at the sleeves. "Because it was exhausted," he says, insulting my intelligence with his pathetic brush-off. "I need to go to Ice."

"Right," I sigh, and start to collect the remnants of our brief picnic, piling the rubbish into a carrier bag. "Actually, no." I toss the bag aside and stand, getting up close and personal with Miller's tall frame. I must look tiny and fragile next to him, but my resolve is huge. He's constantly demanding I share my burdens, yet he's happy to shoulder his own. "I'm not coming to Ice," I say, drilling holes into him, knowing he won't go without me. Not after this morning. He wants to keep me close, which is fine by me, but not at Ice.

"I beg to differ," he snorts, but his tone is lacking its usual confidence and in an attempt to show he means business, he takes my neck and tries to turn me.

"Miller, I said no!" I shrug him off, anger and frustration afflicting me, and hit him with burning eyes of determination. "I'm not coming." I sit down again, kick my flip-flops off, and collapse to my back, swapping the blue of Miller's eyes for the blue of the sky. "I'm going to enjoy some quiet time in the park. You can go to Ice alone." I'll kick and scream if he tries to manhandle me.

I take my arms behind my head and keep my eyes on the sky, sensing him fidgeting over me. He doesn't know what to do. He loves my sass, supposedly. Bet he doesn't now. I settle in for the show, getting comfy, determined not to budge, and find my thoughts drifting back to what had my sass rearing its ugly head in the first place. Miller and his perfect world. My conclusion is simple, and it's nothing to be ashamed of. He had a poor upbringing, with shabby rags for clothes, and now he's obsessive about wearing the finest threads he can buy.

How he came to have the money to buy the millions of suits of armor he possesses is irrelevant. Kind of. Not at all. My conclusion has only led to more questions—questions I dare not ask, not for fear of upsetting him, but for fear of what the answer might be. How did he come to be in "this world"? That house was a children's home. Miller has spoken of no parents and confirmed there is only him. He's an orphan. My fussy, fine, perfect Miller has been alone forever. My heart's breaking for him.

I'm so lost in my sobering thoughts I jump a little when a warm hardness is suddenly pressing into my side. My head falls to the side to find his eyes. He's snuggled right in and after laying a gentle kiss on my cheek, he rests his head on my shoulder and slides his arm over my stomach.

"I want to be with you," he whispers. His actions and his words have my arms relinquishing cushion duties for my head and wrapping around him where I can. "Every minute of every day, I want to be with you."

My smile is sad, because having reached my assumption, I know that Miller hasn't had a someone before. "Us," I confirm, squeezing some comfort into him. "I love your bones, Miller Hart."

"And I'm deeply fascinated by you, Olivia Taylor."

I squeeze him harder. We lie on the fleece blanket forever, Miller humming and painting pictures across my midriff with the tip of his finger, me just feeling him, listening to him, smelling him, and giving him his *thing*. It is quality time, and it's the most blissful quality time imaginable.

"This has been nice," he muses, pushing up onto his elbow, resting his perfectly stubbled chin in his palm. He continues to trace faint lines across my tummy, observing his tender motions thoughtfully. I'm happy to watch him. It's unbelievably pleasurable, total heaven. We're captured in our own private moment, surrounded by the ramblings of Hyde Park and the distant chaos of London by day. Yet totally alone. "Are you chilly?" He looks up at me, then skates his gaze down my little floral dress. The evening is drawing in and a light breeze is whipping up. I look up to the sky and note a few gray clouds slowly drifting over.

"I'm okay, but it looks like rain is on its way."

Miller follows my eyes to the sky and sighs. "And London casts its black shadow," he muses to himself, so quietly I almost don't hear him. But I did hear him, and I know there's a deeper meaning to that statement. I draw breath to speak, but think better of it, and he pushes himself to his feet before I can ask, anyway. "Give me your hand."

I take his offering and let him pull me effortlessly to my feet. He's creased as hell, but apparently not too bothered by it. "Can we do this again sometime?" I ask as I gather up our half-finished salads and place them in a bag.

Miller sets about folding the blanket into a tidy bundle. "Of course," he agrees gladly, with no trace of unwillingness. He really has enjoyed himself, and that warms my contented heart further. "I really must stop by the club." My delicate shoulders sag and Miller spots it. "I'll be quick," he assures me, moving in and dipping to brush our lips lightly. "I promise."

Refusing to let anything more spoil our quality time, I link arms with him and let him walk us across the grass until we hit the pathway. "Can I stay with you tonight?" I'm feeling guilty for my regular absence from home, but I know Nan's not in the least bit bothered by it, and I'll call her as soon as we're back at Miller's.

"Livy, you stay with me whenever you choose. You don't have to ask."

"I shouldn't leave Nan alone."

He laughs lightly, pulling my eyes up his chest to his face. "Your grandmother would put the most ferocious guard dog to shame."

I return his amusement and rest my head on his arm as we amble along. "I concur."

A strong arm wraps around my shoulder and hugs me to his side. "If you'd prefer me to take you home, then I will."

"But I want to stay with you."

"And I'd love to have you in my bed."

"I'll call Nan as soon as we're back at your place," I affirm, making a point to remember to ask her if she minds, even though I know for sure that she doesn't.

"Okay," he agrees on a little laugh.

"Oh, there's a bin." I rustle the bags in my hand and head over to the bin, but my stride falters when I spot a sorrowful-looking man slumped on the bench nearby. He looks tatty, dirty, and vacant—one of the many homeless people who frequent the streets of London. My pace to the trash bin slows as I watch him twitching, and I conclude very quickly that drugs or alcohol are probably the cause. Human nature stokes the compassion within me, and when he raises empty eyes to mine, I stop walking completely. I stare at the man, who's probably barely a man—late teens, perhaps, but life on the streets has taken its toll. His skin is sallow, his lips dry.

"Spare any change, miss?" he croaks at me, yanking tighter at my heartstrings. It's not uncommon to be asked such a question, and I usually find it reasonably easy to walk on by, especially since Nan reminds me every time that by lining their pockets with money, you're also probably funding their drug or drink habit. But this disheveled young man with scruffy, ripped clothes and disintegrating trainers is reminding me of something, and I can't seem to push my legs on.

After spending far too long staring at him, his open palm extends toward me, snapping me from my miserable thoughts and the flashbacks of a lost-looking child. "Miss?" he repeats.

"I'm sorry." I shake my head and continue, but as I lift the bag to drop it into the bin, a warm palm wraps around my wrist and holds it firm.

"Wait." Miller's low timbre strokes my skin and pulls my eyes to his. Without another word, he claims the bag and takes the two half-eaten salads out, then places the carrier in the trash bin before turning and striding over to the homeless man. I watch in astonished silence as Miller reaches him and drops to his haunches, handing the two bowls over, followed by the fleece blanket. Tentative hands accept Miller's offering and a heavy head nods its thanks. Tears pinch at the back of my eyes and very nearly fall when my perfect part-time gentleman lays a palm on the man's knee and rubs a reassuring circle into the dirty leg of his jeans. Miller's actions are delicate, caring, and knowing. They are the actions of someone who understands. He's telling me his story slowly, but with no words. They are not needed. His actions speak volumes, and I'm shocked by them, but most of all saddened.

That lost little boy was still lost.

Until I found him.

I watch closely as Miller rises to his full height and slips his hands into the pockets of his expensive suit trousers, then slowly turns to face me. He just stands there, regarding me carefully as I draw another gut-wrenching conclusion. An orphan? Homeless? I bite painfully on my lip, anything to prevent the threatening sorrow from gushing from my eyes at the sight of my beautifully broken man.

"Don't cry," he murmurs, closing the distance between us.

I shake my head, feeling silly. "I'm sorry."

My forehead meets the crook under his chin when he's near enough, holding my distraught body up, and strong arms surround me in his safety. "Give him money and he'll likely buy drugs, alcohol, or cigarettes," he tells me quietly. "Give him food and a blanket, then he'll sate his hunger and keep warm." He kisses the top of my head and breaks away from me, quickly wiping the stream of tears trailing down my cheeks. "Do you know how many lost children there are on the streets of London, Olivia?"

I shake my head a little.

"It's not all opulence and grandeur. This city is beautiful, but tainted by a dark underworld."

I absorb his quiet words, feeling ignorant and incredibly guilty. I know he speaks the truth. And I know because not only have I skimmed the edge of it, but also because Miller has been immersed in it his whole life.

His eyes remain focused on mine, a million messages passing between us. Him telling me. And me understanding. "I've had a wonderful afternoon, thank you." He ghosts my eyebrow with his thumb and leans in to kiss my forehead.

"Me too."

He smiles and takes his customary hold of my neck, turning me and taking us toward the exit of Hyde Park. "We're going to get caught in the coming downpour if we're not careful," he says, looking up to the sky.

Following his indication, I see the gray clouds have now turned black, and then the huge splash of a fat raindrop on my cheek confirms that Miller is probably right. "We'd better run," I say quietly. Miller's suit is already a pile of creases. Sodden material to boot will tip him over the edge.

And with that thought, the heavens open.

"Oh shit!" I gasp as I'm suddenly pelted with cold, giant raindrops. "Bloody hell!" It's relentless, pounding the ground at our feet and splashing up our legs, the sound deafening.

"Run!" Miller shouts, but I'm so shocked by the sudden chilliness attacking me, I can't figure out if he's alarmed or laughing. But I do run. Fast. Miller grabs my hand and pulls me, and I look up through my wet hair to see his dark waves flattened against his head, water beads coating his face and emphasizing his long, dark lashes.

The sight makes me stop dead in my tracks and causes Miller to lose grip of my wet hand, our skin slipping apart. He skids to a halt and turns the most incredibly bright blues onto me. "Olivia, come on." He's saturated, wet through, totally drowned. He looks obscenely handsome, if a little panicked.

"Kiss me," I demand, remaining static, ignoring the pounding of rain that's now making my flesh numb from the cold.

His stunning brow furrows. It makes me smile. "What?"

"I said kiss me!" I shout over the thundering rain, wondering if he really didn't catch it.

He laughs a little, widening his stance, and then casts his eyes around us and relaxes in his standing pose. I keep my eyes on him. Nothing will pull them away. I wait for Miller to absorb our surroundings, now unbothered and unaffected by the relentless rain.

It's only a few moments before glimmering blue eyes return to me.

"Don't make me ask again," I warn, and then take the longest inhale of breath when he strides toward me, conviction and a ton of pure, raw love overflowing from his mesmerizing orbs. He lifts me up, squeezes me to his wet suit, and takes me dramatically. His palm slides to the back of my head to hold me in place and my legs part and find their way around his waist. It's a no-holds-barred, passionate kiss—full of want, lust, adoration, and comfort, and it signifies everything I feel for Miller Hart.

Our wet lips slip across each other with ease, our tongues battle furiously but gently, and my palms encase his neck, my body pushing into his. I could kiss him forever like this. The cold has been chased away by the heat of our mingling bodies, leaving no room for discomfort, just acres of space for serenity.

I have that serenity, and I know Miller does, too.

"You taste even better in the rain," he says between our hectic tongues, not prepared to stop. "Jesus, fucking divine."

"Hmmm." I could never find any words to describe how he's making me feel right now. There are none. So I show him by hardening my kiss and squeezing him tighter.

"Savored," he mumbles weakly. I hum again as he slows our kiss until our tongues are barely moving. "It turns out that I can worship you in Hyde Park." He pecks my lips and pushes my wet hair from my face.

"Not to your full ability." I keep myself coiled around his drenched body. I'm not ready to let go yet.

"I concur." He turns and starts an unhurried stride out of the park as the rain continues to beat down. "So I need to get finished at the club and get you home so I can show you my full ability."

I nod and bury my face in his neck, letting him carry me back to the car.

If there is perfect beyond Miller's perfect world, then this is it.

* * *

I'm squelching in the leather seat of Miller's Mercedes, sensing a growing concern from beside me at the soggy state of his fine car. The dual temperature control displays a medium sixteen degrees, the right number to keep Miller calm, but the wrong number given how damn cold I am. I'm dying to turn the dial up, but mindful that I'm pushing Miller's boundaries already—what with wet suits, picnics in Hyde Park, and unexpected shopping exhibitions. Turning that dial might be the straw that breaks the camel's back. I shiver and sink farther into my seat, catching Miller out of the corner of my eye sweeping his waves off his forehead.

Tracy Chapman coos about fast cars, which makes me smile as Miller is driving incredibly slowly. The air of calm and the serenity floating around our wet bodies is tangible. No words are spoken and they don't need to be. Today has been better than I could ever have imagined, hiccups earlier in the day aside. Miller has worked through some tough issues, and not only has it filled me with the most incredible amount of pride, but it's also enriched the feelings I have for him. And most satisfying of all, I know that Miller has stepped outside of his perfect box and liked where he's found himself. The fact that I am now freezing in my seat and dare not touch the temperature control of his swanky car is irrelevant.

"Are you chilly?" Miller's concerned tone doesn't grab my attention, but his question does. He's surely not going to give me heat as well as a picnic, *almost* casual clothes, and a kiss in the rain?

"I'm fine," I lie, forcing myself to stop shaking.

"Olivia, you are far from fine." He reaches forward and rotates each dial in turn, ensuring they match, taking the car's temperature to a toasty twenty-five degrees.

My elation soars and I reach over to catch a feel of his lovely stubble, all coarse and scratchy, but familiar and soothing. "Thank you."

He pushes his cheek into my touch, then takes my hand and kisses the tips of my fingers before placing our joined hands to his lap and holding them there, choosing to drive one-handed.

I never want this day to end.

Chapter Twenty-two

Tony." Miller nods in greeting, directing me past his bar manager by my neck and not seeming to notice the worried look on his face. He looks *really* worried, and while Miller appears fine with ignoring it, I'm not.

"Livy?" Tony says it like a question, like he's surprised to see me. He once said Miller was happy in his own precise little world. But I know better. Miller wasn't happy. He may have pretended to be, but I know—because he told me so himself—that he had a lovely time today.

It's clear that Tony doesn't know what to think of this soaking wet, disheveled man before him. I don't speak, just giving a small smile of acknowledgment as we disappear from view.

"He doesn't like me," I muse quietly, almost reluctantly, wondering if my time will be wasted asking why that might be.

"He worries too much." Miller's reply is short, sharp, and final as he guides me through the maze of corridors toward his office. I know Tony is against us, just like everyone else, so I'm not sure why his disapproval bothers me more than the rest of the interferers. The looks? The words? And why isn't Miller more upset about it, like he gets with the others?

Miller taps in the code for his office and pushes the door open, and I'm immediately faced with the extreme precision of his office. Everything is how it should be.

Except us.

I look down at my soaking state, then to Miller's, thinking how wrecked we both look. Strangely, now that I'm surrounded by the familiarity and exactness of Miller's world, I feel all uncomfortable and . . . wrong.

"Olivia?" I look across to Miller, who's at his drinks cabinet pouring a scotch while yanking at his tie.

"Sorry, daydreaming." I shake myself out of my silly reverie and close the door behind me.

"Go sit." He indicates his office chair. "Can I get you a drink?"

"No."

"Sit," he prompts again when I'm still standing by the door a few seconds later. "Go."

I look down at my dress, then to Miller's fancy office chair. It was a trial and a concern sitting in Miller's car while all soggy, and now I'm faced with his lovely leather office chair. "But I'm all wet." I pull at the hem of my dress and release it, letting it slap against my thigh in demonstration. I'm not just wet; I'm dripping.

His glass pauses at his lips as his eyes skip over my body, absorbing the mess I'm in. Or maybe not. His eyes land on my chest and then flip to mine. They've gone all smoky. "I quite like you wet." His glass points at me, his fiery gaze slicing through my chilliness and igniting my dormant desire. My body lights up and my breathing stutters under the heat of cool blues.

He starts to slowly wander over to me, casually, calm, and with a million emotions sparkling in his eyes. Want, lust, desire, resolve, and a ton of others, but I don't get the chance to continue my mental list because his free arm slides under my bottom and lifts me to his mouth. I smell and taste scotch, reminding me of a drunken Miller, but it's easily dismissed under the attention of his divine mouth. Our wet clothes stick together, and my fingers delve into the messy array of his hair. This kiss is slow, meticulous, and soft. He moans his pleasure and nibbles gently on my bottom lip each time he pulls away before lazily pecking me softly and pushing his tongue back into my mouth.

"I need destressing," he mumbles, making me laugh. He's probably the most relaxed I've ever seen him. "What's so funny?"

"You." I pull back and take my time feeling his face—relishing in the harshness of his stubble. "*You* are funny, Miller."

"I am?"

"Yes, you are."

He cocks his head in thought as he carries me over to his desk in one arm. "I've never been called funny before." I'm placed in his leather seat and turned to face his pristine desk, finding a stupid sense of calm when I note everything is in its rightful place, namely the solitary item that always graces Miller's desk—a phone. "You don't have a computer?" I ask.

He taps the section of desk that hides all of the screens, and I mildly smile my acknowledgment. How . . . tidy.

"I promised I'd be quick."

"You did," I agree, relaxing back in his chair. "What do you need to do?" It's only now I wonder where any paperwork is kept, too, or stationery and files.

The silver tie gracing his neck is removed along with his suit jacket, leaving him in his waistcoat and shirt. "A few calls, this and that."

"This and that," I whisper as I watch him place his drink accurately on his desk and kneel on the floor on the other side. He rests his forearms on the white surface and looks at me thoughtfully. It makes me sit farther back in his chair. What's he going to say?

"I have a request."

That doesn't improve my wariness. "What?"

He smiles, obviously at my clear worry as he reaches into his pocket. "I'd like you to have this." He places something on the desk but holds his hand over it so I can't see what's beneath.

My eyes flick up and down, my cautiousness magnifying. "What is it?"

His smile slips a little, and I detect nerves. It only escalates mine. "A key to my apartment." He lifts his palm, revealing a Yale key.

My muscles relax, my mind refusing to center any attention on where my silly thoughts were heading. "A key," I breathe on a laugh.

"You can stay at my place whenever you wish. Come and go as you please. Will you accept?" He looks hopeful as he slides it across the desk toward me.

I roll my eyes and then jump on a gasp as the door flies open and Cassie staggers in. "Shit!" I curse under my breath, my heart speeding with fright. Miller's on his feet in an instant and crossing the room.

"Cassie," he sighs tiredly, his broad shoulders slumping as he comes to a halt.

"Well, hello!" She laughs, holding the door for support. She's drunk, and not just the tipsy, merry kind. I'm not looking forward to this, but however pissed she might be, she still looks sickeningly perfect. Her wobbly gaze is as rooted to Miller as it could be, given her drunken state. She hasn't even noticed I'm here. I'm invisible.

"What are you doing here?"

"My date was canceled." She waves an indifferent hand through the air before slamming the door shut so hard that shock waves ripple up the walls of Miller's office.

My eyes creep between the two of them, back and forth, liking the fact that she's been in here only a second and Miller's patience already seems exhausted. I hope he manhandles her from the room again. What I don't like, though, are Cassie's inquisitive eyes that are rooted on Miller. And I know why.

"Look at the state of you!" She's truly shocked, and I join her in the shock department when she stumbles over to Miller and starts laying her manicured hands all over his wet body. It takes a whole lifetime's worth of restraint not to throw myself across Miller's office and wrestle her to the ground. I want to scream at her to remove her hands from him. "Oh, Miller, baby, you're all wet."

Baby?

In an attempt to distract myself, I start twisting my ring around my finger, over and over until I'm sure I've rubbed a blister into my skin. She's stroking him, cooing and fussing, like he might die because he's got a little wet.

Get your fucking hands off him!

"Miller, what happened? Who did this to you?"

"I did it to myself, Cassie," he says touchily, taking her palms from his chest and releasing them. He steps away, and I relax a little at the distance he's put between them. Not for long, though, because the relentless trollop closes it back up. I'm stiff as a board, conjuring up a pile of verbal abuse to lob across the room, and I'm quite alarmed by it. I force some calming thoughts, but they're fast transforming into blood-boiling fury.

"What do you mean?" she questions uncertainly, eyes and hands beginning to roam again.

"We were having a picnic in the park," I pipe up, no longer prepared to sit back and watch Miller tackle the pressing presence of Cassie alone. "We had a lovely time," I add, just for good measure.

Her hands freeze in place on Miller's torso, both of them gawking at me, Miller tired, Cassie shocked. "Olivia," she purrs. "What a surprise."

I would think she's being sarcastic, but even if her low purr isn't shocked, her face is. Then she turns her incredulous look onto Miller, who exhales his building frustration.

"What do you want, Cassie?" He removes her greedy palms from his chest again and starts unbuttoning his waistcoat. "I don't plan on being here long."

"Well"—she saunters over to the drinks cabinet and pours herself a large straight vodka—"I was hoping you'd take me out for drinks."

My hackles rise, and I shoot a look to Miller, who's now shrugging off his waistcoat. His wet shirt is transparent and clinging everywhere. I cough on a choke. He looks dreamlike, and Cassie has noticed, too. All sorts of conflicting things are happening, my sass telling me to rip a strip off Cassie, my lust telling me to tackle Miller to the floor and eat him alive. Nothing about this situation is comfortable. Then Miller removes his wet shirt, exposing vast planes of taut, smooth, cut leanness, and my mouth drops open, not because of what I'm presented with, but because he's openly offered the stunning sight to Cassie's greedy eyes.

Her body sways as she studies Miller's wet, flexing muscles, her vodka paused at her lips. "I think you've had enough to drink," Miller grumbles, making his way to the bathroom. I watch his back disappear through the doorway, knowing Cassie has followed his path, too. My skin starts to prickle, feeling animosity hitting me. Now she's looking at me, and even though I know I'll probably be reduced to cinders from her filthy look, I can't help chancing a glance.

"What have you done to him?" she spits across the room, waving her glass of vodka at the bathroom doorway.

I need to remain calm. I'm struggling to keep my rage at bay, dying to lash out at her. She's interfering, probably better than anyone. Yet Miller's not displaying the same psychotic flip-outs with Cassie, just like he isn't with Tony. Is he going to tell me that Cassie is worried, too? Yeah, she's worried all right. She's worried I'm going to take Miller away from her, and she'd be right to worry. I bet this woman has cattiness down to a fine art. I'll never match her on that, it just isn't my style, so I keep my focus on her and sit back in Miller's chair. "I've made him see light through his darkness."

She recoils and exhales quietly. I've stunned her, shocked her into silence. It feels good, but I hear footsteps nearing, so I leave Cassie and her disbelief and carry my calm eyes across the room until I find him. He's rubbing a towel over his head, looking at me with sparkly blues. "Come here," he says quietly, his head cocked. I'm out of the chair and across the room to join him without delay. I know that glimmer. Cassie is about to witness a little Miller-style worshipping. This will beat any kind of tongue-lashing that I could invoke. A warm palm has claimed my neck within a heart-beat and warm lips have claimed my mouth a heartbeat after that. His kiss is brief but holds all of the usual qualities and spikes all of the usual reactions, and I definitely don't mistake the shocked inhale of breath from behind me. Yes, he lets me kiss him, and in a sad fit of ownership, I place my hands on his naked chest, just so she can see me feeling him, too. "Here." He drapes the towel across my shoulders and uses the corners to wipe my wet forehead. "Go dry off in the bathroom."

I hesitate, not keen on leaving the room with a drunk and now-silent Cassie on the prowl. "I'm fine," I try feebly, making him smile. After dropping a chaste kiss on my cheek, he strides over to the concealed wardrobe and pulls the doors open, scans the rows of posh shirts, and then yanks one down by the sleeve. Cassie gasps in horror, Miller throws her a dirty look...and I go dizzy with happiness.

"Put this on." He hands me the shirt and turns me in his arms before giving me a gentle nudge in the back. "Give me your dress and I'll have someone hold it under the hand dryers for a while."

"I can do that," I protest, thinking it'll be a perfect chore to pass the time while Miller gets his work done.

"You'll do no such thing," he scoffs, pushing me onward. I turn once I'm in the bathroom, finding Miller pulling the door shut and Cassie still staring, struck dumb at Miller's back. "Five minutes." He nods sternly and disappears from view when the wood comes between us. I frown at the door as the fireworks within settle down, making way for a little bewilderment. I've just allowed him to ship me out of his office with no complaint or protest. Now the fact that he's just manhandled one of his precious shirts and given it to me to wear doesn't feel like progress at all. It feels like distraction. I laugh out loud. I'm stupid, and on that conclusion I open the door and present myself back into the room. Both heads turn, both faces looking heated. They are far too close, probably to keep their conversation from my earshot.

"Oh, for God's sake," Cassie hisses, taking a huge swig of her vodka. "Can't you just get rid of it?"

I cough my disgust as Miller swings around violently and snatches the glass from her hand. "Learn when to shut the fuck up!" He slams the glass down, sending Cassie on a startled stagger. Now I can see his fury, and that is the only thing that keeps my mouth from spilling a torrent of expletives. There's no need for me to put this woman in her place because Miller is about to do it for me. He pushes his face near hers. "The only thing I'll be ridding from my life is *you*." His voice is scathing. "Don't fucking push me, Cassie."

She grabs the cabinet for support and takes a moment to compose herself, her eyes shooting to mine briefly. "You'll be crucified." Her words are factual. I can tell by the stiffening of Miller's naked shoulders.

"Some things are worth the risk," he whispers, uncertainty rife in his tone.

"*Nothing* is worth that risk," Cassie retorts. There's an element of fear in her, and that fear spreads across the room and settles within me. Deeply.

"You're wrong." Miller takes a long pull of calming air and

steps away from her, turning impassive eyes onto me. "She's worth it. I want out."

Cassie gasps, and if I could rip my welling eyes from Miller, then I know I'd see an astounded expression all over her perfect face. "You... Miller... You can't," she stammers all over her words, swiping up her drink and taking a shaky gulp.

"I can."

"But—"

"Get out, Cassie."

"Miller!" She's beginning to panic.

His jaw tightens, his eyes remaining on my frozen form in the doorway as he pulls his phone from his trouser pocket, hits one button, and holds it to his ear. "Tony, come get Cassie."

What happens next leaves me wide-eyed and openmouthed.

"No!" She launches herself at him, knocking him into the cabinet, sending glasses and bottles crashing to the office floor. I flinch, but my legs refuse to carry me across the office to intervene. All I can do is watch in shock as Miller tries to restrain her flailing hands as she screams at him, scratches and begs. "You can't! Please!"

The signs of Miller's frightening rage are all in the room with us, his puffing chest, wild eyes, and sweating form. I hate to think what damage he could do to a woman. I despise Cassie, I hate everything about her, but even *I* am worried for her.

Miller's about to take leave of his senses.

I drop his shirt and run across the room, disregarding the danger I may be putting myself in. I just need to make him see me, hear me, feel me. Anything to divert him from the direction I know he's headed.

"Miller!" I shout, reluctantly accepting this will never work. I yelled at him repeatedly outside Nan's to no avail. "Fuck!" I curse, standing close, watching the frantic wrestling of arms. Cassie is crying now, her perfect hair looking rough and messy.

"Don't you dare leave me," she wails. "I won't let you leave me!"

My eyes widen in alarm. There's more than business between these two. She's flipped her lid, and while I'm fearful for her, I'm quite concerned for Miller, too. Those nails are like claws and thrashing all over him while he tries to seize her and she continues to scream persistently. She's deranged and Miller's heading that way, too.

I try to catch Miller's eye, try time and time again to reach and touch him, but each attempt has me retracting to avoid being caught by a flailing limb. Panic starts to eat me alive but before I can figure out my best move, Tony comes crashing through the door.

His dramatic arrival pulls my attention away from the scrapping of bodies but doesn't interrupt Miller and Cassie. "Tony, do something!" I plead, swinging back toward them, feeling helpless and small. "Miller, stop!"

I reach out when I see a clear path to his torso, my body moving closer, desperate to stop them. "Livy, no!" Tony bellows, but his tone doesn't stop me. I'm getting close, I can reach him, but then the most searing sting spreads across my cheek, sending me flying back on a painful yelp, my hand instantly cupping my burning face and tears stabbing at my eyes.

The blow to my face sends me all disoriented. "Shit!" I find nothing to grab to steady myself, and instead give up on the inevitable, letting my body crash to the floor.

Everything blurs around me—vision, sound—and pain flames the flesh of my face. I try to shake some clear thoughts back into my mind, or at least gain some straight vision, but it takes the feel of strong hands on my shoulders to bring me back into the room.

It's silent.

Deadly silent.

I look up and see traumatized blue eyes scanning my face, eventually settling on my burning cheek. Cassie is by the drinks cabinet, tremors of shock riding through her body and a look of apprehension on her flustered face. She takes shaky hands to the bottle of vodka and skips pouring a glass, instead taking the neck of the bottle to her lips. I'm not certain who struck me, but after a few seconds of watching Cassie through blurred vision, I quickly conclude it's her, and she's now bracing herself for... something.

"Tony?" Miller's voice is rampant with rage.

"I'm here, son." Tony moves in, looking down at me with sorry eyes. I feel stupid, a burden and weak.

"Get that bitch the *fuck* out of my office." Miller sweeps me up from the floor and cradles me in his arms before turning to face Cassie. She's nearly polished off the whole bottle.

"I can stand," I protest, my throat scratchy from my scream of alarm.

"Shhhh," he soothes quietly, pressing soft lips to my temple, all the while keeping burning rings of fury on Cassie.

She's wary and shifting drunkenly, but she still carries that air of superiority. "She shouldn't have got in the way." She dismisses the whole incident easily, gulping down the rest of the vodka.

Tony moves in and takes Cassie's arm. "Let's go," he orders, removing the bottle from her hand and slamming it down.

"No!"

"Get her out!" Miller yells. "Get her the fuck out before I kill her!"

"You wouldn't hurt me!" She laughs. "You couldn't!"

Tony starts pulling her to the door, but she doggedly fights him off. She's relentless. "For crying out loud, Cassie! Sober up and sort this shit out later."

"I'm fine!" She wriggles from Tony's hold and staggers over to the desk, plonking herself down in Miller's chair. I may have only just got my clear sight back, but I definitely don't mistake her flip a scowl in my direction. Even now? She's just clobbered me one, attacked Miller, and she's *still* all hostile. Can she not detect the aggression radiating from every refined pore of my part-time gentleman? Is she stupid? "Give me a fucking break," she grumbles, reaching up to the intricate cross that's always decorating her neck. She fumbles with it, cursing under her breath.

"Cassie," Miller warns. I can feel his chest heaving double in pace under me. "Don't."

"Fuck off!"

Tony's very quickly by her side, leaning down to get level with her, his palms flat on Miller's desk. "I won't allow it, Cassandra."

She turns a defiant chin up to Tony and moves in close, getting nose to nose with him as she continues to play with her silver cross. "Fuck...off."

"Cassie!"

"He wants out! Have you ever heard something so funny? They'll never allow it."

I want to scream that all those women don't have a choice, that he's mine now, but Miller squeezes me to him. It's a reassuring squeeze.

She laughs. "It's fucking hilarious." The metal of her necklace splits into two pieces and I watch in horror as white powder scatters Miller's perfect white desk. I gasp, Tony curses, and Miller tenses from head to toe.

Cocaine?

If I hadn't seen the fine particles drop from Cassie's beautiful piece of jewelry, I probably would never know it was there; the residue is camouflaged perfectly by the expanse of white gloss beneath it. I'm speechless as I watch her snatch a credit card from her bra, along with a note, before she starts shifting the powder around on Miller's desk, encouraging it into a perfect, long line. She's an expert.

Tony's pacing the room, swearing profusely, and Miller is just staring at her while keeping me in his viselike grip. The tension in the room is palpable, and I'm truly anxious about who's going to make the next move. There's an overwhelming need to free myself from Miller, but that would leave him to let loose. Everyone is safer while I'm in his arms, but then I'm suddenly not in his arms anymore. I've been placed on a couch in the corner and Miller is on his way over to Cassie, not that she's aware. She's too busy Hoovering up the powder on Miller's desk through a rolled note.

"Easy, son," Tony soothes, flicking his worried eyes to me. The pain in my face has been replaced by awful apprehension. Every person in this room, except me, is like a ticking bomb. And it's Miller's fuse that's burning the fastest.

His palms hit the desk and his bare chest leans forward, getting close to Cassie. She's now sniffing and wiping at her nose, a smug smile creeping onto her face. "I've asked more than once. If you make me ask again, I will not be held accountable for my actions."

She huffs her lack of concern and relaxes back in his chair. I can see arrogance slinking its way across her face. Fearlessness.

"Smile," she says simply, crossing one leg over the other and... smiling.

I frown. Smile? What is there to smile about? Nothing.

"Miller, come on." Tony's trying his hardest to talk some calm into the situation, and I'm willing him to succeed.

Cassie's perfectly arched eyebrows arch farther. "Want some?"

"No," Miller spits.

She pouts and lets it drift slowly into a sly smile. "That's a first."

I gasp, I cough, unable to halt any of the shocked reactions from spilling from my mouth. He does drugs? On top of everything else, I now have addict to add to my list?

"I fucking hate you," Miller seethes, moving closer.

"She's ruining you."

He leans closer to her, threateningly, his palms twitching where they rest on the glossy white surface. "She's saving me."

Cassie's laugh is cold and sardonic as she moves in nearer to him. "Nothing can save you."

I'm completely numb, trying to process this new blast of enlightenment while desperately trying to cling on to the strength I need to help Miller. I look to Tony, pleading with my eyes for him to intervene.

But it's too late.

Miller launches himself across his desk, grabbing Cassie by the throat.

I scream.

The scene is manic. Unreal. Miller has lost control, and when the crazy woman seated at his desk should be fearing for her life, she's just laughing at him instead.

"For fuck's sake!" Tony throws himself into the mix, getting a smack across his jaw for his trouble, but instead of yielding, he fights harder. He knows, just as well as I do, that this will end only one way, and that'll be with Cassie in the hospital. "Get off her!"

"She's a fucking parasite!" Miller roars. "Life is miserable enough without her help!"

"Miller!" Tony jabs him in the ribs, making Miller shriek and me wince. "Back off!"

Miller pushes away from his desk and swings around aggressively. "Get her out and back in rehab!"

"I don't need help!" Cassie spits nastily. "You're the one who needs fucking help." She squirms free of Tony's hold and starts pulling at her untidy dress, yanking the hem back down to her knee. "You're prepared to risk everything for that?" Her arm shoots out toward me.

It? That? Oh, I might be stunned by the events unraveling before me, but her persistent insolence and insults are beginning to piss me off. "Who the hell do you think you are?" I stand, immediately aware that Miller has halted with his gritty marching. "You think a few temper tantrums and bitter words will break him?" I step forward, feeling my confidence swell, especially when Cassie snaps her rotten mouth shut. "You can't stop him."

"It's not me you should be worried about." Her lip curls. They're just more words, but the acute manner in which they are delivered sends anxious tingles shooting up my spine.

"That's it." Tony intervenes, taking Cassie's arm and leading her from the office. "You are your own worst enemy, Cassandra."

"Always have been," she agrees on a laugh, allowing herself to be guided to the doorway without a fuss or fight. But then she slows to a halt at the threshold and turns leisurely, sniffing as she does. "It was nice knowing you, Miller Hart."

Her parting words cool the heated emotions that are dominating the atmosphere in Miller's office, leaving the air thick with tension. The door slams, courtesy of a riled Tony, and Miller and I are left alone.

He's edgy.

I'm disturbed.

We both remain silent for what seems like forever, my mind playing repeats of the past ten minutes as my wet body and injured face slowly start to register. I begin to shiver and my arms instinctively wrap around my body. It's a protection mechanism. It has nothing to do with my chilly bones.

My gaze is cemented to the floor, not daring or wanting to torture my eyes with the sight of Miller in full-force psycho mode. They've had more than they can handle in the last couple of days. These outbursts are becoming too frequent. He needs help. The stark reality of Miller's life just keeps getting starker.

"Don't deprive me of your face, Olivia Taylor." The softness of his voice is strained, an attempt to instill some ease into me. I'm not sure it can work. I don't think anything can work. I'm again questioning my ability to chase Miller's demons away because as I see it right now, I'm fueling the fire. And I hate that. I hate my constant doubting because of these interferers. "Olivia." I hear the light thud of footsteps approaching, but I keep my eyes down.

I shake my head and my chin begins to tremble.

"Let me see those sparkling eyes." The warmth of his palm connects with my sore cheek, sending a flash of pain coursing through me. I recoil on a hiss, turning my face away from his view. I already know that it will be glowing red from the brute force of the whack I've just absorbed and that will undoubtedly enrage Miller more. He seems to be calming. I need to keep it that way. His hand retracts slightly, hovering just in my field of vision. "May I?" he asks quietly.

I fold, inside and out, my fallen heart crumbling, my weak body collapsing. He's silent as he catches me, like he fully expected my body to give, and he takes us down to the floor, rocking me in his strong arms. The familiarity of his bare chest against me doesn't have its usual effect. I sob—horrible gut-wrenching sobs. It's all too much. The strength that Miller feeds me seems to have been swallowed up, leaving me a weak waif of nothing. I'm no good for him. I can't see him through his darkness because my own world is becoming too dark in the process. William is right. A relationship with Miller Hart is impossible. Apart, we are barely functioning. Together, we're dead and incredibly alive at the same time. We're impossible.

"Please don't cry," he begs, squeezing me to him, his low tone now sincere and unforced. "I can't bear to see you like this."

I say nothing, my sniffles preventing me from speaking, even if I knew what to say. Which I don't. The best part of my existence has revolved around avoiding a cruel world. But Miller Hart has taken me and put me in the center of that world.

And I know I will never escape.

His face is buried in my hair, and he's humming that comforting melody. It's a desperate attempt to pull me round. He feels my despondency. He's worried, and when he's hummed for minutes upon minutes and I still haven't ceased weeping, he growls lowly and stands with me secured against him, then carries me quietly into the bathroom.

He positions me on the toilet, with no need for precision, and pushes my matted hair from my face with the utmost care to avoid my sore cheek. I finally allow my stinging eyes to lift along with my head to face him. His blue eyes reveal horror as they focus on the side of my face, and he takes a deep, calming breath.

"Wait," he orders harshly as he retrieves a face cloth from a small pile beside the sink and runs it under the cold tap. He's kneeling at my feet quickly, the cloth coating the palm of his hand. "I'll be gentle."

I nod my acceptance and wince before he's even connected the cool cloth to my face.

"Shhh." The chilliness hits my tender cheek, making me recoil on a painful gasp. "Hey, hey, hey." His other palm reaches for my shoulder to steady me. "Let it settle." Taking a deep breath, I brace myself for the pressure I know he's about to apply. "Better?" he asks, searching for comfort in my eyes. I can't find the energy to speak, so I give a pathetic nod, depriving Miller of my eyes when I clench them shut in pain. Everything feels heavy—my eyes, my tongue, my body . . . my heart.

Reaching up, I rub at my tired eyes, massaging into the sockets rigorously with the heels of my hands, hoping to work away the lingering visions, not just of this evening's outburst but of all Miller's recent rages and the horrid images of him shoving cocaine up his nose. I'm being naive and ambitious.

"I'll get some ice," Miller murmurs, sounding as pitiful as I feel. He takes my hand and replaces his with mine gently on my cheek before he pushes himself from the floor.

"No." I grab his wrist to stop him leaving. "Don't go."

The hope that flickers through his blank eyes spikes guilt. He falls to his haunches and rests his palms on my knees.

"You do cocaine," I state, not making it a question. There's no scope for denying here.

"Not since I've met you, Olivia. There are many things I haven't done since I've met you."

"You quit just like that?" I know I sound cynical, but it's not something I can help.

"Just like that."

"How bad?"

"Does it matter? I've stopped."

"It matters to me. How often do you use?"

"*Did* I use." His jaw ticks and his eyes clench shut. "Once in a while."

"Once in a while?"

Blue eyes slowly appear again, pouring with regret, sorrow... shame. "It helped me get through..."

I gasp. "Oh God."

"Livy, I've never had a reason to stop doing any of the things I did. That simple. I don't need any of it anymore. Not now that I have you."

I drop my eyes, confused, shocked, and hurt. "Who'll crucify you?"

"Many." He laughs nervously, and it prompts my eyes to find his again. "But I'll never give up on us. I'll do anything you want me to," he vows.

"See a doctor," I blurt without thought. "Please." He can't possibly deal with all these problems. He can't be beyond help. I don't care if he's been told that before.

"I don't need a doctor. I need people to stop interfering." His jaw is clenched, just the mention of meddlesome people spiking the rage that's so very worrying. "I need people to stop making you overthink."

I shake my head on a sad smile. He doesn't see it. "I can learn to deal with interference, Miller." I have to. Miller will take all of the interference personally. Maybe it's paranoia. Drugs make people paranoid, right? I have no idea, but it's a problem and it can be fixed, I'm certain. "It's you who's making me sad."

His hands halt their calming rubs on my knees. "Me?" he asks quietly.

"Yes, you. Your temper." Cassie's hate is unpleasant and mystifying, but it didn't make me feel hopeless like this. That's *his* doing. "I can help you, but you need to help yourself. You need to see a doctor."

Blue eyes deepen as they explore my face, and he drops from his crouching position to his knees. I look down at him, immersing myself in the tranquility that his telling gaze always offers, like right now, even when we're in such a mess—when Miller is in such a mess—the comfort I'm feeling is immeasurable. He squeezes my thighs before he takes my hands in his and brings my knuckles to his soft lips, all the time maintaining the consuming connection of our eyes. "Olivia, do you understand the extent of my feelings for you?" His eyes close tightly, robbing me of the comfort I partly survive on. "Do you comprehend it?"

"Open your eyes," I demand softly, and on a strengthening inhale of air, he lazily pulls them open. "I comprehend the extent of *my* feelings for *you.* If this is how you feel about me, then I get it. I understand, Miller. But you don't see me attacking anyone who threatens us. Our united front is enough. Let *us* do the talking."

Emotional pain invades his perfect face, making his lips press together and his eyes clench shut. "It's not something I can help," he admits, letting his face drop into my lap. He's hiding, ashamed of his confession. I know he takes leave of his senses, but he has to try to stop. I sever the contact of our hands and plunge my fingers into his wet hair, looking down at my touch massaging the back of his head. His palms sweep around to my bottom and cling on desperately, his face turning so his cheek is now resting on my thighs. I can see him staring blankly at nothing, and I transfer my caress to his cheek and gently trace the contours of his profile, hoping my touch will have the same effect as his does on me.

Peace.

Comfort.

Strength.

"Everything I had as a child was taken from me," he whispers, stealing my breath with a hint of willingness to tell me of his childhood. "I didn't have many possessions, but they were dear to me and they were mine. Just mine. But they were always taken from me. Nothing was precious."

I smile wistfully. "You were an orphan." I state it as a fact, because Miller has just told me in his own little way. The photo doesn't need to be mentioned.

He nods. "I was in a home for boys for as long as I can remember."

"What happened to your parents?"

He sighs, and I immediately fathom that this is something that he has never spoken of. "My mother was a young Irish girl who ran away from Belfast."

"Irish," I breathe, seeing Miller's bright blues and dark hair for what they are—typically Irish.

"Have you heard of the Magdalene Asylums?" he asks.

"Yes," I gasp, horrified. The Magdalene nuns were folk of the Catholic Church who claimed to be working for God to cleanse the young women who were unfortunate enough to fall into their clutches—or who were sent there by their ashamed relatives, often pregnant.

"She escaped, apparently. She came to London to give birth to me, but my grandparents eventually tracked her down and took her back to Ireland."

"And you?"

"They dumped me in an orphanage so they could return home, free of the disgrace. No one need know I existed. I've never been a people person, Olivia. I was a loner. I didn't get along with others, and I spent a lot of time in a black cupboard as a result."

My eyes widen in realization. I'm disgusted, but most of all I'm sad. Especially since I can detect the shame he feels. He has nothing to be ashamed of. "They locked you in a cupboard?"

He nods lightly. "I didn't mix well."

"I'm sorry," I say on a guilty gush of air. He still doesn't mix well, only with me.

"Don't be." He smooths his palms up my back. "You're not the only one who was abandoned, Olivia. I know how it feels, and that is only a very small part of why I will never leave you. A very small part."

"And because I'm your possession," I remind him.

"And because you are my possession. The most treasured possession I've ever owned," he confirms, lifting his head to find my dejected eyes. Everything was taken away from him. I get it. He smiles mildly at my sadness. "My sweet girl, don't be sad for me."

"Why?" Of course I will be sad for him. It's an incredibly sad story, and just the beginning of Miller's wretched life up to this point. It's all disjointed—the orphan, the homeless man, and the escort. There are things that connect these stages of Miller's life and I'm scared to death of hearing them. What he's told me, both vocally and emotionally, has taken me to the front line of agony and sadness. What connects these dots may be an enlightenment that will break my fallen heart beyond repair.

Warmth slides across my wet back, onto my hips, and up my sides, until his grip is creeping onto my collarbones and he's encasing my neck. "If my twenty-nine-year tale of misery has led me to you, then that makes every unbearable part of it worthwhile. I'd do it all again in a heartbeat, Olivia Taylor." He dips and sweetly kisses my cheek. "Accept me as I am, sweet girl, because it's so much better than what I was."

The lump in my throat swells, making breathing too difficult.

It's too late. My heart is already broken, and so is Miller. "I love you," I utter pitifully. "I love you so much."

The gaping hole in my chest rips even more when Miller's unshaven chin quivers the tiniest bit. He shakes his head in wonder before rising to claim my whole body, pulling me into him and giving me the most fierce *thing* in the history of *things*. "I thank everything holy for that, and I'm not a religious man."

Breathing into the wet hair sticking to his neck, I close my eyes and sink into the lean planes of his body, taking everything he has to give and returning it. My strength is restored, stronger than ever before, and determination is rushing violently through my bloodstream. He hasn't agreed to seeing a therapist or a councilor, but my widened knowledge of this confounding man and his confessions is the best start. Helping him, pulling him from his self-professed journey to hell will be easier now that I'm armed with the knowledge I need to understand him.

The interfering would seem inconsequential if it wasn't for Miller's extreme reaction to the interferers. He sees me as his possession, and he sees them as wanting to take me away from him. In an ideal world, all of the meddling idiots would disappear with a magic click of my fingers, but being as we don't exist in a mystical realm, other options need to be explored. And the most obvious is getting Miller's temper under control, since it has become glaringly obvious that all of these meddling idiots are not only meddling, but persistent, too. He'll always see interference as people trying to take his possession—his most treasured possession. It's natural for him to react this way.

My bones are being constricted to the crumbling point under Miller's embrace, my lungs being squeezed, too. I'm soaking up the luxury of his *thing* and savoring in it, but my depleted body and exhausted mind are also desperate for rest. We're still at Ice, meddlers are loitering, we're both still wet and disheveled, and Miller hasn't done a thing work-wise.

I squirm a little in his hold, encouraging him to ease up so I can look at him. I find eyes matching my tiredness. "I'd like you to put me in your bed," I say quietly, and drop a delicate kiss on his soft lips.

He swings into action instantly, releasing me and steadying me before stalking off into his office and returning before I have a chance to follow, fastening a dry shirt—all the buttons in the wrong holes. "Do you want a shirt?" he asks, running a quick check over my body. "Yes," he answers for me, turning and disappearing from view again. I sigh and follow him, this time meeting him in the doorway. "Put this on," he orders, flapping a shirt out.

"I have no bottoms."

"Oh." He frowns at my dress and turns undecided eyes onto the shirt. I wouldn't walk out of here in just one of Miller's shirts, even if he allowed it, which I highly doubt he would.

I take the shirt and place it on a nearby sideboard. "Just take me home." I'm on the brink of collapsing.

He sighs, taking up his usual hold of me. "As you wish."

I'm guided out of the club, knowing we're being watched by Cassie and Tony, but our clear closeness speaks for itself—no words or smug smile of victory required. I'm placed in Miller's Mercedes, the heat is cranked up, although with matching temperatures on both sides of the car, and I'm driven to Miller's in silence. He's touching me almost the whole way, not prepared to lose contact, until we're in the underground car park of his apartment block and he has to release me to exit the vehicle. I stay where I am, warm and snug in the passenger seat, until Miller collects me in his arms and carries me the ten flights of stairs to the shiny black door that'll take us into privacy.

"Call your grandmother," he instructs, placing me on a stool. "Then we'll have a bath."

My hopefulness dissipates at the suggestion. Bathing with Miller is beyond blissful, but so is him holding me in his *thing* in his bed, and I'm favoring the latter option right now. "I'm so tired," I sigh, reaching for my phone from my bag. I'll barely muster the energy to speak with Nan.

"Too tired to bathe?" he asks, disappointment invading his face. I don't even have the energy to feel guilty.

"In the morning?" I try, thinking my hair will have dried into something beyond wild by the time I've slept on it, and Miller's will have, too. The mental image brings a small smile to my lifeless face.

He thinks for a few moments, and the pad of his thumb smooths across my eyebrow, Miller's tired eyes following its path. "Please, let me clean us." His face is beseeching. How could I possibly refuse?

"Okay," I agree.

"Thank you. I'll give you some privacy to call your grandmother while I draw the bath." Dropping a kiss on my forehead, he turns to leave.

"I don't need any privacy," I protest, wondering what he thinks we might speak about. My declaration stalls his escape, and he nibbles at his lip thoughtfully. "Why would you think I need privacy?"

He shrugs those perfect shoulders, and those perfect eyes lose a little exhaustion, finding mischievousness instead. I smile warily at the signs of playful Miller. "I don't know," he muses. "Maybe you'd like to discuss my buns."

The stupidest grin stretches to my cheeks. "I'd do that in your company."

"You shouldn't. I get all embarrassed."

"No, you don't!"

A bright smile diminishes any lingering gloom that may have remained, sending me giddy. "Call your nan, sweet girl. I want to bathe and get my habit under the sheets."

Chapter Twenty-three

I can hear talking. It's faint, but it's there. The room is illuminated only by spots of London's nighttime light on the skyline. If I didn't know better, I would think I was outside on a balcony staring out across the city, but I'm not. I'm on Miller's worn sofa in front of the huge glass window, naked and with a cashmere throw draped over me—somewhere better.

I sit up, dragging the blanket with me, and blink back my tiredness, yawning and stretching as I do. The view and my sleepiness distract me from the voices I heard a few moments ago, but then Miller's slightly raised and agitated tone reminds me of his absence from the couch. I pull myself to my feet and make the best job of wrapping the blanket around me before I pad across the wooden floor to the door, pulling it open soundlessly and listening for Miller. He's speaking quietly again, but he sounds irritated. The last time he took a call in the night he disappeared. Flashbacks of our hotel encounter ricochet around my head like a bullet, making me wince. I can't think of him like that. The man I faced in that hotel room wasn't the Miller Hart I know and love. He needs to change his number, make it impossible for these women to get hold of him. He's not at their disposal anymore, although I begrudgingly note that they don't know this yet.

I start toward the sound of his muffled voice, his words becoming clearer the closer I get until I'm standing at the doorway of his kitchen staring at the scratch marks Cassie left on his naked back.

"I can't," he says, resolute and completely fixed. "It's just not possible." His words fill me with pride, but then he collapses to his arse on a chair, revealing another person in the room.

A woman.

My spine lengthens.

"What?" she asks, her surprise evident.

"Things have changed." He reaches up and drags his palm through his hair. "I'm sorry."

I gulp. Is this it? Is this him officially quitting?

"I won't take no for an answer, Miller. I need you."

"You'll have to find someone else."

"Excuse me!" She laughs, flicking her eyes past Miller's seated form and catching me at the doorway.

I jump back out of sight, like she hasn't already seen me. She's mature, but very attractive, her ash-blond, perfectly styled bob fixed in place and her fingers wrapped around a wineglass. She has long, red talons for nails. That's about all I got a glimpse of before I stupidly hid, and feeling very foolish about it, I turn to make my way to the bedroom, trying in vain to steady my erratic heartbeat. He's declining her. My intervention isn't needed and I distinctively recall Miller saying the fewer people who know about me, the better. I hate it, but I have to follow his lead, given that I have no clue where we're headed.

"Well, well." I hear her smooth voice as I'm making my escape, my shoulders jumping up to meet my earlobes. I know she saw me, but a silly little part of me was hoping my stealthy movement removed my body from view before her beady eyes captured me.

Wrong.

Now I feel like a Peeping Tom, when she's the one who has invaded Miller's apartment in the middle of the night. Is she going to hand me his card, too, and tell me to keep it safe? Is she going to offer a share? After everything, I might skin her alive.

"What?" Miller's voice tenses my shoulders further.

"You didn't say you had company, darling."

"Company?" He sounds confused, and knowing I'm completely rumbled, I back up and turn to face the music, showing my face just as Miller looks around to see what's captured his guest's attention. "Livy." His chair scrapes across the marble floor as he stands hastily.

I feel awkward and stupid, standing in a blanket with my hair all over my face and my bare feet shifting nervously.

Miller looks edgy, which isn't surprising, but the woman in his kitchen looks interested as she relaxes back in her chair and holds her wineglass to her deep red lips. "So we're entertaining at home now?" she purrs.

Miller ignores her question and approaches me quickly, turning me in his arms and pushing me gently from the kitchen. "Let me put you in bed," he whispers.

"Is she one of them?" I ask, letting him lead me away. I already know she is. I can tell by the air of superiority surrounding her confident persona and her designer clothes.

"Yes," he answers tightly. "I'll get rid of her and come join you."

"Why is she here?"

"Because she takes liberties."

"She has," I agree.

"Darling!" Her cocky, self-assured voice has the same effect as the last time one of Miller's clients spoke. I tense under Miller's hold, and he tenses, too. "Don't hide her away for my benefit."

"I'm not hiding her," he spits over his shoulder, striding on. "I'll be back in a minute, Sophia."

"I'll look forward to it."

It's only at the mention of her name and the follow-up of her overconfident words that I realize she has an accent. European, definitely. It's mild but detectable. She's like the woman from Quaglino's, except brasher and more confident, and I wouldn't have thought that possible.

When I've been directed into his room, he pulls back the neat covers and lifts me into bed, gently laying me down and resting his lips on my forehead. "Go back to sleep."

"How long will you be?" I ask, uncomfortable with him going back out to that woman. She's arrogant. I don't like her, and I definitely don't like the potential of her drooling all over Miller.

"You're in my bed and you're naked." He pushes my hair from my face and nuzzles into my cheek. "I want to have my *thing* with my habit. Please let me deal with this. I'll be as quick as I can, I promise."

"Okay." I resist latching on to him with my arms because letting go when he leaves will be too hard. "Stay calm, please."

He nods his acknowledgment. One more kiss on the lips and he slips out of the room, shutting the door behind him and leaving me with only the darkness and my thoughts—unwanted thoughts, thoughts that if I give too much time to will drive me positively insane.

Too late.

I'm tossing and turning, burying my head under the pillow, sitting up and listening for a commotion and deliberating returning to Miller, my anger bubbling. But when I hear the door handle shift, I'm lying back down again, pretending I haven't just spent the last ten minutes driving myself nuts with thoughts of rules, restraints, hard cash and worrying about Miller's temper.

Dusky light floods into the room and within only moments, he's pressed up against my back, moving my hair from my neck and saying hello with a wet lick up the column of my throat.

"Hi," I whisper, shuffling over until I'm happy to have his face close to mine.

"Hello." He kisses my nose tenderly and strokes my hair.

"Has she gone?"

"Yes," he answers swiftly and assertively, but says no more, which is fine by me. I want to forget she was ever here.

"What are you thinking about?" I ask when a long silence has stretched between us, him seeming happy to keep it that way but me breaking it to try to drag my mind away from night visitors.

"I'm thinking how lovely you look in my bed."

I smile. "You can barely see me."

"I can see you just fine, Livy," he argues quietly. "I see you everywhere I look, whether it's dark or light."

His words and warm breath on my face settle me completely. "Messy?"

"A little."

"Hum to me."

"I can't hum on demand," he objects, looking a little shy.

"Can you try?"

He thinks for a few moments and then tucks me farther into his chest, resting his chin on top of my head. "You've put too much pressure on me."

"Pressure to hum?"

"Yes," he confirms simply, kissing my hair instead. It's a good compromise, but as the silence stretches and we're lost in a world of peace and comfort, holding each other, he overcomes the pressure of my request and begins to hum quietly, sending me into a deep, peaceful slumber.

* * *

"Livy." His quiet whisper stirs me, and I try to roll over but go nowhere. "Olivia."

My eyes creep open, finding sparkling blues and his signature shadow covering his jawline, now even longer. "What?"

"You're awake." He lifts onto his forearms and rubs his groin into mine, indicating his current hard condition. "Shall we?" he asks, the potential of some Miller-style worshipping waking me up as if Big Ben were ringing from the side of the bed.

"Condom," I breathe.

"Done." His hand wanders down my hip until he's at my entrance spreading my heated wetness on a little gasp of gratification. "Were you dreaming of me?" he asks surely, replacing his hand on the mattress and rearing back.

"Might have." I'm nonchalant, but then he's pushing into me and my attempts to appear casual diminish with one smooth thrust. "Ooh," I groan, lifting my arms and linking my fingers around his neck, the delicious fullness of him within me taking me to places beyond pleasure—just as Miller has promised.

I really was dreaming of him. I was dreaming that this was forever, and not just a lifetime, but beyond that, too—a life of perfect preciseness in everything, especially when he makes love to me. I'm over his finicky nature. It'll always fascinate me, but more significant than that, I'm irrevocably head over heels, painfully and utterly in love with him—no matter who he was, what he did, and how damn obsessive he is.

The gliding of our bodies together exceeds pleasurable. He's looking down at me with total devotion, bolstering my feelings more and more with each and every careful pump of his hips. I'm ablaze, rippling, breathing sharp gasping breaths in his face as my palms dampen from the sweat riddling his nape.

"I'm desperate to kiss you," he mumbles, pushing deep, holding himself as he reins in his labored breathing. "So desperate, but I can't deprive my eyes of your face. I need to see your face."

I squeeze my internal muscles instinctively, feeling him pulse steady and slow.

"Jesus, Livy, you put perfection to shame."

I want to counter his claim, but all of my concentration is going into matching the meticulous tempo of his dreamy hips, each drive firm and flawless, each retreat steady and controlled. The stirrings in the pit of my tummy are preparing to travel farther down, preparing to erupt and send me wild with overwhelming sensations, and not just of the physical kind. My heart is bursting, too.

I'm suddenly moving, being pulled up carefully to his kneeling lap and guided around time and time again. "You fit me just right," he groans, slowly closing his eyes. "The only thing in my life that has ever been truly perfect is you."

In my blissed-out state, I manage to comprehend what that means, especially for a man who craves exactness. "I want to be perfect for you," I pledge, pushing my body into his, planting my face in his neck. "I want to be everything you need." I have no issue with admitting that. In moments like this, I see a man who's relaxed and content, not uptight and broody or unpredictable and dangerous. If I can help to shift some of these attributes from the bedroom into Miller's life when he's not worshipping me, then I will, every day for the rest of my days. The middle part of yesterday was a perfect start.

I feel hypnotized as I pull back and stare into his eyes, clinging to his hair and moving exactly where guided. The power he exudes from being so gentle is incredible, his speed and measure mind-blowing. He gasps, touching our foreheads. "Sweet girl, you already are." His head rolls, taking his lips down to mine, and we kiss fervently, tongues clashing and rolling as I'm lifted and grounded continuously. "You're too special, Livy."

"So are you."

"No, I'm a fraud." His hips buck a little, enticing a collective cry from us both. "Good God!" he yelps, raising his arse from his heels and kneeling, holding me against him with no strain at all. My head falls back as I grapple at his back, my ankles linking to gain more stability. "Don't deprive me of your face, Livy."

My head is too heavy and rolling freely as the pressure accumulates and buzzes. I'm going to burst. "I'm coming."

"Please, Livy. Let me see you." He delivers the words on a lazy grind. "Please."

I force myself to fulfill his plea, using what energy I have to pull against his neck to help me. I cry out.

"Lie back."

"What?" I yell, closing my eyes, feeling my muscles contracting persistently. I can't control it anymore.

"Lie back." His palm rests at the base of my spine, letting me lean against it, and he eases me down until my upper back is on the mattress and my lower body is held against his kneeling frame. "Comfortable?"

"Yes," I gasp, bowing my back and plunging my fingers into my blond, knotted waves.

"Good," he rumbles.

The strain in his face tells me he's close, too, the rippling of his stomach an indication of the tension building. "Are you ready, Livy?"

"Yes!"

"Oh Jesus, I'm so ready." His hips seem to take on a mind of their own as he shudders into me, the smooth fluidness long gone. He's shaking, clearly trying to hold his restraint, and I wonder again if it's a continual battle for him to prevent the hard fierceness that I bore witness to in the hotel.

That line of thought requires a clear mind, which I don't have right now. I'm coming.

"Miller!"

He pulls his hips away and delivers a thrust that sends us both over the edge, Miller on a tight bark, me on a suppressed scream. His fingers are digging into my flesh as he pushes that little bit farther into me, twitching, jerking, and groaning.

I'm wiped out, completely useless, struggling to even keep my eyes on Miller's postclimax, sweaty face. I welcome his weight when he drops onto me, keeping my eyes closed but making up for my loss of seeing him by feeling him everywhere. He's soaking wet and panting in my hair, and it's the most amazing feeling and sound ever.

"I'm sorry," he whispers out of the blue, and I frown through my exhaustion.

"For what?"

"Tell me what I'm going to do without you." He squeezes me ridiculously hard, putting a strain on my ribs. "Tell me how I'm going to survive."

"Miller, you're constricting me." I practically gasp the words, but he only squeezes harder. "Miller, ease up." I feel his head shake in my neck. "Miller, please!"

He pushes up quickly from my body, dropping his head and eyes, leaving me gasping and heaving on the bed. He won't look at me. I rub some life back into my arms, my legs, everywhere, but he refuses to acknowledge the discomfort he's caused me. He looks worryingly beaten. Where's this come from?

I scramble to my knees to mirror him and take his hands in mine. "You don't need to be concerned by that because I've told you how it is for me," I say calmly, reassuringly, quietly relieved that he appears to be as concerned by the potential of separation as I am.

"Our feelings are irrelevant," he says factually. His declaration makes me back up slightly.

"Of course they're relevant," I argue, a coldness I don't like settling over me.

"No." He shakes his head and pulls his hands from my grip, leaving mine to fall lifelessly to my thighs. "You're right. I should have let you walk away from me."

"Miller?" I can feel the panic begin to set in.

"I can't drag you into my darkness, Olivia. This has to end now."

My chest is beginning to crack open slowly. I'm making his world light. What's the matter with him? "You don't know what you're saying. I'm helping you." I try to take his hands again, but he pulls them out of my reach and gets up from the bed.

"I'll take you home."

"No," I whisper, watching as his back disappears into the bathroom. "No!" Jumping up from the bed, I run after him, grabbing his arm and yanking him around to face me. "What are you doing?"

"I'm doing what's right." There's no feeling, no remorse or sorrow. He's shut down on me, worse than ever before, the mask fixed firmly in place—no suit required. "I should never have let it go this far. I shouldn't have come back for you."

"It?" I yell. "You mean us! There is no *it*, or *you*, or *I* now. It's *us*!" I'm falling apart on him, my shaking body refusing to calm—not until he holds me and tells me I'm hearing things.

"There's you, and there is me." He looks slowly up at me. His blue eyes are empty. "There can never be an *us*."

His cold words stab at my splitting heart. "No." I refuse to accept this. "No!" I shake him by the arms, but he remains impassive and detached. "I'm your habit." I start to sob, the tears bursting from my eyes uncontrollably. "I'm your habit!"

He pulls his arms away and steps back. "Habits are bad for you."

My chest explodes open, exposing my shattered heart. "You're talking rubbish."

"No, I'm talking complete sense, Livy." He walks away and steps in the shower, not even flinching as the unheated water pours all over him.

I'm not giving up. There must be something wrong with him. My panic fuels my doggedness and I'm in the shower, pushing at his body as he attempts to shampoo his hair.

"You don't get to do this to me again, not now! Not after everything!"

He ignores me and rinses his hair before he's even really washed it. Then he hastily escapes me, exiting the other side of the shower, but I'm relentless, shouting as I go after him. I'm grabbing at his wet back, trying to stop him, but he shrugs me off, trying to dry himself and fight his way from the bathroom.

I'm deranged, my heart pounding, my body quaking. "Miller, please!" I cry, dropping to my knees and watching him disappear again. "Please." My head falls into my palms, like darkness and hiding might drag me from my nightmare.

"Get up, Livy." His impatient tone only serves to make me sob harder. "Get up!"

I confront his stone-cold face with my tear-drenched eyes. "You just made love to me. I've accepted you. You wanted me to forget that man and I have."

"He's still here, Livy," he grinds harshly. "He's never going away!"

"He was gone!" I insist desperately. "He's never here when we're together." That's not true, and I know it, but I'm falling farther into hell and I'll try anything to claw my way back.

"Yes, he is," he spits, leaning down and pulling my waiflike frame from the floor. "I was stupid to think I could do this."

"Do what?"

He recoils and releases me, waving up and down my body. "This!"

"You mean feel?" I smack him on the chest. "You mean love?"

His mouth snaps shut and he steps back, clearly fighting to control his twitching body. "I can't love you."

"Don't," I murmur pitifully. "Don't say that."

"The truth hurts, Olivia."

"It's that woman from last night, isn't it?" I ask, her smug face suddenly all I see through my fear. "Sophia. What did she say?"

"It's got nothing to do with her." He stalks from the bathroom, and I know it's because I'm working my way closer to the issue.

"Did you really want to stop?"

"Yes!" he barks, swinging around and nailing me with incensed eyes, but he soon backs down, realizing what he's said. "No!"

"Yes or no?" I scream.

"No!"

"What's happened since last night when you came back to bed?"

"Too fucking much!" He's gone from my sight, slipping into the wardrobe. I go after him again and watch as he yanks on some shorts and a T-shirt. "You're young. You'll get over me." He's refusing to look at me or acknowledge my words, the coward.

"Do you want me to get over you?"

"Yes, you deserve more than I can give. I told you from the start, Livy. I'm emotionally unavailable."

"And since then you've worshipped me and given me everything you've hidden from the world." I keep my eyes on empty blues, desperately trying to find something in them. "You've destroyed me."

"Don't say that!" he yells, guilt clear in his tone and expression. He knows it to be true. "I brought you back to life."

"Congratulations!" I scream, outraged. "Yes! You did, but the moment I saw light and hope, you've cruelly slayed me."

He recoils at my words that are nothing but truth, and with no worthy response, he passes me to escape his wrongs, ensuring no contact is made. "I have to go away."

"Where?"

"Paris. I leave at noon."

A sharp inhale of breath chokes me. The city of love? "You're going with that woman, aren't you?" My heart is completely severed now, the thought of Miller, posh women, restraints, money, and gifts...

And all I can see is my mother's beautiful, selfish face. My face. And now Miller's face.

He will *not* do this to me! "I'll get over you." I straighten my shoulders and watch as he halts at the sound of my even promise. "I'll make sure of it."

He slowly turns and gives me warning eyes. I couldn't care less. "Don't do anything stupid, Livy."

"You've just relinquished your right to make requests, so you'll forgive me if I choose to ignore you." I barge past him, fully aware of what I'm doing and totally prepared to see my threat through.

"Livy!"

"Have a nice trip." I retrieve my damp dress and throw it on as I make my way through his apartment.

"Livy, it's not as easy as just stopping." He's coming after me, the sound of his bare feet slapping on the marble floor behind me getting louder as I hurry to the door. He's concerned now, my indirect promise spiking his possessive streak. He doesn't want another man to taste me. "Livy!" I feel him grab my arm, and I swing around, boiling with rage, finding the mask lifting slightly. But the smidgen of hope doesn't stop me from lashing his cheek with my palm. His head snaps to the side and remains there while I attempt in vain to cool my temper.

"Yes! You should have let me walk away from you!" I fire with complete resoluteness. "You should have let me forget!"

His face slowly comes back to me. "I didn't want you to remember me like that. I didn't want you to hate me."

I laugh, stunned by his selfish motives. He doesn't care what anyone else thinks of him. But me? I'm different? "How honorable of you, but you've made a fatal mistake, Miller Hart."

He looks wary as he drops his hold of me. "How?"

"Because I hate you more now than I ever did when you made me one of your whores! Now you're just a coward. Now you're a quitter, a chicken!" I gulp down some calming breaths, feeling ashamed of my desperate behavior and begging. He knows how I feel, and I know how he feels, yet he's the one walking away, when it's me who would be taking the biggest leap of faith here. It's me going against all of my rules and morals. It's me taking on the mountain of flaws this man has. "I'll never let you have me again," I vow. "Not ever." The grit in my tone is a surprise.

"It's undoubtedly a good thing," he barely whispers, taking another step away from me, like he's concerned that if I'm within touching distance, he might contradict his words. "Be safe, Livy."

The double meaning in his statement is an insult. "I'm safe now," I proclaim, turning my back on a man clearly torn and walking away from him for the last time ever.

My despair has vanished at his cowardly words and actions. I know how he feels. *He* knows how he feels—which makes him a weak, spineless coward.

Now all I want to do is hurt him. I want to take the most resilient part of him and destroy it.

Chapter Twenty-four

It's past nine at night, and I'm wiped out by overflowing emotion, but my vengeful mind won't allow me to sleep. I'm being spurred on, encouraged by resentment to stick the knife in and twist it continuously. Four missed calls from William haven't helped my state of mind. If anything, it's only encouraged me. I know without question that I'm about to prove him right once and for all. I'm my mother's daughter.

I no longer have my Ice membership card, but it won't stop me. Nothing will stop me. Bypassing the short queue, I present myself to the doorman, who performs a sigh of exasperation before granting me access without a word. I strut past him and head straight for one of the bars, taking in my surroundings, the music, the happy atmosphere. The music tonight seems dark, and playing right now is Faithless's "Insomnia." It's purposeful. It's apt.

"Champagne," I order, resting my arse against the bar and gazing around at the blue glow engulfing Miller's club. It's rammed full of London's elite, the usual masses of well-dressed revelers filling every available space, but despite the amount of people closing me in from every direction, I know the security cameras will be focused on me and me alone. Miller will have given Tony the heads-up, and I've no doubt the doorman has already advised Tony of my arrival.

"Miss?"

I turn and accept the glass of champagne, ignoring the strawberry and downing it. Then I immediately demand another. I'm handed a fresh glass, and as I turn, I spot Tony striding across the dance floor in my direction. He looks fuming mad, and knowing what's about to transpire, I disappear amid the sea of people, taking off toward the roof terrace.

As I make my way up the frosted glass steps, I glance over my shoulder and smile when I see Tony standing where I've just fled, looking around in confusion. He leans over the bar and speaks to the barman, who quickly shrugs before tending to a waiting customer. I see Tony bash his fist on the glass counter of the bar and swing around, scanning the club. Smug, I continue on my way until I round the corner and break the threshold of the giant glass wall, finding myself among a sea of people laughing, drinking, and chatting, none of them taking a bit of notice of the stunning outlook.

I take a sip of my champagne and wait, and I don't have to wait for long. I catch the eye of a guy across the terrace and smile coyly before slowly turning away from him to enjoy the view.

"Alone?"

I leisurely pivot on my heels, coming face-to-face with him. He's dressed in dark jeans and a white shirt. My eyes drag the entire length of his body until I'm at his face. It's a handsome face—clean shaven and fresh, and his short brown hair is longer on top, combed to the side.

"You?" I ask, relaxing in my pose and taking my glass to my lips.

He smiles a little and directs me to the edge of the terrace, his hand resting lightly on the small of my back. There are no internal sparks ricocheting around my body from his touch, but he's a man and that's all I need.

"Danny." He leans down and pecks each of my cheeks. "You are?"

"Livy." I glance up to the camera and smile as he takes his time introducing himself.

"Pleasure to meet you, Livy," he says as he pulls away. "I love your dress."

I've no doubt he loves it. It's tight and short. "Thank you."

"You're welcome." His eyes sparkle.

We spend a short while chatting and I reciprocate when he smiles and laughs, finding it easy, but not because I'm attracted to him. It's because I know cameras are focused on me from every direction, recording everything and saving it for Miller's eyes once he's returned from Paris.

"Is there a protocol you like to follow?"

I struggle to prevent my brow from furrowing in confusion. "You mean whether I'd like you to take me for dinner or just take me to bed?"

He smirks. "I'm happy to do both."

My confidence wavers momentarily, but I quickly rein it in. "We'll call the strawberry dinner." I tip my flute and catch the fruit, making a point of chewing it slowly and swallowing even slower.

He follows suit and mimics my actions with a knowing smile. "It's a stunning view." He tips his empty glass toward the open space beyond, and I follow his indication to look.

"I agree," I muse, "but I can think of far better ways to spend the rest of the evening." My boldness should stun me, but it doesn't. I'm on a mission—a dangerous mission. Miller isn't the only one with a mask. This is too easy.

Turning my eyes back to Danny, my lips tip seductively and he moves in, slowly lowering his face to mine until our lips brush.

In an attempt to maintain my cool confidence, I close my eyes and conjure up images of Miller. It's weak and pathetic, but it's the only way I'll see through my cruel actions. Danny's lips don't help me achieve my objective; they feel and taste nothing like Miller's, yet I don't hold back. I let him kiss me, and I relish only in the knowledge of what this will do to the man I love—the man who I know loves me but is too much of a weak coward to fight for it.

"My place," Danny mumbles against my lips, slipping his palm onto my bottom. I nod against him and he immediately takes my hand to start leading me from the terrace. Miller Hart has ignited a dormant recklessness. I've proven William right. I'm my mother's daughter, and the realization should send me into meltdown, but the only meltdown I predict is the cold reality of my life without Miller in it. He's a massive mess of complications and challenges, yet I crave him and all of the obstacles that accompany him.

We take the stairs, me following Danny, until we hit the ground floor. He pushes his way through the crowd, eager to escape the roar of people and gain some privacy. But then he halts and stuns me by kissing me again, humming into my mouth on a sigh. "I might do that a few more times before we make it out of here," he says, gently pushing his groin into my stomach.

I don't protest, mainly because I'm jumping all over the fact that there is a camera directly above us, so I wrap my arms around his broad shoulders and let him have his way, my way of saying, *Fine by me.*

Dragging his body from mine, he reclaims my hand and leads on, stopping only a few more paces into his determined stride. But he doesn't kiss me this time. "Excuse me," he says, trying to sidestep someone, only for them to move with him. I can't see who it is. I don't need to see who it is.

"You're not leaving with the girl." Tony's gruff voice makes me sag behind Danny, but it also boosts my resolve.

Danny turns to look at me. "Ignore him," I say tightly, pushing into his back, encouraging him to move on.

"Who is he?"

"No one." I take over the lead, tugging a bemused Danny with me. Tony can't stop me, and that will destroy Miller further.

"Livy, quit the games." Tony's annoyed growl pulls me to a stop.

"Who said this is a game?" I ask shortly.

"Me." He steps forward, flicking warning eyes to a perplexed Danny, who's since dropped my hand.

Danny laughs. "Okay, I don't know what the crack is, but you can leave me out of it." He strides off, leaving Tony and I glaring at each other.

"Smart guy."

"Why do you care?"

"I don't."

"Then why bother intervening?"

"Because you'll get yourself in trouble."

"I'll find someone else," I spit, barging past him, my legs like jelly as I make my way back to the bar. "Champagne," I demand once I've fought my way to the front. Tony appears in front of me on the other side of the bar, shooing away the barman who was set to serve me.

"You're not being served any more alcohol."

My teeth clench. "Why don't you mind your own business?"

He leans over the bar, his own teeth grating. "If you realized the damage you're doing, you'd cut the shit, sweetheart."

Me? Damage? My temper flares into dangerous territory. If I was operating on resentment before, then now it's in pure, raw rage. "That man has destroyed me!"

"That man is shackled, Livy!" he yells, making me recoil. "And regardless of what you and he ever thought, you can't free him."

"From what?" I don't like the resolve in Tony's tone or the look on his round face. He sounds too certain.

"From the invisible chains." He speaks in a near whisper, but I hear the words perfectly over the deafening music and crowds. My throat starts to close off. I can't breathe. Tony is watching me absorb his statement, probably wondering what I'm making of it. I don't know. He's talking in code. He's insinuating that Miller is powerless—a weak man. That's not true. He's very powerful, physically and mentally. I've experienced both.

I remain silent, mind spinning, body shaking, unsure of my next move. I feel distressed and in the dark, my damn eyes beginning to sting with the onset of hopeless tears.

"Go home, Livy. Get on with your life and forget you ever met Miller Hart."

"Impossible," I sob, my face quickly drenched as I lose the battle to retain my grief.

Tony's body deflates through the mist of water clouding my vision, and he's suddenly gone, but my body won't kick into action, leaving me standing at the bar, lost and useless.

"Come with me." I feel a hand gently take my arm and guide me away from the busy bar, through the club, and down the stairs to the maze beneath Ice. Tony's information, albeit vague and cryptic, indicates this isn't Miller's decision.

I stagger and trip in front of Tony, almost disoriented, and when we arrive at the door to Miller's office, he punches in the code, swings the door open, and guides me to Miller's desk. He places me carefully in the chair. "I don't want to be here," I murmur pitifully, blanking out the comfort I gain from being in one of Miller's perfectly precise spaces. "Why did you bring me here?" He should have put me in a taxi and sent me home.

Tony shuts the door and turns to face me. "There's something on the desk for you," he says with zero enthusiasm, and I can tell it's because he doesn't want me to have whatever it is. I cast my eyes across the glossy white surface, seeing the cordless phone in its usual spot, and in the center of the desk is an envelope, placed so accurately, the bottom flush with the edge of the desk, only Miller could have put it there.

Instinct makes me sink into the leather of his chair, putting distance between the harmless piece of paper and me. I'm cautious and certain that I'm not going to want to read what's contained inside. "From him?" I ask, not removing my eyes from the envelope.

"Yes," Tony sighs. "He stopped by on his way to St. Pancras."

I'm not looking at Tony, but I know he's just exhaled a silent stream of weary breath. My hand lifts slowly and takes the envelope, which has my full name scrolled across the front in writing I recognize. Miller's writing. The shakes are unavoidable, no matter how hard I try to control them, as I pull the note from inside. I'm vainly attempting to regulate my breathing, but heart palpitations are making it an impossible task to achieve. I unfold the paper and brush at my eyes to restore my clear vision. Then I hold my breath.

My sweet girl,

How did I know you would end up here? The security cameras have been turned off this evening under my request. If you choose to allow another man to taste you, then it is no more than I deserve, but I could never bear to witness it. Thinking about it is torturous enough. Seeing it could push me to kill. I've hurt you and for that I hope I burn in hell when I arrive there. Of all my wrongs, you are my biggest regret, Olivia Taylor. I don't regret worshipping you or indulging in you. I regret the impossibility of my life and my inability to give you forever. You must trust me and the decision that I've made, and know I've made it with a heavy heart. It kills me to say it, but I hope you can forget about me and find a man worthy of your love. I'm not that man.

My fascination will never die, sweet girl. I can deprive my eyes from seeing you and deny my mouth from tasting you. But there is nothing I can do to heal my shattered heart.

Eternally yours,
Miller Hart

"No," I sob, all built-up air in my lungs rushing from my mouth on painful gasps. The *H* of Miller's name blurs when a tear hits the paper and makes the ink run down the page. The sight of the smudged, distorted letter matches me.

"Are you all right?" Tony's voice breaks into my chaotic thoughts, and I lift my heavy eyes to another person opposed to our relationship. Everyone is hell-bent on breaking us, as I once was, too. And after all of Miller's loss of temper when he'd feared I'd lapsed in fortitude, it's now him.

"I hate him." I spit the hurtful words with total sincerity. This letter hasn't eased the pain. His words are conflicting, making coming to terms with his decision harder to accept. His decision. What about mine? What about me and my willingness to accept him and let him fill me with the strength I need to help him? Or is he beyond help? Is he too close to the depths of hell for me to pull him back? All of these thoughts and questions are only assisting in turning my pain into hatred. After everything we have endured, he shouldn't get to make this decision on his own. I drop the letter to his desk and stand sharply. He's hiding. He has hidden all of his life... until he met me. He showed me a man I'm certain no one else has seen before. He hides behind manners that defy the brusque, arrogant arsehole and suits that defy the relaxed Miller when we're lost in each other. He's a fraud, just like he said.

A red mist engulfs me and I stumble past his desk, practically falling to the drinks cabinet on the other side of his office. I spend a few moments running my eyes across the perfectly placed bottles and glasses, my breathing loud and erratic.

"Livy?" Tony sounds close and *very* alarmed.

I scream, deranged, swiping my arm across the surface, sending every perfectly placed item that adorned the unit smashing to the office floor on a loud crash.

"Livy!" Tony's suddenly grabbing at my thrashing limbs, fighting to restrain me as I continue to shriek and battle against him like a woman possessed. "Calm down!"

"Get off!" I shout, heaving my body from his grasp and sprinting across Miller's office to the exit. My legs are moving fast, in time to my thundering heart, taking me away from Miller's perfection, up the stairs, and out into the midnight air. I all but throw myself into the road, giving a cab no choice but to stop or run me down. I jump in. "Belgravia," I pant, slamming the door and watching as Tony barrels out of Ice, his arms flailing violently at the doorman as he watches me pull away. I fall back against the leather, giving my heart time to recover, my forehead hitting the cold glass as I watch a dark London pass by.

London really has cast its black shadow.

Chapter Twenty-five

His apartment block looks uninviting, the glass-adorned lobby cold and silent. The doorman tips his hat as I pass, my heels breaking the eerie quiet and echoing around the vast space. I don't take the elevator, instead pushing my way through the door that leads to the stairwell, hoping the energy it'll take to get me up the ten flights might dull down some of the anger burning a hole in my gut.

My plan fails. I fly up the stairs and find myself slipping my key into the lock of his shiny front door in no time, with no sign that my temper has cooled. Knowing exactly where I'm heading, I run through his quiet apartment, into the kitchen, and start yanking drawers open. I find what I'm looking for; then I fly down the corridor to his bedroom, taking the first door into his wardrobe.

As I stand at the threshold, armed with the most sinister knife I could find, I cast my eyes around the three walls that are all filled with rails and rails of bespoke and designer suits and shirts. Or masks. I see them as masks. Something for Miller to hide behind. His armor and protection.

And at that thought, I scream, deranged, and start yanking down the rows and rows of expensive garments. I begin slashing at the material, dropping the knife sporadically to rip the expensive fabric into strips. The power in my arms makes my task easy, my anger my friend, the knife only reclaimed and utilized to make random holes everywhere before I tear with my bare hands.

"I hate you!" I scream, slashing through his racks of ties.

I'm bordering the level of psychosis that Miller has shown all too often in recent days, and I only relent when every piece of his clothing is a mess of torn fabric. Then I fall to my arse, exhausted, my breathing labored, and stare at the piles of ruined material surrounding me. It wasn't a given that my mission to destroy all of his masks would make me feel any better, and it doesn't. My hands feel raw, my face is stinging, and my throat is sore from screaming my way through my task. I'm as big a wreck as the mess I've caused. Shuffling back, I find the cabinet that sits in the center of Miller's wardrobe and slump against it, my shoes lost amid the mess, my dress riding up to my waist. I just sit there in silence, heaving and panting, for the longest time, wondering... what now? Being destructive might momentarily divert me from thinking, but the relief is short-lived. There will come a point when I've destroyed everything, possibly even myself. Beyond recognition. Then what will I do? I'm tinkering on the edge of self-annihilation already.

I let my head fall limply back, but jump when a loud crash rings through the apartment. My body stills, my breath catching in my throat. Then the hammering starts. I'm immobilized by a familiar fear, just sitting here listening to the persistent bangs on the front door, my eyes wide, my heart fighting to break free from my chest. I look around at the mess surrounding me. And spot the knife. Picking it up slowly, I watch the blade glimmer as I turn it in my hand. Then I stand on shaky legs. Perhaps I should hide, but my bare feet start moving of their own accord, my hand gripping the handle of the knife tightly. I wade through the remnants of Miller's clothes toward the racket, cautious, wary, until I'm tiptoeing down the corridor and emerging into the lounge. I can see across the room to the entrance hall, and I can see the door physically moving with each hard bang.

Then the banging stops and an unnerving silence falls. I go to step forward, choking down my fear, determined to face the unknown threat, but halt when the mechanical lock on the door shifts and the door bursts open on a loud curse.

I stagger back in shock, my pulse bursting through my eardrums, making me dizzy and disoriented. It takes a few frightening moments to register what I'm confronted with. He looks unbalanced, a shocking thing for me to claim after the time I've just spent in his wardrobe. He's a wreck, heaving and sweating, almost vibrating with anger.

He hasn't seen me. The door is smashed shut and his fist thrown into the back of it, splintering the glossy wood, making Miller roar when his knuckles split open and me stagger back in alarm.

"Fuck!" His expletive bounces around the colossal open space, hitting me from every direction, making me cower on the spot. I want to run to his aid or shout at him to notice that I'm here, but I dare not speak. He's completely unhinged, leaving me wondering what the cause is for his violent lash-out. His own interference? I stand, distressed and disturbed, as his back heaves and the echo of his boom fades. It's only mere seconds before his shoulders visibly tense and he swings his messy body to face me. The perfection that is Miller is lost. The lump in my throat explodes, choking me, and I bite down on my lip to stop a sob from slipping past my lips. The sweat trailing down his temples is dripping onto his jacket, but he's unbothered by the potential of his posh suit being dampened. His eyes are wild as he stares at me; then he throws his head back again and yells to the ceiling before collapsing to his knees.

His head drops in defeat.

And Miller Hart cries—massive, body-jerking sobs.

Nothing could cause me more pain. Years of holding his emotions in check are pouring out of him, and I can do nothing more than watch, my heart aching for him. My own agony has made way for the torture this confounding man is suffering. I want to hold him and comfort him, but my legs weigh a thousand tons and refuse to carry me to him. I'm useless. I try to speak his name, but achieve nothing but an agonized gasp.

A lifetime passes. I cry a lifetime's worth of tears and so does Miller, except for him it's probably literally. I'm beginning to wonder if he'll ever stop when his injured hand lifts and roughly brushes over his stubbled cheeks, replacing the tears with smears of blood.

His head rises, revealing a blemished face and blue eyes rimmed in redness. But he won't allow them to focus on me. He's doing everything to avoid making eye contact with me. Agitated, he pushes himself from the floor and moves toward me, making me retreat, but he passes me, still avoiding my eyes, and makes for his bedroom. After tossing my weapon on the round table in the hallway, I finally convince my dead legs to move and follow him. He strips out of his jacket, waistcoat, and shirt as he strides across his bedroom, heading for the bathroom. His clothes are being tossed aside, his bedroom floor scattered in garments that are being torn from his body. Halting at the foot of the doorway to his bathroom, he kicks his shoes and socks off and then yanks his trousers and boxers from his legs, leaving him naked, his back shimmering in sweat.

He doesn't venture any farther, standing silent in the doorway, his head lowered, his muscled arms outstretched to grip the door frame. Not knowing what to do but knowing I can't bear to see him in this state any longer, I begin to approach him gingerly, until I'm close enough to smell his manly scent mixed with the clean sweat that's dripping from his body.

"Miller," I say quietly, lifting my hand and reaching for his shoulder, but when I tentatively rest my hand on his flesh, I have to resist yanking it back on a gasp. He's boiling hot, but I don't have to withstand the burning heat for too long. He hisses on a flinch, making me wince at his rejection, and paces to the shower, stepping in and turning it on.

He's frantic in his task. After grabbing the sponge and loading it with shower gel, he carelessly tosses the bottle to the floor before scrubbing at his skin. I'm alarmed, not only by his uncharacteristic show of untidiness, but also by his urgency to clean his body, and so harshly. He's scrubbing, working the sponge everywhere, rinsing and reloading with more shower gel. Steam is quickly engulfing the huge space, telling me the shower is far too hot, not that he seems affected. "Miller." I take a few paces, getting more and more concerned the steamier the room becomes. "Miller, please!" I slap my palm on the glass to try to get his attention. His hair is sopping and hanging all over his face, hampering his vision, but he's not deterred. There's a mixture of terror and anger being injected into the desperate motions of the sponge flying across his body. He's going to blister himself. "Miller, stop it!" I try to enter the shower fully dressed, but jump out when the water makes contact with me. "Shit!" It's scorching hot. "Miller, turn the water off!"

"I can't stand it!" he yells, scooping the shower gel from the floor and squeezing the bottle all over his chest. "They make my skin crawl! I can feel them through my clothes!"

My breath catches in my throat, his words registering loud and clear. But that's the least of my worries. He's going to injure himself terribly if I don't get him out. "Miller, listen to me." I try for a calming tone, but my voice is anxious, and I cannot help it.

"I have to be clean! I need to remove every trace of them from me."

I need to get in and shut the shower off, but even from the outside the water is scalding me. "Turn the shower off!" I shout, losing my composure. "Miller! Turn the fucking shower off!" I'm ignored, and when his scrubbing moves from his chest to his arms, I see angry red welts materializing on his pecs. It kicks my scared arse into action and before I can consider the pain I'll endure, I'm in the shower, feeling the wall for the controls. "Shit shit shit!" I yell as I'm attacked by blisteringly hot water from every angle.

I push Miller's body out of my way, snapping him from his insanity, and frantically turn the knob to halt the infliction of pain on both Miller and me. When the water dries up above us, I roll against the wall to my back, exhausted, my skin stinging and sore, and wait for the steam to disintegrate, revealing Miller's naked, motionless form. He's expressionless. There is nothing on that heart-stopping face, not even a hint of discomfort after tolerating the boiling shower for far longer than I did.

I move toward him and reach up to gently stroke the wet strands of hair out of his face as I gather the depleted air that has been sucked from my lungs. "Don't ever try to push me away again," I warn firmly. "I love you, Miller Hart. All of you."

His tortured blue eyes drag slowly up my wet, slumped body and gaze longingly at me. "How?" He asks the simple, reasonable question on a whisper. This man has tested my resilience to the absolute maximum. He's tossed me from crippling despair to crippling pleasure. He's made me reckless, stupid, blind...and he's made me brave.

I can love him because he touches my soul.

"I love you," I repeat, feeling no need to justify it to anyone, not even Miller. "I love you," I murmur. "I won't go down without a fight. I'll take anyone on and I'll win against them all. Even you." My palm cups his nape and pulls his face to mine, watching as he scans my face with blank eyes. "I'm strong enough to love you." My lips push to his, instigating our reunion, and my tongue delicately enters his mouth, coaxing a moan before he pulls away.

"I couldn't do it," he says quietly. "I couldn't do it to you, Livy." He lifts me to his body, my thighs curling around his hips, but I'm mindful of his tender skin, keeping my hands on his shoulders. I can't stop my face from seeking the comfort of his neck, though. I lay my cheek on his shoulder and inhale him into me, feeling the solace he feeds me sink into my body through our contact. He couldn't do it.

"I want to worship you," I say into his neck, my hot breath colliding with his heated skin. The mixture of the two is almost intolerable. I need to remind him of what we have. I need to show him I can do this. That *he* can do this.

"I do the worshipping."

"Not today." I unwrap myself from his body and lead him from the shower, taking him to his bed and pushing him down to the sheets. His tall body stretches across the mattress as he watches me arrange his limbs until I'm sure he's comfortable. Then I kiss his impassive face and leave him to relax while I draw a bath. I ensure the water is only tepid and look through his ridiculously neat cupboard, making sure I don't upset his perfect arrangement of bottles, tubes, and pots until I find some bath soak. The horrific mess that I've left his wardrobe in is likely to make him disintegrate, but I'll deal with that later. I'm not delusional enough to think that a picnic in the park and a kiss in the rain have eliminated Miller's obsessive ways completely.

Leaving the bath running, I remove my sodden dress and wander back into the bedroom, then start to collect his discarded clothes, probably the only ones that he still has intact. I fold them neatly and place them in a pile on a dresser, glancing up when I feel blue eyes burning my naked skin.

"What?" I ask, shifting under his close scrutiny.

"I'm just thinking how lovely you look tidying my bedroom." He shifts onto his side and props his head on his bent arm. "Continue."

The anguish dulls a little more, and I smile, making his blue orbs win a little sparkle back. It's familiar and comforting. "Would you like a drink?"

He nods.

"Any preference?"

He shakes his head.

I feel my forehead crease as I start to make my way from the room, glancing back over my shoulder, finding him following my path closely until he disappears from view. I'm hasty, rushing down the corridor and across the lounge, landing in front of the drinks cabinet.

I swipe up a short glass, certain it resembles the ones that I've seen Miller drinking from. Then I take on a really amateur tactic for picking scotch, closing my eyes, waving my hand, and pointing at a bottle. Satisfied with my random selection, I pour the glass halfway, spilling some as I do. "Shit!" I swear, clattering the bottle against the others when I put it back too clumsily.

Now I'm hopeless for a whole different reason. The charismatic—if a little messed up right now—man in the room down the hall has refinement down to a fine art. I haven't.

I roll my eyes to myself and lift the glass to my lips, taking a big glug and immediately gagging at the taste. "Oh God!" My lips smack together, my face screwing up as I hold the glass up and look at the dark liquid with disgust. "Vile," I mutter, swiveling and trekking back to Miller.

He's still on his side, looking at the door when I enter. "Scotch." I hold the drink up and his eyes travel across to the glass before landing back on me with a bang. But he says nothing, maintaining his quiet state.

I wander over to the bed thoughtfully, holding his eyes, and extend my arm once I've reached him. His muscled arm lifts slowly and takes the glass. Then he blinks painfully lazily, making me cross my legs in my standing position to stop the pulsing from breaking out into a hard throb. Just the fact that these familiar traits are present is delightful, whether he's doing it on purpose or not. My huge bag of intensity is back, his messed-up condition aside. I can see bright, hopeful light.

"I've drawn a bath," I tell him, watching as he lifts the whisky to his lips and takes a languid sip. "It's not too hot."

He looks to the glass for a brief moment before making me melt with a slight tip of his wonderful mouth. "Come here." He flicks his head to follow up his demand, and I slip in beside him, letting him tuck me into his chest so he can sip his drink with one hand and stroke my hair with the other.

"Your knuckles look sore," I say, loving being back in my comfort zone even if the events that have brought me here are killing us.

"They're fine." He pushes his lips to the top of my head and says no more. I can feel and hear him taking frequent sips of his drink, and while I'm happy tucked closely to his body, I'd like to look after him and try to gently coax an explanation from him.

I reluctantly pull myself away from the hard, warm security of his chest and take his hand. He frowns but lets me help him up and lead him to the bathroom, bringing his drink with him. The giant bath is full enough, so I flick the tap off, then signal for him to climb in. He's quiet as he sets his drink down on a nearby counter, and I finally feel it appropriate to spend a few silent moments absorbing his nakedness while he's turned away from me. The muscles of his back are sharp, defined by the spotlights shining down, and the cheeks of his smooth backside are solid, drifting into long, lean thighs, then perfectly formed calves. I ignore the scratch marks. This impeccably formed man is perfectly flawed. He's damaged, more than me, and he believes he's destined for hell. I need to know why he's so adamant about his destiny. I want to be the one who changes his fate.

Miller turns and my gaze that was happily focused on his buns is now staring at something else firm and smooth and . . . ready. My eyes fly up to shimmering blues but a straight face. And I blush. Why do I blush? My cheeks are on fire as he regards me, my bare feet shifting as I'm bombarded by pure, raw, inexorable shots of heated desire. I've lost my poise completely. My earlier resolution is being beaten down by his intoxicating presence.

"I want to worship you," I breathe, reaching back with shaking hands and unhooking my bra, letting it drop down my arms and tumble to my feet. His eyes drop to my knickers and I do as I'm silently bid, removing them slowly. Now we're both naked and his desire mixed with mine is creating a heady cocktail that's rife in the quiet air around us. I nod to the bath. It's that or fall to my knees and beg him to indulge me with some Miller-style worshipping, but I need him to see I'm strong, that I can help him.

Licking his lips is his last-ditch attempt to make me fold. I struggle terribly but manage to sustain my strength, nodding to the bath again. His mouth doesn't smile, but his eyes do. He climbs the steps and settles in the bubbly water.

"Would you do me the honor of joining me?" he asks quietly.

I answer by taking the steps unhurriedly, using the time to weigh up my best position, settling on behind him. A cock of my head tells him to shift forward, which he does with a very slight pucker of his brow, allowing space behind him for me to sink into. I spread my thighs, slide my hands over his shoulders, and pull him back to my chest. His dark, wet waves tickle the side of my cheek and his body is a little heavy, despite the water lightening him, but I'm coiled around him, breathing him into me, giving him my *thing*.

"This feels so nice." His voice is soft and low. Peaceful.

I hum my agreement, encasing his shoulders with my arms, undoubtedly restricting his movement, yet there are no complaints. He answers my constriction by relaxing his head back and feeling out my lower legs that are linked and resting on his stomach.

"This isn't going to be easy." His words are spoken with an edge of pain. They confuse me. I already know that.

"It wasn't easy yesterday or the day before, but you had fight in you. What's changed?"

"A reality check."

I want to see his face, but I worry what I might find in his eyes if I do. "What do you mean?"

"Some decisions I'm not at liberty to make." He utters the words quietly, reluctantly. The stiffening of my body is unavoidable, and I know he's noticed because he squeezes my calves almost in reassurance. I'm not sure Miller feels any reassurance himself, so trying to comfort me is a silly venture.

I try to process what that could mean and come up with no obvious answer. "Elaborate," I instruct sternly, making him turn his face into my cheek and bite down lightly.

"As you wish."

"I do," I affirm.

"I'm chained to this life, Olivia." He doesn't look at me when delivering his shocking declaration, making me gently cup his rough cheek and pull his face up so I can see him, all the while Tony's words bouncing around in my head.

I use his one-word demand again. "Elaborate." Then I kiss him tenderly on his beautiful mouth, hoping I'll give him back some of the strength he fills me with. Our mouths move slowly together, and I know he'll make it last forever if I don't break it, so I do. Grudgingly. "Tell me."

"I'm indebted to them."

I try to keep a brave face, but those words fill me with dread. There are two questions I need to ask in response to his statement and I can't decide which should take priority. "Why are you indebted to them?"

He blinks on an uncomfortable sigh. I can see him becoming more and more reluctant as the conversation progresses and the enlightenments unfold. His minimal answers are a sign. He's making me ask, rather than openly share. "They gave me control."

Another puzzling answer, leaving a huge hole for further questioning. "Elaborate." I sound impatient when I'm trying my hardest not to be.

He breaks free from my palm and rests his head back. "Remember me explaining about my talent?"

I stare down at the back on his head, wanting to remind him of his manners. "Yes." My reply is slow and cautious. It makes him shift slightly.

"My talent earned me a certain amount of freedom."

"I don't understand." I'm beyond confused.

"I was a regular male prostitute, Livy. I had no control nor received any respect." He spells it out, making me flinch. "I ran away from the orphanage when I was fifteen. Spent four years on the streets. That's how I met Cassie. I broke into empty houses for shelter." I gulp back my shock before I can interrupt his flow, but he turns and catches my stunned face. "Bet you never considered your man was an expert lock breaker."

What does he want me to say to that? No, I didn't, but I also never considered that he would be an escort, a drug addict...I halt that train of thought immediately. I could be here a while. And Cassie. She was homeless, too?

Miller smiles a little and turns back away from my startled face. "They found us. Put us to work. But I was beautiful and on top of that, I was good. So I was taken from the lowly and utilized to my full ability. Glamour and sex. I make them a fortune. I'm the Special One."

I go cold, life itself draining from my body, horrible chills jumping onto my wet skin. It's happening too often. And I'm struck dumb. Taken from the lowly? "You're *my* special one." I can't think of anything else to say, other than reinforcing my feelings for him, making him feel like more than a walking, talking pleasure machine. "You're *my* special one, but special because you're beautiful and adoring, not because you give me mind-blowing orgasms." I roughly kiss the back of his head, squeezing him to me.

"But it helps, right?"

"Well..." I can't say no. How he makes me feel physically is amazing, but it comes nowhere close to how he makes me feel emotionally.

He laughs lightly, annoying me, not because it's quite inappropriate to find anything about this humorous but because I can't see it. "You can say yes, Livy."

I yank his face to mine, finding that mild boyish grin. "Fine, yes, but I love you for reasons other than your sexual capabilities."

"But I'm good." His grin widens.

"The best."

His grin falls away instantly. "Tony called me."

I'm tense again. Everywhere. The cameras were off, but Tony saw me. Would he have told Miller? I can't be certain, although Miller's loss of control outside of Ice that time should make Tony's silence easy. He studies me, assessing my reaction. I must look as guilty as sin. "I—"

"Don't tell me." He turns away from me. "I'm likely to kill."

My eyes dart all over the bathroom, mentally thanking every god in existence for Miller's initiative to turn the cameras off. I hate that I reacted that way, and I hate that he predicted it. In an attempt to divert my guilt and Miller's thinking, I prepare my next question. "And Cassie?"

"I convinced them to bring her with me."

I want to resent him requesting that, but compassion halts it in its tracks.

"Being the Special One gives me clout." He sighs. "I choose my clients, arrange dates to suit me, and make my own rules. The no touching was a given. They don't need to touch *me* to achieve their aim, and I was sick of being used as an object. Kissing is intimate." He detaches my snaked legs from his body and leisurely turns over so he's spread front forward on my torso and looking up at me. My hand reaching out and brushing his stray curl off his forehead is natural. "Tasting someone is intimate." He slides up my body and plunges his tongue into my mouth, moaning and biting gently at my lips. "Once I'd tasted you, I knew I was getting into something I shouldn't. But you taste so fucking good."

My legs rewrap around his tight waist and my desire rockets, the feel of him locked securely between my thighs making me wonder if I can ever bear releasing him. I think I understand him a little more now. Discounting our awful encounter in the hotel, he's done nothing but worship me. He lets me touch and kiss him. He wants intimacy with me.

"Who are 'they'?" I ask into his mouth. Tony's confounding riddles are suddenly very clear. He knows. He knows who "they" are.

"I'll die before I expose you to them." He bites my lip and lets it drag through his grip. "Which is why I need you to trust me while I figure this out." His eyes are pleading. "Can you do that for me?"

"What's to figure out?" I don't like the sound of this.

"So much. Please, I beg you, don't give up on me. I want to be with you. Forever. Just me and you. Us. It's all I see now, Olivia. It's all I want. But I know they'll do anything to stop me from having you." Reaching up, he smooths down my cheek with a fingertip and runs his thumb across my bottom lip. He's answerable to someone—someone unpleasant. "I owe them."

"What do you owe them?" That's stupid!

"They took me off the streets, Livy. To them, I owe them my life. I make them a lot of money."

I have no idea what to say, and I certainly can't fathom how "they," whoever *they* are, can keep him in this world forever. A lifetime debt is plain unreasonable. They can't expect that.

"I haven't had sex with anyone since I met you, Olivia. Tell me you believe that."

"I believe you." I don't hesitate. I trust him.

"I know these women. I can't have people asking questions. I can't let them find out about you."

Realization dawns as things begin to make sense, and panic settles deep. "What about that woman in Quaglino's?" I remember her face, the shock, the delight, and then the smugness. She said she wasn't a gossip. I don't believe her.

"I have too much dirt on Crystal and she knows it. I have nothing to worry about there."

I'm not even going to ask what dirt that is. I don't want to know. "Tony and Cassie," I remind him. I don't trust Cassie, not one little bit.

"I don't have to worry." He's adamant, and I'm not sure if that makes me feel better or worse. Tied? Chained? He'll die before he exposes me to these people? Cassie and Tony know these people and they know the consequences of our relationship.

But how many people have seen us together? We've been at the club, shopping, in the park. My eyes are darting everywhere. "Anyone could have seen us." I sound worried, which is just fine because I am.

"I've taken damage control where necessary."

"Wait!" I shoot my stare back to Miller. "That time you found me at the hospital."

He recalls, and I know it because discomfort riddles his wet face, yet I don't bother giving him the chance to either confirm or deny it.

"We were being followed, weren't we? You abandoned your car and took us down to the tube because we were being followed." How many times have we been followed? How many times have *I* been followed? "Do they already know about me?"

Miller sighs. "There are signs. I was careless. I've exposed you. I thought..." He takes a few moments and comes up with no thoughts.

Signs? I don't need clarification. My innocent mind in spinning.

"I've dealt with anyone who may have been an issue."

"How?"

"Don't ask, Olivia."

My lips straighten, jilted. "That woman saw me in your apartment."

"I know."

"So what have you told her?"

He's suddenly evading my eyes, so I yank his chin to me and purse my lips. "I told her you were paying."

"What?" I gasp. "You told her I'm a client?"

"I had nothing else, Olivia."

I shake my head, not believing what he's telling me. Do I look like I would pay for sex? I wince when images of a thousand pounds scattered on a dining table jump all over my tortured mind. "What happened after Sophia left last night? Why the change from coming back to bed to waking this morning?" He totally imploded, with no warning or reason.

"She said some things. Made me overthink." He looks ashamed, and he bloody well should be when I've been repeatedly chastised for doing exactly that. "She pointed out my obligations."

Obligations? My fucking brain is in a whirlwind. "And what happened today?" This I *have* to know. There seems like too many obvious cover-breakers to me, yet Miller seems confident of their silence.

He drops his eyes. "I frightened myself."

"How?"

"If I was punishing with these women before, then now I could be dangerous. I could hurt them."

I frown, wrestling his face up and seeing fear in his eyes, which only serves to escalate mine. "Why?"

He takes a long, controlled breath of air and lets it all breeze out with his words. "Because when I look at any one of them, I see a reason why I can't have my sweet girl." He lets me absorb his words for a few moments. I know what he means. "I see interferers."

I clamp my lips together, tears stinging the backs of my sore eyes.

"I can't risk taking them when all I'm seeing is that. They'll end up dead. But more importantly, I can't do it to us."

A small sob escapes me and he pushes himself into my body, coating me everywhere, my arms locking around his wet back in a vise grip. "You need to hide me," I sob, hating the cold reality that Miller's life signifies.

"I don't want to." His mouth pushes into my neck and sucks softly. "But they're going to make this difficult and I have to protect you. I've tried to walk away from you, I know I should walk away, but I'm too fascinated by you."

I smile through my sadness. "I'm too fascinated by you to let you."

"I'm going to fix this, Olivia. Don't give up on me."

I'm feeling strong and determined and I'm going to transfer some of that into Miller. "Never. I'm going to worship you now," I declare, turning my face into his. I don't know what lies ahead and that scares me, but a life without Miller *terrifies* me. I have no choice but to trust him and trust he's doing what he thinks is right. He knows these people. It's not just the women I need to worry about. "Savored, not rushed," I whisper.

His face slowly moves toward mine. "Thank you," he murmurs, and then he swallows me up with a long, unhurried, delicate kiss, our tongues swirling dreamily as he rises and pulls me to his kneeling lap.

"I want to worship you," I mumble against his mouth, feeling him taking over with his worshipping ways.

"Your request has been noted," he assures me, but doesn't relent on the kiss that he has complete control over, his hands running over every square inch of my back. "And ignored." He lifts from the water, taking me with him, holding me firmly against him as he negotiates the stairs and carries me across his bathroom, blindly collecting a condom from the cupboard before he heads into his bedroom. But he bypasses the bed, making me frown while he keeps up the delicious pace of his tongue. We're in the hallway briefly before Miller opens the door to his studio and carries me in. I smile, the disorder and chaos of the room warming me. He picks up a black device while holding me and presses a few buttons, and I nearly break down when Imagine Dragons's "Demons" begins to seep from somewhere.

"Oh Jesus, Miller," I sob against his mouth, letting the words settle into the deepest part of me.

"Let's paint perfect," he breathes, resting my wet bum on the edge of the table that's running the length of a wall. I feel my body collide with things, sending them scattering across the surface, but there's no gasp of horror or rush to replace them.

Our kiss is broken, leaving me wheezing in his face as his lips part and he pushes me down to the cold table. The chilliness of the hard surface barely registers over my wet, blazing skin. I'm burning up. Spreading my thighs, he positions himself between them. "Shall we?" he asks, reaching forward and circling a nipple, sending a thrilling surge of blood to the tip of my sex. He really is the Special One. I could climax now.

I nod, pulling in a sharp breath when he tweaks one of my tingling nubs, only gently, but my breasts are sensitive, hungry for his touch.

"I've asked once." His voice is rough, his question serious as he removes the condom and slides it on, his jaw tense.

My back arches and my heels push into his arse, pulling him into me. "Please," I beg, forgetting all plans of me worshipping him. My hands grip the edge of the table, my eyes clenching shut.

"You're depriving me, Olivia." My nipple is taken and twirled between his thumb and forefinger gently. "You know how that makes me feel."

I do, but he's sucking all of the reason out of me. My head starts shaking and my hands leave the edge of the table, delving into my sopping wet hair. I'm losing my mind, and when his hand shifts down to the inside of my thigh and strokes a teasing circle close to my pulsing center, I make my despair known. "Miller!" My stomach muscles contract, pulling my shoulders from the table, and my arms fly out to the side, knocking pots of brushes and trays of paint everywhere. I'm too sidetracked to be bothered and Miller is most unconcerned by the added mess, his eyes glinting, oozing victory. I'm reduced to a convulsing mess of twitching muscles and erratic breaths. And he hasn't even touched me in my most sensitive place yet. It's all too much—his touch, my thoughts... the profound lyrics.

"I make you feel alive." He drives two fingers into me, his action pushing all breath from my lungs. I collapse back down to the table, looking up at his straight face. I might be mindless with the pleasure he inflicts on me, but nothing would distort the vision of penetrating blue eyes as they watch me writhe under his touch. They are hooded, but each blink is executed as slowly as ever, taking forever to close before being drawn back open. "I make you wonder how you'll survive without my attention to this exquisite body." Pulling his fingers slowly out, he circles his thumb over my twitching bud before surging forward again. "Scream my name, Olivia," he orders.

It's almost impossible not to close my eyes, but it *is* impossible to bite back my scream. I climax. My body goes into shock, my hands grappling at nothing on the table as all air rushes from my mouth on a loud, piercing wail of his name in hopeless pleasure. He watches me, his face remaining impassive and his eyes remaining victorious, while I ride out the throbs and contract persistently around the fingers he's holding within me, deep and high. He keeps them there and lowers his torso over me, getting his face close to mine. "And I constantly wonder how I'd ever survive without the privilege of giving you this attention." He kisses me sweetly on the lips. "Especially this part." I let him devour me while he gently thrusts his fingers in and out, slowly helping me down from my high, leisurely working my mouth on constant hums of appreciation.

I could never worship him this well. I'm sure I couldn't make him feel this good and safe and secure.

"I'm going to take my time making love to you now." He nuzzles into my hair and peels his torso from mine, exposing my wet skin to the cool air of his studio. "I'm going to show you just how much you fascinate me."

My eyes follow him up and we regard each other while he withdraws his fingers and wipes them across his bottom lip. Then he licks them slowly. Then he just gazes at me. For a long, long time. His close scrutiny doesn't make me feel uncomfortable, but as always, it makes me wonder what's running through that multilayered mind of his.

"What are you thinking?" I ask quietly, not resisting a little brush of my fingertip down the rippling muscles of his stomach.

He follows its path, letting me feel him for a time before taking my hand and lifting it to his lips. Each fingertip is kissed, my palm flattened, and my hand placed gently on my breast. "I'm thinking how lovely you look on my paint table."

I smile mildly, and he starts to move my hand, encouraging me to follow his guidance and mold my breast. A moan trickles past my lips and I sigh, long and peacefully.

"You look lovely everywhere." He moves his free hand down to his groin, gasping a little when he wraps his palm around the girth of his arousal. His jaw sharpens. "You're just too fucking lovely." Looking down, he guides himself to my opening and brushes across my entrance. I start to pant, motivating him to deliver another teasing, feathery tickle. It's too much.

"No!" I shock myself with my little outburst and Miller's eyes flying to mine display his alarm, too. "Don't drive me crazy, please!"

His stunned eyes drift into knowing.

"I know it delights you, but please don't torture me." I'm a desperate wreck and entirely unbothered by it. After today and everything that has happened, I don't need to be tormented or teased.

He says nothing and slowly pushes into me, transferring his hands to my hips and lifting me slightly. My worry diminishes, being replaced immediately with a serene, blissful sensation of calmness. Taking my other breast, I relax and let him carry me to ecstasy—that place where our troubles and challenges don't exist. That place I want to lose myself in forever with Miller Hart. His worshipping. His mouth. His eyes. His thing.

His tall, powerful body pumps lazily into me, controlled, measured, his muscles rolling with each rotation of his hips, his lips parting as he watches me. There's no strain right now, nothing but easy pleasure, but his talent for delivering such exquisite gratification will quickly send me delirious, the heaviness in my groin already beginning to fight its way to my epicenter. I want this to last. I want to go on and on, so I clench my teeth and squeeze my muscles to try to halt the inevitable, or at least delay it somewhat.

His concentrated gaze isn't helping. Neither is the sight of the cut perfection of his body. Alone, each of Miller's addictive qualities is powerful. Combined, they are deadly. "I love seeing this body trying to fight off the inescapable." His palm releases my waist and splays across my throat, slowly dragging down the center of my chest to my stomach. I moan my pleasure, arching my back, as he continues to flow into me, seeming to find it easy to maintain his steady pace, whereas I'm on the brink of giving up fighting it off. "I love how every muscle tightens." He strokes soft circles over the tense muscles of my tummy, and I whimper, battling to keep my eyes on him when I want to throw my head back and scream his name. "Especially here." He pulls out and reenters firmly, shifting his hand to my hip again and pausing while I rein in my shouts. He's panting, too, now, his wavy hair damp with sweat. "Is it working, Livy?" he asks cockily, knowing the answer.

"Nothing works." I wriggle under his hold, my hands leaving my breasts and beginning to flail to the side. I hit something again, but this time I feel a new wetness and I glance to the side to see my hand covered in paint and a pot of water tipped on its side, the murky paint-stained solution trickling down the table toward me. "Oh God! Miller!" I throw my hands up and brace them on his forearms, digging my nails into his flesh. His jaw tightens, his face distorting, his head dropping back. But his eyes don't shift. I hold my breath, the sparks winning and fighting their way to my core.

I get rewarded with his continued, neat rhythm. Lazy advances. Lazy retreats. Lazy grinds. Everything is slow and so purposeful.

"How?" I cry, the mystery spiking annoyance in my wanton state. "How can you remain so controlled?"

He moves, shifting his feet to gain more stability, and takes my hands, threading his fingers through mine and clamping down. "Because of you." His arms are used as leverage, pulling my body up slightly with each smooth thrust. I bite down on my lip, accepting drive after drive. "I want to treasure every moment I get to spend with you." His strong arms pull hard and hurl me up, sending him deeper on a shout, me on a cry. Our chests collide and he stills, letting me adjust to the inconceivably deep penetration. He breathes in my face, shallow, labored, pleasure-filled gasps. "I taste you and I want to relish in every moment I get to indulge in you." His lips capture mine in a ravenous kiss, his groin swiveling, finding its earlier tempo. "Jesus, Olivia, I wish I could devote every moment of the day and night to worshipping you." The softness of his luscious mouth loses a bit of tenderness when he pushes farther into me, his kiss now carnal.

My craving for my confounding part-time gentleman intensifies. But our reality dulls it. He can't devote every moment of the day and night to me. He's chained, and it makes me feel so incredibly helpless. "One day," I push the words through our sensual kiss, moving my mouth and biting at his lip before plunging my tongue back in, pushing my breasts into his chest.

"Soon," he says, nudging my head to the side, homing in on my throat and sucking on my clammy skin. "I promise you. I won't let you down," he whispers into the crook of my neck, kissing softly before encouraging me to pull away from the security of his chest. He gazes at me, filling me with determination and strength. "I won't let *us* down."

I nod and then let him lower me back to the table. My hands are released and he reaches to the side of me, collecting something and returning his hands to my stomach. I look down and see the tip of his index finger caked in red paint. Slightly bemused, I flick my eyes to his, seeing him focused on my tummy. Then he slowly drags his finger across my skin, starting to gently thrust into me again, reviving the lingering climax. I begin to tingle and take immense satisfaction from watching Miller concentrate on his task while he effortlessly lets his body flow into mine.

He's calm and slow in both of his missions, drawing on my tummy *and* making love to me. But I'm running out of time. "Miller," I gasp, my spine bowing, my fists balling. I'm tipping the edge, bubbling.

"I love feeling you," he whispers, his hips bucking a little, enticing a yelp from me and a gruff shout from him. "You're pulsing around me," he pants. "Fucking hell, Olivia!"

"Please!" I plead, my head beginning to thrash as I'm tossed into a whirlwind of intense sensations. I can't escape it. I'm going to shatter. Both of his hands grab my thighs and start pulling me onto him, not incredibly hard, but considerably more powerful than his usual composed tactics. "Oh!"

I'm desperate to pull myself together, gain a bit of control amid my crazy pleasure, just so I can focus on his face as he climaxes. I look up to him, going dizzy when he throws his head back, his jaw set to crack from the pressure of his teeth gritting. Now our bodies are slapping together, each collide spiking shouts of pleasure.

And then it happens.

For both of us.

Miller slams into me on a roar, stilling and pushing deep, and I scream his name. I burst. I can't see straight, my internal muscles going into spasm to match my body.

"Oh my God," I exhale on a long, satisfied rush of breath, finally gaining something close to normal vision, finding his chest pumping and his face dripping in sweat. Looking down to my stomach, I catch a glimpse of a few lines, but his palm is quickly covering the letters and smudging them, spreading the paint everywhere, the words now a big smear of red dye.

Then his body collapses onto me, his lips finding mine. "I lost it. I'm sorry. I'm so, so sorry." Paying some special attention to my mouth, he smothers me. Body. Mouth . . . Heart.

I smile and embrace him, taking him in my arms and returning his kiss. "There was feeling," I say quietly into his mouth. The absence of it during my encounter with the punishing escort was the issue, not necessarily how hard he took me. It was how unloving and detached he was.

His face hides in the hollow of my neck. "Did I hurt you?"

"No," I assure him. "The only pain I feel is when we're apart."

He slowly lifts, revealing his chest covered in paint. "We just painted perfect, sweet girl."

I smile on a breathy exhale. "Hum to me."

He matches my smile, giving me one of his most beautiful traits. "Until there is no breath left in my lungs."

Chapter Twenty-six

There's something to be said about making the perfect cup of coffee, but I'll struggle without the aid of an all-singing all-dancing coffee machine, and leaving Miller's apartment without him is not an option right now.

I stand in my knickers and one of Miller's black T-shirts, scanning the lengths of the worktop in his kitchen looking for a kettle... and don't find one. In fact, I don't find much at all—no toaster, chopping boards, kitchen towels, or *any* kitchen-related gadgets, for that matter. Every available space is free from clutter. Deciding Miller's obsessive tidy habit must mean he's hidden *everything* away, I start opening cupboards on the hunt for a kettle. I work my way around the rows of base and wall cabinets, swinging each open in turn, getting more and more exasperated with each cupboard that I venture into. All of the contents are stored too perfectly, although it does mean I can quickly see what's hidden within. But I still find no kettle. I close the last cupboard on a frown and begin tapping my fingers on the empty work surface, but I'm distracted from the mystery of an absent kettle when my skin starts to tingle mildly. My fingers pause and I smile, keeping my back to the doorway, the tingles building up into a delicious flurry of internal sparks.

"Boom," he whispers onto the back of my neck, making every nerve ending explode. Firm hands slide beneath my T-shirt and take my naked waist, turning me in his arms. I come face-to-face with a nude, sleepy Miller. "Morning." His lips move sleepily, too, hypnotizing me momentarily.

"Morning."

He smiles, swooping down to claim my mouth. "I just had quite a shock," he says against my lips, nibbling between words.

"Why?"

"Because I ventured into my wardrobe." He pulls back and eyes me while I press my lips together, shame and guilt attacking me. Oh God, he's...calm. I relax but feel wary of his reaction to his shredded wardrobe. His head tilts. "Or I suppose rag shop is more apt now."

"I'll replace them," I promise sincerely, thinking my mother's mass of stored cash probably won't even cover it. "I'm sorry."

His palm slips into my locks at the back of my head and I'm pulled forward until his lips meet my forehead. "I've already forgiven you. Looking for something?"

"A kettle," I answer, lifting my eyes to his, staggered by his calm persona.

"I don't have one."

"How do you make hot drinks, then?" My hands slide up his arms to his shoulders as he lifts me onto his worktop.

He doesn't answer, instead leaving me on the counter and moseying over to the sink. I'm curious, but not enough to convince my eyes to watch what he's doing, rather than watch the incredible vision of his backside tensing with each step. My head cocks thoughtfully on a satisfied smile, and then he turns and I'm suddenly not focused on his buns any longer.

"Earth to Olivia." His soft tone has my line of sight diverting up his torso slowly, eventually arriving at a knowing hint of a smile. He flicks his head in indication for me to look, and I see him press a button on a chrome, state-of-the-art tap. Steam immediately billows from the head. "Instant boiling water."

I roll my eyes and rest my hands in my lap. "How very tidy," I muse mockingly. "I bet you peed your pants with excitement when that was invented."

His lips purse in an attempt to prevent his smile. "It's a damn good idea, wouldn't you agree?"

"Yes, for obsessive-compulsives like you, who hate clutter, it's perfect."

"There's no need for insolence." He flips it off and immediately gets a cloth from under the sink to wipe away the water drops that his little demonstration has left behind. It doesn't escape my notice that he fails to challenge my reference to OCD, and I don't bother telling him that there really is a need for insolence, choosing to goad him further instead.

"I'm proud of you," I tell him, casually casting my eyes around his kitchen with interest, knowing he'll be studying me curiously.

"You are?"

"Yes. You've placed me on your work surface, making it look a little messy, and exposed yourself to some risks." My eyes arrive back at Miller's naked, inquisitive form.

"I'm good at assessing and mitigating risks." He takes a few steps toward me, his eyes turning hungry. "But I need to know what the risks are in order to do so."

"Good point." I nod agreeably, stopping my stare from dropping below his neck. I can see from the smoke in his eyes that he'll be firming up. Catching a glimpse will toss me into surrender mode and I'm having too much fun poking fun at him. "I'll tell you the risk."

"Please do," he whispers, low, deep, and seductively. My nipples pucker.

I slowly remove my T-shirt and swing my bare legs onto the counter, lying flat on my back, my body spread along the length of marble. Maintaining my nonchalance is difficult with a naked Miller in such close proximity, and even harder when the cold of the marble spreads across my skin. I hold on to my gasp of shock and turn my head to the side to see him.

He's smiling, and it punches the stored air from my lungs fast so I can mirror his happiness. "I don't see this as a risk." His eyes skate from my face, all the way to my toes and work slowly up my horizontal body again. The lust in his gaze hits me between the thighs like a sledgehammer. I'm squirming under his obvious intent that's seeping from his every naked pore. "I see this as an opportunity."

I grip my bottom lip between my teeth and follow his remaining steps until he's looming over me.

"Raise your knees," he orders gently, his instruction making the pressure of my teeth increase on my lip. "Now, Olivia." That authoritative tone is all it takes. I have no shyness, no reluctance or holding back. My knees lift until the soles of my feet are flat on the counter, anticipation for his touch consuming me. I'm zinging from head to toe. He slips his fingers into the top of my knickers and lazily draws them down my thighs, encouraging me to lift my feet when he reaches them. The small, cotton garment is folded neatly and placed accurately on the side before his palms rest on my thighs and pull them apart. I gulp down air and close my eyes, waiting for his next move. "Fingers or tongue?"

"I don't care," I exhale on a breathy gasp. I'll take anything. "Just touch me."

"You sound desperate."

"I am," I admit, unashamed. He winds me up into a coil of desire and desperation, then teases and tortures me with his expert worshipping ways. It's excruciating and wonderful all wrapped into one.

"Fingers," he decides, tickling my entrance with a skim of his thumb across my heated flesh. My back bows violently, and I cry out. "That way I get to kiss you if I choose."

My eyes open and I find him braced on one arm over me, his face hovering close to mine and his wayward wave of hair tickling his forehead. I remain quiet and endure the agonizing wait for another dash of contact as he scans my face. And then it happens and I find my head lifting without thought to capture his lips. Only one finger is half submerged within me, and my greedy muscles try their hardest to hold on to it, tensing harshly, but he pulls out and separates our mouths. I moan despairingly, letting my head rest back down as I pant and twitch.

"You don't call the shots, sweet girl," he warns cockily, stirring my impatience.

"You always say you'll do anything I want." I'm using his own promise against him, even though I know full well he wasn't referring to sexual acts.

"I concur." He gets his lips as close to mine as they can be without touching. "But you haven't told me what you want."

"You." I don't hesitate.

"You have me already. Tell me what you want me to do to you." He's just as speedy with his counter, making my cheeks flush as I grasp his intention. He wants instructions? "Come on, Livy. Think of it as a method statement to support our assessing and mitigating of risks." There's an element of mocking to his tone, which both deepens my blush *and* sparks a bit of sass. So on a long, confidence-boosting inhale of oxygen, I locate that sass and mentally grab it with both hands, ensuring it can't disappear on me.

"Enter me."

"With what?" he deadpans.

"Your fingers," I breathe, seeing instantly that he doesn't just want instructions. He wants exact, step-by-step commands.

"Ooh, I see." He conceals his amusement well, glancing down

at his hand hovering between my thighs. "Hadn't I ought to check your"—he pouts and thinks for a second—"condition?"

Damn him! I'm growing aggravated, my own fingers prepared to do the job if he doesn't get on with it. "Miller, please." I immerse myself in darkness, closing my eyes in desolation. I'm bursting at the seams with need, the heaviness between my thighs pushing deep and starting to throb eagerly.

"Focus, Livy." He pushes my thighs apart again when I attempt to close them to suppress the pulsing.

"You make it too hard!" I shout on a futile thrash of my body. Two big palms press into my shoulders, holding me still, and I open my lids to come nose to nose with a triumphant glimmer in deep, satisfied blues. My hand instinctively reaches up and grabs his hair, giving it a bold yank in frustration.

It has zero effect. He pries my fingers from his dark waves and places my hand on my tummy, giving it a little warning squeeze on a serious face. "I love your sass," he whispers, ghosting his lips across mine, flirting, and though I know I won't get blessed with a heart-stopping kiss, my body responds and lifts in a vain attempt to catch them anyway.

"You want to taste me?" he mumbles, only allowing a slight friction of our mouths, denying me the full-on contact. "Do you want to swallow me up and lose yourself in me forever?"

"Yes!" My frustration grows as he continues to refuse me the contact I'm demanding.

"Do you remember who can sate this unyielding need?"

"You," I moan as I squirm beneath the brief contact of his fingers at my entrance.

He pulls away from me quickly, his sanctimonious expression morphing into something else. I'm not sure what. But I can only compare it to glory. He looks like he's struck gold. To anyone else, his face is expressionless, blank... untelling, but to me it's spelling a million words of happiness. Miller Hart is happy. He's content. And I know for sure that *that* has never happened in the history of Miller. "I don't *just* want to be the man who can give you mind-blowing orgasms."

My pleasure and musing is interrupted by his statement, and I immediately notice the glory in his eyes has fallen away. I'm a trifle confused. "You always say it," I argue quietly, my fizzing settling under his uncertainty. I've vowed to make him feel like more than a walking, talking pleasure machine, yet he seems to be happy with the praise he's rewarded with when we're intimate. He demands it, working me up into a frenzy and basking in the begging he draws. He deserves it, by God, he needs a medal, but I never considered for a moment that I might be making him feel used. He likes me pleading for his touch. It makes him feel wanted. Needed.

Everything dies within me when I consider the horrific thought of him pinning the same statement to every woman he's taken. Does he deliver such compelling words to them? Probably. It's his job. Does he make them feel as amazing as he makes me feel? I know he does.

Miller is broody when in the heat of the moment, and he's flaming hot when armed with a belt and a four-poster bed. "Do you express this much passion to every woman you've ever taken?" My question shocks me, especially since I only planned on considering it silently. My subconscious wants an answer.

"Everything you get from me is natural instinct, Olivia Taylor. I've never been fascinated before. I've never given all of me before. You get all of me. Every fucked-up little piece. And I pray every second of every day that you'll never give up on me, even if I do." He pushes his lips gently to mine and leaves them lingering for what seems like forever, injecting me with strength, intensifying my love. "Keep me in this beautiful light place with you." He releases me and hits me with pleading eyes. "Don't let me fall back into darkness, I beg you."

I absorb his words, immobilized under his clear blue gaze. Hearing him reaffirm his feelings, express himself so well, should hold my contentment firm. But I heard the negative line in his statement. *Even if I do.*

I'm too aware of Miller's recent actions. The right words from the wrong people could send him spiraling back into that dark place and only my strength can pull him back.

"Stroke me," I order softly, "with your fingers." I take his hand and guide it to the apex of my thighs. "Then enter me and thrust gently."

He nods in wordless acknowledgment and braces his hand on the counter as his touch finds me. My breath catches. "Let me taste you," he whispers, bringing our faces closer together.

My response is mechanical, no thoughts necessary, and I lift and seal our mouths on a groan, wrapping my arms around his neck. Every muscle I possess hardens in preparation, my thighs dropping farther open, inviting more of him into me. His efforts are lazy and measured, two fingers gliding perfectly across my flesh and working me up deliciously. I'm breathless, my kiss becoming predictably harder as my pleasure builds.

I gasp, sucking at his bottom lip before letting my head fall back to the worktop.

His eyes are hooded, his labored breathing matching mine, as he maintains the steady slipping of his fingers over my throbbing flesh. "Jesus, Olivia." His head drops limply as he finally breaches the threshold of my entrance with his fingers and puts some weight behind his caresses, pushing into me on a low moan.

My chest flies up on a delirious shout. "Miller!"

"Fuck! I love hearing you scream my name." He withdraws and thrusts forward again, the power of his drive not just evident by my continued moans and cries, but clear on the cut edges of his strained face. I'm fighting the urge to squeeze my eyes shut, desperate to lose myself in dark pleasure, but more desperate to watch him. There's wonder past the dark desire of his addictive eyes, but I lose the glorious sight when he dips and encases my tingling nipple with the heat of his mouth. It catapults me into sensory overload. I start to shake.

"Oh God!" My hands in his hair apply pressure, pushing him onto my breast, and my hips start lifting, meeting the pumping of his fingers. Every nerve ending is buzzing uncontrollably, my head shaking, my thoughts scattered. I begin to feel my climax take hold, the pleasure dominating every inch of me shifting to one spot, set to explode. And with a nip of my nipple and a deep rotation of strong fingers within me, it happens.

The world ceases to rotate on its axis. Life stops. My mind goes blank. There's a distant sound of groaning and once I've overcome the initial onslaught of harsh pleasure, I drop my head to the side in exhaustion and peel my eyes open to find Miller at full height, looking down at me as he strokes me softly between the thighs, easing me lightly down. His arousal is thick, pulsing and protruding proudly from his groin.

I don't speak, mainly because I haven't the energy, but I *do* find a little strength to reach to the side and take a gentle hold of him, wiping my thumb across the swollen head to smear the bead of cum that's leaking from the tip. Miller hisses, the muscles of his chest quivering aggressively while he battles to cope with my touch. He's pulsing incessantly, and I can see his heart pounding in his chest. It takes just one delicate swipe of my fisted hand around him to tip him. He knocks my hand out of the way and lifts to rest his iron length on my tummy, groaning, his head rolling as he spills all over me. The warmth of his essence coating me has my body relaxing back into the marble on a lengthy, gratifying sigh. I'm floating in a magical land of perfection.

"Sleepy?" His rough voice tickles my ears, and I hum, closing my eyes. His hand gently breaks away from between my thighs and rests on my tummy. Then he spreads his cum everywhere, up to my boobs and down to my legs. I'm coated. And I couldn't care less. He dips and pecks my lips, encouraging me to open up to him. I let him drench my mouth with his attention. I could fall asleep here on this solid work surface.

"Come on." He pulls me up to a sitting position and muscles between my spread legs, all the while keeping up our kiss. My arms are positioned over his shoulders; he cups my bum and pulls me in. "You can help me make breakfast."

"I can?" I blurt, making him pull back on an inquisitive frown. Messing up his worktop, his clothes... me. And now I can help him make breakfast in his perfect kitchen, where tasks are carried out with military precision? I'm not sure I'm up to it, and quite frankly, interfering with his obsessive ways to that extent kind of scares me.

"Let's not make too big a deal of it," he warns.

But it's a massive deal. Huge. "You can do it," I offer, feeling a little overwhelmed. He's given me so much already. I don't want to push my luck.

"You can't shirk me that easily." He gives my cheek a reassuring flutter of his lips and pulls me down, turning me in his arms so my back's pressed into his chest. His chin rests on my shoulder. "But first, a quick wash."

He urges me forward with his palms resting on my tummy, his steps guiding mine until we're standing before the sink and he's turning on the tap. He dampens a towel, pumps in some liquid soap, and efficiently wipes down my front, then kneels down to swipe up my legs. It's all I can do not to throw my head back and moan for more.

After washing our hands together, he leans over me and wipes the sink down while I look on with a smile. "To the fridge," he whispers, pushing me gently on until we're before the giant mirrored doors. Miller's nakedness is concealed. But mine isn't. "Stunning view." He nips at my shoulder, keeping his eyes on mine, and lets his hand slip below my stomach to my entrance. I hold my breath and push my cheek into the side of his face, squirming. "So warm and inviting," he whispers, and then licks his bite mark on my shoulder and spreads my dampness with all four fingers. The slippery friction on my sensitive nub of nerves has me moaning as I watch his eyes darken. "You're still pulsing, sweet girl."

My bum pushes into his groin, causing Miller to mimic my sounds of ecstasy. "You wanted to feed me," I remind him, quite stupidly. I'll take more worshipping over the mundane task of eating any day.

"Correct, but I can't promise I won't make the most of your inviting condition while we prepare breakfast." He circles around my clitoris slowly, accelerating the dulling pulse.

Oh God, help me!

"Miller," I squeeze my eyes shut briefly, retreating, my body folding in on itself to escape his inconceivably skillful touch.

He pushes his mouth to my ear. "I might make a habit of preparing our meals with my habit stuck to my chest."

If he does that, then we might not ever eat. My need for him is my undoing and I make to turn.

And go nowhere.

"Nuh-uh-uh." His hand pushes into the soft flesh of my tummy and his fingers walk up my front slowly until they are resting at the corner of my mouth. Our eyes hold as he wipes my wetness across my lips. "Lick."

When his order should probably make me decline shyly, it has my craving multiplying instead. I follow through on his demand, lapping slowly at his fingers while he holds me in place, more with his thirsty eyes than with the firm clamp of his hand.

"Good, wouldn't you agree?"

I nod, but I'm more inclined to think that the flesh beneath the wetness is tastier.

"Enough for now." He withdraws his fingers and slides his

palms down my arms until he's at my hands. "This could take some time."

"Only if you can't keep your hands to yourself," I reply quietly, wishing I didn't have to go to work so we could prepare breakfast all day.

He lifts our hands and threads our fingers so we can open the fridge door together. "You wouldn't want me to, so this will be a pointless discussion."

"Agreed." I'm confronted by the contents of Miller's fridge, noting shelves of neatly stored food—mostly fruit, or something equally healthy, and bottled water. He takes our hands to the basket of strawberries, and I smile. "Chocolate for breakfast?"

"That would be extremely unhealthy."

"So?"

He nips at my earlobe as he takes the fruit out of the fridge. "For breakfast we have strawberries with Greek yogurt."

"Doesn't sound as tasty," I grumble, and I bet it's fat-free, too.

I'm ignored, the slight straightening of his lips telling me to quit complaining without the need for a verbal warning. A gentle nudge of his hips into my lower back followed by his backward steps has my feet shifting, mirroring his steps and taking us away from the reflection of the fridge doors. His eyes are glued to mine, scorching my naked flesh, and remain that way until he's forced to turn us. We move across the kitchen as one, collect a chopping board from one cupboard, two bowls from another, a colander from another, and finally a paring knife from a drawer before everything is placed neatly on the work surface. Our hands work together, although every motion is instigated by Miller, me happy to let that happen because then I can't do anything wrong. He's humming his sweet melody in my ear absentmindedly, seeming so peaceful, which warms me to the core and beyond. He's happy and content, like me preparing breakfast to his standards and following his *way* could possibly be the most fulfilling thing in the world. To Miller, it might just be. He helps me lift the knife and covers my hand with his while collecting a strawberry and placing it on the chopping board. Then he guides my hand to lift the knife and directs the blade across the top, removing the stem. He pushes the discarded piece to one corner, halves the red, plump fruit, and places a loving kiss on my cheek before he pops the pieces in the colander.

"Perfect," he praises, like he hasn't just influenced the string of accurate motions we've undertaken, down to the handling of the knife. But if it keeps Miller's perfect world turning on its perfect axis, then I'll happily comply. He collects another strawberry, keeping his chin on my shoulder. The nearness of his steady breathing in my ear as he hums is past comforting. This must be the closest one can come to heaven while still on Earth.

"I thought you could stay with me today," he says quietly, guiding my hand to the strawberry. A gentle pressure on my hand splits the flesh, revealing its juicy, mouth-watering center. I wouldn't dare do something as silly as sneak a piece, not under my finicky Miller's watch, so I'm utterly gobsmacked when he collects one of the halves and brings it to his mouth. Frowning, I follow its path, momentarily distracted by the slow parting of his lips before he slips it between them. Only momentarily, though. Displeasure soon snuffs it.

"That's—" I get no further into my objection, Miller's mouth silencing me. He bites down and juice bursts between our kiss, truly making it the tastiest kiss ever. Miller and strawberry. "Hmmm," I hum in pleasure, juice dribbling down my chin.

"I concur," he whispers, breaking our kiss and licking a delicate wet stroke up my chin, fulfilling his self-appointed role of cleaning up our mess. It might be pleasurable for him, but it's still tidying of some nature, so it figures Miller would jump at the role.

"I have to go to work today," I murmur under his penetrative gaze. My body is on fire and a whole day locked in Miller's apartment, the world shut safely outside, is almost impossible to resist, but I can't shirk work again.

He kisses my nose on an accepting sigh. Too accepting. "I understand, but promise me you won't venture off on your own." His plea drags my contentment and comfort into worry. I'm being followed. "I'll take you and collect you."

"How long do you expect to have to chaperone me?" I ask. While I'm more than concerned by the revelations of an unwanted shadow, I also appreciate that Miller can't babysit me forever.

"Just until we have established who and why." He resumes chin on shoulder and strawberry slicing.

"Who's 'we'?"

I definitely don't imagine a hesitant pause before he answers. "You and I."

I'm suspicious. I hate being suspicious. Suspicion is dangerous and it also spikes curiosity. And I hate curiosity, probably more than suspicion. "I can't establish anything unless you give me the information, which you won't, leaving *you* to establish things."

"Well, that's how it should be," he states matter-of-factly, increasing that wretched suspicion and curiosity. "I don't want your lovely mind worrying about it." He affirms his claim by pushing the knife through another strawberry and kissing my temple. "We'll be leaving that line of conversation right there."

"Where?" I ask on a roll of my eyes. I've been put firmly in my place, kind of, yet I can't help a sarcastic quip.

"There's no ne—"

"Miller," I sigh. "Loosen up!" It's one step forward, a million back.

"I'm perfectly loose." He pushes his groin into my lower back and bites my neck, making me squirm and laugh, and just like that, he contradicts my previous thought.

"Stop it!" I gasp through my laughter.

"Never."

But he does stop, and I stop laughing instantly, too, snapping my head up in attention. "Was that a doorbell?" I ask, intrigued. I've never heard the sound before.

"I believe it was." Miller sounds as interested as I am.

"Who could it be?"

"Well, let's find out." He pries my hand off the knife and lays it parallel to the chopping board before releasing me. Then he tidies his workstation promptly but accurately and collects my folded knickers and T-shirt.

He takes my hand and paces through the apartment speedily. We're in his dressing room in no time, and I hear the doorbell sound again as he mutters under his breath, something about disturbances. He pulls a pair of fresh black boxers on, gets the piles of black T-shirts from his drawer, and starts a new pile; he actually begins to rotate the damn T-shirts while the doorbell rings persistently in the background. I'm silent and watching him grow more and more agitated by the second as he yanks his T-shirt on. He takes my hands and kisses my knuckles. "Take a shower." A chaste kiss is dropped on my forehead and he's gone, leaving me standing like a plum in the middle of his dressing room, with curiosity my only companion. It's bombarding me, and not prepared to remain alone for it to drive me nuts, I throw my knickers and a shirt on and follow quietly behind Miller, his long, powerful legs eating up the journey to his front door fast.

Aggression pours from him as he yanks the door open, and it only seems to multiply by a million when whoever's on the other side is revealed. I can't see, Miller's tall frame is blocking my view, but judging from the ice that emanates from Miller's refined physique, we don't want to see this person.

"You can fuck off now, or stay and allow me the pleasure of snapping every bone in your body." The hatred in his tone is profound. Frightening. Who is it? I watch Miller's back heaving, steam virtually pouring from his ears. He's going to take leave of his senses at any moment. Good God, hasn't he listened to anything we've spoken about? He simply cannot control it.

"I'll stay."

The man's voice sets my heart racing in my chest. He's come looking for me? Miller's fists clench, making the veins of his arms bulge. Shit, he's getting ready to charge. I move forward, conflicted—intervene or stay well away.

"As you wish," Miller replies casually, like he hasn't just committed to murdering our guest.

"I wish you'd back off, too, so my girl can think straight without your influence."

Miller moves forward. It's threatening and intended to be. My anxiety accelerates, as does my heart rate. "I'll say this once," he seethes, fists clenching and releasing into balls. "I have never made Olivia do anything that she doesn't want to. She belongs with me. She knows it. I know it, and you need to fucking know it, too. If I go anywhere, she's coming with me."

I find my courage and creep up behind Miller, sliding my palm onto his back before circling him and placing my body in front of his. A black eye, bruised cheek, and split lip greet me.

"Gregory," I breathe nervously, feeling Miller giving off all sorts of worrying vibes. He's rigid against my back. "Are you okay?"

Brown eyes soften at my presence, his face almost relieved. "Amazing," he jokes, flicking a filthy look to Miller. "We need to talk."

A strong palm grips my neck and begins massaging. If it's an attempt to knead some of my anxiety out of me, then he'll fail. It's swirling through me uncontrollably. Nothing will lessen it, let alone eliminate it. "Talk, then," Miller orders.

"Alone," Gregory hisses, eradicating any sniff of a hope I held that he was here to fix things with Miller. I feel helpless.

"Hell will freeze over before I leave Olivia alone with you."

"Afraid she'll leave you?"

"Yes." Miller's fast, brutally honest answer shocks me, and obviously Gregory, too, because no counter is coming Miller's way.

Gregory's eyes absorb me for a few thoughtful moments before he finds some words. "Would you like to talk alone?" he asks, stiffening every muscle in my body. I do. I'm not afraid of what he will say or that he'll try to convince me to leave Miller, which he probably will. It'll be wasted energy, and Gregory must know this by now. He's been pummeled twice for his dedicated interfering, and quite badly. He's surely not going in for a third round. "Well?" he prompts when I'm still standing silently, mentally figuring out how to handle this. Or handle Miller.

My blank face is suddenly looking up at Miller after he's turned me in his arms. All rage and stress has gone, his eyes clear and concerned. "Would you like a moment alone with your friend?"

I'm stunned. Totally dumbfounded. I nod, unable to get any words past my shock. Miller nods, too, exhaling deeply and dipping to kiss my nose as his palm cups the back of my head. He's prepared to allow someone the opportunity to interfere?

"I'll take a shower," he says quietly. "Take as long as you need." The uncharacteristic display has thrown me for a loop, and I know Gregory is slightly taken aback, too. I can practically hear his shock in the form of a surprised, thumping heartbeat. I'm about to nod again, but I'm quickly considering how uncomfortable Gregory might feel remaining in Miller's apartment. And me, too, for that matter. Miller lurking in the background ready to attack should he overhear some words he doesn't approve of will do nothing to relax me.

"We'll walk down to the coffeehouse," I utter, less confidently than I would have liked, my heart sinking when Miller starts shaking his head with worried eyes. "I'll be with Gregory," I add with a pleading gaze, but with no faith that *that* will sway him. Gregory must be wondering what's going on. I can't land him with stalker news, not on top of everything else. "Please." My shoulders sag, defeated.

The confliction riddling him is plain and clear and written all over his face. "Okay," he agrees reluctantly, nearly knocking me to my backside in astonishment. His soft eyes leave mine and harden the moment they find Gregory. "I trust you'll guard her with as much care and attention as I do."

I cough on a choke and gape at his perfectly straight face, knowing he'll be getting the same look from Gregory. He really isn't helping his cause. I understand him. I get him. I see past his uptight persona and hear past his confounding way with words. But no one else can.

"What?" Gregory asks, amusement mixed with pure exasperation clear in his tone.

Miller twitches, his eyes narrowing. "I don't like repeating myself."

"For fuck's sake." Gregory laughs. "Where the fuck did you find this twat?"

"Greg!" I gasp, spinning around and backing up into Miller's chest to prevent the inevitable.

"Well, give me a break, please!"

"I'll *break* your fucking neck!" Miller scathes, punching holes through my beaten friend with raging eyes over my shoulder.

"Enough!" I shout, throwing my hands up violently. "Just… enough!" There are a million words I want to throw into the mix, ones for Gregory *and* for Miller, but at the risk of escalating the situation further, I take some calming breaths and close my eyes to gather a bit of patience. "Gregory, wait in the kitchen." I chuck my arm out in gesture. "Miller, come with me." I grab his hand and start pulling him away. "I'll be ten minutes," I call over my shoulder, not giving either man a chance to retaliate. I'm not leaving them alone. I'll return to pools of blood and discarded bones.

"I'll wait in the hallway," Gregory spits, and I hear the door slam viciously, shaking the apartment walls.

Miller splutters, pulling me to a halt. "Did he just slam my fucking door?" His eyes are wild and he makes to turn, his face screwed up in disgust. "He just slammed my fucking door!"

"Miller!" I yell, diving in front of him. "Bedroom! Now!" I've lost it, madness churning in my gut, heat rising to my face. Now he's being fastidious for the sake of it. "Don't make me repeat myself!" I'm shaking. I've reached the end of my worn tether with these two, each behaving like a bulldog, letting their egos cloud what matters. Me! "I'm going for coffee with Greg!"

"Fine," he says, looking sulky, "but if a hair on your head is damaged when I get you back, I won't be held accountable for my actions."

"I'll be fine." What does he think will happen to me?

"He better make certain of it," he scoffs.

What? "You sound like a conceited idiot!"

"Olivia." He dips and gets nose to nose with me, his eyes burning bright with fervor, while mine are burning bright with frustration. "You know how I feel about people interfering, and you know how I feel about them upsetting you. Not only will I break his spine if you return to me physically harmed, but I'll hold that promise if he upsets you."

My whole body slumps dramatically. It's intentional, just so he can physically see how much he frustrates me.

"Overthinking," he whispers, sliding his palm onto my nape and pulling me forward, closing the minuscule gap that remained between our mouths and sealing our lips.

"I won't overthink," I promise, letting him suck my annoyance out of me. I'm past that now. "And after everything you've put me through in the last twenty-four hours, Miller? I'm having coffee with a friend."

I feel his lips purse against mine. "As you wish." He can't argue with that. He wraps me in his arms, disconnecting from my mouth so he can sink his face into my wild blond hair. It's like he knows that a Miller *thing* can magic some strength into me. It never fails. "I count on your strength, my gorgeous girl."

I embrace him and let him squeeze me strong. Or stronger. I might have been hugely annoyed with what's happened since Gregory rocked up, but my strength didn't waver. I'll never run away from us. "I should take a shower."

He releases me. My hair is pushed over my shoulders and arranged just so as he scans my face. "Don't leave me without you for too long."

I smile and gently break away from him, taking myself to the shower while mentally preparing for another onslaught of interference from my best friend.

Chapter Twenty-seven

Gregory is leaning up against the wall in the hallway when I leave Miller's apartment, scrolling through his phone. "Hey," I say, pulling the door closed behind me.

He looks up and pushes away from the wall on a strained smile. "Hey, baby girl."

Those words alone make me want to sob. "What's happened to us?" I ask.

Gregory looks to Miller's shiny black door and back to me. "The coffee hater happened."

"He's more than a coffee hater," I argue quietly. "And it was only my first coffee that he hated, so we can't technically call him that anymore."

"Cocksucker."

"That one's reserved for Ben. Seen him lately?"

His broad shoulders go rigid. It's guilt. "We're not here because of *my* fucked-up love life."

I nearly fall over as a result of his cheek. "My love life isn't fucked up!"

"Get a grip!" He's up in my face with two easy strides. "That in there"—he points to Miller's front door—"is fucked up and he's rubbing off on you!"

My hackles rise, my face twisting with infuriation. "I'm not listening to this." I pivot on my heels, set to abandon our "talk" in favor of some solace from my fucked-up, OCD-suffering, demon-holding, possessive, damaged, drug-using, ex-notorious-male-escort/part-time gentleman. Okay, so he is kind of fucked up, but he's *my* fucked-up, finicky Miller. And I love him.

"Olivia, wait!" He grabs the top of my arm a little harshly, but quickly drops it when I yelp. "Shit!" he curses.

I swing around, rubbing at my arm on a scowl. "Take it easy!"

He looks truly nervous. "I'm sorry, I just didn't want you to go."

"Then tell me so."

He casts his brown eyes to my arm. "I hope I haven't marked you; I quite like my spine where it is and in one piece."

I press my lips together to prevent my grin at his sardonic joke. "I'm fine."

"Thank fucking God." He shoves his hands in his pockets and looks down sheepishly. "Can we start again?"

Relief floors me. "Please."

"Great." He looks up to me, remorse rife in his brown eyes. "Can we walk and talk? I'm not all that comfortable bad-mouthing your coffee hater when he's in such close proximity."

On a roll of my eyes, I link arms with him and lead him to the stairwell. "C'mon."

"Is the elevator broken?"

I skid to a halt, frowning to myself. I haven't even realized that I'm picking up on Miller's obsessive habits. "No."

Gregory's frown matches mine as we stroll over to the elevator and board as soon as it arrives. His face looks dreadful, but I'm not sure it would be wise to acknowledge it or ask how he is, given that we're both smiling now, so I plump for something entirely different. "How's work?"

"Same old," he mutters unenthusiastically, killing that line of conversation dead in its tracks.

I think hard again. "Mum and Dad okay?"

"All right."

"How are things with Ben?"

"Fragile."

"Has he come out?"

"No."

I roll my eyes. "What the hell did we talk about before I met Miller?"

He shrugs as the doors open, and I lead on, desperately searching my empty mind for anything to talk about, other than Miller and the inevitable interference that's on the horizon. I come up with zilch.

Nodding politely at the doorman and ignoring the reflection of Gregory's dragging body behind me, I push through the doors and emerge into the bright, fresh London air. I would have thought the vast open space engulfing me would instill a sense of freedom, but it doesn't. Nowhere near. I feel suffocated under the impending interrogation from Gregory, desperate to run back to Miller and take my freedom from being smothered in his apartment. In his *thing*. In him.

I turn on a sigh, finding Gregory shifting awkwardly behind me, obviously stumped for what to say or do. He insisted on a talk. He must have things to say, and even though I don't particularly want to hear them, I wish he'd just get it over and done with so I can tell him that he's wasting his energy... again.

"Are we going for coffee or not?" I ask, indicating down the street.

"Sure," he mumbles grumpily, like he's aware that he's about to waste his breath. He joins me and we begin to stroll down the street. There's at least three feet separating us and unrest is filling that gap. It's never been like this between us, and as there's no conversation happening, it gives me too much silent reflecting time to wonder how it came to this. Our silly little fumble in my bedroom that time was a cause for concern, but with the animosity and battling between Miller and Gregory, that's fallen by the wayside, which is undoubtedly a good thing.

We cross a road, quite easily, given the early hour, and continue at a leisurely pace, Gregory drawing continuous breaths of air to speak but never actually saying anything, and me looking eagerly for the sign that'll tell me we're nearing the coffeehouse. The discomfiture squeezing us is becoming unbearable.

"Just tell me what it is about him." Gregory pulls me to a stop, and I open and close my mouth, trying to figure out how to word it. It's all clear as daylight in my mind, but trying to voice it to an outsider stumps me. I don't need to justify myself to anyone, yet the profound need to make Gregory understand why I'm still here is suddenly very important to me.

"Everything." I shake my head, wishing I could come up with something better.

"The fact that he's an escort?"

"No!"

"Money?"

"Don't be stupid. You know I have a bank account full of cash."

"He's intense."

"Very, but it has nothing to do with that. He wouldn't be Miller if he didn't have issues. Every part of that man is a result of his life so far. He was orphaned, Gregory. His grandparents dumped him in a questionable children's home and forced his young mother back to Ireland, leaving him behind because of the shame he'd bring on the family."

"Doesn't mean he can behave like a total twat," he mutters, scuffing his boots on the concrete beneath his feet. "Everyone has problems."

"Problems?" I fume indignantly. "Being orphaned, becoming homeless, having OCD, and resorting to prostitution to survive isn't a problem, Greg. It's a fucking tragedy!"

My friend's eyes widen, making me frown. "Homeless?"

"Yes, he was homeless."

"He has OCD?"

"Not confirmed, but it's pretty obvious."

"Prostitution!" he shouts in delayed reaction.

I realize my error immediately. Escort. Gregory didn't need to know that Miller had been a regular prostitute, and although there's really not much difference, the latter is far more appealing. Which is utterly ridiculous. "Yes." I raise my chin, daring him to pass comment, thinking what he'd say should I add drug addict to the list.

My ploy fails on every level. "It gets better!" He laughs, but it's a nervous laugh. "And I'm pretty sure he's psychotic, too, so you really do have your very own head case."

"He. Is. Not. A. Head. Case." I punctuate each word on a hiss, my blood beginning to boil. "You don't see him when we're alone. No one does, except me. Yes, he can be uptight, and so fucking what if he likes things a certain way. He isn't killing anyone!"

"He probably has."

I recoil in disgust, words collecting and sticking to my tongue, my brain not quite sure which expletives to hurl at Gregory first. "Fuck off!" It settles on a good all-rounder, and once I've lobbed it in his face, I turn back toward Miller's apartment block, my angry feet pounding the pavement harshly.

"Ah, Livy, come on!"

"Piss off." I don't look back. There's likely to be explosions if I do. But then I think of something and swing around. "Where did you get Miller's card?"

He shrugs. "That black-haired bird who was at Ice's opening night. Hot as fuck!"

Cassie.

I feel my hackles rise and the pressure in my head mount. The bitch! I steam off, worrying about my mounting fury. I want to hit something. Hard.

"Oh!" My yelp is high-pitched as I'm captured and tossed upward so I'm lying across his arms. He changes direction and strides off down the road, back in the direction of the coffeehouse, ignoring my incredulous look.

"Sass," he says simply. "I'm kind of glad you've hung on to it."

My body lets up on the tension stored and I relax in his arms. "I love him, Gregory."

"I can see that," he admits begrudgingly. "And does he love you?"

"Yes," I answer, because I know for certain that he does. He just doesn't say it so straightforwardly. But that's his way.

"Does he make you happy?"

"More than you'll ever know, but I'd be so much happier if people just left us alone." I feel him deflate beneath my suspended body on a sigh.

He stops and places me on my feet, then takes a solid grip of my petite shoulders. "Baby girl, I get a bad vibe. He's so..." He pauses, his hand reaching to his forehead and rubbing in a clear sign of worry.

"So *what*?"

His lips purse and he drops both hands to his side where they hang lifelessly. "Dark."

I nod, taking a deep breath. "I know every dark thing there is to know about him. I'm making it all light again. I'm helping him and whether you agree and accept it or not, he has helped me, too. He's my someone, Gregory. I'll never give him up."

"Wow." My friend exhales, his cheeks puffing. "Those are some strong words, Olivia."

I shrug. "That's how it is. Don't you see? He isn't holding me captive or forcing me into anything. I'm there willingly and because I'm supposed to be. I hope you find your someone someday, and I hope you feel as consumed by them as I do Miller. He's special." I mentally wince at my own words, tossing that thought far, *far* away.

Peace seems to settle over me under the evident realization in Gregory's expression. I'm not sure if he understands, and maybe he never will, but acceptance would be a good starting point. I don't expect them to be bosom buddies. I don't think Miller could be bosom buddies with anyone; he's not a people person. He doesn't mix well with anyone, least of all interferers. But the least they can do is be civil. For me, they should find the strength to do that.

"I'll try," Gregory whispers, almost reluctantly, but it still makes my heart dance with happiness. "If he's willing to try, then I'm game."

I smile, probably the brightest I ever have, and launch myself into his arms, making him stagger back on a small chuckle. "Thank you. He cares about me, too, Gregory. Just as much as you." I neglect to mention that he probably cares more, knowing that won't help my cause.

There are no more words, just us hugging each other with the energy of too many weeks' worth of lost time until I finally pull out of his hold, victory and elation spiraling through my whole body. His willingness, of course, is riding on Miller agreeing, but I have no doubt that he will. As long as there's a promise of zero interference and my happiness, then we should be good. I kiss his handsome cheek and link his arm, turning to continue our journey to the coffeehouse.

And freeze.

The blood drains from my head and Gregory grabs me with his spare arm to steady me. "Livy? What's up?"

The white BMW parked at the curb is unfamiliar, but it's not the swanky car that has my interest. It's the woman leaning up against the side who holds my attention, watching us as she draws on a cigarette. I've seen her once before and I'll never forget her face.

Sophia.

She has a beautiful raincoat on that's as polar white as her vehicle, her lips are bloodred, and her blond, sharp bob is as perfect as it was the last time I had the pleasure. I feel sick.

"Livy?" Gregory's concerned voice shakes me back to life, pulling my eyes away from the smug look splattered all over her flawless face. "Shit, you're all white." His hand rests on my forehead. "You gonna throw up?"

"No," I insist weakly, considering the high possibility that I really will. This woman, above all the others in Miller's life I've encountered, I'm wary of most of all. For one thing, she's been in Miller's apartment in the middle of the night. She was also sipping wine, all at home, and that thought hasn't crossed my mind until now. There's something different about this one, and I don't like it. Not one little bit. After clearing the air with Gregory, the last thing I need is her making a scene, warning me off or belittling me.

Trying desperately to gather myself, I force a smile and tug on Gregory's arm. "Are we ever going to make it to the coffeehouse?"

"I was just wondering that myself." He smiles and follows my lead, not appearing to have noticed anything untoward, other than me having a strange moment. Sophia could screw that up, and when I hear the clicking of designer heels on the pavement behind me, I know immediately that she's about to.

"Olivia, I believe," she purrs, making every muscle in my body tense. My footsteps falter, my eyes clenching shut in silent hope that if I ignore her, she might go away. I doubt it, but I'm willing to give it a go. I continue walking. Gregory's speaking, yet I can't hear a word, just the distant hum of his tone rattling on in the distance. I can hear her, though. "Or do you answer to *sweet girl* these days?"

My heart stops in my chest and my feet stop beating the pavement. There's no escape, and when Gregory glances over his shoulder in curiosity, I know I'm about to be forced into a confrontation.

I slowly turn, finding her just a few steps behind me. She takes a slow draw on her cigarette, watching me closely.

"Can I help you?" I ask, as evenly and casually as I can muster, not bothering to look and gauge Gregory's expression. I know it'll be inquisitive, and I can't rip my wary gaze from a knowing, haughty one, anyway.

"Oh, I think you can," she replies, flicking the butt of her cigarette into the gutter. "Let's take a drive, shall we?" Her arm extends toward the BMW and I look to find a driver holding the back door open.

"Who's this?" Gregory finally speaks up, moving in closer to me.

"Just a friend," Sophia answers for me, alleviating the pressure of dreaming up a convincing answer before Gregory probes further. Except I'm not sure her explanation of who she is will wash.

"Livy?" Gregory nudges me in the shoulder, forcing me to confront him. His brow furrows in question.

"A friend," I mumble feebly, my mind racing in search of my next move. I'm coming up with nothing. She referred to me as *sweet girl*. Miller's been speaking with her, and he's been speaking with her about me?

"I haven't got all day." Sophia breaks into my thoughts with her impatience.

"I've got nothing to say to you."

"But I have plenty to tell you—at least, if you care anything for Miller at all..." She trails off provocatively, and my legs shock me by automatically carrying me toward the car, the enticement of her words and potential information pulling me in.

"Livy!" Gregory calls, but I don't turn back. I don't need to see his face and I don't need him deterring me from doing something that could be incredibly stupid. "Olivia, what are you doing?"

I look behind me and see Sophia's driver intercept Gregory, stopping him from coming after me.

Gregory frowns at him. "Who the hell are you? Get out of my way."

The driver's hand lifts and settles on Gregory's shoulder. "Be wise, boy." His tone is oozing threat, and Gregory peers past him, still frowning, confusion rife on his handsome face.

"Olivia!" He starts to struggle with the driver, but he's a big man. A threatening man. I get in the car.

The door shuts and a few moments later, the other rear door opens and Sophia sinks into the leather. I must be stark-raving mad. I don't like this woman, and I know for sure I'm not going to like what she says. But there's an obscenely unreasonable desire for knowledge rippling through me. If she knows something that can help, I have to find out what it is. More knowledge. Knowledge that'll likely break my fallen heart, or possibly just break me.

The car pulls away from the curb, just as Gregory starts hammering on the window next to me. I hate myself for it, but I ignore him.

"Boyfriend?" Sophia asks, smoothing down her coat.

I'm about to snap a retort, something along the lines of Miller being my boyfriend, but something stops me. Instinct? "He's my best friend. He's also gay."

"Ah!" She laughs. "How very idyllic. The gay best friend."

"Where are we going?" I ask to change the subject. I don't want her to know anything more about my life.

"Just a pleasant drive."

I scoff. Nothing about being with Sophia is pleasant. "You said you had information. What is it?" Let's cut to the chase. I don't want to be in this car and now I'm determined to remove myself from it fast. Just as soon as this woman divulges exactly why I'm in it.

"First and foremost, I'd like you to walk away from Miller Hart."

It's a request, but delivered in such a way that there could be no mistaking the threat. My heart, my soul, my hope, it all sinks. But Miller's words—everything about damage control and diversion is suddenly all I can hear. No one can know about us, and although it kills me, I know what I must do. "There's nothing to walk away from. I saw him a few times." I feel like I could shut down, give in, and she's only just getting into her swing. She has lots more to say; I can feel it.

"He's not available."

I frown, focusing on blue eyes that scream victory. This is a woman who always gets her way. "That's of no interest to me."

"Oh." She smiles. It makes my skin crawl. "You're rather close by to his apartment."

I nearly falter, but just catch my composure before it rumbles me. "My friend lives nearby."

"Hmmm." She opens up a structured Mulberry handbag and reaches in, pulling out an engraved silver cigarette case. Her condescending hum riles me. I can feel irritation overriding the uneasiness, and I conclude that to be a good thing. Sass, damn it, don't fail me now! Her long fingers select a cigarette from the neat row held tidily under a silver brace, and she taps it on the lid before slipping it between pouting lips. "Miller Hart hasn't got time to be wasting on a curious little girl."

My neck retracts on my shoulders as she lights up. "Excuse me?"

Taking a long pull on her cigarette, she regards me thoughtfully and blows out a stream of smoke in my direction. I ignore the cloud of putrid air that engulfs me, keeping my eyes on her. I'm not backing down. My sass appears from nowhere and stands strong by my side.

"Most women have fun with Miller Hart, *sweet girl*." She emphasizes Miller's term of endearment for me. "And some, like you, stupidly think they'll get more. You won't. In fact, I believe he called you 'just a little girl who's too curious for her own good. I've taken her money, had fun with her, nothing more.' "

Her claim makes my stomach turn, adding to all of the other unwanted reactions she's spiking with her cruel words. "I know what to expect from Miller. I'm not stupid. It was fun while it lasted."

"Hmmm," she hums, regarding me closely, nearly making me look away. But I don't. I stand firm. "No one knows him like I do. I know him well," she claims.

I want to slap her. "How well?" I don't know where that question came from. I don't want to know.

"I know his rules. I know his habits. I know his demons. I know everything."

"You think he's yours?"

"I *know* he's mine."

"You're in love with him."

Her hesitance tells me all I need to know, but I know she'll confirm it. "I love Miller Hart deeply."

The pressure around my neck increases, yet I manage to register the fact that she hasn't claimed that Miller loves her. That knowledge strengthens my resolve. I'm not just some fling, some "curious girl." Maybe in the beginning, but our equal fascination changed that very quickly. He can't stand Sophia. He scrubbed, and I was there to care for him when he was in such a state. I have no fear that he loves this woman. She's a client. She wants to be more, obviously, but to Miller she's just another interferer who he'll likely hurt should he see her again. She wants what she can't have. To Sophia, Miller Hart is unobtainable, just as he is to every other woman. Except me. I already have him.

As the car pulls up to the curb, she turns in her seat, facing me full-on, lifting her chin to exhale some smoke toward the roof of the car, this time sparing me the disgusting cloud. She shows a small amount of thoughtfulness through her layers of expensive makeup as she runs disapproving eyes up and down my body.

"We're done." She smiles as she signals to the door, a silent order to get out, which I do, eager to escape the chilly presence of this awful woman. I slam the door shut and turn as the window slides down. She's sitting back in her seat, all casual and pretentious. "Nice talking."

"No, it wasn't."

"I'm glad we've established where we stand. Miller can't be getting caught up with silly little girls. It'll be his demise." The window slides shut and the car pulls swiftly away, leaving me a trembling bunch of nerves on the roadside. I'm struggling to breathe past my fear, and however hard I try to calm myself, tell myself that she's just trying to put the fear of God in me, I can't help the tiniest fragment of worry from settling deep. No, it's not a tiny fragment. It's a meteor. Huge and damaging. And I'm scared it's going to destroy us. Demise?

Reaching up to my neck through my fuzz of uncertainties, I begin a soothing rub over my flesh, but pause the moment it registers that there's a reason I'm performing this action. I lift my hand and the hairs jump back up, making me swing around in search of my shadow. There are pedestrians everywhere, most moving fast, but no one looking particularly suspicious. My fear snakes up my spine, straightening my back. I'm being watched. I know I'm being watched. I'm frantic as I swing one way, my hair whipping my face, then the other in the hopes of something catching my eye—anything that will stop me from believing that I'm going stark-raving crazy.

There's nothing.

But I know there's something.

Sophia. But she's gone. Or is this just the lingering aftereffects of her recent presence? It's possible; the woman has an unwanted lasting air about her.

I spin, my eyes darting as I try to gauge my surroundings and soon realize that I've been dumped a good mile away from Miller's. Panic runs riot through my veins as I turn, running at full speed toward Miller's apartment block. I don't look back. I sprint through the streets, dodging people, crossing roads without looking until I see his apartment block in the distance. It doesn't give me any sense of relief.

Flying into the foyer, I run straight into a waiting elevator. I'm frantic as I smash the button for the tenth floor repeatedly. "Come on!" I yell, holding back from abandoning the elevator in favor of the stairs. Adrenaline is overwhelming me, and it'd probably carry me up the stairs faster than this elevator can, but the doors begin to close and I slump against the back wall, my impatience growing. "Come on, come on, come on!" I start pacing the small space, like my movement might hurry it up. "Come on!" My face is pressed up against the doors when they open, and I squeeze through as soon as the gap is large enough for my lithe body.

My feet barely touch the ground. I rocket through the hallway, my legs moving so fast I can't feel them, my hair sailing behind me, my heart set to explode out of my chest in fright, fear, anxiety, desperation...

His door's wide open, and I hear yelling. Loud yelling. It's Miller. He's taken leave of his senses. My need to get to him spirals, my legs now numb from being overworked, and I crash through the doorway, my eyes darting until I find his naked back. He has Gregory up against the wall by his throat.

"Miller!" I scream, my knees giving out when I come to an abrupt halt, making grabbing the nearby table essential if I'm to remain on my feet. Tears burst from my eyes, every emotion piercing me collecting together and putting too much pressure on my ability to cope.

He swings around violently, his eyes wild, his hair wild, his movements wild. He looks like a feral animal—a dangerous feral animal. He *is* dangerous. Unforgiving. Notorious.

The Special One.

Gregory is released without delay, and his gasping body slides down the wall lifelessly, his palms clenching his throat on a wince. My desperation won't allow room for guilt or worry for my friend.

Miller's long legs eat up the distance between us in a nanosecond, his eyes remaining dark but relief clear in the swimming blues I love so much. "Livy," he breathes, his naked chest heaving relentlessly. I throw myself forward when I'm sure he's close enough to catch me and land in his waiting arms, my stress reducing by a million levels at simply being in his hold.

"I was followed," I sob.

"Oh, fucking hell," he curses. He sounds in physical pain. "Fuck!" He lifts me from my feet and holds me tightly. "Sophia?" The anxiety in his hoarse voice raises those stress levels again. He's too frantic.

"I don't know." And I don't need to ask how he knows it was Sophia. I expect he's strangled a description out of Gregory. "She dropped me off streets away. I felt them after she left." I shake my head, keeping my face stuck to his neck. It's silly, but I concentrate on breathing him into me, hoping that surrounding myself with all of my comforts will chase away all of my distress. I'm shaking like a leaf, no matter how secure he holds me, and through my uncontrollable body movement, I can feel his heart punching into my chest. He's delirious with concern and that only heightens my ever-growing fear.

"Come here," he rasps, like he doesn't have full control of my motionless form. He carries me farther into his apartment, my nails digging into his shoulders. There's a brief attempt to detach me from his body, but when I silently refuse, increasing my grip, he relents and sits on the couch with me still stuck to his body. He fights to maneuver me, shifting my legs to one side until I'm cuddled on his lap, my head buried under his chin. "Why did you get in that car, Olivia?" he asks, no scorn or anger in his tone. "Tell me."

"I don't know," I admit. Stupidity. Curiosity. They must be the same thing.

He sighs, mumbling under his breath. "Don't go near that woman, do you hear me?"

I nod my acceptance, wholeheartedly wishing that I never had. Nothing good came of it, except some undesired knowledge and aching questions. "She said you told her I was a bit of fun." The words, although free from my mouth, leave a rancid taste behind.

"You mustn't see her," he grates, wrestling me from his chest. I give in this time, needing to see his face. There are a million emotions etched on every perfect piece of it. "She's bad news, Olivia. The worst. There's a reason I told her what I did."

"Who is she?" I whisper, fearing the answer.

"An interferer." His answer is simple and tells me everything I need to know.

"She loves you deeply," I tell him, although I suspect he already knows. He nods, shifting his wayward wave. It draws my eyes to it very briefly, screaming for me to push it back, which I do. Slowly.

My chin is grasped and pulled toward his face until our mouths are a hairsbreadth apart. "You must understand my hatred for her."

I nod and his eyes close slowly, he breathes in slowly, and he releases the air slowly. "Thank you," he whispers, nuzzling his nose into my cheek. I immerse myself in his evident appreciation, seeing things exactly how they are. Scorned women. Women who have come to depend on the attention that this damaged man gave them. No one said my relationship with Miller would be easy, but no one said it would be near on impossible, either.

I immediately correct myself. One person did.

"What did you tell her?" Miller asks.

"Nothing."

He pulls back. "Nothing?"

"You said the less people know, the better."

His face twists in pain and he yanks me to him. "You beautiful, smart girl."

Silence falls, and so does the heavy burden of a million worrying issues. They need to be resolved, dealt with, whatever, but right in this moment in time, I can't bear it. I'm happy hiding from the cruel world we're trapped in by remaining submerged in the comfort Miller provides—the comfort I've come to depend on.

"I won't lose, Olivia," he vows. "I promise."

I don't move from his clutch, instead nodding my acknowledgment while he cuddles me fiercely.

"Well, well, well."

The cocky greeting freezes the blood in my veins, and both Miller and I snap our heads up. I don't like what I see, and I definitely don't like the angry lines cutting into his handsome face.

"There is little point in me furnishing you with a phone, Olivia, if you don't answer it."

"William," I breathe, feeling Miller's body turn to lead beneath me. Oh God, Gregory, William, a ton of shit from Sophia. This situation couldn't get any worse. I feel anarchy on the brink of explosion, and the instant hostility pouring from Miller at William's arrival doesn't lessen my trepidation. This could turn very ugly, very quickly.

William strides into the room, his phone in hand, flicking a quick unfriendly look to Gregory as he passes. Poor Gregory is still slumped against the wall, his hand still rubbing at his neck. But the appearance of my mum's ex-pimp has his immediate interest.

I'm suddenly standing, and Miller straightens to full height, his torso puffing out like a gorilla set to charge. "Anderson," he virtually growls, reclaiming me and pulling my back into his bare chest.

William helps himself to a scotch, musing for a few moments before selecting a dumpy bottle from the back. "You said you'd call me, Olivia."

I ignore his observation and wait with bated breath for Miller to launch into obsessive orbit at the sight of an interferer, someone who is not only interfering with his relationship, but also with his precisely placed liquor bottles. He's going to flip his lid. "What are you doing here?" I ask.

William turns slowly and swirls the dark liquid in the glass before sniffing it and giving a sharp nod of approval. I feel Miller's hackles rise and I know William feels it, too, even from across the room. But he ignores it. He's goading him. He knows about Miller's OCD. "Miller called me," William states matter-of-factly.

"He did?" I blurt, escaping Miller's hold and swinging around to face him. He invited William to interfere?

Miller's nostrils flare and he nails me in place with annoyance. "I thought you'd been abducted."

"You thought I'd been kidnapped?" I press. "By Sophia?" Why the hell would she do that? And why did he call William? Miller hates him, and I know the feeling is totally mutual.

His face is poker straight, but those eyes are still exuding pure, raw fear. "Yes."

I'm robbed of words.

And breath.

Then something hits me like a bullet to my temple. "You told William about my shadow?" I brace myself for Miller's answer, even though I know for sure what it'll be.

He nods. The urge to reach up and free my neck of the invisible noose is too much, and I find myself feeling around my throat, prompting Miller to move in and take my frantic hands.

"Olivia?" William's silky voice, which is still laced with antagonism, pulls my attention across the room. "When I say I'll pick you up at a certain time from a certain place, I expect you to be there. When I call, I expect you to answer."

It takes every ounce of my remaining patience and strength not to drop my head back in exasperation, but even with the lack of visual disrespect, William still picks up on my impudence. I don't care, especially not now. "I'm not a fucking child," I hiss, my fists balling in Miller's grasp. I yank myself free and spin away from him. Anxiety is being washed away with the tirade of shitty newsflashes that I'm being assaulted with.

"You should have listened," Miller says softly from behind me, making me swing back around. I'm getting dizzy from all this shocked spinning.

"What?" I yell. I can tell from his steely gaze and the reluctance of his tone that it kills him to admit that.

His arms are hanging limply by his sides, his wide shoulders slumped, his stance threatening but yielding all at once. I don't know what to make of this. "If Anderson makes a request, Livy, you should listen."

Just when I thought nothing else could stun me, he says that? "He wanted to pick me up. I was with you! And I should listen? Like I should have listened to him when he was telling me continuously to walk away from you?"

Miller's eyes turn vicious and flick to William across the room. "Never listen when he tells you that," he seethes.

My head falls back and I look to the heavens for help, wondering who and what I should be listening to. "Why do you think Sophia would kidnap me?" I can't believe the questions falling from my mouth. I know I need sass to survive Miller Hart, but not a black belt or...I gasp, realization sucker punching me. "Self-defense."

"It's a necessity."

"In case one of your jealous whores tries to abduct me?!"

"Olivia!" Miller yells, enraged, making my mouth snap shut, startled.

Gregory is suddenly in my line of sight, and I focus on him for a moment, finding his mouth agape, his eyes full of alarm. "I can't believe what I'm hearing," he splutters. "Are we on the set of *The Godfather*?"

I close my eyes and shift to the sofa, letting my backside fall in exhaustion to the squidgy cushion. "But she didn't hold me against my will." I inhale, searching for sensible questions in a mind awash with craziness. "Getting caught up with me will be your demise." I look up at him. "That's what she said." And while I previously appreciated the absurdity of the warning, Miller's straight face and telling eyes now make me appreciate the reality. I sit up and swallow hard, not wanting to ask the question tickling the end of my tongue. "Was she . . . did she . . . is it tr . . ." I pause and collect the words together in my mind and let them tumble out on an apprehensive whisper. "Is she right?"

Miller nods, blowing my already crumbling world apart. The fear that was lost to shock and anger resurfaces and immobilizes me. My stomach turns. I hear Gregory gasp. I feel Miller stiffen. And I sense William's . . . sadness.

Sophia knows the consequences if Miller quits? He's shackled, and not just by the women relishing in his sick web of hedonism. I feel ill. His demise? Who are these people?

The sound of a mobile phone pierces the heavy atmosphere and William wastes no time answering it. He looks regretful as he speaks quietly to the caller, and his refined, gray-suited body is shifting uncomfortably on the spot. "Two minutes," he says tightly before hanging up and penetrating me with his silver gaze. It's full of sorrow. My stomach turns. "Take her and go," he murmurs as he watches me. "Now."

My brow wrinkles in confusion, and I stand, throwing my eyes to Miller. He's nodding in understanding. "What's going on?" I ask, not knowing how much more I can take.

Miller approaches me and slides his palm around my neck, resorting to his tactics of calmly massaging my nape. I'd shrug him off, but I can't possibly move. He turns to William. "Do you have the package?"

William reaches into his inside pocket and pulls out a brown envelope. He's thoughtful for a few seconds before he hands it to Miller, who shoves it under his arm and reaches in, pulling out two passports and a pile of paperwork. He uses his mouth to open one of the burgundy books to the photo page and runs his eyes over it. It's me. I choke on nothing, unable to speak as I watch him check the next, seeing a shot of him this time.

"You'd better go," William presses, glancing down at his watch.

"Watch her." Miller releases me and jogs off toward his bedroom, leaving me to continue choking on my panicked breaths. I'm suffocating, a cruel world closing in on me and sending my life into mayhem.

"What's going on?" I finally ask, my voice matching my body in the shakes department.

"You're leaving," William answers simply and swiftly, now detached, all emotion long gone.

"I don't have a passport."

"You do now."

"It's fake? Why would you have a fake passport for me?" And where would he get one? I almost laugh to myself, but a lack of energy prevents it. This is William Anderson. There's no limit to his capabilities. I should know that.

He approaches me carefully, one hand resting in his pocket, the other holding his tumbler of scotch. "Because, Olivia, from the moment I discovered your involvement with Miller Hart, I knew this would be the end result. I didn't intervene to be difficult."

"What would be the end result? What's happening?" Why are people talking in code?

William seems to consider something for a moment before he looks down at me with sympathy filling his wonderful grays. He knows everything about Miller's darkness. Restraints and a bad temper aren't the only reasons William has been so persistent in his endeavors to keep me away from Miller. It's all so clear. He knows the consequences of our relationship, too. He smiles a little, taking my cheek in his palm and smoothing the pad of his thumb across my cold flesh. "Maybe I should have done this with Gracie," he says quietly, almost to himself, reminiscence rife on his distinguished face. "Maybe I should have taken her away from the horrors. Taken her away from this."

I stare at a remorseful face, but I don't ask the obvious question, which would be to ask what *this* is. "Do you regret it?"

"Every day of my wicked life."

Concern makes way for sadness. William Anderson—the man who loved my mother with a passion—lives with daily regret. It's potent and alive. It cripples him. I can think of no words to ease his pain, so I do the only other thing that feels right. I reach up to the powerful beast of a man and cuddle him. It's a silly attempt to lessen his lifelong pain, but when he laughs a little at my action and accepts my embrace, holding me tightly with his free arm, I think I might have at least made a minute's difference.

"Enough now," he says, the authority back in its rightful place. I'm detached from him, and as the room comes into view, I spot Miller hovering a few meters away, standing next to Gregory. My best friend looks like he's in a trance, and Miller looks unusually calm, considering what he has just witnessed. He has on gray sweatpants, a black T-shirt, and trainers. It's an unusual getup for Miller, but after the massacre of his masks, I guess he has no other option. Then the sports bag suspended from his hand catches my eye, and I allow a moment to process the earlier appearance of passports and William's words.

"Go," William utters, flicking his head toward the door. "My driver's parked on the corner. Take the exit from the second floor and use the fire escape." Miller doesn't swing into action, which prompts William to go on. "Hart, we've spoken about this."

I flick confused eyes to Miller, instantly wary of the ferocity rolling off of him in waves. His jaw beneath his stubble turns to rock. "I'll crucify them all," he promises, his voice drenched in violence. It makes me swallow hard.

"Olivia." William says my name on a simple breath. It's a reminder, and Miller looks down at me, cognizance seeming to wrestle past the anger. "Get her away from this fucking mess until we can figure out what's going on. Don't drag her any farther into danger, Hart. Damage control." William's phone sounds from his hand and he curses as he answers. "What's the deal?" he asks the caller as he looks to Miller. I don't like the guardedness on his face. "Go," he says urgently, remaining on the phone and pacing toward us. Miller seizes me and leads me to the door in the blink of an eye, William following directly behind.

I'm disoriented. I'm confused. I'm allowing myself to be hauled out of Miller's apartment with not a clue as to where I'm being taken.

We're in the hallway fast, Miller guiding me to the stairwell. "No!" William shouts, making Miller halt sharply and snap his head back, eyes wide. "They're coming up the stairs."

"What?" Miller roars, breaking out in a stressed sweat. "Fuck!"

"They know your weaknesses, boy." William's tone is dark, and so are his eyes.

"What's going on?" I ask, breaking free of Miller's hold, my eyes batting back and forth between him and William. "Who are *they*?" I don't like the cautious look William throws Miller's way, not that Miller will notice. He's beginning to tremble, like he's seen a ghost, his skin paling before my eyes. "Answer me!" I scream, making Miller jump and lift his brilliant blues slowly. They are haunted. It robs me of breath.

"The ones who hold the key to my chains," he whispers, sweat trickling down his temples. "The immoral bastards."

A sob rips through me like lightning as his confession settles hard and fast. "No!" My head starts to shake and my heart rate rockets. I don't want to ask. He looks truly frightened, and I don't know whether it's because they, whoever they may be, are on their way or because his escape is blocked and he needs to get me out. Intuition tells me it's the latter, but it's the former that has my heart squeezing in trepidation. "What do they want?" I brace myself for his answer, wincing as he fights the symptoms of a meltdown, and when he finally speaks, it's on a mere whisper.

"I've handed in my resignation." He holds my eyes while I let the enormity of his statement sink in. And then my eyes flood with salty tears.

"They won't let us be if we stay?" I ask, choking all over my question.

He shakes his head slowly, pain invading his beautifully perfect face. "I'm so sorry, my gorgeous girl." The bag drops to the floor and I see defeatism grip him. "They own me. The consequences will be shattering if we stay."

My whole body shakes under the somberness of his shaky promise, my cheeks stinging and sore as I wipe at my face, searching for my strength to replace Miller's loss of it. I'm in deep—deeper than I ever imagined. And I plan on drowning with him if necessary. I suck in an unsteady breath and pace over to him, hauling the bag up from the floor and taking his clammy hand. He lets me, but as soon as he figures where we're headed, he stiffens and I hear the beginning of panicked breathing. He's putting up some resistance, making it harder for me to pull him to where I need him. But we make it.

I press the Call button for the elevator and silently plead for it to be near the top of the building. I'm looking back to the stairwell exit constantly.

"Olivia?"

I glance to my side, seeing Gregory has joined William. He looks lost. Confused. Shocked. I smile at him, trying to ease his worry, but I know I've failed. "I'll call," I promise, just as the doors slide open and Miller steps back, taking me with him. "Please tell Nan I'm okay."

I throw the bag into the elevator and turn, taking Miller's other hand so we're joined by both. Then I start to take slow steps back, aware our time is ticking, but more acutely aware that this is not something I can rush. He's staring past me into the enclosed box, his whole body heaving violently, and it's in the intensity of this moment that I wonder how I could have been so cruel those times I used this fear against him. I fight off the tears that the guilt spikes and continue with my backward steps until our arms are at full length and the space between our bodies is wide.

"Miller," I say quietly, desperate for him to focus on me instead of the monster he sees behind me. "Look at me," I plead. "Just look at me." My voice quavers, no matter how greatly I'm trying to keep it together. Relief swamps me when he takes a tentative step forward, but then he starts shaking his head furiously and takes two steps back. He's swallowing repeatedly and his hands are becoming increasingly hot. The waves of his lovely hair are becoming heavy under the weight of the sweat pouring from his scalp, his forehead, just about everywhere.

"I can't," he pants, gulping. "I can't do it."

I look across to William and see concern as he constantly checks his phone and looks to the stairwell, and when I look to Gregory, I see something that I've never seen from my best friend when Miller is in the picture. Compassion. I bite my lip as the tears begin to fall, choking on a sob when he looks at me and gives me eyes full of encouragement. Then he nods. It's only just detectable, but I see it and I understand it. I feel hopeless. I need to get Miller out of this building.

"You go," Miller says, pushing me into the elevator. "I'll be fine, you go."

"No!" I yell. "No, you are not giving up!" I throw myself onto him, snaking my arms around him and silently vowing never to let go. I don't miss the letup in tension from his body under my hold.

My *thing.*

His *thing.*

Our *thing.*

I squeeze him, my lips on his neck and his face in my hair. Then I let go and pull more forcefully on his hand, begging with my eyes for him to come to me. And he does. He takes one slow step forward. Then another. Then another. Then another. He's on the threshold. I'm in the elevator. He's trembling, still gulping, and the sweat is relentless.

And then I hear a loud sound from the stairwell, followed by William's colorful curse, and I do what instinct tells me and yank Miller into the elevator before smashing the button for the second floor and throwing my arms around his gasping body, immersing him in our *thing.*

The frantic pace of his heart beating in his chest must be verging on dangerous. I'm looking over his shoulders to the hallway as it slowly disappears with the closing of the doors, and the last thing I see before we're alone in the terrifying box is William and Gregory stepping into sight, both watching quietly as Miller and I vanish from view. I smile at them through my sadness.

It wouldn't be a surprise if the ferocity of his heartbeat hitting my chest leaves bruises. It's relentless, no matter how hard I squeeze him. My attempts to calm him are fruitless. All I need to do is concentrate on keeping him upright until we reach the second floor, which right now is easy. He's rigid as I watch the digital monitor tick down through the floors, each number seeming to take eons to appear. We're in slow motion. Everything seems to be in slow motion.

Everything except Miller's breathing and heart rate.

I feel him jerk under my hold, and I attempt to pull out but get nowhere. He's not letting go of me, not for anything, and I'm suddenly panicked by the potential difficulty of getting him out of the elevator once it stops. "Miller?" I whisper, low and calm. It's a vain attempt to fool him into believing that I'm composed. I'm far from it. He doesn't respond and I take another glimpse at the floor indicator.

"Miller, we're nearly out," I say, pushing into him to force him to step backward until his back is at the doors. The judder of the elevator when it stops makes me jump, and Miller lets out a weak whimper as he pushes against me. "Miller, we're here." I struggle against his fierce resistance, hearing the doors begin to open. It's only now I consider the possibility of *them* waiting for us on the other side of the doors, and panic flares, my body stiffening as the doors begin to open. What if they are? What will I do? What will *they* do? My breathing pattern changes, catching up with Miller's as I peek over his shoulders, my feet beginning to ache from staying on my tiptoes.

The doors open fully, revealing nothing but an empty hallway, and I try to listen for any signs of life.

Nothing.

Pushing against Miller's dead weight, I get nowhere in my urgent need to shift him. How will he be once we're out of this box? I haven't got time to coax him out of this elevator, let alone the building.

"Miller, please," I beg, swallowing down the lump of desperation in my throat. "The doors are open." He remains frozen, stuck to me, and tears of panic begin to overwhelm my eyes. "Miller," I whisper, my shaky voice tarnished with defeat. They'll be on their way back down soon.

My whole body goes limp in his arms, but then a chime sounds and the doors begin to close again. I don't have time to shout for

Miller to get out. He seems to jump to life, the sound of the doors closing undoubtedly the cause, and he drops me fast, his body flying back as if someone has launched him from a cannon. I hold my breath as I watch him. He's drenched, his hair stuck to his head and his eyes wide with fear. And he's still shaking.

Not knowing what else to do, I reach down to retrieve the bag and move to the threshold of the elevator, all the while keeping my worried eyes on him as he looks around him, familiarizing himself with his surroundings. And it's like the shattered pieces of my world suddenly fuse, bringing hope crashing back into our reality, as the mask falls, wiping away every shred of fear, and Miller Hart is back.

He flicks empty eyes up and down my body, catching sight of the bag, and it's gone from my grasp in the blink of an eye. Then my hand is claimed and I'm out of the elevator just as quickly. He breaks into a run, forcing my little legs to sprint in order to keep up with him, and he glances back every few seconds to check on me and for anything behind us.

"You okay?" he asks, no signs of exertion showing.

I, however, have misplaced the adrenaline that was fueling me. Maybe my conscience has registered Miller's resurrection and wants to relieve me of the pressure to hold things together. I don't know, but exhaustion is taking hold and my emotions are screaming for release. But not here. I can't lose it here. I nod, keeping up my pace so I don't hinder our escape. Showing mild concern on his perfect face, he throws the bag up to his shoulder as we near the fire exit and releases my hand, his body charging at full speed into the door. It crashes open loudly, and the daylight beyond attacks my eyes, making me wince.

"Take my hand, Olivia," he demands urgently.

I seize it, allowing him to pull me down the fire escape and onto the side street. A car horn blares immediately, and I spot William's driver holding the back door open. We dodge cars, trucks, and taxies, most honking their horn in annoyance, as we weave through the busy London traffic, charging toward William's car.

"In." He gives a curt nod to the driver and takes over his hold of the door as he barks his order at me and throws the bag in. I waste no time, flinging myself onto the backseat, Miller following behind. The driver is up front before I know it and screeching off down the road, his madcap driving skills alarming me. He's an expert, dipping and weaving through the traffic with ease and coolness.

And then the enormity of what has just happened hits me like the wickedest of tornados and I cry. I bury my face in my palms and break down, so many thoughts whirling through my poor, overwrought mind—some reasonable, like I need to call Nan. What about Nan? And some unreasonable thoughts, like where did this man learn to drive so capably? And does William need these types of driving skills?

"My gorgeous girl." His strong palm wraps around my nape and tugs me over to him, pulling me onto his lap and securing me in his arms so my soggy cheek is buried in his chest. I cry relentlessly, jerking in his hold, unable and unwilling to even try to avert it any longer. The last half hour has taken everything out of me. "Don't cry," he whispers. "Please don't cry."

My fists clutch the material of his T-shirt at his pecs until my hands ache and I've cried rivers of confused, gut-twisting tears. "Where are we going?"

"Somewhere," he answers, wrestling me from his chest to find my eyes. "Someplace where we can lose ourselves in each other with no interruptions or interference."

I can barely see him through the pools of tears blurring my vision, but I can feel him and hear him. It's good enough. "Nan."

"She'll be taken care of. You don't need to worry yourself with that."

"By William?" I blurt, thinking all kinds of shit will hit the fan if William rocks up to Nan's. Jesus, she'll go mental!

"She'll be taken care of," he repeats, short and sharp.

"But I'll miss her."

Reaching up, he slides his fingers into my hair, cupping the back of my head. "It's not for long, I promise. Just long enough to let the dust settle."

"How long will that be? And what if they don't let the dust settle? Will William be involved? Does he know them? Who are they?" I pause to draw breath, wanting to spit out all of these questions before my tired mind shuts down and I forget them. "They won't hurt Nan, will they?" I gasp as something slams into my racing mind. "Gregory!"

"Shhhh," he soothes, like I haven't just abandoned my best friend in Miller's apartment when God only knows who are on their way up. "He's with Anderson. Trust me, he'll be fine. And so will your grandmother."

Relief swamps me. I *do* trust him, but he hasn't answered any of my questions. "Talk to me," I plead, not having to elaborate on that gentle demand. His lovely blue eyes are trying desperately to reassure me, to eliminate my unease. It's working in a strange sense.

He nods and pulls me back into his embrace. "Until there is no breath left in my lungs, Olivia Taylor."

* * *

Heathrow is chaotic. My mind races, my heart pounds, my eyes dart all the way to the departure gate. While I fidgeted through check-in and security, Miller looked completely composed, holding me close, probably in an attempt to conceal my shakes. I haven't paid much attention to what's happened since we were dropped off at Terminal 5. I don't know where we're going or for how long. I called Nan, armed with a story of a surprise trip from Miller, only to have William answer the call. My heart stopped in my chest, and then restarted when Nan came on the line, cool as a cucumber. I didn't understand, still don't, but she told me persistently how much she loved me before making me promise I'd call when we arrived wherever we are going.

And all of that brings us to now.

I'm standing at the gate, gazing up at the monitor, open-mouthed. "New York?" I breathe, resisting the urge to rub at my eyes, just in case I'm seeing things.

Miller doesn't humor my awe, instead gently guiding me to the lady who'll let us pass once she's checked our passports and boarding passes . . . again. I stiffen. Again. But she smiles and ushers us on.

"You would make a terrible crook, Olivia," Miller says seriously.

I allow my muscles to relax as he leads me down the tunnel toward the plane. "I don't *want* to be a crook."

He smiles down at me, his eyes twinkling. All signs of the terrified creature have disappeared, restoring my finicky, refined Miller to his former glory. And he really is glorious. I sigh on a long, sated exhale and rest my head on his arm, looking up to see an overly happy stewardess smiling brightly at us. I could growl in exasperation when she asks for our passports and boarding passes. You would think I'd be used to it after the millions of other times they have been requested since we arrived at Heathrow. But no. I'm beginning to tremble again as she flicks through before glancing at each of us to check we match the photograph. I force a nervous smile, convinced she's going to scream *fake* and then call for security. But she doesn't.

She checks the boarding passes and smiles as she hands them back to Miller. "First class is this way, sir." She gestures to the left. "You've just made it on time. The captain has ordered us to secure the doors."

Miller gives a brisk nod, and I turn to see another stewardess pulling the doors shut.

And every drop of blood drains from my head as I glance down the tunnel, toward the departure gate. It's an illusion; it has to be. My curiosity gets the better of me and I creep forward as the closing door begins to hamper my view, wanting to get as close as I can, blinking the whole time, convinced I'm seeing things.

Then I stop.

I'm rooted to the spot, my mind empty, my blood freezing in my veins.

And I'm staring at me.

It's definitely me . . . just nineteen years from now.

TO GUARD HER, HE'LL BREAK EVERY RULE.

TO HAVE HER, HE'LL TAKE ANY CHANCE.

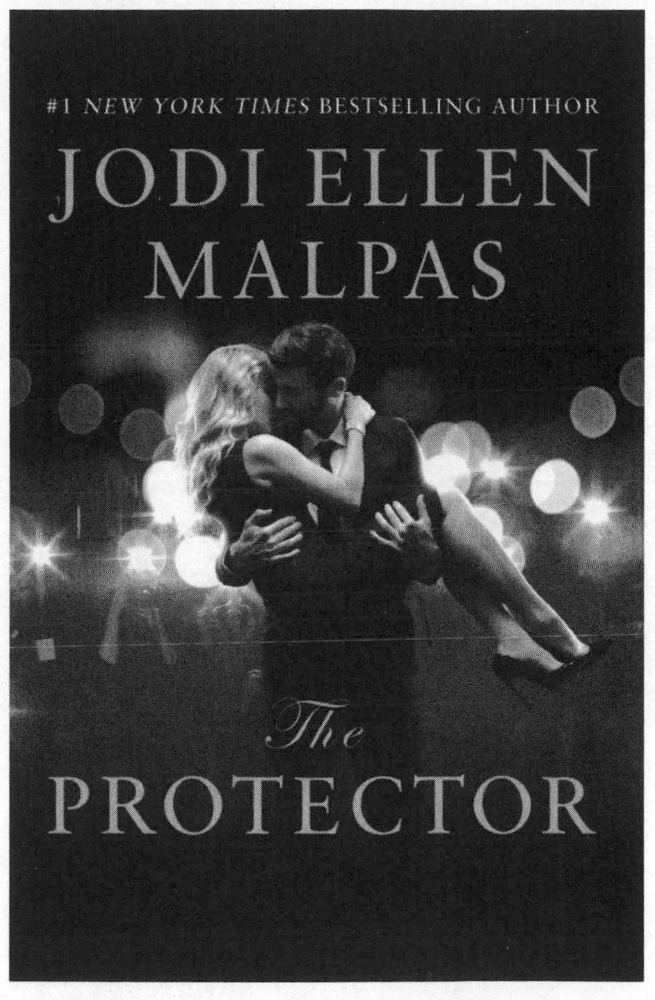

On sale September 2016